THE
LOST SONS
OF THE WEST

THE
LOST SONS
OF THE WEST

A.L. BUXTON

Published in paperback in 2017 by Sixth Element Publishing
on behalf of A.L. Buxton

Sixth Element Publishing
Arthur Robinson House
13-14 The Green
Billingham TS23 1EU
Tel: 01642 360253
www.6epublishing.net

ISBN 978-1-912218-08-0

British Library Cataloguing in Publication Data. A catalogue record for this book is
available from the British Library.

This is a work of fiction. Names, characters, businesses, places, events and incidents
are either the products of the author's imagination or used in a fictitious manner.
Any resemblance to actual persons, living or dead, or actual events and places is
purely coincidental.

A.L. Buxton asserts the moral right to be identified as the author of this work.

Printed in Great Britain.

To Athena Buxton

MAP OF REQUIRIUM

CHAPTER 1
A NEW BEGINNING

The peaceful night's breeze blew softly against the crackling embers that bounced up from a neatly built fire. Gideon Destain sat by the fire with his legs spread and his elbows tucked comfortably on his knees. Gideon had long dark hair, brown of colour and long in length. He had tiny paper slit eyes and a rough black beard. He was broad and big, tall and strong, everything that a warrior should be.

He was sitting quietly, thinking deeply whilst his brothers and many others slept around him. He fiddled happily with a small piece of straw that he plucked from the grass beneath him.

A soldier emerged out of the dark bushes that surrounded the camp. He crept carefully over all the sleeping bodies and made for Gideon.

"Young swordsman," whispered the man elegantly as he rested his gloved hand on Gideon's shoulder.

Gideon looked up to find the soldier standing over him with a message.

"Commander Frankel has eyes on Rhoden. He awaits your presence."

Gideon smiled at the young soldier who went by the name of Braceum. He was Commander Frankel's right hand man and second in command.

"I will be right there, my friend," replied Gideon.

Braceum bowed his head softly before turning back around and heading back towards the treeline. He ducked beneath a hanging tree branch and disappeared into the darkness.

Gideon leaned forward and reached for a stone that lay on the grass. He picked it up and lobbed it at Nuallan with perfect accuracy.

Nuallan jumped up, cursing viciously as he attempted to discover his attacker.

"Quiet, Nuallan, let the others rest for a short while longer," said Gideon as he tried to calm his older brother.

Nuallan gathered his senses and stood. Nuallan was a man of similar resemblance to his younger brother, Gideon. He was broad and tall with long black hair and a bushy beard. He wore a dark shaded black bandana around his meaty head. He looked down with envy at Andrus who was lucky enough to indulge himself in slumber a little longer. Andrus, the youngest of the brothers held no resemblance to either of his brothers. He was shorter, still broad but not as big. His hair was a light shade of brown and only dangled by his shoulders. His face was smooth and without hair.

Nuallan muttered to himself as he stepped over their younger brother and followed Gideon off into the treeline. Together they ducked down and slipped out of sight.

The two brothers mooched through the dark vines and bushes in search of Braceum. In the half-light of the night, they noticed some footprints imprinted on the damp dirt that blotched between the grassy plain. The prints led to the base of a filthy uneven mud mound that led up to the vantage point where the Commander awaited them.

Nuallan and Gideon slipped through the trees and tackled the hill, quickly aided by Braceum who came sliding down the mound to seek the brothers' whereabouts.

"Hurry, you two, the Commander wants to execute the attack soon whilst it is still dark." Braceum offered out his hand and hoisted Nuallan up first and then Gideon.

The three of them dug their heels into the mud and began climbing. It took them no longer than a minute to reach the top where the Commander greeted them.

"Young swordsman, here, quickly. Come and have a look, son," said Commander Frankel.

Gideon scraped his body up off the mud and sneaked behind a battered rock that sat upon the hill's peak. He planted himself beside the Commander and the other men that spied on Rhoden.

Commander Frankel was a tall man in his early fifties, well over six foot with short grey hair that glistened like the moonlight. He was from a town called Vanghale, and he trained and led Vanghale's army. Their leader was Earl Oswald, an ambitious but reckless Earl. He had the Commander lead his army to Rhoden and other surrounding settlements to reap their profits, rape their woman and plunder their towns.

"Look there, Earl Julius has still not learnt his lesson. His guard is still weak, no more than half a dozen soldiers patrol the town's wall," pointed out the Commander.

Earl Julius was the Commander of the small town of Rhoden, his old age preventing him from becoming a powerful leader. No one in Requirium really feared him, but with age he had become wise. The Bothsom mines sat a little north from his town and he reaped them well. Most of his army were stationed at the mines to protect them but this meant that Rhoden was left unprotected.

"Go over your new plan with me, lad," said Commander Frankel as he continued to scan Rhoden's walls for any hidden troops.

Gideon stretched his head up to take a proper look around. He leaned his arms on the rock and began to explain. "Nuallan and Andrus will tackle the walls with a couple of your men. They will take the rope and claws and rappel up the wall to gain entry that way. Once they have taken care of the patrols, they will open the main gate. There, me and my company will be waiting along with you and the rest of your army."

The Commander smirked half-heartedly before nodding. "A fine idea, as long as we execute this without being noticed. You persuaded me to bring only forty men, young swordsman. If this plan fails, it's on you. Got it," he said sternly.

The Commander would usually attack with a few hundred men. They would break through the main gate and go in loud and recklessly, but Earl Oswald didn't like the amount of casualties his men were suffering so he demanded a different approach.

"It will work, I assure you," said Gideon confidently.

The Commander looked satisfied. He then twisted round and signalled his men. One by one they crept over to the hill's edge and slid down back into the bushes. The Commander brushed his fingers through his silver hair and launched himself down the hill behind Gideon and Nuallan.

The scouting party returned to camp to find the rest of the men feasting on their supply packs.

"Finish up, men, the time has come," declared Frankel.

Gideon walked back over to the fire to go over the plan with Doxass, Faizer and Andrus. The three of them sat, legs spread, on a horizontal tree trunk, eating away their ration packs.

"Andrus, you are going with Nuallan. You are to climb the wall and take out all the patrols. Once they are taken care of, make your way down to ground level and open the gate. I spotted a bell at the end of the wall on the eastern side. If one of the guards shouts or reaches that bell, it's mission failed," explained Gideon.

"And what of us?" questioned the rather large Doxass.

"I am taking you, Josanne and your brother Faizer with me across the field and in through the main gate," Gideon said as he looked around in search for Josanne. "Where is Josanne?" he asked with confusion.

"She went to fill up the water pouches down by the lake. The bitch shouldn't be too long," mocked Doxass.

"This bitch will take your water pouch back down to the river and throw your fat arse in after it," cursed Josanne sarcastically as she emerged from the shadows.

She walked elegantly through camp, dropping a water pouch

into each of the Company's welcoming paws. She threw the last one at Doxass who erupted into a tune of heavy laughter.

Josanne had beautiful long red hair that was messily plaited at the bottom. It grew right down and rested on her peachy backside that curved round like a ball attached to two long stilts. She was in her late thirties but still carried beauty. She was from the eastern city of Brigantium, the daughter of an eastern noble who was respected and extremely wealthy thanks to the King.

Faizer took a deep bite of his apple and chucked the remainder away into the fire. He picked up his long fancy sword and sheathed it in his scabbard. "A few more months of fighting for Earl Oswald and we should have enough gold to travel across the 7th and start a new life," he said to Doxass as he helped him up.

"Aye, brother," replied Doxass as he again burst into a roar of laughter.

Doxass and Faizer were brothers from a town called Vaughan, close in bond but different in appearance. They were both tall but Faizer had short black hair with a neat short beard whereas Doxass had very long blond hair with a messy plaited beard. Vaughan was about one hundred miles west of Vanghale. A terror hill tribe had been terrorising the town of Vaughan for months, killing, stealing and raping as they came. Doxass and Faizer began building a resistance group to fight off the pagans and before long they had a sizeable force that was able to protect Vaughan. One day they tracked a pack of the tribe members until they eventually found them, ambushing a group of travellers on the road. Doxass and Faizer slaughtered the men and saved the travellers. They took them in, sheltered them, fed them and listened to them. They were so intrigued by their story they swore to dedicate their swords to the three travellers. Andrus, Nuallan and Gideon gladly accepted and so the company was created.

"Do you intend to waste more of the precious night, you fool?" snapped the Commander as he towered over Nuallan who still sat on the trunk finishing his ration pack. "Grab your comrade and get to it. You have a fucking job to do."

Nuallan paused his chewing and slowly looked up at the armoured Commander. He glared viciously for a moment before taking another bite of his food. The Commander grew impatient. He slapped the sloppy slab of meat out of Nuallan's greasy hands and attempted to grab his black overthrow to yank him up. Nuallan pushed Frankel's silver mitts away and dived up into the air, ripping out his blade in a state of rage.

"I do not take orders from you, Frankel, you worthless town whore. I will gut you where you stand, and your army of peasants if you lay hands on me again, you cunt," exploded Nuallan, causing dozens of Commander Frankel's men to draw their swords and head over towards the commotion.

Gideon, who'd only just become aware of the conflict, ran over and desperately tried to separate the two ferocious beasts. Doxass and Faizer however leapt into action and stood supportively behind Nuallan.

"Put away your weapons, you fools. We are allies," said Gideon.

The Commander smirked psychotically as he seemed to thrive on the danger. He took a few steps back and raised his hand, signalling his men to stand down.

"Now you, Nuallan, put away your sword," urged Gideon.

Nuallan grunted with frustration and did as instructed. "Fucking cunt, we shouldn't even be here. Come on, Andrus, apparently we have a fucking job to do." Nuallan tightened the black bandanna that covered most of his forehead, and the two of them scurried on out of the camp and burst through a big opening in the treeline's belly.

The Commander nodded at Braceum who was standing eagerly behind him. Braceum and another soldier called Bray bowed to Commander Frankel and then tracked Nuallan and Andrus's route. They were to accompany them on their mission.

"Now that we got that out of the way, we can get to it ourselves," mocked Frankel insultingly. Portions of his men began laughing as they made their way into the dark hole and down to the field below.

Gideon and the remainder of his company remained straight-faced, displeased by the minor insult that the Commander had just produced.

"Fucking cunt. Come on, let's move out," Gideon stated and led his followers into the daunting treeline.

The remainder of the company and Frankel's men spread out at the base of the forest, using whatever they could for cover but with most left lying in the open flat on their bellies. They looked ahead, trying to plan their mobilisation onto the field, various boulders and ditches offering potential cover options for when they would make their way across the field towards Rhoden.

The wide untended flat was all that sat between the forest and the town. The defensive wall was positioned very well. It was a perfect square except the main gate was sucked right in which meant anyone who decided to attack the gate would be surrounded from the wall on the left and the right. Earl Julius could command his archers to position themselves upon the walls and take out most of the attacking force before they even reached the gate. Unfortunately for Earl Julius, he did not have the numbers to carry out such a defensive manoeuvre.

"Right, young swordsman, we remain here until your companions take the wall," whispered the Commander who lay about five feet away from Gideon. His expensive armour was blackened from the muck beneath his belly.

Gideon rolled his overthrow sleeves right down and tugged his hood over his head. He then raised his head slightly above the long grass and attempted to spot his brothers.

"Where are they? Have they reached the wall?" asked Faizer.

Gideon ignored him and kept on scouting. All of a sudden his eyes widened as he spotted four shadows creeping close to the western side of the wall.

"I see them. They have made it," Gideon said with relief.

"Good, now it's time to move up a little bit. Use whatever you can for cover and stay low. If any of you gets discovered, I will personally rip your cock from your balls," threatened Commander Frankel fiercely.

The men moved forward. Slowly but surely they slid, wriggled and shifted their bodies through the shivering grass towards Rhoden.

"Give me the claws quickly," Nuallan said. "I will go first then one at a time follow me up. Get tight against the wall and stay quiet."

Braceum listened before throwing forward a filthy brown bag that contained the claws. Nuallan held onto the bag and then crumpled his body up until he got his knees pressed against the dirt. He took one last look to make sure no guards were present then satisfied that he could make the journey, he came up off his knees and dived the small distance to the wall. Silently but swiftly he made it and instantly pressed his big body up against the wooden planks.

Next Andrus leapt out of the grass like a preying lion and launched himself up and over to the wall also, Bray travelling next without a fuss. Braceum jittered up and attempted to run until something startled him. His run broke down and he collapsed back to the floor, dropping the long brown rope down beside him. Nuallan and the others pressed up even tighter against the wall as they realised that Braceum must have seen a soldier upon the wall. The flaring torches upon the wall lit the area slightly where Nuallan and the others stood; if any guards were to take a proper look down, they would discover the pack.

Andrus carefully slid a sharp defined dagger out from his brown cloak that warmed his nervous body. Andrus was an excellent shot with a throwing knife or a dagger. Before the war he would enter competitions within Meridium. His father would call him a girl for using such a weapon but Andrus was the most stubborn one in the family, and his father's words never swayed him.

"Did you hear that?" asked a guard who was walking to the edge of the wall.

"No, it was probably a field mouse or a boar," replied another guard who looked out into the field from his position upon the wall.

"Come on back to the eastern side in case any of them fucks from Vanghale storm our gate again. They are due another visit," added the guard before leading his accomplice away.

Nuallan held his hand out towards Braceum, signalling him to stay put for a few more seconds, and moments later Nuallan waved Braceum on. Braceum darted out of the grass, dragging the thick brown rope along with him. The men instantly got to work. They untied the bag and pulled out the claws, tied the hanging string that dangled from the metal claw hooks round the end of the chunky rope, and once secure they all took a risky step away from the wall and chucked the rope up. Their aim was true and accurate, and the claws wrapped tightly around the wall's mucky worn pillars.

"Right, here we go, lads, up we go," said Nuallan as he latched himself onto the rope.

One at a time, the men followed Nuallan and slithered up the rope quietly.

Nuallan was the first to reach the top. He grabbed hold of one of the wooden pillars and swiped his legs up and over the wall. Instantly he tracked the two guards that were walking with their backs to him. He crept as fast as his legs would allow him without creating too much noise on the creaky cracked decking that ran along the inside of Rhoden's wall. The two guards spun around as he got close, but it was too late. Nuallan grabbed hold of his first victim, tightly gripped his head and twisted his neck powerfully, breaking it with one tug. The other soldier responded by drawing his sword. Before his sword fully revealed itself from its scabbard, the battle was lost. Nuallan swung him round like a bear savaging a child. He bashed his head hard off the wall until the man resisted no more. Nuallan threw the body over the wall and made for the gatehouse. Metres before he arrived, three men walked out and saw him.

Nuallan tore a great longsword from a case that was hidden on his back beneath his large black overthrow. He lowered it and then slashed up, cutting the first attacker's belly open. He controlled it brilliantly as he parried away both of his opponents' attacks and timed his counter attack perfectly. He slashed down on the soldier to his right and then swung round and lunged powerfully into his last enemy.

"Save some for us, comrade," Bray whispered as the rest of them caught up.

Nuallan ignored him, quietly opened the gatehouse door, and the four of them moved in.

Two men were sitting at a rigid old table playing a strategy game with some small carved rocks. The bloodthirsty Bray and Braceum claimed these kills, tackling the men off their chairs and engaging into a fight. Nuallan allowed the Commander's men to quench their thirst on these men, wasting no more time inside as he opened the opposite door and ran out onto the eastern side of the wall, his young brother following him eagerly. Four soldiers were standing guard on the wall, one pretty close and then the other three about halfway along the wall. Nuallan also saw the warning bell hanging at the far end of the eastern wall. If a soldier made it to that, the quest would fail.

Nuallan got to work. He crept up to the first soldier and took the man down, withdrawing quickly into the shadows. The remaining three soldiers hadn't seen anything. They had to be taken out as one, lest one had time to shout a warning. Nuallan waited quietly until Andrus appeared, having finished off the man who was lying on the floor and chased after his brother.

Gideon had always urged his company and his brothers not to kill unnecessarily but sometimes they had no choice. None of them enjoyed killing but it was what they had to do to get by, especially since they began selling themselves to Earl Oswald.

They waited until one of the men started to wander off on patrol, then moved silently together to engage the two left in front of them.

They had to take them out quickly and quietly.

Andrus struck his opponent a heavy blow to the back of the head as Nuallan tackled his.

Nuallan glanced up. The final guard had turned, realisation flaring in his expression. He spun, reaching for the warning bell.

"Andrus, after him quickly!" Nuallan hissed desperately.

Andrus quickly bypassed Nuallan and his opponent. If the man shouted, they were done for. The warning bell was within distance for the Rhoden man. Andrus drew a knife and threw it in one fluid motion.

It struck as the man was reaching out for the rope, his hand stretched out without clasping. He coughed and gulped hard, and slowly the distance between himself and the bell extended. Andrus's blade had stuck him in the neck, the blood that splashed from his wound dripping from the bell that had almost rung out a warning. Andrus crept up slowly, pulling his blade from the suffering man's spine and neatly cutting his throat to put him out of his misery. He then put away his blade and closed the man's eyes.

"I am sorry, my brother," he whispered to the dead soldier.

"No time to lose. We must get the gate open," Braceum said as he caught up to Andrus and Nuallan, but he was ignored as Andrus continued to look at his most recent victim.

Nuallan popped his head over the wall and looked out into the open to scout out the assault party. Dozens of dark shaded figures were scattered about in the field.

"They are in position." Nuallan wiped his filthy bloodstained hands onto his mucky overthrow. "Let's move down to ground level and get the gate open."

Braceum jolted for the stairwell with excitement. "Let the raid begin, my friends, let the raid begin."

CHAPTER 2
RAIDERS

The dry grass slapped off the legs of the pursuing soldiers as the wind speed increased. The company ran out first into the open, made for the gate and managed to do so without being discovered. Next a large portion of the Commander's soldiers hopped out from the grass and charged the wall, and finally the Commander himself and the final portion of his men made for their destination. If anyone were to look over the wall, even slightly, the party would be discovered.

"I hope your comrades took out all of the watch, " said Frankel as he arrived.

"They won't disappoint. Just be patient, we will be inside the walls soon enough," replied Gideon confidently.

The men swayed from side to side in an attempt to pump themselves up for a fight in case any resistance awaited them on the inside. The men of Vanghale thrived off an atmosphere like this, raiding was all they had known; the Commander had trained them to be ruthless, vicious and merciless. They were skilled enough with a sword to defeat the Rhoden guards but they lacked any proper tactical training or strategic education.

"Where the fuck are they? We risk discovery if we linger here much longer, you fool," snapped the Commander, slightly raising his voice.

He caught the attention of Gideon who wriggled through some

of the men to confront Frankel. "Hold your fucking tongue. My men will get us inside," he hissed in defence of his brothers.

The pair stared each other out venomously until the awkward silence was broken by a heavy latch being lifted on the large gate.

"Knock it off, you two, the gate is opening. Prepare yourself," interrupted Faizer.

The pair silently put aside their differences for the time being and prepared themselves to breach Rhoden. All the men took a step away from the gate as it slowly opened up. Frankel pushed his way to the front of the pack and faced his savage mob. He clenched his fist and hovered it against his armoured chest plate. He then bowed his head respectfully to all his soldiers who responded by mimicking the expression. It was a traditional salute that the men of Vanghale gave each another before engaging in combat.

"How heroic," muttered Faizer to his beastly brother Doxass who sniggered quietly.

The gate opened up even further and a small gap started forming. Gideon squeezed through first and entered into the torch-lit little town of Rhoden.

"Brother, here, come over here," said Nuallan gently as he greeted his brother.

Gideon swivelled round and spotted his two brothers bent down beside the opened up gate. He marched over and joined them.

Nuallan gestured. "I spotted a church and a tavern close by. I think they would prove profitable settlements."

"Josanne, will you raid the tavern with Nuallan whilst the rest of us take the church?" asked Gideon as he turned to his arriving company member.

"Of course, but first shouldn't you do something about that?" she said as she pointed over to the Commander. He was already getting carried away, kicking over his third fire bowl that spewed out flames all over the courtyard.

"House to house, men. Slaughter anyone that stands in your way," he commanded ruthlessly. His troops began spilling out of the courtyard and into the surrounding streets. The men trampled up the unswept stairwells that provided access to each front porch and began smashing down the doors and bashing in the windows.

The screams of the innocent civilians of Rhoden gushed out into the cold windy night, the screams echoing so loudly that it awoke more of the sleeping. The streets filled with panic as the people ran for their homes, locking themselves inside. This was how the men of Rhoden would raid. They did not fight with honour or respect, they were not trained to fight in a formation or to fight as a unit. They knew only how to scavenge, beat and frighten their foes.

The Commander too was causing destruction to the town. He grabbed hold of a fleeing child and smashed him hard in the back as the youngster tried to run into an alleyway.

Gideon watched unhappily but he did nothing as the Commander's eyes caught his vicious gaze. He smiled wickedly back at Gideon before running further into the street and up into a burning house.

"What do we do? Do we stop him?" asked Faizer who seemed to be getting worked up at the Commander's actions.

"You cannot stop him, you fool. This is how we raid. Now, don't we have a church to plunder?" said Braceum arrogantly. He smiled at Bray and signalled him to follow him. They took off and made for a dirty alleyway that tightly linked up beside the eastern side of the wall.

"Fucking cunt, I should take his head off where he stands," cursed Doxass as he watched Braceum and Bray run off into the ally.

"Braceum is right, that is how they raid, they have their ways of doing things and we have our ways. Now come on, let's get to it before them two fools blow our cover completely," said Gideon calmly.

The company tracked Bray and Braceum into the ghastly alleyway, a disturbing stench flooding out of it causing Andrus and Josanne to block their mouths with their hands. The pair of them took point and led the company into the narrow space. They picked up the pace and began jogging and sidestepping through the piss and dirty rainwater that no sunlight had managed to dry up. Suddenly the clash and bang of swords alerted the company.

"Quickly!" ordered Gideon as he sought to put an end to the noise before more soldiers heard it. One by one the company washed out into another street to find Braceum and Bray duelling with three Rhoden guards. Braceum swiped from left to right as he battled against two of them whilst Bray fought beside him against a single guard.

Andrus quickly threw his quick-witted skills into play. He skipped over and latched onto one of the soldiers fighting Braceum. He lifted his arms up from behind and began shaking him about in an attempt to drag him to the ground. Bray, who'd just finished off his opponent, offered assistance. He hopped forward on one leg and dug his sword deep into the guard. The sword split the man's chainmail and set free a gush of blood.

Andrus, who never intended for the guard to die, released his hold and watched as the body slid down to the floor.

Gideon quickly intervened in attempt to save Braceum's opponent. He leapt forward and grabbed onto the man's armour, swinging him round and pulling out his sword. Gideon slid his hand up behind the man's head and forced his sword handle into the face of the battered soldier. He smashed him hard three times in the nose before launching him over a fence that protected a small house on the street.

"What do you think you're doing? I had that covered," barked Braceum furiously.

"If we go around killing every man we come across, there will be no town left to raid," countered Gideon.

Braceum still looked furious but he was wise enough not to argue anymore.

"Nuallan, Josanne, get rid of the bodies and make for the tavern then meet us back here," commanded Gideon.

The tavern sat at the bottom of the road, a few abandoned

huts and stalls standing between them and the tavern itself which was dark, the shutters closed.

"We will meet you back here once we have plundered the settlement," Nuallan said.

"Agreed. Now, the rest of you with me," ordered Gideon.

The church sat right before them. It gleamed beautifully in the night, the torches shining elegantly all around the outside wall as the flames collided nicely with the multi-coloured windows that littered the front face of the building.

The company poured through a small wooden gate. They quickly scattered up the smart stone stairwell and up to the doorway. Gideon rested his hand gently on the smooth black handle, turned it and entered.

They spread out as they went in, the raid not beginning immediately as each one of them was absorbed in the church's beauty. The golden furniture glistened magnificently, even the pews were delicately carved but one thing in particular caught Gideon's eye. A dominating cross hung proudly at the far end of the church, and Gideon looked at it with guilt. Back home in Meridium, everyone including the King worshipped the gods. There were dozens of churches scattered around the city and everyone honoured and respected them.

"Here we are, lads, take one of these and get to it," Bray said with excitement as he handed each man a thick rough sack.

"Fill them up good and proper, and the Earl in return will fill your pockets," yelled Braceum from the opposite end of the church. His sack was already a quarter of the way full, as he rammed goblets, and even some of the more hardened prayer books into his bag.

Gideon nodded to his left at Doxass and Faizer, giving them permission to begin. They both immediately tackled a tall statue-like lamp in the corner and worked together to dismantle all the smaller parts. Gideon observed the raid for a few seconds until he was forced to squint his thin eyes as he noticed the handle twisting on a small door beside the huge cross. The door opened and a man dressed in white robes limped out.

"Leave this house, you pagans," shouted the old man. "Stop this madness or the gods will strike you down!"

Braceum, who was standing only a few metres away, paused. He dropped his sack, pulled out his sword and ran over to the priest. Bray quickly did the same, the two of them circling the man like wolves sizing up their prey.

"Braceum!" Gideon screamed from the entrance to the church.

Braceum looked over to Gideon and smiled with malice, a smile that Gideon was so used to seeing from the Commander.

"You let him go, this is not how we do things," Gideon said.

Bray lowered his sword slightly but quickly raised it back up when he realised Braceum had not yielded.

"No, young swordsman, this is not how you do things," hissed Braceum. "I have different orders." With one quick slash, he cut open the priest's chest and rotated his sword, sticking it deep into the priest's belly.

The innocent old man dropped to the floor, causing a bang with the impact.

"No!" erupted Gideon as he lost full control of his temper. He yanked out his longsword and raced through the pews and over to Braceum and Bray.

Braceum faced the oncoming beast and raised his sword, but Gideon moved too quickly. He lashed out before Braceum even had a chance to attack. He sliced across Braceum's chest and positioned himself behind his wounded foe. With one powerful move, he slowly drove his blade through Braceum's back.

The scream of pure pain echoed round the marble room.

Faizer and Doxass leapt into action, cornered Bray and closed in.

"Please, no, I won't say anything to the Commander, I swear it," Bray begged desperately. "Braceum died in combat, yes, that is what I will tell him."

Faizer and Doxass put away their swords and grabbed hold of him, Doxass delivering a hearty punch to the gut before throwing him down to his knees before Gideon.

"Please, I swear by the gods, I will not speak of this," cried Bray again.

Gideon walked slowly around him whilst making full eye contact with Andrus.

"We cannot trust him," Andrus said. "If he were to speak out, the Commander would inflict pain upon us. My wife and children live among the people at Vanghale, I would not risk harm coming to them."

Gideon nodded lightly at his youngest brother before taking a deep breath and tightening his grip. With one sudden explosive movement, Gideon whipped his body round and cut down, tearing open Bray's throat barbarically.

The company watched, shocked, as the limp lifeless body fell to one side.

Even Faizer and Doxass looked shocked at what they had just witnessed. They had never seen Gideon kill anyone that wasn't at least trying to kill him before. This was the first time they had ever really seen the true anger and wrath of the Meridium Prince and heir.

Gideon spared no thought for his two recent victims as he dropped down to his knees beside the priest. He shut the dead man's eyelids and kissed him on the forehead.

"We have raided enough," he said. "Take the sacks and go. We tell Frankel his men died in combat."

The company didn't wait about. They each picked up their sacks and made for the door.

Gideon wiped the blood from his sword on Braceum's cloak and picked up his sack.

"Wait!" he said as he picked up a light jog to catch up to his comrades.

The company stopped.

"Do you hear that?" He crouched slightly and crept towards the door, bypassing Andrus whose hand had just grasped the door's handle. Gideon gently pushed Andrus aside and put his ear against the door.

"The screams, I hear them," confirmed Doxass as he listened intently.

The wind was thrashing powerfully through Rhoden as the night's storm heightened. It drowned out most of the screams that echoed through the streets. Gideon turned the handle ever so gently and peeked his head slightly outside to scout out where the screams were coming from.

"What is it? Are there more soldiers?" asked Andrus, confused.

Gideon sighed impatiently and ripped open the door, startling his allies slightly. He lashed out into the open as he yet again lost control of his temper.

"Wait, what is it?" Andrus said as he moved out into the open, and to no one's surprise it was the Commander, out in the open, cutting down civilians.

Faizer and Doxass tracked Gideon down the stone steps and out into the street. The Commander's men were dragging women off into alleyways whilst the rest of the men slaughtered anyone that attempted to stop the vile crimes.

"Frankel, you wild pig. Stop your men!" shouted Gideon as he punched one of the Commander's men down to the ground, the soldier foolish enough to get in Gideon's way as he approached Frankel.

"We will be no part of this," he shouted again.

The Commander turned to Gideon and smiled arrogantly. "This is how we do things, young swordsman. Now pick a woman and go fuck her whilst your men slaughter the peasants of this town."

"We will do no such thing, you evil fuck," screamed Doxass as he came charging through the men and attempted to run at the Commander.

Three of the Commander's men attempted to stop him by intercepting him, but they stood no chance against the sizeable warrior. He smashed the first attacker in the face, knocking him out cold.

Andrus and Faizer dived into play as they collided with the other two. The Commander still had his sword drawn and so did a dozen or so of his men. The women and wounded men of Rhoden quickly escaped whilst the Commander's men were occupied with the company.

"Do we have a problem here, young swordsman?" barked the Commander who yet again seemed to be thriving from the danger around him.

"Aye, it appears we do, you fucking worthless town whore," snapped Nuallan who appeared behind the Commander's men along with Josanne. The pair of them dropped their hefty sacks and drew their swords. The sacks were splitting at the sides. Nuallan and Josanne must have stripped the tavern clean.

Men on both sides now shouted and cursed at each other, everyone but the Commander and Gideon, who both just kept solid eye contact with each other. It was a regular occurrence for the two of them to disagree on a raid because of how different they were to each other. But Gideon knew that Earl Oswald would side with Frankel over himself any day, after all Gideon and his company were outsiders to them.

Gideon fought hard to resist the urge to engage in a fight with the Commander's men because he knew their odds were slim. He would not risk the lives of his kin, so he decided it was time to leave.

"Sheath your swords, men. This savage is not worth our trouble. Pack up and let's get out of here," he declared wisely.

"You will do no such thing. There is plenty left to be plundered, you cowering dog," insulted Frankel.

Gideon struggled to contain his fury. He wished for nothing more than to be able to put his sword between the Commander's eyes, but he resisted again. He picked up his sack and swung it over his shoulder.

"Let's go," he muttered.

The Commander realised he wasn't going to get a reaction out of Gideon so he changed his tactic and turned his aggression towards Andrus. "You dare to disobey my command? If you do not fight, your wife and children lose their place back at Vanghale."

When the company had offered their swords up to Earl Oswald, they'd made a deal. They would follow the Commander's orders and fight, plunder and steal from any location that he desired, and in return they could keep twenty percent off whatever they plundered and Andrus's wife and children would be given a house inside Vanghale.

"Maybe I ought to pay them a little visit upon our return," the Commander said.

Gideon dropped his sack of gold and turned back around, but he had no time to act as Andrus leapt across the pavement and headed straight for the Commander in a state of rage.

Andrus was never good at controlling his temper, especially when threats were directed towards his family, but suddenly he came to a standstill as something startled him. He stood frozen to the spot, staring with confusion past the Commander and up to the top of the street.

Gideon and the others watched him, puzzled, and then they saw it.

"Time to go?" said Faizer as he began shuffling backwards.

"We're leaving now. Get the bags and make for the gate," commanded Gideon.

Andrus scorched a horrified look at Commander Frankel before spinning around and collecting his bag.

The Commander looked eagerly up to the top of the street to see what had startled the company so much.

"Men, create a line and prepare yourself!" he yelled as soon as he turned around. A defending force had gathered and they were being rallied by their leader, their Earl. Earl Julius.

Gideon led his company away from the imminent bloodbath, passing the tavern that Nuallan and Josanne had just raided and heading to the eastern wall. They could still hear the curses that the Commander yelled at them, his words echoing horrifyingly off the walls of Rhoden.

Sweat dripped from the heads of them all as the burning buildings blazed out of control.

Faizer wiped his forehead. "The mad fuck. The whole town is alight. Wasn't the whole point of this mission to get in and out unnoticed?"

"He is a fucking wild one. Best stick a blade in him the first chance we get," suggested Josanne.

Gideon halted his run and held up his clenched fist. The company swarmed round him, all of them looking for a way through the flames, most of the alleyways and smaller streets burning dangerously.

"What do we do?" Nuallan said. "We cannot travel this way. We must go back."

Faizer pointed. "That building there, the library. A building that size will have two entrances, one in the front and one in the back. I bet my sack of gold that the back entrance will bring us right out beside the main gate."

"You're right," Gideon said. "Let's move."

They fell in behind him, hopped over the wooden fence that surrounded the library and sprinted towards the door. Doxass took control by stepping in front of Gideon, taking one step back before kicking his heavy foot against the door. It almost snapped in half as it swung open.

"Inside," ordered Gideon. "Go," and the company ran into the building all with their hands over their mouths against the heat and smoke from the burning books.

"Over there, I see the door," Doxass said, quickly putting his hand back over his mouth.

They went quickly but carefully as the structural beams above them began to creak and crack as they gave way. The first beam bellowed loudly as it broke in half and came crashing towards the ground.

"Watch out!" Faizer warned as he leapt forward taking Gideon down to the ground, the beam plummeting towards them hard. It slammed to the side of them, close but causing no harm. They dragged themselves to their feet with aid from Nuallan and made for the back door that Doxass had just smashed open.

Doxass patted down his blond beard with panic as some

burning ash had flown into his facial hair, as the rest of the company spewed out of the burning library and fell out onto the grass, the choking and coughing drowning out the shouting and clashing of swords that could still be heard coming from the Commander's fight.

"By my beard, Faizer, you were right," Nuallan said as he dived to his feet. "The main gate is right there."

Gideon's eyes twinkled with relief at their glimmer of hope. They were to survive the burning deluge around them.

"Come on, lads, let's get out of here," he said.

Everyone got to their feet, dusted themselves down and yet again began running from the flames. They entered the courtyard and went through the slightly open gate.

The sun was just rising beyond the mountains. They had completed their side of the mission on time. They all trekked back over the dying field, dodging the ditches and clumps of hay that they had previously used for cover, back into West Foolong Forest.

In single file, the company climbed the sloped hill back up to camp. No words were shared as they struggled to tackle the hill after the night's antics had taken it out of each and every one of them.

Gideon was first to reach the top. He marched straight over to the fire and threw his sack of gold down. The fire was dying down, only embers remaining. He was frustrated, mind dwelling on the Commander's words and actions.

Everyone else dropped their sacks and took a minute to catch their breath. Andrus noticed Gideon's strange actions so he attempted to seek out the matter, walking over carefully and resting his hand on his brother's shoulder.

Gideon spun round in a snapping motion, launching Andrus's hand away. He began patrolling up and down with frustration, and it was not too long until the other members of the company noticed Gideon's change in mood.

"What's the matter?" asked Nuallan.

Gideon didn't hesitate or wait to unleash his answer. "That

fucking Commander, this fucking town and that fucking Earl sat back at the shit hole we all call home."

Nuallan and Andrus had never seen Gideon so worked up before. He was stubborn and aggressive most of the time but it was rare that he would go on like this. This reminded them of their father Artaxes.

"You make no sense, you fool, gather your thoughts and speak plainly," said Nuallan who seemed to be getting a bit frustrated himself.

"Is this the life we live now, from fur blankets and great halls to condemning the death of innocents and sleeping in a shit pit?" Gideon was shouting.

"This is the life we have now, Gideon," Andrus said. "What has been done cannot be undone. It's been like this for seven years now, why is it suddenly taking its toll on you?"

Gideon calmed himself and slowed his pacing, deep in thought.

"I have always tried to make a good life for us out here, but we have nothing. I realised that tonight. Look at what we have to do in order to survive. The Commander's men were raping and murdering innocent people just for a few lumps of gold." He slowly began losing his temper again. "This is not who we are!" he exploded. He dropped to his knees beside the flickering fire and breathed in deeply. "We shouldn't even be here. We are the Princes of Meridium, we are the sons of the great King Artaxes, Guardian King in the West." He paused and steadied his voice. "And look at us now."

Andrus tiptoed lightly towards him and put his hand back upon his shoulder. "The gods command this of us now, and I have more than just ourselves to worry about. I have a family, Gideon."

Gideon smiled back at him and picked himself back up. They embraced each other for a moment until something startled them.

A heavy snap came from out of the treeline. Everyone quickly looked around in the direction of the noise to find the Commander standing there.

"That explains a lot, very interesting indeed," he muttered.

Gideon and his brothers' secret had been discovered. After seven years of fighting for Earls and working for barons, their secret had finally came out.

The Commander stepped carefully out of the bushes, his armour stained and bruised with blood and muck, only a few men remaining.

"All this time, the people thought the three lost sons of Meridium were dead, but you're not dead. All this time you have been here fighting, with us." The Commander tilted his head down as he thought hard, and after a few seconds he lifted it back up and smiled dangerously.

Gideon clenched his sword and prepared himself to cut down the weak link.

"Gideon, Nuallan and Andrus Destain stand right before us, lads," announced Frankel. "So who are these? Your bodyguards?" Frankel looked towards the brothers from Vaughan and Josanne.

"Loyal friends," snapped Andrus who was readying himself with an intimidating stance. He held his damp cloak to the side revealing his throwing knives.

"You know, there is a very heavy bounty on your head," said the Commander.

Nuallan twisted his face at the half-hearted threat. "Enough of this," he said, growing impatient with the uneasy tension. He reached for his blade and pulled it out. "Let's fucking have you then, you cunt," threatened Nuallan.

"You are mistaken, young Prince. You are, after all, the heirs of the western throne. We in fact owe you our allegiance," said Frankel.

Gideon glared at the Commander, searching his mind for answers. Was the Commander saying this to save his back now that he didn't possess the numbers to defeat the company, or was he in fact declaring his allegiance to his superiors? Gideon decided to test the Commander with a question. He walked between his brothers and stood calmly in front of Frankel. "No one can know who we are. If we return to Vanghale, will you swear that you and your men will keep this secret, until the day we leave?"

The Commander glared back with that demonic smile that turned every man's stomach. He then leant his head down, bowing honourably. "You have my word."

Everyone in the company was shocked at the way the Commander so quickly yielded and honoured his Princes.

"Good, then there is no need for any more bloodshed," announced Gideon, leaving the matter alone for now.

The Commander leaned over his shoulder and signalled his men to pack up. "Prepare the horses, we ride for Vanghale." He watched Gideon walk away, then Frankel looked around to make sure no one was watching him. Once satisfied, he walked back off into the treeline and rested against a bark-cracked tree. He looked hard between the waving branches and leaves, glaring through the roof of Foolong Forest and up into the sky.

His mind was working overtime. He didn't know what to do.

Hand the brothers over, earn massive respect from his Earl and claim the substantial sum from the bounty the High King of Darchem offered? Or, honour his word. After all, they were his Princes. Meridium ruled all of the West and every Western Earl, Baron, and man paid taxes and submitted to the Guardian King. It would be treason to go against his Prince, but the Commander and his Earl had never honoured the rule of Artaxes and his spawn. They too sought expansion and power.

Frankel looked over his shoulder and watched Gideon pack his gear beside his comrades. He watched more until he began smiling to himself. He had made up his mind.

CHAPTER 3
THE WESTERN AFTERMATH

The golden-haired General walked through one of the palace's largest halls, his silver armour jingling and ringing powerfully with every solid step. Koos spotted the two King's Guard dressed in full armour.

They both had a long blue cape streaming down their backs and a white lion imprinted on their chest plates, the symbol of the King's Guard. They were awaiting him by the double doors that led to the King's throne room. Koos changed his direction and headed over to them.

"Dariuss, Havada," greeted the young General.

They both bowed to him before addressing him. "General," they said one after each other. Both of the King's Guard's appearances were hidden due to their strangely styled helmets but small blond strands of hair could be seen hanging out of the bottom of Havada's helmet as it rested on his shoulders. Dariuss was the same, but his hair was black.

Koos stood before them, extremely nervous. "Is he in there?"

"Aye, he is," said Havada, "but I warn you, he is not in a good mood."

"At least you won't be there to see him cut off my head, I need you elsewhere," replied Koos sarcastically.

"You plan to go through with it then? You know he won't approve," Dariuss said.

Koos ignored Dariuss's negativity and averted his attention to Havada. "Go down to the courtyard, your men await you. Ride for Brigantium and deliver this message." He reached into his long blue cloak and pulled out a rolled up scroll. "You must ride to the eastern city and place this scroll in the hands of Tobias Ringfold. No one else's, only his. Do you understand?"

"Of course," Havada said, "but what if King Artaxes does not give us his blessing. I cannot defy his wishes, and you know of his hate towards the Horse Lords in the East. He would see Tobias buried in the ground before he would accept aid."

"Once I have spoken with him, I will come down to the courtyard and give you your orders. Do not leave until you see me, understand?"

"Yes, General," confirmed Havada. He bowed his head, tucked away the scroll in his blue cape and turned away.

Koos turned back to Dariuss. "Shall we?" he suggested as he held his hand out allowing Dariuss to walk into the throne room first.

Dariuss walked towards the gigantic heavy doors, rested a hand on each door and pushed forward with all his strength. They slowly separated causing a hollow creak. He walked in and mimicked Koos's expression by holding his hand out in front of him, gesturing Koos to go first.

Koos chuckled to himself and walked through the doors and past Dariuss. Dariuss followed Koos and walked beside him along the red carpet that travelled right through the throne room.

On each side of them stood enormous columns that towered right up to the ceiling, the detail of the ridges along the sides of the columns magnificent. An armoured soldier stood motionless at the base of each column, each equipped with a square shield and a sharp spear.

Bright beams of light shone in through the clear open windows that patterned the smooth white walls, gleaming off the marble floor and making it look even more beautiful. A figure could be made out sitting on the far end of the throne room on a risen platform, King Artaxes, on his throne. Artaxes was into his late fifties now, and the grey had taken over his head, although with age his physical appearance had not suffered. He was tall still, well over six foot one. He was not as broad as most but still just as strong.

"Good luck," said Dariuss as the pair of them reached the glistening set of steps that led up to the King's platform.

Koos tackled them first, his armour rattling as he climbed the stairs one at a time. Dariuss soon overtook him on the staircase and quickly reached the top.

"My King," greeted Dariuss.

The King nodded at him. Dariuss then walked past the King and stood in line with the other three King's Guard and the First General that were standing behind the King's throne. Each one was wearing the blue Meridium cloak with the white lion imprinted on their chest plate. The First General was the overall second in command. His name was Lucifer, First General for over thirty years, and Artaxes's most trusted and favoured soldier among his army.

Artaxes slouched in his silver throne miserably. He was sitting sideways on, holding onto a blue bit of thread that dangled off a smaller chair beside his own. It was his wife's throne.

Koos stood before the King with his hand rested on his sword handle and his other hand clenched in front of his heart. He clapped his feet together and bowed, then took a few steps towards the King and attempted to engage him in conversation.

"Good morning, my King. I have a serious matter that I must discuss with you," said Koos politely.

Before the King was willing to listen to his General, he interrupted him and pressed a matter of his own. "Tell me, General, do you remember my wife?"

Koos looked back with confusion. "Yes, of course I do, my King. She was a true woman of Meridium."

"Indeed she was. She was the heart of this city, you know. She gave me the strength and will that I needed to bring balance to my Kingdom."

Koos looked at the King strangely. Everyone knew the King

had lost his mind slightly when his wife Claudia Destain died, but why was he speaking of it now? Surely he knew how important the matter was that Koos was trying to press.

Brushing off the King's strange comments, Koos tried to speak to the King again. "King Artaxes, I have word from a squadron of men who arrived in the city this morning from Villach." He was forced to hold his tongue once again as the King interrupted him with a more deranged story.

This time as Artaxes spoke, he tightened the hold on the thin blue fabric that dangled from his wife's seat. "And do you remember my son, Nuallan?" he asked as his jaw tightened and his cheeks wriggled.

"Of course, he was my friend and captain at a time."

"Then you will remember him killing my wife, do you not?"

Koos took a step forward. "Your wife was not killed by your son, my King. She was murdered by a hill gang from the south."

Artaxes didn't take to Koos's traitorous words well. He erupted from his throne, balancing himself onto his long legs.

"You fool, and how do you think she ended up in the hands of the hill gang? Your clumsy murdering friend gave her to them."

Koos dared to argue back. "If you believe that, then you are the fool, my King. Whether you like it or not, you must get over the past. What is done is done. You have more important things to think about right now, like thousands of Oakland Musters sacking your ports and raiding your defensive cities. Villach is lost."

Artaxes raised an eyebrow before sliding back down into his throne. "The Oakland musters are no threat to us. I will drag their beloved forest down into The Sink if I must."

Koos was growing impatient. He took another step forward towards his King. "Not a threat? How can you say this? They control Oggsfleet Port and the city of Villach. In the space of two days, they successfully attacked, raided and gained control of these positions. You must call for aid. I have Havada at the ready. He awaits your blessing."

Artaxes showed his first bit of interest in Koos's warning.

He pulled himself up until he was sitting upright. "Blessing for what?" he asked patiently.

Koos took a deep breath before announcing his plan. "I have informed him to ride for Brigantium to ask for aid from Tobias Ringfold. If he would come with just a small portion of his men, we would crush the Musters with ease."

Artaxes frowned and slid back into a slouching position. "Tell me, you fucking halfwit, where was Tobias and his mighty Horse Lord followers seven years ago? We needed him then. We do not need him now." He leaned forward and said loudly, "Your father would spit on this idea of yours if he were but here to listen to it, you silly boy."

"But he's not," Koos said, teeth clenched, close to losing his temper all together, even the King shocked that he had broken from his usual calm stable mind. "He is not here, my King, neither is your wife, or the heirs of Meridium, and they never will be. It's just you and whatever remains of your poor mind."

The King stood up and walked towards Koos calmly. He rested his lips on the General's ear and said, "If any man rides for Brigantium, I will cut off their head."

Koos wavered in fear, the shock of the threat truly affecting him. The person who had acted like his father for most of his life had just threatened to kill him should he carry out his desperate mission. He watched, horrified, as his King turned from him and walked away, Lucifer and the rest of the King's Guard following the King down the steps and off through a small door at the back end of the throne room. Only Dariuss halted for a moment to spare a look of sympathy towards the young General.

Frustrated and angry, Koos stormed out of the throne room. He burst out of the doors and marched through the northern halls, ignoring all the greetings that soldiers and various priests shouted at him as he passed. He clattered down the steps and broke out of the palace's main entrance and out into the open city of Meridium.

What a sight it was. The city was broken up into three city sections, the palace sitting at the most northern point of the city above all the sections. City section one was on the western side of the city where all the trading was carried out, hundreds upon hundreds of stalls, salesmen and wine merchants gathering there every morning, and trading until the sun went down.

City section two was in the middle of the city, separated from the King's palace by a wooden wall. Most of the city's buildings were built here, armouries, libraries, taverns, stables and many others. Churches however were built in every section. The people of Meridium were very religious and it was the law to attend a church at least once a week.

Section three was the housing section, the poor, rich and middle class all lived in different parts of the section, people flooding into the other sections every morning to trade. The tight roads and pathways thinned out the city's streets neatly, alleyways offering shortcuts through the streets and into others. But the once great city struggled to hold onto its beauty. The white buildings were now blackened with the smog that floated out from the blacksmiths' chimneys, vines grew through the cracked brick, and most houses and roads were unevenly laid. Since the war, the city had lost that many men and boys to High Darchem, few remained to carry out the jobs. Artaxes had also lost the will to tend to his city as much as he used to.

Meridium was crumbling.

Koos quickened his escape from the palace grounds. He stormed through the gatehouse and into section two. He headed down the main street that ran right through the city section until he arrived about halfway down, going in and out of all the people scurrying out of the town and vanished into an alleyway. He followed the pathway until he came to a little open area, a nicely built stable sitting in a dead ended street.

He pulled out a key from inside his blue cape and unlocked the latch on the door, walking in and going straight over to a table underneath a smudged window. He slammed his fists deep into the table and began shaking angrily.

He had to think deeply for a solution. Havada could not be sent against the King's wishes and he himself would be executed if he went. He untied the string on his armour and positioned it on the table, folding it neatly and rolling up the sleeves on his light blue under thermals. He began searching around the cold hollow stable, messing up the shelves and ripping open the lids on various storage boxes within the building. Eventually he found a brown leather saddle with gold hoop buckles. He went to pick it up but stopped as a creaking sound alerted him.

A short man opened the door the rest of the way and walked in confidently. His name was Cassius and he was a Captain of the Meridium army, although he acted more like a scout and a spy than a Captain. His father was a business owner in Meridium, held close by Artaxes many years ago before his death, and once Cassius was old enough to fight, his father begged the ear of Artaxes, persuading him to allow Cassius to be trained among the more skilled and wealthy soldiers. That was how he obtained the rank of Captain.

As time went on, Cassius would suck up to the King by informing him of all his sons' whereabouts and dealings, and now the middle-aged spy kept a watchful eye on anything that went on inside Meridium's walls. He had short black hair and his beard was dark and trimmed, his black leathers and cape matching up with his dark venomous eyes.

"Going somewhere, General?" asked the snaky Captain.

"If I were, it would be of no concern to you," hissed Koos.

Cassius smiled delicately and wandered through the stable and over to Koos. He peered behind Koos and looked into the box, spotting the saddle that Koos had discretely tried to stash.

"Word is that you plan to ride for Brigantium," he said.

Koos slammed the box lid shut and squared up to him. "In case you were not aware, Captain, the western cities and ports are being terrorised by the Oakland Musters. We do not have the numbers to defeat them. The Horse Lords of Brigantium do, and together we will trample the filth." He couldn't keep the frustration from his voice.

"And does the King give this quest his blessing?" asked Cassius sarcastically.

Koos looked blank. He turned back around and reopened the box, pulling out the saddle and walking over to the table.

"He does not, but his mind is blurred. He no longer sees a threat as a threat, but the city will fall if we lose any more of our outer defences," insisted the young General.

"I agree," said Cassius surprisingly. He followed Koos to the table and reached his hand around the back of the General. "But the Brigantiums are cowards. We share no alliances with them and if you remember, it was them, the almighty Horse Lords from the East that abandoned us on that field seven years ago. You of all people should not forget that," he whispered as he dug his finger into Koos's chest, tracing out his scar, rubbing it punishingly until Koos spun around.

"Forget? I couldn't forget even if I wanted to. How could I? Look around you. The crumbling city, the deranged King, the lack of horses, soldiers and siege equipment reminds me of it. Everywhere I look, I am reminded of that day."

Cassius smirked at him as he listened, his attempt to wind up the young General successful. "Everyone in the city admires your bravery and loyalty, lad, including myself, but if you ride for Brigantium, the King will be informed." Cassius made the threat as he turned and walked for the door. He pushed it open and stepped out. "Be wise and stay," he added. "Meridium needs a soldier like you for the dark days that lie ahead. I won't have your blood on my hands." He left the room completely leaving Koos standing puzzled and alone.

Koos stood wondering for a moment, taking in Captain Cassius's threats and also his advice. But he knew what he had to do. He sorted the saddle and hung it over his arm, and leaving the mess behind, he left the stable and walked back through the pathway and out onto the street.

Koos marched, interested to notice if any of Cassius's men were watching him, but none seemed to be in sight. The General continued his journey through section two towards the silver grey bricked courtyard. It was a big opening plain of silver concrete, dozens upon dozens of statues of the Meridium King standing proudly around the courtyard. Large watchtowers stood scattered along the inside of the wall that protected the courtyard and the rest of the city. The wall was at least forty foot high, equipped with ballista missiles and trebuchets positioned on platforms that hung out of the front face of the city's wall. Archers and spearmen stood guard upon it, taking shifts so that there was always a sufficient number of guards. It was a system that had never seen an enemy cross or breach the wall.

Koos strode down into the courtyard and walked over by the gate where Havada stood holding the reins of two horses.

"General, the party is ready to leave at once," Havada said eagerly. "Did the King give us his blessing?"

Koos met him and took hold of one of the reins. He shot his saddle over the back of the black horse and began knotting the strings tightly.

"Koos, what did he say?" begged Havada again.

"He called for the head of anyone who rides for Brigantium," Koos replied.

Havada looked disappointed. "Then I cannot go, my General. I am a King's Guard and my life and loyalties are indebted to the King."

"I understand that, I would not ask that of you. I ask only that your men will accompany me off the Meridium outskirts for protection."

The three men who were already mounted and ready to leave had no objections to his request, and sat happily waiting for a command. Havada turned to look at his men before looking back at Koos. In an instant, he leaned forward, snatching the reins of the horse that his General was preparing.

"You will go?" he asked unsurely.

"I will. I will return in less than a week with Tobias and his army."

"But you said it yourself, Artaxes will take your head. Koos, do not be mistaken, the King is a vicious man."

Koos finished off preparing his horse's saddle. He tucked his sword neatly between the saddle and the horse's thick black belly and then turned to face his friend.

"My father was one of the King's closest friends, more of a brother than a friend. He will not harm me," Koos assured as he climbed up onto the horse. "I will not watch the Kingdom of Meridium endure any more suffering. We must all do our parts in order to save the Kingdom. One day the heirs of Meridium will return and restore balance and honour to this once great city, but until then we must all make sacrifices." He said it boldly, causing one of the soldiers at the back of the party to chuckle to himself.

"The heirs of Meridium will never return, they are dead," the man stated harshly forcing Koos to turn around venomously.

"No, they are not dead!" he snapped.

Havada interrupted the dispute. "Very well, my men will escort you to the outskirts. Good luck, my friend." Havada reached out his hand.

Koos met his hand and latched onto it perfectly. "Rise and rise again, my friend," he said.

"Rise and rise again, General," replied Havada.

These words were spoken often since the war. They indicated that the Meridiums would always stand back up and regain glory after defeat, the words shared amongst many in the Meridium army but never the King.

Koos dug his heels into his horse's hip, signalling it to take off, and so it did. Havada watched the young General and the three mounted escorts ride off out of the main gate and off into the field. He watched until they were out of sight, and then turned and began his long walk back up to the King's palace. As he travelled, he noticed a character standing by a stall with four rugged men, Captain Cassius and his runabouts. They glared at Havada in a way that seemed to be an attempt to provoke a reaction out of the King's Guard, but none came. Havada ignored them and continued his journey back to the palace.

CHAPTER 4
AN OLD TALE

The emerald green leaves fluttered sharply in the gusty wind that attacked the entrance to West Foolong Forest. Gideon and his company made an appearance as they led the pack that flooded out of the forest's mouth. Commander Frankel's horse however walked calmly towards the rear of the returning raiding party. The victorious pack travelled along the short dirt road that led to Vanghale's gate, a parsley green field surrounding Vanghale just like it did at Rhoden. The difference between the two was that this field was tended to far better, dozens of farmers working on it everyday. Large parts of the terrain had been sectioned off so that crops could be grown and harvested.

The large town was shaped in a perfect square, protected by high walls. There were four gates to the town, one at the north, south, west and east. All the gates were guarded but the northern one had the most men on watch. It faced the west entrance of Foolong Forest because if an attack came, it would probably come from that direction.

The only way to get into the town was by one of the drawbridges that had to be lowered down since a full circular ditch surrounded the town. The ditch was tight against the wall and about fifteen feet deep.

The men of Vanghale had carved and stripped huge logs converting them into thick pikes, which had been sunk into the ditches facing upwards. This was an excellent defensive mechanism against any enemy that attacked.

"What is your plan upon arrival?" asked Faizer whose horse had just caught up to Gideon's.

Gideon looked at Faizer and then tilted his body round to spot out the Commander. The Commander had been staring at the back of Gideon and his horse for most of the journey.

"I do not know. I will go and speak with the Earl immediately. You and Nuallan will accompany me," decided Gideon quickly.

"Not Andrus or the others?" asked Faizer, surprised.

"I want to go up there and find out his intentions. If he wants to continue his raids on Rhoden and the other towns, changes must be made. I need to make my point clear, otherwise we are leaving." He lowered his voice. "Also I need to find out if the Commander has informed him of our secret. I don't want to go up there and end up in another fight. The others have sharp tongues and I need my wisest men."

Faizer looked at him with confusion. "Then why are you bringing Nuallan?" he asked.

Gideon smiled. "Just in case a fight does break out."

Faizer laughed back but was soon silenced as the Commander trotted past with his men, crossing the northern drawbridge into Vanghale first.

"Well, he seems to be in a hurry," growled Faizer.

Gideon watched the Commander viciously. He knew Frankel was trying to get an audience with the Earl first, but why?

"Where is that cunt going in such a dash?" snapped Nuallan who had caught up to the leading pair.

"Where do you think?" hissed Gideon as his horse trod onto the drawbridge.

The company fell into single file as they crossed it and broke into Vanghale. They passed through the rectangular gate and swarmed out into the courtyard.

Gideon slid off his horse and handed the reins to Josanne who dismounted next.

"Andrus, head home and see your family. Doxass and Josanne

are to meet you there once they have tended to the horses," he ordered.

"You're going to see the Earl now?" asked Andrus.

"Aye, I need to speak with him. Save us a bowl of stew and we will meet you at your house presently."

"Save me two," joked Doxass with a pleasant tone as he walked off towards the stables.

Andrus stood with a look of jealousy upon his face, confused why his brother wanted Faizer to accompany him and not himself. Over the years, Andrus had grown a little envious towards Faizer. He didn't like how Gideon chose him as his right hand man over himself and Nuallan. Too tired for an argument he brushed off the situation, and made for home.

Nuallan grabbed hold of Gideon who was storming out of the courtyard, leaning in towards his ear. "Care to fill me in?"

Gideon walked away without revealing anything to the others. He paced quickly until there were no guards of Vanghale present. Once satisfied, he slowed his march and allowed Nuallan and Faizer to catch up. They walked out of the small courtyard and headed for the Earl's keep in the centre of the town.

The streets of Vanghale ran up in single rectangular streaks, all leading to the centre of the town. There, the Earl's keep sat amongst the stalls and a few open taverns. There were no churches or libraries inside this town. The people of Vanghale only believed in raiding and taking without mercy. They were just simple scavengers with no ambition.

Nuallan attempted to force answers out of his brother again as they walked up one of the central streets towards the square.

"Gideon, care to fill me in now?" asked Nuallan a little more pleasantly this time.

"I need to speak with the Earl about the Commander's actions. If he is not willing to tame his wild dog then we will no longer raid alongside these animals."

"By pressing a matter like that, you risk the Commander spreading word of our true identities. You do understand this, yes?" countered Nuallan.

Gideon, seeming very certain of himself, replied quickly. "He will not say anything."

Nuallan looked even more worried. "How can you be sure?" he pressed.

"I just know it," Gideon said. "Now, don't worry yourself. Just let me do the talking and be ready for anything."

Nuallan sniggered lightly to himself before speaking. "If there is one thing I have learned since our banishment, it is to always be ready for anything."

The three of them reached the end of the street and walked out into the town's square. The atmosphere was rather cheerful as the children ran around playing. The tradesmen yelled out their offers on their fruit and vegetables and the ale merchants offered out free testers of their products. Gideon and his two companions slid in and out of the crowd and made for the medium-sized shack at the back end of the square.

It wasn't much to look at considering it was an Earl's keep. The wooden walls were chipped and gnawed, the door was cracked and beaten, and the roof was riddled with holes that seemed to be filled up with nothing but cloth and straw.

"Let me do the talking, brothers," Gideon said as he walked up to the door, but he was quickly stopped. Two soldiers that were standing guard crossed their spears, blocking the doorway.

Nuallan took charge quickly. "You have two seconds to move out of the way before I rip out both your throats," he threatened.

Both the guards looked nervous but refused to stand down.

Faizer quickly involved himself in order to prevent a scrappy brawl. "Lads, we have just returned from the raid. We seek to discuss matters with the Earl," he said.

One of the soldiers who seemed to be very young looked to the other for assistance in what to do. He was met with a worried look from his companion who eventually broke, stepped aside and allowed the group access. The three of them walked in, Nuallan brushing himself up against the youngest guard as he slid past and into the keep.

The atmosphere inside the keep was dull, nothing like the one outside. Groups of men stood scattered all around the room, supping ale grossly, most of the men wild of beard and rather rough looking. The floor was scattered with wolf skins and other furs from butchered animals, skins hanging up on the walls in an attempt to provide the room with warmth, but it wasn't working as trapped rainwater dripped from the roof and ran down the walls, ruining any cosy homely feeling.

The air was mucky and a carnival of foul scents fluttered in the air unpleasantly. The only form of comfort that lurked inside the keep was the warm creamy feeling that fluttered from the molten red embers that sat nicely inside a stone fire pit that was filled with branches and logs.

Gideon mooched through the groups of chattering men and headed for Earl Oswald. He was sitting in his leather chair with the Commander behind him watching the bags of gold. Earl Oswald was a man in his sixties, the grey creeping into his long blond beard overrunning the tiny blond strands that once lived there, his long frizzy hair also struggling to control the conquering grey. The Earl respectfully pulled himself to his feet to greet his mercenaries.

"Welcome back. A successful raid, I hear." The Earl looked back to his Commander.

Gideon stepped forward and slowly began approaching the Earl. "I have a few things I would like to discuss," he requested, leaving out the greetings and formalities.

"Oh yes, and what's that, young swordsman?" replied the Earl sternly.

"Your Commander. I do not know what orders you had given him but I believe the actions he carried out were not by your word. I am here to tell you that if his ways do not change, my company will retire from your raids."

The Earl sighed and turned round again to look at his Commander who stood straight-faced hawk eyeing Gideon.

"I grow tired of listening to you two groan and moan about how each of you do things when out on a raid. You must understand that my people do not have the same morals as you and your followers," said Earl Oswald, making Gideon grow impatient as he spoke.

"So you condone the raping of innocent woman and the slaughter of men and children, all for a couple of sacks of golden goblets and spoons," snapped Gideon.

"My men follow my commands and orders and carry out my tasks. What they do on the raids is none of my business or yours. As long as they bring home the prize, it does not faze me." The Earl smiled. "Now you should learn your place. A fine addition you and your wild pack of animals have become, but do not be mistaken, young swordsman, my men would raid just fine without you. I have nearly two thousand loyal men at my disposal. You see the house I provide and the gold I let you keep, you need that more than we need you."

Nuallan snarled viciously as he stood behind Gideon. "Are you threatening us, old man?" he barked, forcing Frankel to step in.

The Commander pulled out his sword and stepped forward, many of the men standing in groups around the keep dropping their ales and drawing swords also, some of them shouting and cursing as they did so.

The slithering sound of dozens of swords being unsheathed forced a nervous look upon Faizer's face, but Nuallan and Gideon seemed unfazed, the two of them were always up for a fight. Earl Oswald leapt up as quickly as his old body allowed him to with his hands raised.

"Put them away, lads, there is no need for this. And as for you two, you and Frankel will set aside your differences. I have another raid planned but this time the prize is way bigger," said the Earl to Gideon. He slid back down into his chair and began to explain.

Gideon and the others all listened with eager interest.

"In three days time, we will attack Rhoden again, but this time we will hit them where it hurts, the Bothsom Mines. If we take the mines, we can then control the town. Earl Julius's men will be forced to fight for me, what remains of them anyway," explained Oswald.

The Commander and the surrounding men smiled and chattered happily amongst themselves, even Nuallan seemed slightly won over.

"Are you aware over four hundred men guard that mine, and military camps are set up all along its borders. It will be a tough fight," Faizer said.

"Do not worry, my dear boy, we will have sufficient numbers. A small force will be sent to attack the town whilst half my army will attack the mines, one thousand men," said the Earl.

"The men of Rhoden will be outnumbered massively. They stand no chance," added the Commander involving himself into the conversation.

Gideon thought hard on the offer, seeking to dismiss the promise of gold and attempting to see why Oswald really wanted to control Rhoden. "Once you have Rhoden in your mitts, what will you do then?" he said. "The other towns surrounding the Midlands offer no rewarding loot. Your raiding days will have to come to an end."

"Indeed they will, I have grown ambitious," the Earl said. "If I unite all the surrounding towns to my side, I will have a rather sizeable force. The lands further to the west grow weak. I hear now that the Oakland Musters torture the Meridiums. I hear even the city of Villach has fallen. How long do you think it will be until the city of Meridium itself becomes available?"

Gideon's face dropped and so did Nuallan's.

"Villach has fallen?" muttered Nuallan recklessly.

"Yes, lad, you all seem rather upset about this news." The Earl regarded them, a horrifying smile taking over his face.

Gideon instantly panicked, a sickly feeling in his stomach. He couldn't believe it, the Commander had revealed their secret.

"Not upset, just surprised," insisted Faizer quickly. "We heard stories you see, of the great Artaxes and the Western Kingdom."

The Commander puffed out with a small chugger of laughter at Faizer's failed attempt to cover up the already revealed secret.

"Oh, I'm sure you did, but who told you the stories, hmm?" countered the Earl as he pointed towards Gideon.

"Whatever you are indicating, you are mistaken," Nuallan attempted desperately.

But Gideon put his hand up in front of his brother to silence him. The Meridium heir played it smart and attempted to strike a deal with Oswald.

"A large bounty lies on our heads," he said. "But the plunder you would receive from the Bothsom Mines is far more than any amount the High King of Darchem would pay you. Will you turn us in?" Gideon couldn't help but notice the demonic smile that was sitting on Commander Frankel's face as he spoke.

"Did you not hear me, Gideon Destain of Meridium? This is not about money. I have grown ambitious. You pledge yourself to me and I will one day take you back to the very gates of Meridium. We all know the story. That your father disowned you all, threw you out into the wilderness with nothing but each other," the Earl said painfully. "You must seek revenge, do you not, young Prince?"

Gideon's heart warmed to the sound of the word. It had been a long time since he had been referred to as a Prince. He thought for a moment alone whilst Faizer and Nuallan remained silent, too scared to say a word in case they endangered themselves more.

After some thought, Gideon raised his head and with his right hand he brushed his brown stringy hair behind his ear. "Aye, we will fight, but I take no order from your Commander." Gideon pointed in the Commander's direction, the man still smiling pleasantly.

The Earl pounced to his feet ecstatically. "Done. From this day onwards, in Vanghale, you will be named Commander Gideon. You and Frankel together will train my armies and lead them into battle."

Frankel's smile finally faded. He tilted his head in the Earl's direction and looked with confusion. He now had no power over Gideon and the company.

"My company will be ready in three days," announced Gideon sharply. He spun round and stormed off out of the keep, Nuallan and Faizer left standing shocked and alone with the Earl until they quickly scattered out of the keep and chased Gideon down.

The Earl again fell back into his chair, and this time it was him with the wicked smile upon his face.

"You would treat me as an equal to this foreign prick?" snapped Commander Frankel as he lurched round to the front of Oswald's chair.

"Don't worry yourself, Commander. The people of this town know of your loyalties and your backbone. Now I want you to follow them, watch their house. If anyone attempts to flee Vanghale, report to me immediately. They are too valuable now."

The Commander smiled half-heartedly and walked out of the keep.

"Gideon, what do you think you're doing?" shouted Nuallan from across the square as he chased down his brother.

Gideon ignored him and turned to storm off, trampling up a set of steps and bursting through the door of the local tavern.

"Where on god's earth is he going?" groaned Nuallan.

"Come on, let's just get after him," said Faizer.

The two of them tracked Gideon's steps, striding in and out of the people that still swarmed the blazing square and into the tavern.

The stench of the air quickly changed as they entered, the mixture of foul breath, cheap ale and smoke lurking unsettlingly within the tavern. People stood swaying all over, cursing and laughing like crazed men.

"There he is," said Faizer, pointing.

Gideon was sitting with his head in his hands at a wobbly old table at the back end of the tavern.

Nuallan and Faizer walked over quickly and sat down in the spare seats.

"Gideon, what do you think you are doing? You have no right to accept the Earl's commission without consulting the rest of the company," barked Nuallan with fury. "You just agreed to go to war with our own people."

"Nuallan, settle yourself. I have a plan," Gideon said finally.

Nuallan's eyes widened, slightly embarrassed at his previous statement. "In that case, I will get the ales in." He jumped up and charged over to the bar.

"So this plan, speak to me," demanded Faizer eagerly.

Gideon put his head back into his hands and rubbed. He took a deep worrying breath in. "We are leaving, tomorrow if possible."

"But you just agreed to pledge yourself to the Earl and accepted a promotion. Forgive me for speaking out but there is no way he will allow you to leave now."

"He was never going to let us leave anyway. I fear he may already have sent message to Darchem of our whereabouts."

The conversation was interrupted by a drenching bang as Nuallan slammed down three overflowing tankards of ale. He sat back down and pressed for answers.

"So, come on, what is the plan?"

"We will return to Andrus's house tonight and have a meeting," Gideon said. "We need to leave as soon as possible. But where we go I do not know."

"Anywhere but west. I will never go back to Meridium, Gideon," Nuallan said sadly. "Besides, father would kill me if I did."

Faizer's face tightened with confusion as he took in Nuallan's comment. "Why would your father kill you?" he asked. "I don't understand?"

Gideon quickly made eye contact with Faizer and shook his head slowly and secretively.

Faizer was more confused at Gideon's warning.

"Because he blames me for the death of our mother, and who can blame him?" revealed Nuallan.

"What happened on that dark day was not your doing, Nuallan. Every sane person in Meridium knows that," Gideon said.

"I don't think I dare ask anymore," Faizer said.

"No, I will tell you," said Nuallan surprisingly.

Gideon reached over the nutshell brown table and put his hand on Nuallan's thick forearm.

"You don't have to, brother," he said, but Nuallan snatched his arm away and insisted.

"He deserves to know. He is as much a brother to us as Andrus is," countered Nuallan as he prepared to tell the story.

Faizer pulled his ale close and chugged it hard as he waited to hear Nuallan's story.

"It was eight years ago, not long before the war. King Tobias Ringfold from the Eastern Kingdom was hosting a royal wedding for his cousin who was marrying some noble's daughter from the south. You see, our Father was never fond of Tobias and his Horse Lords, so when my mother revealed she was attending, he refused. Our mother was a very, very traditional woman and also very fond of the Brigantiums. She would travel there once or twice a month." Nuallan paused. "So, whenever she would go on her adventures and travels, father would stay put. It would allow him the freedom to sack the western tribes without mother yelling in his ear that it was wrong." He stopped again to take a slurp of his ale.

Gideon sat with his head down, staring at nothing. He disliked the story and took no enjoyment in listening to it.

"So once I heard of mother's plan to travel, I quickly went to see father about planning and leading the escorts, except I had my own way of wanting to do it. I was at the age where I was trying desperately to prove to the people I was the rightful heir and that I was worthy of the throne once father died, because of course at that time I was in fact the heir to Meridium. So I put upon father a plan to get our mother to Brigantium without anyone knowing. Father had been putting so much pressure on the tribes and gangs that occupied the Hushwood Forest just outside Meridium's borders, that it was causing the tribes and gangs to flood out and set up camp in the open. I knew of this so I changed mother's route, shrank the escorts in order to not draw attention, and I took charge of the convoy over First General Lucifer, the man in charge of organising her departures and keeping her safe usually." Nuallan stopped his story as a woman arrived at their table to reignite the candle's flame that seemed to have died out.

"Any more ales, gentleman?" she asked.

Gideon shook his head as he continued to look down. Faizer however handed her his empty tankard and then shooed her away.

Nuallan waited till the woman left before continuing. "So father eventually agreed, but he made it pretty clear what would happen if anything went wrong, and it did. It went terribly wrong. The new route that I selected was occupied by a large hill tribe that father had terrorised and mocked for years. Their scouts must have seen us so they waited and planned an ambush. I had only selected six mounted guards and myself to accompany my mother and her carriage. It wasn't nearly enough. The first we heard were screams and chants coming from the forest's belly. Twenty or so of them ran out of the forest and attacked us. I was pulled from my horse and knocked unconscious. I was awoken by one of my men splashing water into my face some time after. Only him and myself had survived. My mother was gone, taken by the tribe." Nuallan took a break, sipping at his ale and looking at Gideon before continuing. "We scoured the forest for hours searching for her but there was no sign. Eventually we returned to Meridium and informed father. He tore the throne room to bits with his bare hands." Nuallan's voice broke as a tear trickled down his face. He dropped his head down in shame.

Gideon took over the story. "You see, Faizer, our mother was the heart of Meridium. The love our father shared for her was like no other. He has never smiled again or laughed since."

"My heart goes out to you, Nuallan," said Faizer sympathetically. "To never get to say goodbye to your mother must be devastating."

Gideon sighed strangely and coughed. Faizer noticed his strange behaviour and looked back to Nuallan.

"I did get to say goodbye, from afar," muttered Nuallan. "The next morning we were awoken by the city bell ringing. We all ran to the city's gate and climbed up onto the wall. Father was already there. He had been there all night. Still to this day I will never forget the horrified look upon his face. The tribe had brought my mother to the gates so that we could watch. She was there, naked, bloody and beaten. They had raped and beaten her so badly that they had to drag her across the ground because her legs no longer worked. My father screamed and screamed for his guards to mount their horses and ride out to save her but before they even made it down the steps, the tribe's leader slid down from his horse and cut her throat in front of us."

Tears were streaming down Faizer's face as well as Nuallan's. Only Gideon stayed strong.

"You poor, poor man, I am so sorry that this happened to you," Faizer said.

Nuallan brushed his tears away and clawed back his dark messy hair. He picked up his ale and finished it off. "My father beat me so badly it took Gideon and three other guards to drag him off me. Later that day I was forced to denounce my claim to the throne. That is why Gideon here became the heir to the Western throne."

Faizer fell from his forward leaning position and slouched back into his chair with his hands resting on the top of his head.

"Now to more urgent matters," Nuallan said as if everything was normal. "Andrus and the rest must be informed of the plan, should they not?" He lifted himself out of his chair and walked away from the table, exiting the tavern door.

Gideon and Faizer sat for a moment longer, staring into each other's eyes. They spoke no words but sadness filled the minds of both.

CHAPTER 5
A SPY IN THE SHADOW

Gideon walked quietly up the creaking staircase in Andrus's house. As he reached the top, he made for a window at the end of the landing and pulled in the old, worn latch on the scabby window, blocking out the night's breeze. Now that the wind could no longer blot out the noise coming from the room beside the window, Gideon could hear voices from inside. He pushed open the door slightly, listening carefully to Andrus as he tucked his two young sons into bed.

Andrus was sitting at the end of his eldest son, Oslo's bed. Oslo was sixteen years old and had already started his training with his father and uncles. He was well on his way to becoming a great warrior like them. His thin, medium length brown hair matched his father's.

In the other bed was Armel, Andrus's youngest boy, who was only eight. Armel was still confused as to why he had always been on the move, without explanation, but Andrus had chosen not to tell Armel their story as he believed the boy was still too young to understand.

"Listen up, lads," said Andrus, "within the next couple of days we may have to move again. I want you both to know that everything is okay. It's just what we have to do."

"Where will we go this time?" asked Oslo.

"I do not know, son. I am speaking with your uncles tonight.

Armel, I need you stay up here with your brother and get some sleep."

Armel ruffled about in his sheets as he turned to face his father. "I like it here," he said. "Why do we always have to leave?"

"It's just our way of life, my boy. Now go get some sleep, I must speak with your uncle," he said, ruffling the lad's hair.

At this point, Gideon kicked open the door and leaned inside. "We have a long day tomorrow, lads. Listen to your father and rest," he said, smiling.

Oslo and Armel smiled back and sank deeper into their beds.

Andrus, however, looked worried. "Goodnight, lads," he said as he walked over to Gideon. He put his hand on Gideon's back, steering him out of the bedroom then shut the bedroom door.

"Nuallan gave me a brief on the plan that you suggested," said Andrus.

"You do not agree that we should leave?" snapped Gideon.

"I have more to worry about than just myself this time," growled Andrus, pushing past Gideon and storming down the stairs without waiting for a reply.

Gideon shook his head sadly then followed his brother downstairs.

The downstairs room was a sad room, so dull, damp and cold. The furniture was old and rotten and the darkness conquered the room as the scattered candles failed to brighten up the space.

Andrus's wife, Ornella, was scurrying around placing big, hot bowls of soup on the table for each person. The whole company was present. They sat at the oak-chipped table, slurping away while awaiting Gideon and Andrus.

Gideon walked over and sat himself down in the only available seat, next to Faizer. He was quickly rewarded with a piping hot bowl of soup as Ornella slammed an overflowing bowl down, before skipping back around the table to Andrus.

Everyone's eyes were on Gideon. They had received a brief explanation from Nuallan on what Gideon intended and they were all eager to hear what more he had to say.

Ornella looked around the table. She was like Andrus in a way, with her stubborn and pushy personality. She brushed her silky brown hair out of her face and tucked it behind her tiny ears, growing impatient.

"Well, they won't say it so I will," she said. "Leaving this place is a mistake. Look at what we have… it's the best we have had in seven years. By a long shot."

Gideon looked around the table into everyone's eyes. He could tell it wasn't just Ornella who was thinking this, so he attempted to back up his plan. "We have no choice. The Earl knows who we are now, Ornella. We are no longer safe here, your children are no longer safe."

"So your plan is to jump back out into the wilderness, scavenging what we can like the old days. The Earl has offered you a position here as Commander… take it and let us live happily," spat Ornella.

Faizer joined in and defended Gideon's decision. "I stand by Gideon. You weren't there and I was. I saw the look in Earl Oswald's eye. I wouldn't be surprised if riders from Darchem were already on their way here," he said.

Andrus leapt to his feet. "And tell me, Faizer," he barked, "why were you there? I am struggling to understand why your council was needed instead my own."

He glared into Gideon's eyes.

Doxass lost his patience and pushed his chair outwards, jumping up also.

"Watch your tongue, little man," he said ferociously.

"Sit down, Doxass," said Gideon, trying to calm his comrades. "Andrus, please sit."

The pair stared each other out for a few moments before slowly dropping back into their chairs.

"We can sit here all night arguing," said Gideon, "but let me tell you this… even if the Earl doesn't hand us over and we stayed here and continued to raid, are we really okay with raping women and killing children? Is that what we have become now? Animals?"

Ornella dropped her head as she was slowly being won over.

"No? No one?" said Gideon. "So, we vote. Vote to stay or leave."

Faizer stood first. "I choose to leave."

Doxass stood up next. "I stand by my brother and Gideon. We should leave."

Nuallan, who had been rather quiet, stood next. He stared at Andrus, then spoke. "This is the safest option. We must go on surviving. I vote to leave."

Josanne smiled and remained seated. "This place smells like cow shit anyway, leave," she said.

All eyes now looked to Andrus and Ornella.

Ornella spoke first. "You have got us this far, Gideon. If you are certain of the danger that is to come, then I respect your decision, but my loyalties lie with Andrus. His decision is my decision."

Andrus stood up slowly, patting the dirt from his grey overthrow, as he spoke. "If any harm comes to my family," he said, "I hold you responsible, Gideon. I vote leave."

"Good, it is decided then," said Gideon, looking pleased. "We leave tomorrow."

Josanne looked up at him. "You really think Oswald and Frankel will let us walk out of here after you accepted his offer," she said.

"I have a plan," said Gideon. He slid his untouched soup to the side and rested his elbows on the table. "Listen up. Josanne, I need you to take Doxass and make for Otterly Road. You still have contact with the black market tradesmen, yes?"

"Yes," she said, "I still know Marco."

"Good. At first light, go see him," said Gideon. "Take the bag of the loot that we plundered from Rhoden, get as much gold you can for it… barter. I will go on a hunt with Andrus and Faizer. We'll disguise ourselves with all of our hunting equipment, but instead of hunting deer, we'll go to Cobbler's Farm."

"Cobbler's Farm?" said Josanne. "Clever. You seek to buy horses to make our getaway easier."

"Aye, horses," confirmed Gideon.

"You have me somewhere else?" said Nuallan.

Gideon looked to his left where Nuallan sat. "Yes, brother. You have the morning watch upon the wall and gate tomorrow morning, do you not?"

Nuallan nodded. "Aye, I do."

"There is a small storage compartment beside the wall," said Gideon. "Ornella and the children will wait there for your signal. You know of the long hanging tree that curves out of the forest and over onto the field?"

"Yes, I know it," said Nuallan.

"Keep a watchful eye upon its trunk. I will tie a piece of white fabric around it when it is time for you to move. As soon as you see it, gather Andrus's family and make for the forest. Stop for no one. We will be there, waiting with the horses."

Gideon now turned back to Josanne. "Once you have the coin, make for Cobbler's Farm. We'll wait beneath the bridge that leads onto his lands."

"Okay, got it," said Josanne.

Ornella's face filled with confusion. "Hold on," she said "once we escape the borders of Vanghale, where do we go?"

No one spoke, but looked around at each other with the hope that someone had a solution.

"We could go east," suggested Josanne.

"I will go anywhere but west," said Nuallan. "The further away from father, the better."

"There is nothing in the east for us," said Gideon.

"Well, we could go to Brigantium," said Josanne. "You have no quarrel with Tobias Ringfold. I have family there that would put us up. We'd be as safe as we've ever been."

Nuallan and the rest didn't look too sure about this.

"We'd be identified," said Nuallan. "The people there know our faces, Josanne."

She was quick to respond. "Is that really a bad thing? You have hidden for long enough. Maybe it's time you let the people know that you still live. Whether you want to see your father again or not, word will spread."

"I agree with her, Gideon," said Faizer. "It is the right move for us."

It was very rare that Faizer would side with someone else over Gideon, so most of the company were rather shocked when he backed up Josanne's plan.

Gideon folded his arms and rested back in his chair, thinking hard on the subject.

Then Ornella offered some advice to sway him.

"Oslo and Armel will be safe," she said. "They can get an education and I can get work. We will no longer be a burden. You and your brothers can create new paths for yourselves... no more scavenging, stealing or fighting."

Gideon looked won over but then Andrus said, "And what if they hand us over to the High King? Or even hang us upon arrival? You know the Eastern Horse Lords and the men of Meridium are not exactly known for their friendship. There is much hostility between our two kingdoms."

Andrus's words affected them all.

"Must we take another vote?" groaned Ornella.

Gideon looked to Andrus who shook his head.

"Then we make for Brigantium tomorrow," said Gideon. "Get some rest, my brothers and sisters." He looked over at Nuallan. "Nuallan, can I speak with you outside?"

Nuallan nodded and rose up out of his chair to follow Gideon from the room.

"What is it?" said Nuallan, as Gideon walked out onto the porch.

The porch encircled the house and was made of murky wood that creaked and hummed with every step. Gideon stepped across it, walking past Nuallan to lean on the porch's wooden handrail. He stared out into the sky, observing the audience of silver petal-like stars that swarmed the moon. A moon that, on this night, looked like a white disc floating around on an ocean of black.

"Are we making the right move here?" said Gideon.

Nuallan barely heard Gideon's question... something else had his attention. He thought he heard rustling in the bushes around the porch.

"Something wrong?" asked Gideon.

Nuallan paused then shook his head. "No, nothing," he said, turning back to Gideon. "The right move? I don't know, brother. You have always led us and made our choices and decisions for us. I trust your judgment. If you think we should go then we go, if you think we should not, then we will not."

Gideon smiled and rested his hand on Nuallan's shoulder.

"I want to thank you for your loyalty, Nuallan. After everything that's happened, you still stand beside me. It's remarkable. But this time the decision is not mine. Our friends made it for us so I will trust their judgment."

Nuallan smiled, stood up straight and brushed his fingers through his long, black hair, adjusting his black bandana before walking back off towards the door. "Brigantium it is, then," he said before entering the house.

Gideon looked over at him. "Aye, Brigantium. Rest well, brother. Tomorrow will be a long day."

The pair of them smiled at each other then Nuallan went inside.

Gideon stared into the night and dived deep into his thoughts. The idea of Brigantium brought warmth to his heart. If Tobias was to grant them entry to the city, they would once again experience riches, comfort and safety. He smiled to himself as he thought of the fresh meat and warm blankets he would once again indulge himself in.

As he blew the cold night air out through his lungs and continued his ruminations, he was completely unaware of the spy that sat in the bushes.

Someone was watching him.

Someone had been listening to his conversation.

But who?

The noise Nuallan had heard proved to be no ordinary noise… it was Commander Frankel. He sneakily popped his head out from the bushes, peaking over the porch like a tiger sizing up a gazelle. He stalked Gideon with a psychotic look on his wrinkled face.

He had heard the plan and dared not risk discovery by lingering too long, so he stepped quietly back into the darkness, disappearing with yet another one of the company's secrets locked in his mind.

CHAPTER 6
CLAUDIA

King Artaxes walked with haste through the eastern halls of his Palace as he headed off to attend his council meeting. Two of his Guard stormed after him, struggling to keep up.

Artaxes had called a meeting to decide what action to take against the Oakland Musters. Although he hadn't shown much interest when he was warned about the Muster attack from Koos, it had bothered him.

The eastern halls were extremely beautiful at night time, the open-walled windows allowing the glimmering stars access to the walls. Many sculptures and monumental statues had been carved into the walls of the eastern halls, some of famous Meridium heroes doing battle… some of the King upon his throne and some of the old queen, Claudia Destain. The artwork was magnificent.

Artaxes and his guard marched past the beautiful paintings and the figures until they reached the end of the hallway, where Artaxes pressed heavily on the two double doors that led to his council chambers.

The doors slid silently open.

"My King," chorused Dariuss and Havada, as Artaxes entered. They leaned on the battle map that lay spread out across a beautiful table. The table was not the only thing of worth within the chambers; the room was laden with Meridium memorabilia.

Hanging from the varnished walls were famous swords that had done great deeds in battle, along with ornamental shields, spears and many blue Meridium sigils. The far back wall was exquisitely painted with a map of the West, all the forests, cities, towns and fields beautifully rendered.

First General Lucifer, who was also present, quickly dashed around the table to greet the King. Lucifer was a legend of Meridium. He had short, silver hair like his King and was of similar age. The First General was wearing his full armour and a blue cape like all the King's Guard and Generals were obliged to do.

Many stories got passed around the taverns and brothels of Meridium about the great warrior. He had fought a lot of battles and was a hero of Meridium that children and military recruits looked up to.

Lucifer handed the King a scroll.

Artaxes took it, noticing the worried look upon Lucifer's face, over to the table and unravelled it. He had barely even looked at it before he lifted his head back up, disappointment in his eyes. "Are these numbers accurate?"

"They are," said Lucifer. "That is all we can spare. We have already left the City Watch weak. If the Musters had half a brain about them, they could take this city as soon as we march west."

Artaxes looked back at the scroll before rolling it back up and dropping it on the table.

"Eight hundred and seventy men… we're lucky we're fighting the shits from the Oakland and not anyone else," groaned Artaxes.

Whilst Artaxes and Lucifer spoke, Dariuss had begun moving small battle statues about on the map to indicate how he thought they should attack.

"We can set up camp here just South of Villach," he said. "Our scouts inform me that over three thousand Musters occupy Oggsfleet Port and a thousand have Villach. It would be a wise choice if we were to take back the city first."

Artaxes nodded, walking around the table so he could access the statues. He gathered six little white lion models that represented his force. He pushed them into one clump and stood them on the picture of Villach on the map.

He turned to Lucifer. "How many cavalry will we have?"

"About seventy," said the General.

"Infantry and spearmen?"

"Three hundred infantry and five hundred spearmen."

Artaxes looked back down at the map. If he attacked Villach, his men would be outnumbered by about three hundred. But this didn't bother him, he knew his force was way more superior than the savage Musters from the Oakland. He started separating the statues, spreading them out.

"Dariuss," he said, "I want you to lead the main assault... four hundred spearmen and two hundred infantry will be at your command. Have the spearmen lead the charge. No doubt the Muster filth will have sacked our city by now so they may have our horses. Your route of attack is the main gate. Break it down." He slammed his fist down into the table, then looked to Havada.

"Havada, while Dariuss carries out his attack, you will take one hundred infantry and one hundred spearmen to the wall." He stared at Havada, noting that the man seemed a little disheartened, most likely about his chances of survival. "You will be equipped with proper siege equipment. Set up the ladders and take the wall as quickly as possible. As for Oggsfleet Port, that can wait," continued Artaxes, leaving Havada still a little uneasy at the mission he had received.

But Havada knew better than to question the King's command.

It was Lucifer's turn to speak. "You understand that without Oggsfleet we have no way to feed our army, we need a source to deliver us resources until it's retaken."

"Right you are, First General," said the King. "I want you to ride for the city of Sandown, seek out their Commander Milano. Tell him we need resources and make sure they deliver, also inform them that I might call upon their army to help retake Oggsfleet in the coming days."

First General Lucifer bowed neatly.

The city of Sandown was a little north of Meridium but still classed as a western city. It was, in fact, one of the largest cities in the west. Most of the men that died in the war were from Sandown.

Artaxes looked up and away from the map. He walked over to a table that was angled in one of the corners of the room and picked up a silver jug of wine. He poured a measure of it into a petite goblet then took a sip as he looked around the room, happy with his plans… until he realised someone was missing from the council.

"Where is Koos?" he asked with confusion.

Lucifer shrugged. "I assumed he was down at the armoury accounting for all the weaponry."

The King angered. "I gave no order."

He looked over at Havada who, in turn, looked down at the map in desperate need to avoid the King's gaze. Havada was spared any more of the King's glare as the double doors to the council room suddenly swung open and everyone looked to the door to find Captain Cassius and a group of cloaked accomplices and spies entering the room.

"King Artaxes, I bear news," barked the snaky Captain.

"Well, go on, speak quickly," said the King, taking another sip.

"It's General Koos," said Cassius. "He has ridden for Brigantium. An escort of three rode him over the border before returning. The men are in the tavern of section two, as we speak."

Artaxes closed his eyes and shivered with anger. "Then he has decided his fate," he said. "Go to the tavern and grab the escorts. Hang them publicly."

Captain Cassius smiled before exiting the council chambers.

Havada filled with fear as his King slowly glared him up and down.

"My king, those are good men. Spare them," he said in a desperate attempt to reason with the King in the hope of saving the lives of the escorts that rode out of Meridium with Koos.

Dariuss and Lucifer stayed quiet as Artaxes walked around the table until he was face to face with his Guard.

Artaxes slowly lifted his goblet up, above Havada's head. Then he tilted his wrist, pouring the wine onto Havada, the blood red liquid staining the man's long, blond hair.

"You worthless fuck," spat Artaxes. "Koos came to me and told me you were to deliver a message for him. I see he has gone in your place. That means you knew of his departure and didn't inform me. Why?"

"The General means well, my King," stuttered Havada.

In an instant, the King smashed the goblet down onto Havada's head. The long-serving King's Guard dropped to the floor in agony, but the King showed no mercy. He pounded down again and again, bursting Havada's top lip and breaking his nose.

Dariuss took a step forward to attempt to stop the brutal attack but he caught the gaze of Lucifer who shook his head. Dariuss forced himself to standstill and wait out the attack.

Finally, Artaxes dropped the goblet and spat gruesomely down on Havada, who was by now barely conscious. The King then brushed back his silver hair and knelt down beside his victim.

"You are a King's Guard," he said. "That means you have dedicated your life, your sword and your soul to me, boy. If you ever break your oaths again, I will take your cloak and demote you, and you will live out your days taking orders from Captain Cassius."

The King stood up and looked over to Dariuss.

"Have him seen to, then report back to me to make preparations. We ride for Villach tomorrow."

He threw one final glare at the whimpering Havada before he walked out of the council chambers and down the hallway.

Artaxes stalked along the eastern hall, deep in thought, until something startled him. A demonic shadow flickering in the shape of a woman. It stood beside one of the sculptures of his wife, Claudia Destain.

He looked with complete disbelief at the figure, before he eventually wandered carefully over. In a sudden puff, the shadow disappeared, causing him to flinch and cower back. Startled and confused, he put his hand on the foot of his wife's monument and looked down.

"Claudia?" he whispered, as he spun around in search of the shadow.

Artaxes felt he was almost losing his mind as he desperately searched the hallway for the petite figure, hoping to get a glimpse of her once again.

"Claudia!" he screamed.

The fuss that the King was making attracted two of his King's Guard. They had followed him out of the council chambers, and ran out to aid him.

"My King, are you alright?" asked one of them, urgently.

Artaxes held his hand out, signalling the man to be quiet.

"Artaxes, look at what you have become," whispered a ghostly voice.

Artaxes dashed up and down the hall in search of the voice. "Do you hear that?" he asked.

The two Knights looked at each other with pure confusion.

"Hear what, my king?" one of them asked.

Artaxes slowed his search and calmed himself down, brushing his fingers through his messy hair before readjusting his tunic until it sat comfortably. The two King's Guard remained silent in fear that their King may lash out at them like he just had with Havada.

"It's nothing," Artaxes muttered, a semblance of sanity returning to his eyes.

This was not the first time Artaxes thought he had seen his dead wife appear, and it would not be the last. His mind was damaged and corrupt, the loss of his wife and the loss of the war troubled him beyond repair, and with none of his sons there to help keep him stable, it was only a matter of time before he would completely lose his sanity.

CHAPTER 7
COBBLER'S FARM

Gideon took point as he led Andrus and Faizer through the green of East Foolong Forest. Not many people travelled or hunted in the forest anymore so the vines and bushes grew out of proportion in every direction. Gideon was forced to take out his sword to remove the obstructing nettles that blocked their path. The sunlight struggled to gain entry through the top of the trees causing the air to stifle. Even on the hottest day, the dying forest would make a man shiver.

"How far till the road?" asked Andrus who seemed to be growing tired of the hike through the damp terrain.

"Half a mile," muttered Gideon as he stopped to check out the area ahead.

They had stumbled through a wall of leaves and onto an open plain of grass. Some trees still blocked their way but not as badly as before. With intent not to arouse suspicion, the three of them had chosen to enter Fooling Forest through the side and not through the eastern entrance, meaning they had to travel to the road that ran through the centre of the forest the long way.

"This is slowing us down. We must run the rest of the way," decided Gideon. He took off, leaving Andrus gasping for air, with no choice but to follow him and Faizer.

The three members of the company began creating an awful lot of noise, the branches beneath their feet snapping rhythmically as they pounded over them. They had almost reached the road. Gideon sidestepped around a sticky bush and pressed himself up against a bark chipped tree that was thicker than him in width so he was hidden behind it well.

Andrus and Faizer realised that Gideon, who was slightly ahead of them, had noticed something, and one at a time they slid down and took cover behind a mound of grass and mud. Andrus rolled his body over and away from the pike-like sticks that were prodding him. Faizer however was too eager to see what had startled Gideon. He saw his opportunity and dived up, leaping over the mud mound and gliding over the open space to eventually slam himself up against the tree alongside Gideon.

"What is it? What do you see?" he asked.

Gideon continued to peek around the tree, looking towards the road that could now be seen, leaving Faizer without an answer to his question.

The road was a pale yellow dirt path that ran right through Foolong Forest, leading to Rhoden, Cobbler's Farm and some other settlements.

Since Gideon didn't give Faizer a reply, he decided to look for himself. He peeped round the opposite side of the tree and looked to the road. About fifty or so men, women and children were walking along the road laughing and joking as they passed. They were all wearing a light brown uniform. The men carried spears and shields and even some of the woman were armed.

Faizer raised his eyebrows when he saw the man bearing the flag at the back of the pack. It was a long brown pole leading up to a lighter brown piece of fabric dangling with two clashing swords upon its quilted face.

Faizer swirled back round the tree and into cover.

"The Lure Alliance. Gideon, these people pose no threat," he said with a puzzled look upon his face.

Andrus, who just about heard Faizer's remark, popped his head up from behind the mound.

"The Lure Alliance? I've heard stories," he said with excitement.

Gideon turned round and held his finger against his own lips.

Andrus huffed with frustration before attempting his manoeuvre, crawling round the mound and slithering towards the tree.

"Victor Stran leads the alliance. He is an enemy of the High King Duran and the whole of Darchem. Faizer is right. They pose no threat. Why are we hiding?" he argued.

"It's just easier if we get through this unnoticed by anyone, no matter who they are," Gideon said. "Besides Victor is unpredictable." He really did not want to be spotted by the Alliance members.

He came out from behind the tree once the coast was clear, and the three of them walked freely through the last part of the trenchy terrain and out onto the road.

"I wonder why the Alliance was so far south," Faizer said. "I heard that thousands of them occupy the Square Wood Forest way north of here."

"Twenty thousand of them, I heard," Andrus added. "They must be expanding."

"The High King of Darchem has hunted Victor for fifteen years," Gideon said. "The further away from him and the Alliance the better. If the Lure Alliance is here, that means that Darchem hunting parties will be also." He looked up. "Now, there is the bridge. Let's move."

He jogged off and began sidestepping down a small hill so he could get under the bridge that offered passage across a shallow river. He ducked down and kicked some stones into the river, creating himself a soft seat on the floor. Once he was satisfied it was comfortable enough, he sat down, but his wish to avoid discussing the Lure Alliance with his comrades any more was in vain as Andrus and Faizer both came down the hill, swinging under the bridge and planting themselves down beside him.

"Tell us, Gideon, tell us the story of Victor Stran," begged Andrus who was super keen on their fight for freedom. Andrus was obsessed. He was first introduced to their story by his father. Victor was one of the only men in Requirium that had the respect of Artaxes Destain who would speak of him often. The way he defied the High King, betrayed the crown and then finally rose up against him excited Artaxes. He had passion for bravery and also a hatred for The High King, but he never explained properly about what happened between Victor Stran and Duran Harall, despite Andrus's constant requests.

Faizer tossed a stone into the river from his seated position. "I heard he was a traitor."

Gideon tossed a stone in after Faizer's as if he was trying to hit his stone. "He is, believe it or not, an honourable man," he said. "See, Victor Stran was high among the High King's ranks once. He was born and raised in Darchem, brought up with Duran Harall. They were best friends their whole lives but eventually Victor got sick of Duran's obsession with sailing across the 7th to conquer the foreign lands. Victor started to grow tired and guilty of enslaving and killing innocent people, so one day they began arguing and Victor struck Duran. Duran out of respect for their friendship spared his life but ordered him to leave the city. He gave permission for any of Victor's followers who wanted to leave with him the chance to do so, and many did. But once they left, the High King sent riders to slay Victor."

"What a waste of time. Why not just kill him then and there?" asked Faizer.

"Because the people loved Victor. Duran feared that if the people of Darchem knew Victor was killed by the King's hand, there would be an uprising. Or worse, a civil war. Like I said, Victor had many followers."

"And he survived?"

"Oh yes, all the riders were killed and Victor took refuge in the Square Wood, a ginormous forest with one hundred miles of bushes, fields and dark pathways in every direction. A few hundred followers left with him and started a new life there."

"How did they manage to survive for so long living in a forest, and how did he manage to raise an army whilst in hiding?" Faizer asked as he picked up a handful of stones and began throwing them into the river.

"Two very large towns sit on the outskirts of the forest, both wealthy and indebted to the Alliance, Willow Dale and Woodpine," Gideon said. "Victor is a freedom fighter. He basically fights crime by helping and aiding everyone. In the early days of the Alliance's creation, he defeated many bandits and raiders that sacked the two large towns. In return, they agreed to become trading partners. Now they trade timber and stone for coin, and as for building his army, word spreads. Once people heard of the Alliance, they fled their homes to join it. Some soldiers even deserted their kings to join the cause."

"A true legend of Requirium," Andrus said. "I would like to meet him one day."

"One day you might."

Andrus smiled and sat back with his back against the bridge's support beam.

"Gideon," whispered a weak voice.

Gideon leaned forward and rose to a crouching position.

"Gideon, it's Josanne."

The three of them stood up fully and climbed out from under the bridge as the familiar voice washed away any thought of resistance.

Josanne and Doxass were at the top waiting for them.

"Coin?" asked Gideon quickly.

"Four hundred gold pieces, I couldn't barter any more from him," said Josanne sadly.

Gideon looked disappointed. "No matter, we should still be able to get a few horses." He began walking over the bridge.

Cobbler's Farm was just on the other side of the small bridge. The company crossed it and walked onto Cobbler's land.

"By God, business must be bad," Faizer said as the farmhouse became visible.

The farmhouse sat inside an unstable fence. There was a barn and a few animals wandered freely. The company picked up the pace as they crossed the field leading towards the property.

Gideon spotted a large gap in the fence and started striding over towards it. "Andrus, Doxass, await us on the perimeter of the fence. Keep watch," he said as he bent down, forcing his body through the gap in the rigid brown fence.

Faizer and Josanne follow him in.

"It doesn't look like anyone lives here anymore, Gideon. We should leave," said Faizer nervously.

The house was so badly tended to that it looked like it could collapse at any given moment. It was originally painted white but the paint had faded so much that the brown underlay was peeking through at multiple spots on the house. The windows were sealed shut by bent brown shutters that seemed to have been nailed on over the window. The barn house was no better. The red paint on that had faded and one of the doors was completely gone.

Gideon peeked his head round the remaining door as they walked past. The straw was scattered all over and the some of the hooks dripped with blood.

"Be on your guard," he warned as he continued past the barn and up to the door of the main house.

Josanne lowered her hand down and gripped her sword handle, ready to unleash it if needed.

Gideon took one last look around before he knocked on the worn white door to Cobbler's house.

"Who goes there?" barked Cobbler who came diving out from round the back of his house with a brown fence pole in his grasp. Cobbler was barely five foot tall, very old and very fragile. He was bald on the top of his head but the back and sides grew in length.

"We mean no harm," said Gideon, holding his hands out in front of him. "Horses. We are here to purchase horses."

He looked to Josanne and signalled her to get out the coin. She released her hold on her sword handle and ruffled about in a brown sack upon her back. She lobbed a heavy pouch of gold to Gideon who caught it well.

Cobbler's eyes glistened at the sight. "Horses?" he asked keenly.

"Aye, give us four, a hundred per horse," said Gideon, forcing a mad chuckle from the old farmer.

"One hundred and fifty coins per horse," he snapped in a wicked tone.

Gideon looked around at his surroundings again. He sympathised for Cobbler deeply so he opened the bag and counted out his gold. He left three hundred in the bag and exchanged his remaining one hundred into a smaller pouch that Josanne handed him.

"Okay, give us two horses, three hundred gold," he offered.

Cobbler's eyes glistened even more. He was acting like he had never seen a gold coin before. He began fidgeting with the sides of his all in one brown rugged jumper.

"Yes, yes, three hundred," he stuttered.

Cobbler shuffled over to Gideon and snatched the pouch off him, startling him slightly. He then scurried back off around the house and disappeared out of sight.

"He's fucking lost it," said Josanne who seemed stunned by Cobbler's behaviour.

"What has happened here?" muttered Faizer as he took himself for a tour around the yard.

"I don't know. Could be Darchem hunting parties," said Gideon who seemed like he desperately wanted to leave.

The trailing footsteps of Cobbler alerted the three of them yet again, as he came wandering round the corner with two horses at his side. He handed the reins over to Gideon who retrieved them and handed the reins from one horse to Josanne and one to Faizer.

One of the horses was a beautiful creamy brown colour with yellow hair running down the back of its neck. The other was a tall black beast that huffed and puffed through its heavy nose. Cobbler took a few steps back and stood gazing at Gideon, waiting for him to leave.

"Thank you, friend," said Gideon. He turned to walk off but yet again found himself observing the farm. He spotted a sheep dog pissing up against a tool shed. Its ribs were visible and its face was thin. It was starving, Cobbler could barely afford to feed himself never mind his animals.

Gideon turned back around and walked over to Cobbler who seemed intimidated and frightened at Gideon's return.

"Two horses, three hundred gold," the old man growled as he stepped back, but Gideon meant no harm, instead he slid his hand in his pocket and pulled out the small money pouch with his remaining coin. He tossed it at Cobbler who caught it gratefully, ripping it open and looking inside, his face lighting up again.

The old farmer looked at Gideon with confusion. He didn't understand Gideon's offering. No one in Requirium acted as kindly as that, not unless they wanted something in return, but before Cobbler could press his questions, Gideon turned and walked away.

"Why give him the rest of the coin," asked Josanne. "We may have need for it?"

"He needs it more than we do, now let's find a way to get these fucking horses through that fence," Gideon said as the three of them approached Andrus and Doxass.

"Two horses?" asked Andrus, disappointed as Gideon and the others reached the gap in the fence.

"Aye, only two, enough for you and your family to make a run for it should we be pursued by the Earl and the Commander," said Gideon.

Andrus didn't argue. He shrugged and grabbed hold of the fence, pushing it slightly back to make the gap in the fence a bit wider, Doxass helping by latching onto one of the hanging planks that dangled from the snapped fence. He lifted it high so that Josanne and Faizer could guide the horses through. Once everyone was through the fence, the company began their journey back to the forest.

"Let's hope Nuallan hasn't fallen asleep on his watch again," said Faizer.

Andrus didn't find it funny. He was the only one who didn't laugh, but the laughter was soon silenced as the company were alerted by the sound of snapping branches coming from the forest.

"Spread out, draw your swords," commanded Gideon.

Everyone pulled out their swords and prepared themselves for a fight.

The snapping noise got louder and heavy footsteps could be heard. It was someone running at speed. Suddenly a hooded character burst through the green wall of vines that separated the forest from the road.

It was Nuallan.

He dragged off his hood, shocking everyone on the bridge, as he was covered in blood and sweat, exhausted. He ran into Gideon's welcoming arms.

"Speak, Nuallan, what's happened!" Gideon demanded.

Nuallan struggled to get his words out. He glanced up and became aware of Andrus who approached slowly.

"Where is my family, Nuallan?" he asked cautiously.

Nuallan sent a devastating look at Andrus. "I was upon the wall waiting for the signal when I looked down and Frankel and his men were raiding the storage building. They dragged them out. I ran down and tried to fight them but there were too many. That's why I came looking for you." Nuallan was trying desperately to control his breathing.

Andrus almost burst into tears and in a state of rage, turned to Gideon and went at him, pushing so hard he nearly fell over. He screamed out psychotically with anger, barged past Nuallan who was just pulling himself to his feet and pushed Faizer away from his horse. He dived upon its back and stabbed it with his heels. The horse flew off down the road back towards Vanghale.

"Wait, Andrus, we must plan this!" shouted Gideon desperately, but it was too late, Andrus was gone.

Nuallan dropped to his knees, sobbing.

"I couldn't save them, Gideon. I couldn't," he whimpered.

Gideon dropped down to his knees to press for more answers. "Tell me, do they live, Nuallan, are they alive?"

"They do, but they are taking them to the square. They are to be hung. All of them," cried Nuallan. "Gideon, how did he know? By the gods, how did he know?"

Gideon forced Nuallan's head into his chest and replied, "I do not know, brother." He looked up at his horrified company. "Back into the forest, we're going to get them!"

CHAPTER 8
THE RETAKING

The sun rose peacefully over the western lands, brightening up the Meridium camp. Artaxes and his small army had marched through the night to the outskirts of the outer defensive city of Villach. The men were spread out over a leaf-carpeted terrain not even a mile away from the city.

Some Oakland Archers could be seen standing upon Villach's wall awaiting the attack. The Musters only had three hundred or so men more than Artaxes, so the King was confident his army would be victorious. His tent as usual was positioned at the back of the camp behind his force. Dariuss was out in the field signalling his portion of the army to begin preparing themselves for battle whilst a couple of Lieutenants wandered around shouting inspirational words at the men, hoping to rile them up for the fight. Meanwhile inside the King's tent, Artaxes went over his plan and began suiting up.

"Do I need to go over it again?" asked Artaxes. He was standing over a table with a battle map upon it, a similar table to the one he had in his council chambers back at Meridium, except the wood was not as rich and the legs were not as thick.

Havada stood on the other side of the table beside Cassius, and guarding the doorway were the other two King's Guard.

"No, my King," said Havada whose bruised face was still painfully swollen.

"Good. Now, Cassius, ready my horse and have the cavalry mounted immediately."

"As you wish," said Cassius. He bowed quickly and darted out of the tent.

"A chance for you to redeem yourself, Havada. Retake the wall quickly and you will regain a little honour," said Artaxes as he separated his legs and held out his arms.

His two King's Guards tended to the King's armour, bringing over the grieves first, tightly strapping them onto his forearms, and next attaching his chest piece and armouring up his legs. The black of the King's tunic and trousers quickly dissolved out of sight as the silver and shine of his battle armour swallowed it up.

"I will retake the wall, my King, and I will kill many enemies upon it," said Havada passionately as he watched the silver devour the King's body.

Artaxes smiled as he reorganised his scabbard belt and sword.

"Good lad, now go prepare your force. We attack soon."

Havada bowed and made for the exit.

As he slid out, Cassius peered back in. "The cavalry is mounted and ready for you, my King," he said.

Artaxes smiled at him before speaking. "You will ride with me today. I expect to see your sword dripping with blood by noon." The King then clattered over, brushing past Cassius as he left the tent.

"A fine morning," whispered the King to himself as he received a soldier who was waiting with the King's horse. He stood before Artaxes, holding his head in a low bowing position until Artaxes took the reins.

The King scanned the sky as he breathed in hard through his nose, the cold moist air filling up his lungs quickly. There was no wind, no rain and no clouds. It was a very calm and quiet morning. All that could be heard was the eagles that chirped with excitement overhead. They knew the battle would soon commence.

Artaxes's army was ready. Most of the tents had been pulled down and packed up, and all of the fires has been stamped out. The separated regiments of soldiers were standing waiting to mobilise, all that was left was for the king to parade through his men and then link up with his cavalry unit. With one bursting leap, Artaxes dived and swung his legs up and over his horse. He ruffled around until his pelvis sat in the saddle comfortably.

Artaxes looked at his army but they did not look back. They stood magnificently straight-backed, facing forward, the silver shadow of the men blotting out the green earth beneath the camp. The King leaned forward on his war horse so that it moved, forcing many men to break from their statue-like stance to greet the King as he began patrolling through the middle of the two regiments.

Artaxes nodded and saluted the odd soldier, all the time keeping a huge excited smile upon his face. Artaxes truly did love a good battle. He was born for days like this.

The King reached the front of his ranks, observing his small cavalry unit that stood towards his eastern flank. Once the foot soldiers mobilised towards Villach, the cavalry would swarm the King and ride in beside Artaxes.

Artaxes tugged on the reins, causing his horse to rotate so that it was facing his army. He looked to his left where a large portion of his men stood behind Dariuss who was mounted upon a luscious brown horse. Next he turned to his right where a smaller portion of his men stood patiently behind Havada who was mounted upon a night-black horse. Both sections of the army had the spearmen at the front and the infantry swordsmen at the back. Although they had different uses, they still all looked identical.

Each man wore a silver shade of armour that covered their waist upwards and their legs were covered in chain mail that stopped above the men's armoured boots. Their helmets were so delicately forged, that the sharp waving edges that stuck out of the top of the tightly fitted helmets could be used as a weapon if needed. Like the battle seven years ago upon the Gantry, no man shivered with fear, instead they all stood eager to retake their city.

Artaxes pulled out his sword and pointed it at his army.

"Today is the beginning of a long campaign for you, men of the West," he said plainly. "Today is the day that we retake our lands from the Oakland Musters. For years now we have suffered because of our defeat upon the Gantry. But no more, our campaign, our new beginning starts here today! We will retake this city and then we will retake Oggsfleet port, and eventually drag the Oakland Forest into ruin."

With one rhythmic thrust, his men launched their spears and swords up into the air.

"We will reclaim our lands, our honour and our glory!" erupted Artaxes with ferocious passion.

The Meridium army roared with ambition as the King's words fired them up. Artaxes waved his sword through the air in Dariuss's direction and then in Havada's, giving them the signal to mobilise. In a perfectly synchronised step, both regiments moved forward.

Two box-like formations instantly picked up a light jog and began crossing the field towards the city. They looked like two sparkling clouds fluttering across the ground. A squadron of men at the back of Havada's force carried a stack of long wooden ladders. This was Havada's ticket into the city. A squadron at the back of Dariuss's force carried a long wooden battering ram that was strung into a thick wooden frame, a white head of a lion encrusted onto the end. That was Dariuss's ticket into the city.

The glistening force increased the distance between themselves and the King, allowing his cavalry unit to swarm in around him.

"Do you think two hundred men will be enough to take the wall?" asked Cassius as he trotted round the back of Artaxes.

"Perhaps," replied the King as the rest of the cavalry unit continued to gather around the King, forming two long straight lines behind Artaxes and Cassius.

The King and his squad watched the attack unfold from a distance, as both regiments reached their targets.

As the first bang of the ram slamming against the city's heavy gate roared around the field, Artaxes smiled, pleased. He then looked to Havada's force that neatly flanked left and attacked the stone wall. Havada's horse had taken an arrow meaning he was now on foot.

A constant blizzard of arrows had begun hurdling down towards Havada and his men. Luckily, the men were equipped with lengthy shields that deflected a lot of the arrows. Artaxes squinted harder as he watched Havada's attack unfold, but the erection of the ladders was delayed, and this bothered Artaxes.

"They're losing too many men. They need to get the ladders up," pointed out Captain Cassius.

Artaxes didn't speak, but continued to observe his King's Guards attack. It wasn't easy to make out what was really going on from the King's position. He could just see a group of silver suited men scrambling about at the foot of the wall.

The observing force were startled slightly as a hefty smash rattled the surrounding land.

"He's through, my King. Dariuss is in," announced Cassius with excitement.

But Artaxes ignored him and continued to watch Havada. He needed the wall to be taken. It would be too dangerous for the King and his cavalry to ride for the gate whilst the Musters still controlled the wall. The Meridium cavalry were not equipped with shields, just a sheathed sword and a lancing spear. The enemy's arrows would slaughter the men and their horses.

Cassius turned on his horse. "What do we do, my King?" he asked eagerly, but he was once again left without a reply.

Artaxes watched silently for a few more moments until his eyebrows raised and a gentle smile took over his face. In an instant dash, he jetted off to his left flank.

Cassius quickly looked back out into the field to seek out what the King had seen, and there it was. The wooden ladders were going up against the walls.

The first batch of ladders slammed against the wall, granting Havada and his men access to the city wall. Instantly, the ladders become invaded by the silver smudge that was the Meridium men. Their strategy was working.

Artaxes sat facing along the frontline of his horses. He held out his sword without speaking a word. Every soldier on the first line responded quickly by poking their spears past their horse's head, pointing them outwards. Artaxes broke his silence and shouted out boldly as he kicked his horse in the ribs, ordering his wintery horse to move. It pelted instantly across the frontline whilst Artaxes slammed his sword off every spear that he passed. An ear-ringing clash echoed around the field as the King smashed his sword off the final spear. Artaxes's horse jeered up, flicking its sheet metal hooves out in a scissor motion, the king holding his posture perfectly as he remained seated.

There was no more time for speeches or chatter, the King had begun the assault. His horse raced towards Villach like it was fleeing for its life, pelting and pounding across the field as it went. Cassius and the cavalry unit quickly charged onto the field after their King, keeping a perfect lined formation for some of the journey until gradually more horses began taking over the slower ones.

Each man desperately attempted to catch up to their King's stallion who might as well have been flying it was travelling so fast. This was not Artaxes's usual plan of attack, normally he would charge out to inspire his men and then gradually slow down allowing his force to hit first, but this time his mind filled with rage. He craved blood.

The horses now flanked slightly to the right as they aimed for a straight piercing run towards the gate where a bloodbath was taking place. The silver stone ground beneath the gate was lubricated with guts and blood that produced a foul stench around the entrance to Villach. Dariuss seemed to be making good progress. He had already pushed through the gate and was slashing away at the misty bunch of Musters that were attempting to hold position, but with the cavalry rapidly approaching, it would only be a matter of minutes before the city's walls and gate once again belonged the Artaxes Destain.

CHAPTER 9
A HEAVY LOSS

"There I see the horse, Andrus's horse!" shouted Doxass.

Gideon and the company had made it back to the treeline of East Foolong Forest. They were all laid camouflaged by the bushes, spying on Vanghale.

"By the looks of it, Andrus must be inside the town," said Gideon who was sprawled out beneath some razor sharp vines. He slithered his body out from underneath and addressed his company.

"This must be carried out with extreme caution. Josanne, you will come with me into the town, the rest of you wait here."

"No," said Nuallan who was still distraught, "it is my mistake. I will go and fetch them."

"Have you all lost your minds?" exclaimed Faizer. "We must go in together. It will be impossible to take on the Commander in a small group or alone."

Gideon groaned with frustration. "We do not have time for this," he snapped. "If we go in as a group, we will be forced to fight. A small group of two may go unnoticed. I will go with Josanne!"

Faizer put his hands upon his head and rolled back, leaning against a tree.

"Now, Nuallan, give Josanne your overthrow," said Gideon.

His brother slowly undid the laces at the side of the grey

overthrow and pulled it over his head, wiping the stream of tears from his cheeks and tossing the overthrow at Josanne. She slid it on and pulled up the hood. Gideon also pulled up his hood.

"It's time. On three we race for the gate," Gideon said.

Josanne set herself into a squatting position before confirming Gideon's plan with a deep nod. The pair of them edged themselves right onto the border of the forest, both with a worried look upon their faces, and rightly so. Earl Oswald would no doubt have a large amount of guards on duty.

"Okay, you ready? One, two, three!" The pair leapt out of the bushes and sprinted across the level green ground towards Vanghale.

The high beaming sunlight flared down on all below. Sweat dripped from Gideon's greasy dark hair as he approached the gate with Josanne. Luckily no guards could be seen upon the wall at all. Josanne hopped across the dirt road and slammed up against the town's gate first. It had been left slightly open which was very surprising. Gideon drove into it next.

"No guards," whispered Josanne. "Where are they?"

The northern entrance to Vanghale was the most well protected gate in the town. For there to be no guard or watch at all was extremely strange.

Gideon slithered around Josanne quietly. He shoved open the gate the remainder of the way and peeked his head out into the courtyard. Body after body lay gutted and bloody upon the courtyard's dusty floor. Andrus had already been here. Gideon walked in to investigate with Josanne at his back.

"He's killed them all on his own? How?" muttered Josanne in disbelief as she looked uneasily at at over fifteen dead bodies that all lay around the town's gate.

Gideon couldn't believe what he was seeing. "I have no idea. We must find him quickly. Let's head through the alleyways."

There were very few men in Requirium that could take out fifteen men on their own, but a man that is fighting for the lives of his family, is a dangerous man at that.

The pair stepped over the bodies as they trod quietly over

towards a tight alleyway, that led right up through to the streets that circled the square of Vanghale. That was where the execution would be taking place. That was where Andrus would be.

Josanne quickly tried to prized Andrus's beloved throwing daggers from some of the dead bodies. Six or seven of the dead men were victims to Andrus's excellent throwing ability.

"A nice gesture, but no time," said Gideon as he disappeared into the murky alleyway.

Josanne slid the one dagger that she managed to retrieve into her overthrow pocket, and then charged towards the alleyway.

Slowly but surely Josanne and Gideon made progress through the diabolical alleyway that led them through the poorest part of town, dozens of tiny houses packed up together on either side of the passage. People had poured piss and shit from their top windows out onto the floor, making their journey through a little unpleasing, but luckily enough they had still gone unnoticed by anyone, although no one seemed to be around.

"Told you this place stunk of shit," whispered Josanne as she crumpled up her smooth face.

Gideon ignored her remark completely, holding out his hand as he came to a standstill, silencing his partner instantly.

"Do you hear that?" he asked as he squinted to pinpoint the noise.

"Drum roll!" Josanne said urgently.

Gideon raised his eyebrows shockingly. "It's beginning. Let's move!"

They both charged down the alley, hopping and skipping over the piles of filth as they went. The walls of the houses that they now passed seemed a lighter shade to the rest. The sun was gleaming in the ally and onto the walls. They had almost reached the end.

As they arrived, Gideon took the lead by pushing his body up against the corner of the wall. He peeked around the corner to see if anyone was around, but still no one was.

"Wait here, and wait for my command," he instructed. He took a deep breath and dashed out.

He crept across the large street with ease, yet again unnoticed, pushing himself up against a mud-stained building that sat on the corner of the street. Slowly he bent his head around the corner. Yet again there was no sight of anyone. He leaned back in and waved over Josanne. She slipped out of cover and ran over towards Gideon, her long naked legs carrying her swiftly across the road.

"Where is everyone? I don't understand?" she said as she pushed up beside Gideon.

"The Earl must want everyone to see the execution, to set an example," he said.

"Then we can use the crowd to our advantage, surely?" she suggested.

Gideon raised an eyebrow with satisfaction. "Aye, we could. You see that alleyway over there?" He pointed across to a street that intertwined with the one they were on.

"Aye, I see it!"

"That will bring us right out into the square. We can then blend in with the crowd and try to stop the execution."

"Okay, then let's move," she said and pushed past Gideon, quickly checking if any guards were in sight. Once satisfied, she pelted out into the open and raced for the alleyway. Gideon tracked her quickly.

The two of them didn't tackle this passage with the same caution as the last one. They splattered through the puddles and shit in desperate need to reach the square before it was too late. The cheer of the crowd and the beating of the drums was heightening as Gideon and his accomplice reached the open street, leading to the square. They skidded to a standstill and cushioned up against the wall one last time, Gideon tightly pulling up his hood and dipping his hands into his pockets. Josanne did the same.

"Follow my lead and do not draw any unnecessary attention," Gideon said. "Let's find Andrus and figure out a way to get his family."

Josanne nodded nervously.

"Okay, come on," he ordered and stepped out into the open,

feeling bare and naked without his cover of the shadows. He stepped out onto the road and walked shiftily towards the crowd that erupted with applause as the Earl stepped out onto the execution frame. They sped up their walk in an attempt to reach the back of the crowd that was swarming the town's square. A monstrous amount of people had filled up the square in order to watch the execution of Andrus's family, even children were present.

Gideon and Josanne blended in at the back of mob just as the Earl reached the centre of the podium in order to speak out.

"Behold the people of Vanghale, witness today what happens to criminals who defy and betray the hand that feeds them. Bare witness, and watch what happens to those who chose to do so," announced Earl Oswald viciously.

A large man, wide and tall, dressed in all, black wandered over to the three individuals upon the podium. He pulled the hoods off all three revealing their identities. Gideon watched with hate as his nephews and sister in law's faces were revealed. Even some people in the crowd gasped with horror as they saw the two young boys standing before them.

The executioner's podium was a heavy wooden frame that was supported by structural beams and wooden staircases. There were three trap doors in the centre of the structure which Ornella, Armel and Oslo all stood over waiting to die, each one of them crying hysterically. Ornella could be seen whispering to Armel, telling him that he was going to be safe and not to worry, but even she couldn't hold back her frightened tears.

Gideon had to act. He quickly shifted through the crowd that no longer screamed with excitement. Instead they began to groan and moan at the sight of the woman and the two young boys. Josanne held on tight to Gideon's overthrow as he pushed through the people in an attempt to reach the front.

"There are over fifty guards here," she whispered. "It will be impossible to get them out."

The guards were positioned all around the crowd as if they were closing in on them like a pack of wolfs.

Gideon and Josanne slid through the final stretch of people in order to reach the front, until only a small fenced barrier stood between them and Andrus's family, but it was too early to strike.

"Do you see Andrus?" asked Gideon.

"No, but I see the Commander," Josanne said with disappointment.

"Where?"

"To the left, over there." She pointed.

Gideon tilted up on his toes in order to spot him, filling with aggression and fury just at the sight of him. Commander Frankel was standing with a handful of guards surrounding him whilst he looked out into the crowd.

"By the looks of it, he is looking for us. Be careful," warned Gideon.

The Earl stepped down from the podium and walked over to the Commander. The execution was about to begin.

"We're running out of time," groaned Josanne. "What is the plan, Gideon?" But she received no answer as Gideon seemed to be without one.

The drum roll began again, now rumbling louder than ever. Gideon didn't know what to do. He looked around for some help but nothing came to his aid. They were left with only one choice, they would have to fight their way through.

Gideon lifted up the bottom of his overthrow and reached for his sword, grasping the top of the fence with his other hand. He bent his knees and readied himself to execute the jump to save Andrus's family.

"He is here! Kill him!" screeched the Commander.

Gideon panicked. He ripped the overthrow over his head and pulled out his sword. The people around him gasped and cowered back but no guards engaged him. The kill order was not directed at him. It was directed at Andrus.

Andrus came slithering out of the crowd that faced the side of the wooden podium, a storm of sizzling throwing knives gliding between the people and into the flesh of the guards.

Gideon froze for a moment until he realised what was happening.

"Gideon, behind us!" shouted Josanne, bringing him back to reality.

Dozens of guards were bulldozing through the crowd to get to Andrus.

"Take care of that, I must get the boys," he yelled back before jumping the fence, and sprinting for the podium. But he was quickly engaged as the soldiers noticed him and began running at him.

He twisted his wrist back and slashed hard at the first man. Gideon dashed left to right, cutting deep into every guard that attacked. These simple town guards were no match for the heir of Meridium.

Andrus noticed an opening to the staircase that would take him up the podium. The guards that stood there had engaged Gideon.

"Go quickly, get the boys. I will take care of these!" shouted Gideon.

Andrus spun round to see who was aiding him, a twinkle of delight washing away the deranged look from his face as he laid eyes on Gideon. He was relieved that his brother was there. He nodded at Gideon gratefully as the guards swarmed in around him.

"Move in, move in, you dogs!" bellowed the Commander who was trying to push through the crowd to involve himself in the fight, but he was making the journey alone, near enough every guard that entered the crowd in an attempt to push through the middle could no longer be seen. They had fallen victim to Josanne.

Josanne was wandering sneakily through the crowd with the throwing knife she had retrieved from Andrus's victim back at the gate. She was stalking and assassinating every soldier that tried to force his way through the panicking crowd. The cover of the people was working to her advantage, over ten bodies lay bleeding in the muck. But her cover was fading, the frightened people were spewing out of the square to retreat to their homes, leaving more open ground for the Vanghale soldiers to pursue her.

Andrus noticed Josanne in the fleeing crowd, and he also spotted the guards that had spotted her. They were targeting her, but he could not help. He turned from his rescuers and charged up the wooden staircase towards his family. He was almost out of time.

The executioner, although fat and slow, was charging for the lever that would release the trap doors sending Andrus's family to the after life. The wooden decking shattered with every step as he bounced towards it.

"Father!" called Oslo desperately. He was the first to notice his father pelting across the podium in an agonising and desperate attempt to stop the executioner. Oslo was the closest to the lever. He bided his time and waited for the hooded executioner to waddle past, and in a perfectly timed swing, he lifted up his legs allowing the rope to tighten round his neck. He swung his legs forward and then back, kicking the executioner as he passed. But the brave act failed as the size difference was too large. Oslo merely made the executioner stumble slightly. It was not enough.

Andrus had one last chance to save his family's lives. He pulled out his last throwing knife and threw it accurately towards the executioner who was grasping the lever. The knife slid through the warm air and hit the back of its victim's skull, the crack of the bone drowning out the noise of clashing swords beneath. Andrus and his family all held their breath as they watched hopefully as the executioner died, but his hand rested lifelessly on the lever and his body was slipping forward.

Andrus quickly darted into action, completing the rest of his journey across the podium, but he was too late. The executioner's body fell forward before Andrus could reach him, pushing the lever all the way down, triggering the trap doors to open.

In a split second, Andrus whipped his cloak to the side, pulling his short sword from its scabbard. He slashed quicker than lightning strikes, cutting the rope around Oslo's neck. The eldest son of Andrus Destain dropped the short distance through the trap door, crashing hard on the sandy floor beneath. Armel and Ornella were not so lucky.

"No!" screamed Andrus painfully as the crack of their necks sent a chilling shiver through his heart. Armel and Ornella hung lifeless, both their necks cracked and bent from the impact of the drop. Still he cut both their ropes, allowing their bodies to crash down beside Oslo.

A scream from down below echoed throughout the square as Oslo crawled over to his dead mother and brother. He had only just hit the ground himself before he was met by their broken bodies.

Andrus however remained hopeful. He threw himself from the podium which was roughly a twelve foot drop. He crashed down on his ankles and threw himself to the floor beside his dead wife and boy. He shook their bodies roughly, hoping they would wake up, but they were gone.

Oslo who still screamed with horror, tugged on his father's leg, but Andrus was lost, sitting on his knees, staring into the eyes of his dead wife.

"Andrus, we need to leave! Hurry!" screamed Gideon as he still fought with the scrappy Vanghale soldiers. But Andrus remained motionless on the floor. Gideon and Josanne were left to fight off the guards alone and it would only be a matter of time now before they too fell.

The Commander and his guards created a circle around the two of them and one at a time his men ran in for the attack. The Earl however had fled to call for reinforcements.

"It's over, my Prince. Accept your fate," mocked the Commander as he tightened the circle around his victims.

Gideon composed himself as he targeted the Commander. Himself and Josanne were outnumbered at about ten to one, but if he timed his attack right he could engage the Commander with only a couple of soldiers getting in his way.

A soldier recklessly broke from the circle and charged Josanne. She cut him down with ease. As he hit the floor, she dived backwards, pushing her back up against Gideon, and the two of them shuffled around with their backs connected.

"Frankel, you murderer!" exploded Andrus from the base of the podium. He stood facing the pack that swarmed his allies, his legs widely spread and his posture intimidating. His hair was drenched in sweat and blood as it hung helplessly over his forehead, his cheeks were jewel blue from the soaking wet tears that had cascaded down his face. It was a sight that would scare the bravest of men.

Andrus took one step forward and then another, and before long he had broken out into a full scale sprint. He anticipated the attack from various guards that broke from the circle to engage him, slicing at them viciously whilst screaming in a horrifying tone. Gideon suddenly had an opportunity, and he took it without a second thought. He dug his heels in to the mud like a bull preparing to charge, then bent his knees and leapt forward, sprinting at the Commander.

Gideon moved so quickly that the Commander didn't realise he was coming, he was still observing Andrus gutting his guards brutally. Gideon charged into Frankel fiercely, lifting him at least three foot from the ground, twisting his shoulders down, and launching the Commander to the ground along with himself. Gideon and the Commander both quickly brushed off the hit and pulled themselves to their feet, ready to engage each other.

Josanne was now left to fight off the remainder of the guards alone. Seven of them now gave chase. She knew she could not win by fighting them in an open space so she ran for the podium. She took deep strides and managed to reach the stairwell before one of them could attack her, then she ran up the first wooden steps before spinning round sword first.

She gouged deep into the crazed guard who screamed with agony, before she brushed him aside, knocking him over the staircase railing. Andrus who had finished off his attackers came to her aid, stabbing the man at the back of the pack so hard that the sword ripped out of his chest. The Vanghale guards were now trapped. Josanne stood halfway up the stairs, stabbing constantly at every man who was forced further up, whilst Andrus stood at the bottom, stabbing upwards at everyone who tried to come down. It wasn't long before the bronze steps were painted molten red.

"Is that all you have got?" barked Commander Frankel as he duelled with Gideon. Every slash and lunge was so perfectly timed and executed that Gideon had begun to struggle. Frankel spotted a chance to end him. He stepped to his left, parrying Gideon's attack before countering with a slash. Frankel, who completely had the upper hand, followed his slash with a devastating elbow to Gideon's jaw, knocking him to the ground.

The Commander's armoured elbow piece had nearly taken Gideon's head off. He lay there on the floor barely conscious. Frankel stepped over the floored Prince and raised his sword up, smashing down heavily. Gideon with all his might heaved his sword up to block the oncoming blow, but the Commander didn't stop, continuing to pull his sword back, lashing down and down repeatedly. Gideon was weakening. His tired wrists couldn't hold his sword for much longer, each bash of the Commander's sword causing his arm to stiffen up. His grip was loosening, he wouldn't hold out much longer.

With one last effort, Commander Frankel hacked down his sword, but it was stopped. Not by Gideon but by Andrus. He had parried his attack by holding his short sword in the way of the Commander and Gideon. Frankel retaliated instantly by shifting his whole body weight to the side, unleashing his armoured hand across the face of Andrus. But Andrus wasn't alone. Josanne swerved under the Commander and slashed at his side, dealing a deep cut above Frankel's hip, causing him to scream out painfully before swinging his sword round to engage her.

Gideon watched from the ground. His vision had blurred from the devastating blow he had received. He squinted his eyes so that the fight in front of him could be more visible. Together Josanne and Andrus bashed away at the Commander, but he successfully blocked every attack, swinging his sword from left to right and forcing away his opponents' swords. He created a chance for himself to gain control of the fight as he lunged at Josanne forcing her to cower back, and once she did, he swiped to the left, bashing Andrus again in the face and causing him to bend down. Frankel grabbed hold of his hair and pulled him in close.

Josanne quickly tried to save him, running forward with her sword raised, whipping it around and attempting to cut at the Commander's side, but he anticipated and planned the move. As she reached him, he threw Andrus towards her, knocking her off balance, and then dashed forward, gashing down at her bare leg and cutting it wide open. The slash was so quick that the muscles in her leg instantly gave way, and she collapsed to the floor in agony.

Andrus tried to pull himself back up but he was met with a swift kick to the face, knocking him onto his back. He was beaten.

The Commander took a moment to gather his composure. He breathed in deeply and observed the now ghostly square. Just minutes ago, there were hundreds of people, and now it was deserted. Only the dead remained an audience to the Commander's victory. He bent right down beside Andrus and grabbed his face, pulling him in close.

"Now you will watch your brother die, spawn of Artaxes." The Commander slammed his head back down and spit on Andrus's sweaty face. He stood back up and walked over to Gideon who still lay there as dazed as the day he was born.

"Now you die, Gideon Destain, son of Artaxes Destain," hissed Frankel as he squatted down, sitting on top of Gideon's broken body. He clenched his fist and delivered the first of many blistering blows, one hand at a time slamming down into the broken face of Gideon. The thud of the Commander's armour connecting with the young Prince's skull crackled around the square horrifyingly.

"Frankel!" bellowed a familiar voice.

Commander Frankel refrained himself from beating the Meridium Prince to death to see who was so rudely interrupting him. He looked up and saw Doxass standing there with his axe in his right hand. The Commander groaned impatiently. He looked back down to his bloodstained victim and muttered. "It won't be long, my Prince. Soon your precious company will be nothing but a boring memory."

Before he could finish speaking, Doxass executed his attack, screaming like a crazed man as he bombed over to Frankel. The Commander quickly rolled over Gideon's body and grabbed his sword, quickly launching himself to his feet just in time to block the axe's venomous bite.

Doxass was wobbled slightly as the sword and axe connected. He spun right back round, launching his axe wickedly at the Commander, but Frankel easily dodged every swing until Doxass got complacent.

Doxass made his first and last mistake. He threw one diagonal swing which allowed the Commander to duck under him, and so he did. Frankel slid around the back of Doxass, grabbing hold of the scruff of his blond ponytail hard, tightening his sword grip and firing it upwards.

Doxass screamed out like a skewered pig as the Commander's blade tore through his tough skin, crushing every bone it passed before ripping out of Doxass's chest.

The sword's tip was as red as the autumn leaves.

"Doxass!" cried Josanne who had to watch the event take place from her curled up position on the floor. Andrus who had also regained consciousness, glared at Doxass's dying body with pure shock.

Frankel wiggled his sword about a few times whilst making eye contact with Andrus, and Doxass screamed no more as the blow finally killed him, his body sliding slowly off the sword and crashing onto the floor.

"No!" screamed Josanne, desperately trying to drag her wounded body along the floor towards her lover's body.

Frankel wasted no more time now. He was done playing games. He wanted Gideon dead so he stormed towards his prey with his sword aimed down.

"You will watch and then you will both hang, just like your

peasant wife and child!" stated the Commander as he drifted past Andrus.

He stood above Gideon and lifted up his sword. Gideon didn't even move, he couldn't move. He lay there waiting to die. With a deep thrust, the Commander slammed his sword down towards Gideon's chest, but for some strange reason, his hand paused, his grip beginning to loosen.

His fingers released their hold, allowing the sword to tumble onto the floor.

Frankel groaned painfully.

A river of blood ran out of his mouth as he screamed.

Someone had stuck him.

As Frankel dropped to his knees, his killer was revealed. It was a tall teenage boy wielding a short sword that Andrus had dropped by his dead wife. It was Oslo.

The boy still cried and whimpered, pulling the sword from Frankel's spine, and immediately he readied himself for another blow, aiming the sword at the top of his opponent's back again.

"This is for my mother and brother," he said before sticking his blade into Frankel's back again, allowing more blood to flow out of the new wound. Oslo tore it out and dropped it on the bloodstained ground.

He had killed the Commander.

He stood there, looking down at the floor aimlessly, waiting for some comfort or reassurance, but he received none. His father Andrus simply pulled himself up and stumbled over to Ornella and Armel, where he sat silently staring at their bodies beneath the podium.

Josanne was absent also as she laid beside Doxass, murmuring sadly as she stroked his bloodstained beard.

"We have to leave," whispered a frail voice.

Oslo looked down. His uncle was slowly trying to roll over to pull himself up to his knees.

"The Earl will be coming with reinforcements. We have to leave," he whispered again.

"Yes, uncle." Oslo lifted one of Gideon's arms round his

shoulders. It was a tough task but he managed to lift Gideon to his feet, carefully and slowly guiding his uncle over to Josanne.

"We must go. Uncle says more guards are coming. We have to leave him," the boy said.

Josanne continued to stare at Doxass's body. She leaned down and kissed him on the head.

"I don't think I can walk," she said. "Just leave me. Get your uncle and father out of here."

An alarming racket echoed from one of the western streets. Reinforcements were on their way.

"Just go, get your father and go, Oslo!" she repeated.

Oslo turned to look for his father whilst angling Gideon round with him as he turned. Andrus startled him slightly as he barged through without saying a word. He grabbed Josanne's arm and pulled her to her feet, causing her to scream out in pain, but he did not sympathise.

Andrus lifted her up and balanced her on his shoulders, all the time still remaining silent as he picked up a fast pace and began making his way back to the gate.

Oslo quickly limped after him with his uncle still hanging from his shoulder. They were nearly out of time.

Oslo managed to drag his uncle into the final alleyway before they reached the gate. Gideon was managing to walk a little better, making the load a little lighter for his nephew however Andrus had completely taken off ahead leaving his son and brother behind.

"How much further, uncle?" asked Oslo, exhausted.

"Just to the end of this passage."

Suddenly out of the darkness of the alley came Andrus, without Josanne, and again he spoke no words, he just hoisted Gideon onto his back. Gideon was way bigger than Andrus in height and in width, and it was remarkable that he was carrying him so easily. Oslo stopped for a moment's rest. He leaned his back against a dirty wall and began to control his breathing. He looked down at his bloodstained hands. He didn't feel guilt but he felt regret. Commander Frankel was the first man he had killed. Wiping the thought from his troubled mind, he rubbed his hands on his brown trousers and jogged off down the remainder of the alley.

Oslo flooded out of the alleyway, instantly met by Nuallan who came bounding over.

"Quickly now, get on the horse," he ordered, marching him over.

Nuallan and Faizer had ridden in on the horse once they realised Doxass had sneaked off. Faizer was sitting waiting on the horse with Josanne in front of him. She struggled to contain the pain she was in as her leg wound was bleeding more and more. Faizer however looked in just as much pain as she was, his eyes glistening as he held his tears back, straight-faced, staring into nothing. He had received the news of his brother.

"Up you get," said Nuallan as he boosted up Oslo.

The horse swivelled off balance slightly as the weight of three people added more pressure upon its mighty back.

"Go to Cobbler's Farm, we will meet you there," commanded Nuallan, and he slapped the horse on its backside hard. It jiggled from side to side as it made for the gate, eventually breaking out into a gutsy sprint carrying the three of them away.

Nuallan watched the horse leave, and once he was happy with the distance between the horse and the town, he turned to his little brother who was standing beside Gideon who was leaning against the gate weakly. Nuallan wandered over nervously and confronted him.

"Little brother, I am sorry," he said sadly. "I... I couldn't save them."

Andrus slowly lifted up his head and looked into Nuallan's eyes. It wasn't a look of hatred or disappointment, it was a look of a lost man.

Andrus didn't seem himself at all. He had just lost his wife, son and a close friend. His mind seemed to have dissolved. He wouldn't speak or show emotion.

Nuallan just looked at him with worry. He grabbed his cheeks and lifted his brother's face back up, staring into his eyes and seeing nothing. But he had witnessed something like this before, an identical reaction to the one of his father when his mother died.

CHAPTER 10
THE ESCAPE

"Come on, brothers, we must hurry," urged Nuallan. He led the pack through East Foolong Forest, trying desperately to increase the distance between themselves and Vanghale. Gideon, who was slowing them down massively, managed a slight jog, but his bruised bones prevented him moving with any real speed. Andrus however dawdled behind his two brothers, moving without a worry in the world.

"Not much further, just keep moving," said Nuallan. He had stopped beside a tree in order to give Gideon and Andrus a push on the back as they both waddled past. Nuallan knew that if the guards of Vanghale had chosen to pursue them, they would soon be upon them.

Blood still ran from Gideon's nose, dripping off his chin and onto the leaf-covered ground, and, if the Vanghale soldiers were in fact laying chase, they would have a colourful trail to track.

Nuallan was beginning to worry. He knew they were moving too slow and that they were making too much noise. Gideon was too battered to move with care... instead, he trailed along, creating an awful racket. Nuallan really needed the help of Andrus, but he still hadn't spoken a word or shown any reaction. He was completely traumatised.

Nuallan sprinted off so he could scout ahead, leaving his

two trailing brothers behind. The fluttering leaves and branches whipped at his knees as he ran past, the odd one slicing into his black pants. He dodged in and out of the pike-like trees that grew thinner the deeper they travelled into the forest.

He rested for a moment between two thin trees, yet again waiting for his brothers. This time he didn't give any inspirational words to help speed them up, instead he waited till Gideon had passed before latching onto Andrus. He swung the soulless body around and slammed him up against the tree, hard, inspecting Andrus's face, staring into his eyes and then checking his body for wounds. He needed to make sure it wasn't a physical injury causing Andrus to behave so strangely. But he found nothing. It was, without a doubt, mental.

"Come on, speak, lad, speak!" said Nuallan. "Listen, I know what you have been through is truly heartbreaking, but I need you now. If we don't get Gideon back before the guards find us, more death will be upon us."

Andrus simply remained silent and even as Nuallan pushed him up tighter against the tree, he didn't even so much as blink.

"Speak!" shouted Nuallan, releasing his hold on his little brother at the same time. He was worried. He didn't want Andrus to end up the same as his father.

Andrus, meanwhile, pulled his body from the tree, and curled around it before jogging off after Gideon, who had managed to pick up his pace a little.

In fact, he was almost at the road and Nuallan was now the one playing catch-up. The worried brother glided, hopped and pounced between the trees and mouldy mud mounds that obstructed his path. His journey became a little bit easier as he reached the wall of green vines that Gideon had cut down.

Nuallan burst through the wall of green and stumbled out onto the road… the last to arrive. Andrus stood on the bridge, staring out over onto Cobbler's land whilst Gideon gasped for air, his lungs whistling out of tune with every breath that he took.

"Not long now," said Nuallan. "We can get you patched up in about another mile."

He rubbed Gideon's bent over back whilst he coughed up a dribble of blood.

"He hasn't half laid a beating on you, hasn't he, brother?" said Nuallan.

Gideon wheezed as he tried to speak. "He won't be hurting anyone ever again. Three grown men couldn't kill him, yet a fifteen year old boy managed to sneak up and stick him." He laughed gently but soon stopped, grabbing at his chest in pain.

Nuallan once again patted his brother's back.

"Who goes there?" barked a dry voice.

Nuallan spun around to find a man, a boy and a woman aiming long spears at him and Gideon.

"Speak! At once!" said the man. He was of medium height and dressed all in brown.

Nuallan held up his hands while Gideon did the same with his right arm, his sprained left arm still clutched into his chest. Before Andrus became aware of the situation, a man grabbed him from behind and rested a sword over his throat.

"Release him at once!" shouted Nuallan.

"Speak honestly and quickly and he will be released," said the stranger.

The man was clean-shaven and wore a small brown leather helmet with full leather amour, also brown. They were members of the Lure Alliance.

"We are travellers. We are injured and need help," said Gideon, standing up as straight as he could, brushing his hair out of his face and glaring at the man.

The man's eyes widened suddenly.

"Gideon Destain of Meridium?" he said, then he nodded to himself. "Aye it is. And you're Nuallan Destain." He called over to the man who had Andrus. "Release him, brother, release him."

The man took away his sword and sheathed it, then wandered over to his superior.

"The Destain family, you say?" he asked, excited. "So you are alive? Well, I'll be damned."

"How do you know who we are?" said Nuallan.

"I was born in Meridium," said the man. "I fled. Deserted, if you will. I joined Victor Stran and his Lure Alliance the day the Darchem dogs rode for Meridium to steal our city's boys."

The stranger, who seemed to be the leader of the squad, turned to the woman and boy, ordering them to lower their spears by simply raising his hand in their direction.

"Apologies, I am Lurgan," he said, "and this is Cally and Vossan."

"And I am Drediar," added the ex-Meridium man.

All four of the Lure Alliance members had identical armour on. Tailored brown boots, sharply defined armour and tightly fitted helmets. The light brown texture of the fabric was excellent camouflage.

"You look like you have seen better days, my Princes," said Lurgan. "What has happened to you?" He pulled a pouch of water from a brown rug sack and handed it to Gideon.

"Rather not say," said Nuallan, "we really must get going."

Lurgan looked at him, a suspicious look on his face. "Have you come from Vanghale?"

"Aye, we have," said Gideon, handing back the water pouch.

"Nah, keep it," said Lurgan, "you need it more than I do. As a matter of fact, we are heading to Vanghale right now. Victor wants to extend our trade income. We seek to barter with them, protection for coin."

Nuallan chuckled. "You're wasting your time. You'll get no warm welcome there. They just murdered half of our company."

Lurgan stared at Nuallan in shock. "We heard that the Earl that runs that town was an old frail man."

"Oh he is, but he is wicked," snapped Nuallan.

Lurgan turned and walked over to his companions, leaning in to quietly confer with them for a few moments, leaving Nuallan and his brothers looking at each other in bafflement. Eventually, Lurgan broke away from his friends and re-joined Nuallan in the middle of the dirt path.

"We will return to Victor," he said, "and inform him that our information was not correct about Earl Oswald. I will have to tell him that we bumped into you along the way, mind. But do not worry, Victor has no quarrel with the men of the West. I would gladly take you to him if you are in need of aid?"

Nuallan thought for a moment, until Gideon answered for him. "Thanks but no thanks," he said. "We have others waiting for us and we really must be on our way."

Gideon looked secretly back at Andrus, half expecting him to leave with the Alliance. He was so obsessed and fascinated with them that it would not have come as a surprise. But it seemed that he hadn't even heard the conversation, he'd been simply staring back into the forest the whole time.

Lurgan bowed his head lightly at Gideon.

"Very well. Stay safe, young Princes," he said, then he turned and waved his followers on and they vanished quickly back into the trees.

Without another word, Nuallan put Gideon's arm over his shoulder and they limped on, over the bridge with Andrus at their backs. As yet, there had been no sign that anyone from Vanghale had followed them and Nuallan was starting to think that they may have escaped the wrath of Earl Oswald.

"Come on, in you get," said Nuallan, as they arrived at a crack in the fence.

Gideon leaned his weight onto his leg so he could duck beneath it, whilst Nuallan held up the fence a touch more so that Andrus could slide through. Finally, he himself went through.

"They made it back. There's the horse," said Nuallan.

The horse was tied up beside the barn house. Cobbler must have been putting Gideon's gold to good use.

"Andrus, hold him up, will you?" said Nuallan.

Andrus walked slowly over and latched onto Gideon, who was now so drained and in need of medical attention that he was nearly collapsing. The heat wasn't helping either. Even though the sun slipped slowly behind the mountains, it still gave off a face-drenching blast of heat.

Nuallan walked up the steps and raised his fist to knock on Cobbler's door.

"They are all inside, just go in," said Cobbler, startling Nuallan slightly. He had emerged from the side of his house, carrying an overflowing bucket of water.

Nuallan nodded and opened the door.

He walked along the dark hallway, sideways on because of how thin the passage was. Eventually, he reached the end and leaned on the wooden door. He entered, breathing a huge sigh of relief, to find everyone sat there.

The mood inside, however, was not a good one.

Josanne was sleeping on a made-up bed of sheets and straw in the corner. Her leg was bound with white tissue and cloth, stitched and cleaned. Faizer was awake but as quiet as Josanne, looking out of the window watching the setting sun.

Nuallan aroused the attention of Oslo who was crouched in the corner sobbing lightly. He jumped up at the sight of his father, Andrus, who followed in after Nuallan.

Nuallan took over the care of Gideon once more so that Andrus could embrace his son, but he didn't. Oslo wrapped his arms tightly round his father's waist, but Andrus didn't respond, he simply stared down at the top of his boy's head as if the child was a stranger.

"Father!" said Oslo.

Andrus ignored him.

"Father!" repeated Oslo, crying desperately out for some attention from his father, but still he was ignored. He released his hold and smacked into Andrus's chest.

"Father! Father! Father!" he screamed.

Nuallan set Gideon down onto a leather chair that sat miserably in the centre of the room, then dashed over, prizing Oslo away from Andrus.

"Come on, lad," he said. "He just needs time. Leave him be."

He picked up Oslo and carried him off into the corner of the room, then slid down the wall with Oslo beside him.

Nuallan was exhausted. With Gideon spending most of the day barely conscious, he had had to take charge. Which he did well, but he wasn't used to it. He was physically drained.

"Where is he?" said Cobbler, bursting into the room. "Wake him up. He needs treatment."

He shoved Andrus aside and rocked Gideon's sleeping body.

Andrus simply wandered over to the window, staring out as the last moments of the day slipped away. Faizer who now sat on the end of Josanne's bed looked over at Nuallan and Oslo, who looked back at him but spoke no words.

The atmosphere was miserable. This was the first time the company had experienced a tragedy as severe as this, three dead in one day. The conditions of the room added to the stress. It was so cold and dark. Light could only get in through the one window, which Andrus blocked, plus the silver disked moon was now replacing the oval sun.

Only one candle flickered in the room, struggling to provide much light or heat. The room felt dead, the only noise coming from Gideon's moaning body as Cobbler strapped up his sides and cleaned his bloody face.

Once Cobbler had finished off tending to Gideon, he packed away his bandages and stuffed them in a bag behind the double chair. He then waddled over to the only seat left in the room, dropping down into the single wooden chair and pulling out a pouch of wine, supping at it hard before he caught the gaze of Nuallan and Faizer.

Cobbler took one more swig then passed it down to his right where Faizer sat.

Faizer sucked hard before throwing it over to Nuallan.

Nuallan took the biggest gulp out of everyone, then he offered the pouch to Oslo who sat depressed beside him. Oslo took the pouch and gently took a sip.

"You handle it well, little man," said Faizer.

Oslo smiled half-heartedly before leaning over and handing the pouch back to Faizer, who took another drink of the wine before he finally returned it to Cobbler.

"Was it you?" said Faizer. "Did you kill the Commander?"

Oslo lifted his head up and nodded.

Faizer smiled. "Your first time?"

Oslo nodded once more.

"It gets easier," added Faizer. "The more men you kill."

Oslo turned to face Faizer, more interested now.

"The quicker you get used to it, the better," said Faizer. "In the coming days, I suspect many more men will feel the wrath of your sword, young'en."

At this, Nuallan glared over to Faizer and stared at him angrily.

Faizer caught his gaze and looked quickly down. It was far too early for anyone to be speaking of such things but he risked a few more words before silencing himself for the rest of the night. "I thank you for avenging my brother."

Oslo didn't know how to take Faizer's words so he went back to looking at the floor.

"So much pain," muttered Cobbler, "so much sadness in one room, I have never seen anything like it. Your friend did me a kindness, so I will repay you all with a bit myself. You can stay here for a couple of days until you rest up. I will feed you and change your bandages, providing no one comes here looking for you."

"He's my brother," said Nuallan, "and thank you. We will leave in a couple of days."

Cobbler nodded and finished off the wine, then he stood up and walked toward the door. "I have to go feed the animals before it gets too dark," he said. "Rest up and get better. I have bandages and more wine to help heal your wounds, but I have nothing for that one there." He pointed at Andrus.

Nuallan frowned at Cobbler. "He just needs time, that's all."

Cobbler shrugged and left the room.

"He just needs time," Nuallan muttered again to himself, whilst watching his little brother standing motionless and looking out into nothing.

CHAPTER 11
QUALITY OVER QUANTITY

The entrance to Villach reeked with Meridium victory. Dariuss had successfully forced his way through the obliterated gate and into the courtyard of stone. The middle-aged King's Guard chopped skilfully at the backs of the Musters as they attempted to retreat. Dariuss's armour was as red as the day it was forged, every slash staining his armour even more.

"Make way, make way for the King," called one of the soldiers.

Dariuss yanked his sword out of an opponent before turning around to find his King riding towards the gate. He thrust his sword into the air and waved it as his men mimicked his chant for their King.

Artaxes glided through the gate, swirling around his men and instantly giving chase to the retreating Musters. He hung off the side of his white stallion, slicing into every fleeing Muster. Already the bodies were piling up around the streets that led away from the courtyard. The King fought alone, most of his horses were jammed between the gate and the back of the eager Meridium regiment, but it did not matter, Artaxes needed no assistance as none of the Musters even fought back. They were scattering to the winds, disappearing into various buildings.

"My King, we should hunt down the stragglers before they cause more dishonour to this city," said Dariuss, as he caught up to his King's horse.

Artaxes settled himself down and slid down from his horse, handing his reins to a soldier. Before he could speak, he looked to the concrete stairwells that were flooded with silver men. Havada had wiped out the men on the wall and was now regrouping with Dariuss's force.

Havada plummeted down the stairs and ran straight for the King. He rushed in and out of the fired up soldiers until he reached Artaxes.

"The wall is taken, my King," he said, "but I have news. From upon the wall I could see the Musters regrouping to the western side of the city."

"How many?" said Artaxes.

"No more than three hundred, my King."

"Good work, Havada," said Artaxes. "Now take the remainder of your force and go house to house and rid the streets of this filth. Dariuss, with me."

Havada nodded and retreated back to his regiment.

"Battle Formation," ordered Dariuss, repositioning his helmet and marching after his King.

Artaxes marched down into a heavily built street to the western side of Villach, Dariuss and now Cassius behind him, one to the left and one to the right.

All the cavalry units had demounted and joined the back of the regiment. Dariuss had barely lost a hundred men when he took the gate and they almost outnumbered the Musters two to one.

"Halt!" called the King.

Everyone stopped immediately.

The regiment instantly adapted to their surroundings, forming three perfect lines at the front, the back and at both sides, creating a large rectangular block with an open square in the middle.

This formation was so the King and his King's Guard could sit in-between the regiment without being harmed.

The street was long and wide, nothing like the streets in Rhoden or Vanghale. This was a city. Big, glimmering buildings towered above the street on each side. There were stalls, huts and even a stage for plays to be put on.

Artaxes remained at the head of his army, suspecting an ambush or a trap.

"My King, should we fall back behind the shields?" said Cassius.

"No, there won't be much action going on inside the formation now, will there? Didn't I tell you I wanted to see your sword dripping with blood by noon? It looks pretty dry to me, Captain."

Cassius gulped hard, dread striking into his heart.

"Ah, here they are," said Artaxes, laying revengeful eyes upon a fur-quilted man who had just wandered out into the open about one hundred feet away from the blockade. The man was long of hair and wild of beard. In fact, he was the Chieftain of the Muster army. He dragged a long wooden pole across the cracked pavement, a heavy stone block attached to the end. The Chieftain hoisted up his peculiar weapon, thrusting it repeatedly in the air with both hands, screaming and cursing as he did so. Suddenly, the street swarmed as dozens of Musters poured from the alleyways and the shadows, forming up behind their Chieftain.

"The destruction of the Oakland Musters begins here," said Artaxes, loud enough for his army of five hundred to hear, "with the death of this animal and his pets. Now, hold the formation and prepare for battle."

Artaxes took up a stance alongside Dariuss and Cassius. The first row of men were stood, spear first, only a couple of feet behind them as they awaited the Muster charge.

The Chieftain began walking towards Artaxes, his pace quickening with every step until he was soon at full sprint. Artaxes anticipated the Chieftain's movement, but as the Musters got closer, the Chieftain drifted to the left. He was not to be the King of Meridium's first challenger.

Artaxes tightened his sword grip, counted to three in his head and then swung upward, ripping open his first attacker. Dariuss and Cassius mimicked his movement by slicing in the same style, also knocking down their bloody enemies. The Meridium frontline chanted out loud as they stepped forward. Next, the two frontlines spewed forward and hacked out at the Musters. The King was swarmed by his enemy's and his allies... a full-scale bloodbath had erupted.

Artaxes fought with pure ferocity. He had hungered for a chance to get his hands bloody ever since his defeat upon the Gantry, and every bit of anger, regret and shame he had went into every thrust. The pile of dead enemies was now increasing in front of him. Many of the Oakland Musters attempted an attack on the King, but each one ended up with a limb missing or a bloody slash across their body.

Artaxes was on form. He took a moment to assess Cassius's progress, noting that he too had destroyed all of his challengers. Artaxes was spared a few moments, as his frontlines had already obliterated most of the attackers, until another demented sound echoed through the now deserted street. The Chieftain was standing on top of a stall, thrusting his giant hammer into the air, signalling the ambush.

All of a sudden, dozens more Musters swarmed out of the abandoned alleyways and out from under the trashed stalls, diving into the western flanks of the Meridium regiment. Seconds later, more smashed into the eastern flank.

The Meridiums were surrounded. Although the regiment was holding its position well, Artaxes felt that he had to do something so he cut between two Musters and made for the Chieftain, but he was no longer there. Artaxes stood glaring towards the stall with confusion, puzzled as to the enemy leader's whereabouts. He turned around and tried to pick him out, but he was suddenly struck.

A giant warhammer came crashing around, smashing him straight in the chest. Artaxes glided through the air, and smashed down across the floor. He was paralysed, dazed on the floor, hit so hard that a lightning bolt crack had formed down the centre of his chest piece. Luckily, his frontlines still continued to destroy the Musters and not many were left around to finish the job.

Dariuss still fought admirably alongside the frontlines, completely unaware that his King was in need of assistance. Fortunately, Cassius was already on it. He had witnessed the attack and was charging through the blood-crazed crowd towards the Chieftain. Cassius engaged him before he could get anywhere near the fallen King.

The Chieftain quickly swung his hammer around, but it was too heavy and he was too slow. Cassius slammed his sword toward him, slicing his side open, but the Chieftain was strong and he kicked out, hitting the Captain between the legs. The Oakland leader now took control of the fight as he slammed his hammer down towards the King's saviour, only missing slightly as Cassius rolled to the side. He dived back up, waving his sword from left to right, but each attack was parried until the Chieftain deemed it fit to counter.

He flung the bottom end of his hammer out, thumping Cassius on the nose. The Captain knew he had to be swifter than he had been in order to defeat this foe. He knew that the soldiers would be watching. This was his time to prove his worth, to show the people of Meridium that he was more than just a spy or a coward. He quickly shrugged off the blow and leapt back in.

Many of the Oakland Musters had started pulling out, meaning a lot of the Meridium warriors were without an opponent. But it was a tradition in Meridium that if two ranking officers engaged in combat, no one was to interrupt.

Cassius filled with confidence as a small pack of Meridium soldiers watched the fight.

"Fucking kill him!" screamed one of them.

Cassius took in the confident cheers and used them to his advantage. He fought harder and began to gain the upper hand. Cassius had dipped in and out of every swing and had given himself an opening. He sliced down at the Chieftain's leg, opening it widely. The Chieftain dropped to his knees.

The crowd cheered and waved their swords in the air at the Captain's victory. Cassius felt on top of the world but before he could bask in his glory, he had to finish the job, so he walked around and faced his defeated foe. Only the defeated Chieftain remained, as what was left of the Musters had fled the city, pursued as Havada's sweeping force gave chase.

"Now, you die," said Cassius as he raised his sword.

The Chieftain coughed heavily before erupting into heavy laughter.

"The battle may be lost," he said, "but its events will live forever in the minds of your women and children."

Cassius frowned with confusion as he paused his swipe.

"My cock has been in every single one of them," growled the Chieftain, laughing hysterically. "This city will now breed an army worthy to fight among our ranks."

Cassius had heard enough. He slashed down, cutting deep into the Chieftain's neck. He then yanked hard on the sword, pulling it back out. With one last swing, he revisited the wound, taking his foe's head clean off. The head rolled to the feet of Artaxes, who was back up and on his way over to Cassius.

Artaxes stopped the head dead by resting his foot on it. He rolled it around, inspecting the face. Then he looked over at Cassius, who looked back in the hope that he would receive some appreciation or, even better, a compliment.

"Mop up the city," said the King. "I want every dead rebel burnt by nightfall. Once that is done, drink and eat yourselves into a deep slumber."

The men obeyed, most dropping their shields and spears before beginning to drag their victims' bodies into piles.

"My King, all the rebels are dead," said Havada, who came through the crowd of victorious men. "The keep has been cleared out and a feast is being prepared for you."

Artaxes sheathed his sword and began fiddling with the crack in his chest piece.

"My King," said Havada again.

The King looked up at Havada strangely. "Yes, very well," he said. "I want you and Dariuss to head up to there now. You have earned it."

"As you wish," said Havada. He tapped Dariuss on the back,

interrupting him from dragging a body over to the newly built pile. Havada informed him of his reward before leading him up to the keep.

"Come on," said Artaxes, tapping Cassius on the shoulder.

Cassius had still received no compliment or show of gratitude for his victory. He began to grow curious.

Artaxes led Cassius away from the men, marching him back across the courtyard and into the eastern streets where the keep dangled over a peak. There were hundreds of steps to be climbed in order to get there, not ideal for any man who had just participated in a battle.

"You fought well today, my King," said Cassius. "A true inspiration to all the men, what is our next..." Before he could finish speaking, Artaxes grabbed hold of his throat and slammed him against the wall. Cassius was forced to stand high on his toes to stop himself from choking. Artaxes just glared down at him with fury.

"Tell me, you snake," hissed Artaxes, "when is it that you plan to overthrow me?"

Cassius looked up at his towering King with confusion.

"What?" he stuttered.

"Do not think me a fool, you little worm," continued Artaxes. "I saw what you did back there. You seek to gain the respect and confidence of my men... but why? Oh, I know why. Yes, I do."

Cassius grew frightened at how crazed the King had become.

"I only seek your approval, I only attempt to impress you in combat so that I may be favoured and more involved. Like Dariuss is."

Artaxes exploded with laughter. "No, no, I will not play your games," he mocked, glaring into the Captain's eyes. "I'm afraid this is the end of the line for you, my little snake."

Cassius whimpered and closed his eyes, awaiting the blow that would end his life.

But it did not come.

Captain Cassius reopened his eyes.

Artaxes was still standing over him with his hand around his throat, but the King's attention was elsewhere. He was staring off into an alleyway... an alleyway so dark that if you looked for long enough it would give you the darkest nightmares.

Cassius turned his head as much as he could to see what was there but he saw nothing but pure darkness.

Suddenly, a tear rolled down Artaxes's cheek.

"No, my love," he muttered. "You are mistaken."

Cassius filled with hope as the King's grasp weakened.

"I am strong," continued Artaxes, "but I was stronger when you were by my side." This time, he released Cassius and began walking over to the alleyway.

Cassius dropped to the floor, desperately trying to cushion his coughing so that he would not attract the attention of the deeply-crazed King.

Artaxes walked calmly to the entrance of the hell-like alleyway. As he arrived, he suddenly came to a standstill, then turned back and looked at Cassius.

"You fought well today, Captain," he said.

Then he walked into the alleyway and out of sight.

Cassius was in a state of shock. He now truly understood the depth of the King's insanity... that Artaxes was no longer in control. He quickly gathered his thoughts, dried his tears and reorganised his grey chest piece, then jumped up and made for the keep.

He was very frightened and very confused.

CHAPTER 12
ONCE A MONTH

Faizer lunged his spade deep into the worn ground around the barn, Oslo and Cobbler also helping tend to the abandoned plain of grass. It had been three days since the company had landed back at Cobbler's Farm for help.

"With help from both of you, we will have my vegetable patch back up and running in no time," said Cobbler with excitement.

Oslo, Nuallan and Faizer had been helping Cobbler dig up his nettle riddled soil patch for the last two days. It was hard work digging in the sun, but they all needed something to take their minds off the recent events.

Nuallan was not present at that moment, he was out in West Foolong Forest scouting out the route ahead, the route they would take the following morning towards Brigantium. Faizer noticed Oslo struggling to penetrate the dying ground with his spade, groaning and huffing as he slammed the spade bluntly downwards. He smiled and wandered over to the boy to aid him.

"Watch, lad," he said. He took the spade off Oslo and positioned it sharply on an angle before stamping down on the spade's head. The spade ripped through the ground, splashing up some balls of mud. He handed the spade back to Oslo and observed him. Oslo copied the angle of Faizer's instructions, and with a lunging stamp, he forced the spade deep into the earth. He smiled as he conquered the task.

"Thanks, Faizer," he said as he continued to bash into the ground.

"What happened here?" Faizer asked Cobbler as he walked back to the old man. "The first time we came here the place was a mess."

Cobbler frowned, standing his spade up tall and leaning on it with his bony elbow.

"You know, Faizer, women are the most under-rated creatures upon God's green earth," he said strangely. "Do you have one?"

"A woman? Oh no," replied Faizer. "After what happened to Andrus, I don't think I ever want one."

Cobbler pivoted round on his spade and glanced over at Andrus who was standing quietly to the far eastern side of his farm. He was leaning on the fence staring out over East Foolong Forest in the direction of Vanghale.

"He still hasn't spoken then?" asked Cobbler.

"Not a word. Gideon and Nuallan say the same thing happened to their father many years ago, when their mother died."

Cobbler listened to Faizer before deciding to tell him of his own wife. "My wife died. When she passed, I stopped tending to the fields and animals. The place was never the same. Her passing destroyed this land."

"Sorry to hear that."

"Well, her and the Darchem hunting parties," added Cobbler surprisingly.

Faizer's eyes widened with worry.

"Darchem hunting parties? Why?" he asked nervously.

"Aye, they hunt the Lure Alliance. Word has it that members of the Alliance now seek to expand into East and West Foolong Forest. Darchem parties ride past my farm almost every day."

This news bothered Faizer deeply.

"What did they have to do with your farm?" quizzed Faizer as he struggled to understand Cobbler's facts.

"A bloody lot, I will tell you that much. Since they began venturing so far south, the High King demanded taxes from privately owned settlements, such as taverns, bakeries and farms.

I unfortunately fall into that category, so once a month soldiers come to my farm to claim their taxes. Some months I couldn't afford to pay them, so they stole my livestock, crops and any food and water that they could find."

Faizer instantly dropped his spade and marched towards Cobbler, grabbing the old man's arms tightly.

"Cobbler, when are they due to return? We cannot be here when they arrive," barked Faizer in a state of hysteric panic.

Cobbler went to speak but stopped as something caught his eye beyond Faizer.

"Speak!" yelled Faizer as he shook the old man's weak body.

Cobbler looked down with worry before whispering the worst possible words. "Now."

Faizer spun around instantly as the sound of horses sickened his stomach. A squad of five men pounded along the field and entered through Cobbler's main gate, a different route than Gideon and the company usually took. Faizer was stunned. He needed to warn Gideon urgently, but he had no time, the pack had already entered the farm and were galloping over to him.

Every mounted rider was dressed in thick red armour. Black leather under armour could be spotted on the weak points where the dominating blood armour could not reach. All their helmets were identical. Red, thin and light. The men's lower faces were on show but the metal of the helmet curved around their eyes, making it difficult to identify the shape or colour. Faizer quickly turned around to Cobbler, but he could no longer risk speaking any words as the riders glided past him.

All the riders dismounted, two of them standing by the horses whilst three approached Cobbler.

"Who are these two? I've never seen them before?" asked one of the soldiers sternly.

"This is my son. He travels a lot seeking work where he can," said Cobbler. He still had no idea why Faizer wanted to avoid the Darchem party, but he was wise enough to play along in order to get the men to leave.

"And this is his young boy. He travels with him," added Cobbler.

A man who seemed to be in command of the squad took five steps forward, leaving the other two soldiers standing a few feet behind. He inspected Faizer with his eyes, not convinced.

"Over ten trips I have made to your precious farm, Cobbler, and not once have I seen these long lost family members of yours." The soldier walked over to Faizer pushing his face close to his own.

Faizer could feel the fiery breath of the Darchem man burning onto his flesh.

"For all I know, this man could be holding you against your will." The soldier smiled sarcastically.

Faizer desperately resisted the urge to panic or lash out. As long as he remained calm, the soldier would not have a clue about who himself and Oslo really were, but then it hit him. He remembered that Andrus was standing a couple of hundred feet, staring out over the fence. The Darchem guards would recognise him for sure.

Faizer was now struggling to contain his worry. He began to sweat, his palms became moist and his eyes were beginning to flicker nervously.

Luckily the soldier turned from Faizer before he had chance to notice his nervous expressions. Faizer had a moment of freedom to quickly look over to the eastern fence to spot out Andrus, but he was no longer there. He had vanished.

"Fifty gold coins, Cobbler. Please tell me you can pay up this time. It seems like you're running out of animals for us to snatch," groaned the Darchem superior.

"Yes, I have the coins here with me." Cobbler began rummaging around in his pockets until he was interrupted by the front door of his house swinging open, Josanne walking out.

Josanne was completely unaware of the soldiers that were present. She had simply come outside to speak to Faizer. As she limped out of the door and spotted them, she froze. Josanne knew straight away who they were. The soldier who noticed her began walking away from Cobbler and over towards Josanne, intrigued by her.

"My, she's a pretty piece. I love me a good redhead," he said filthily as he undressed her with his eyes.

"I didn't know you had a daughter as well, Cobbler, you old cunt," laughed the superior.

Cobbler instantly came to her aid, shuffling over and offering the soldier the coin.

"She's my daughter in law, my son's wife. Now here is your coin." But a hand did not greet his own, the coin was not to be accepted.

Josanne stood perfectly still. She had been a victim many times to perverted men, she was used to it but the fact that she was now half crippled and unable to defend herself worried her slightly. It wasn't just the superior Darchem man that glared with hunger, the other four soldiers were also.

"Here, take the coin and go," repeated Cobbler, but again his offering was rejected, the soldier waving his hand in Cobbler's direction.

"No coin needed. This shall do nicely," he hissed.

Faizer instantly dived into action. He ran forward and attempted to tackle the soldier, but he was quickly restrained. The two soldiers on foot intercepted him and began beating him to the ground. The superior now leapt up and latched onto Josanne's red wavy hair, dragging her down the steps and then onto the floor.

"You, you bastard can watch the first of many cocks that will enter your beautiful wife," yelled the soldier brutally.

Faizer screamed in an attempt to alert Nuallan or Gideon but the position he was pinned to the floor at restricted his breathing, causing his warning to be muffled.

"Now be still, bonnie lass," whispered the soldier as he crawled on top of Josanne.

One of the soldiers released his hold from Faizer as he became aware of Cobbler's resistance. He darted over to the old man, delivering a hefty punch to the side of his head. Cobbler dropped to the floor heavily. Next the soldier charged for Oslo who had begun racing over to the superior with his spade in his grasp. The Darchem red cloak intercepted him and grabbed him by the throat, picking him up high, and with devastating power slamming the boy to the ground.

Josanne screamed desperately as the soldier attempted to rip away her brown armoured skirt. He yanked at it powerfully again and again, loosening it slightly, until he suddenly stopped. The hold he had on her weakened. Josanne wriggled away as best as she could, until she noticed her hand was drenched with red blood. She slowly turned her head to discover the heavy body upon her motionless and dead with a throwing knife buried deep in his face.

The two soldiers guarding the horses noticed the knife, paused their laughing and turned around. Before they could turn the full distance, a throwing knife gushed into both of their throats. One at a time, they dropped to their knees, squirming for air. Oslo knew immediately who was throwing the knives, so he timed his involvement perfectly. He waited until his attacker focused his attention on the incident behind him. The soldier stood up and began walking cautiously back towards his only remaining ally, who still lay on top of Faizer.

Oslo took advantage of his opportunity. He pulled himself to his feet, ignoring the splintering pain that ran up his spine, and ran quietly but quickly behind his victim with his spade equipped. Oslo raised the spade and bashed it hard over the back of the soldier's armoured head, knocking him to the floor. He quickly finished the job, smashing the wounded soldier in the head repeatedly until his face was no longer recognisable.

Oslo's attack inspired Faizer to challenge his man, the last of the Darchem soldiers. He began tussling viciously around the floor in an attempt to seize the soldier's sword, but he failed. The soldier bashed him in the head before jumping up and attempting his get away, but he was trapped. Andrus now revealed himself from round the side of the house. He sprinted past the horses, jumping over his choking victims, and blocked the retreating soldier in. The Darchem survivor had his back against the barn wall, his sword raised and ready to take life, but he stood no chance.

Oslo now lingered to the man's left, preventing him from escaping in that direction.

"You're going to die today," muttered Faizer as he closed in from the right hand side. He wiped his bloody lip.

The red cloak realised his odds of survival and dropped his sword, cowering back.

Oslo, Faizer and Andrus now all stood in an oval shape a few feet from the soldier.

"Wait!" signalled a very familiar voice. Gideon had finally heard the commotion and came outside to see what was going on. He walked down the steps, instantly noticing Josanne on the floor, trying cover her bare backside and he realised what had nearly happened here.

Without another word, Gideon stormed over to the barn. He slid between the oval of allies, taking Andrus's sword as he passed. He gripped it tightly and slashed down the face of the now kneeling soldier. The man's face opened up like a volcano erupting its lava. Gideon slashed down again, completely mutilating the man's body, every single slice causing the body to wobble, and eventually tumble down to the blood-drenched floor.

Cobbler's newly tended field now ran like a river of red, the grass and soil stained with the blood of the Darchem soldiers.

"What have you done, you mad men?" blurted out Cobbler who was trying to pull himself to his feet.

Gideon dashed over and assisted him. "We had no choice. Those men knew who we are."

"Knew who you are? Why would they care about a couple of travellers?" replied Cobbler as he rubbed his jaw gently.

"Inside, Faizer. Gather our things. We leave now," ordered Gideon before turning back to Cobbler. "Listen, if more soldiers come and see this, they will kill you. You must leave too. Gather what you need and ride west. Ride for Meridium."

Cobbler looked confused as he received Gideon's orders.

"Scout out a General called Koos. Tell him Gideon Destain sent you. Tell him we live."

Cobbler's eyes bulged out of his face as he took in the rest of the command. "My god, you three are the lost sons of Meridium, aren't you?" he said with confusion.

"Well, not me, Nuallan is the other one," interrupted Faizer as he came back out from the house.

"Nuallan," Gideon whispered to himself. "Where is he?"

"He went into the forest hours ago to scout out the route ahead," said Josanne who had made herself more presentable.

"Which direction?" asked Gideon.

"East. He won't be far," she said.

"We will pick him up along the way. Everyone get ready to leave in a few minutes." Gideon raced over to the barn where Cobbler had wandered. He slid through the red door and raced through the straw-scattered building.

"You must be quick. Do you know the way to Meridium?" questioned Gideon urgently.

Cobbler, who seemed to be in no hurry, nodded with frustration. "Yes, yes. You go, lad. Don't worry about me, I will be alright."

Gideon looked at his new friend and smiled. "Thank you for all you have done for me and my family." He held out his hand.

Cobbler shook Gideon's hand and smiled back.

"Rise and rise again, my friend," said Gideon and he turned to leave.

Gideon closed the barn door behind himself and jogged over to the others. Faizer and Josanne had commandeered the Darchem horses and attached all their belongings to them. Josanne mounted one of the black armoured horses with Oslo on the back, Faizer climbing onto another one, and Andrus on the one next to him.

"What the fuck has happened here, Gideon?" said someone from behind the barn.

Gideon looked quickly to find his brother Nuallan standing

119

there, covered from head to toe in mud. Gideon sighed with relief. He went over and hugged his brother hard.

"Thank god you're back. We need to leave right away. Did you scout out the area ahead?"

"Aye, it's clear," replied Nuallan as he looked with horror at the mutilated Darchem red cloak. "I recommend taking a route along the side of the forest. It's safer."

"We can be in Brigantium as early as tomorrow midday now we have these horses," predicted Nuallan.

"Indeed. Now let's go," said Gideon as he ran over to the horses, hanging onto the side of one and pulling himself up.

Nuallan ran over, jumping onto the last horse. The four Darchem beasts began swivelling around behind Gideon.

"Nuallan, lead the way," ordered Gideon.

Nuallan smiled pleasantly, happy to be given a little authority over the company. He whipped his reins hard, triggering the horse to fly off, and one by one, the company drilled off down the path and spewed out of Cobbler's gate. Their journey to Brigantium had begun.

CHAPTER 13
WHEN BROTHER
TURNED ON BROTHER

A galaxy of flies harassed the company as they trekked exhaustingly towards Brigantium. Gideon and the others decided that it would be safer to travel through the outskirt fields of West Foolong Forest, especially now that Darchem hunting parties were scouring the area. They used the side of the treeline as a guide whilst marching across a field that sloped awkwardly. The long wavy grass would act as camouflage for the company if any Darchem soldiers were to make an appearance.

Nuallan led the group with Andrus at his back, the rest lingering beside Josanne who was struggling with the journey. She was without her horse as she was forced to release it into the wild along with everyone else, leading the horses through this field too heavy a burden for everyone.

"It's fine. Stop looking at it," she said quietly.

Gideon's protective nature was kicking in. He stuck close to Josanne and had been monitoring her injury from the second she dismounted the horse. Her wounds had still not healed, unlike his own. Apart from a few bruises and aching bones, he was fit as a fiddle.

"It doesn't look fine. You're limping. Let me take a look," argued Gideon.

Josanne came to a standstill, groaning impatiently. "We don't have a lot of time. We must keep moving if we want to reach Brigantium by tomorrow."

Gideon stopped, and so did Oslo and Faizer. Gideon whistled in order to alert his two brothers who continued to hike through the tricky terrain. They stopped immediately and began mooching back in Gideon's direction.

"We must stop for a moment to look at Josanne's wound," he said. "Will you two scout ahead to that treeline? Find somewhere suitable to set up camp?"

"Aye, we're only about a mile away. We will set up there," decided Nuallan.

"Okay, build a small fire but keep it limited," Gideon said. "I don't want it to be visible. It will be dark within the hour."

"Sure." Nuallan tapped Andrus on the chest and began gallivanting toward the emerald fortress.

"Right, lay down," ordered Gideon as he flattened down some of the grass.

Faizer and Oslo helped Josanne down. She desperately tried to hide her pain, but the reaction on her face revealed the seriousness of the wound as Gideon unravelled the bandage, sliding it down.

"It isn't infected, yet," he said. "But it will be soon. We needed more time to recover at Cobbler's Farm." He leaned his elbow on his knee, and with his other hand he scrubbed back his hair.

Faizer dropped down onto his knee and inspected Josanne's leg. He lightly tapped her thigh before speaking out. "You will be fine," he said before redirecting his attention to Gideon. "Do you think Cobbler got out in time?"

Gideon looked at him with uncertainty. "I hope so." He tucked the bandage back and helped Josanne up. "One more mile, then we can rest." He bent down behind her, latched one arm onto her back and the other round the back of her tired legs, hoisting her up and shuffling about until she lay comfortable along the top of his strong arms.

Josanne didn't speak any words. She was embarrassed by the

fact she was being carried. Her whole life she had been treated like a man, and now she was being treated like a woman. She wasn't used to it and she certainly didn't enjoy it. From a young age, her father and brothers taught her how to fight and how to survive. She had only ever been around men. Even when she left her home, she was the same. Right up until she met and joined the company.

It wasn't long before they reached the treeline. The trees there were more bare because the leaves had fluttered off like a flock of birds leaving for the winter.

"We will have to keep the fire low," said Gideon as he dropped Josanne to her feet. He ducked deeply under the prickly branches and began crouch walking through. Faizer and Oslo entered next, guiding Josanne through carefully.

"Rethink those logs, Nuallan," said Gideon as he approached his two brothers.

Andrus and Nuallan had begun building a small wooden fire out of dirty logs that they found lying around. They had flattened the grass and kicked the larger rocks and stones away, creating a suitable area for the company to sleep.

Nuallan, who was crouched around the heavily stacked fire, looked up to Gideon.

"We are too close to the treeline. Anyone close to the field will spot it a mile away." Gideon pointed back to the way they had come in. The camp was a little more than thirty feet from the treeline.

"Very well," replied Nuallan. He began tossing the logs back off into the trees, leaving only a few upon the pile of straw and twigs.

"It's going to be a cold night," groaned Josanne as she watched Nuallan toss the branches back into the wild.

Faizer and Oslo carried her into the camp and planted her down on a long chunky log that Andrus had dragged out of the bush. Oslo planted himself down beside her, leaving one seat for Gideon who wandered over. Faizer looked up to the sky, the bald trees making it easy for him to watch the clouds fade and the sun disappear.

"I would say we have about fifteen minutes of light left. Little man, fancy a practise?" He smiled down at the seated Oslo.

The boy smiled and dived up. He lashed out his sword and began bashing away at Faizer.

Andrus sat down beside the fire and attempted to light it. Nuallan planned to reap the warmth as much as possible. He ruffled up Josanne's back pack and placed it beside the fire. He then lay flat and rested his head on it.

He looked up into the darkening sky and began thinking about what tomorrow may hold. He then looked to Josanne and Gideon who were chuckling at the spar going on between Oslo and Faizer.

"Tell me, Josanne, tell me a little about Tobias Ringfold," said Nuallan.

"You have never met him?" she asked.

"No, never. Gideon was usually the one that would attend meetings for father."

Gideon looked at Josanne. "I met the man a few times. He's a good man."

Josanne seemed pleased with the compliment. She was very smitten with King Tobias, he was her King after all. She looked down to Nuallan. "So what do you want to know?"

"I don't know, I just need to know what to expect tomorrow. We still don't know if he will embrace us. He could send us away."

Gideon frowned slightly. He knew Tobias rather well, and he knew Tobias would not send them away.

"Well, you don't need to worry about anything like that," Josanne said. "We will be lucky if we receive an audience with him. He will be extremely busy."

"And why is that?"

"His son Hector is nineteen. His Selection will be coming up in the coming weeks."

Nuallan paused his response. He had heard about the tradition of Selection that the Brigantiums honoured, but he couldn't quite remember. He looked at Josanne with confusion. "Remind me again, what is Selection?"

Gideon remained silent. He knew all about Selection, but he respected the fact that Nuallan and even Andrus seemed eager to hear about it.

The light clash of swords that rang lightly in the background was all that could be heard as Josanne prepared herself to explain.

The birds of the day had banished themselves to their nests and the owls of the night had not yet made an appearance. Josanne shuffled herself to the edge of the log and began to explain. "Every Kingdom in Requirium passes down the throne to an eldest child, usually a boy, but not the Brigantiums. Their eldest children have to earn the throne, and if they don't before the age of twenty, the throne passes to one of the other royal families of Brigantium, in this case the Badstuber family, or the Chalk family. They have hounded Tobias and his family for decades. They crave the throne."

Nuallan seemed to be a little confused, so Gideon intervened for a moment. He leaned forward and faced Nuallan. "Basically if Hector does not pass his Selection, soon, the Badstuber family will have earned the right to the throne, once Tobias dies of course."

Nuallan seemed a bit more enlightened. "I see, yes, I remember now. So, more to the point, what does the Selection entail? I got told by father many years ago, that it is some sort of duel."

Josanne began shivering a little as the night's freezing air began taking its toll. She slid down the side of the log seat and shifted towards the fire before continuing her story. "Kind of. The Prince fighting Selection has to go up against eleven other opponents. His identity is not revealed to the other fighters to prevent them all allying up to wipe him out. They are handpicked mercenaries, volunteers, desperate men who are nothing really of worth. It is a fight to the death. For whatever reason, the other fighters are desperate to win the victor's purse. They either have nothing to lose or they're foolish enough to think they can win. It's ten thousand gold pieces if they are the last one standing."

Faizer took a moment away from training to have his input on the conversation. "Ten thousand? I think I might put my name forward," he said with a grin on his face.

Josanne laughed sarcastically, causing the fire's flames to flicker wickedly. "I'm afraid Hector would cut you down, Faizer."

Faizer walked around the fire and pulled the rug sack out from underneath Nuallan's head. He pulled the water pouch out from the sack and stuffed it back before Nuallan had time to moan.

"That good, huh?"

"Almost as good as his father, they say," she responded.

Faizer drank his water and launched the pouch over to Oslo. Faizer had had enough of training. He lay down by the fire, wriggling annoyingly until he got comfortable, and once he did, he closed his eyes.

Nuallan sat up from his relaxed position in order to press for more information. "Tell me about Tobias's Selection?" he asked with interest.

Oslo was sitting next to his father by the fire, the two of them listening also with interest.

Josanne looked to Gideon as if offering him the honour of telling the story, so he did.

"Tobias was sixteen years old when he passed his Selection. Four years early. He had three brothers, one of whom was nineteen, Helix. Helix had his Selection coming up, he had trained well and the people were confident he would pass, but Tobias craved the throne. He offered himself up weeks before the event took place. The nation was shocked and their father was distraught, but he had no choice but to allow it. So the ceremony took place as normal in one of the arenas inside Versidia. All the noble families attended including all the Kings of Requirium. Tobias and Helix decimated the other challenges until it came down to the two of them."

Everyone continued to listen with eager interest.

"Wait, so he killed his own brother?" asked Nuallan.

"He did. They duelled for a couple of seconds before Tobias planted his axe through the top of Helix's head, completing

Selection and earning the right to the eastern throne of Brigantium, which he claimed five years later once their father died." Gideon threw a twig onto the fire as he finished.

Nuallan looked to be affected by the story. "I'm not sure how I feel about this man. I mean, killing your own brother for the throne?" he said sadly.

"Tobias knew that his older brother would rule for a long time, and he would bare children also meaning Tobias would never ever sit upon the royal chair. He was ambitious, you could say," defended Gideon ruthlessly.

"Ambitious, you say, more like psychotic," retaliated Nuallan. He lay flat and closed his eyes.

Josanne tapped Gideon passionately before closing her eyes also, attempting to fall asleep.

"Hold on," said Nuallan as he sat back up. "How do you know all these stories about Tobias. From what I remember, father would throw a fit if Tobias or any of the Eastern Horse Lords' names came up in conversation."

"Well from mother's bedtime stories. You know how much she respected and admired the Eastern Lords. All my stories were about Tobias, and his followers," Gideon said happily.

Nuallan looked back at him with confusion, even Andrus had tilted his head a little.

"No, I never heard about Tobias," said Nuallan. "My bedtime stories were always about father or uncle Havideous, many also about Koos's father Tidus."

The two of them stared at each other puzzlingly.

Nuallan looked to Andrus again. "Did you ever hear about Tobias?"

Andrus slowly shook his head, but before Nuallan could ask another question, he lay flat and closed his eyes. Oslo did the same, shuffling over beside Josanne and going to sleep leaving only Nuallan and Gideon awake.

The two of them sat there thinking about why they were told different stories by their mother, but only for a moment. It wasn't a massive issue.

"Well, tomorrow then, Brigantium, eh?" stated Nuallan.

"Aye tomorrow."

Nuallan lay back down and whispered some rare words. "I love you, Gideon."

Gideon raised an eyebrow surprisingly. Affection was rarely shown between Gideon and his brothers. It surprised him. He had only ever heard those words from the mouth of his mother. Gideon halted his reply as he lay down and wriggled until he was comfortable. "I love you too, brother."

CHAPTER 14
DARIUSS'S PLAN

Artaxes sat slouched in his wooden chair at the head of the long rectangular table, glaring impatiently at the doorway. A feast of untouched food sizzled upon the table, but no one was allowed to tuck in until Artaxes said so, and he was waiting.

"That chicken looks good. What is he waiting for?" whispered one of the King's Guard, sitting at the far end of the table staring hungrily at the food.

"Shut your mouth, boy. You will eat when I say," snapped Artaxes.

The King's Guard stiffened and sat up straight. He hadn't expected the King to hear him.

Artaxes now sat a little more neatly in his chair as the sound of footsteps interested him. The pace of the approaching visitor slowed, insinuating that they were preparing to enter the dining hall. The latch twisted and the doors swung open.

"First General Lucifer," addressed the King.

Lucifer walked in with his helmet tucked under his armoured arm. He slammed it down before sitting at the head of the opposite end of the table, some of the Lieutenants nodding respectfully at him as he sat. Artaxes waved on the servants that had been standing at the side of the room waiting to serve the food. In a hurry they all scattered over and began filling up the plates of all the ranking officers.

Dariuss and Havada sat on the right side of the table, the only two that refused to eat, the pale sickly look upon their faces explaining how wild their victory night had been. They had both nearly drank themselves to death.

Lucifer spoke out loudly so that the King could hear his words over the crunching and munching coming from the mouths of the officers around the table.

"Nine hundred men, my King. Nine hundred men are all that Sandown has to offer."

The King seemed rather pleased with the offering despite Lucifer's concern. He then looked to Dariuss for a military report.

"How many casualties did we suffer whilst retaking the city?"

"A little more than two hundred and fifty, my King," replied Dariuss. He then looked up to the ceiling and began calculating the remaining men. "I think we have about six hundred or so men left, ready to fight."

Artaxes began thinking. He fancied his chances.

"The men from Sandown, and our remaining force means we have around one thousand five hundred troops," added Dariuss.

Artaxes smiled. He hadn't had command over this many men in a long time, but his smile soon faded when he remembered the size of the Muster army. He looked down the long food-filled table and quizzed Lucifer.

"The scouts informed you of the Muster force at Oggsfleet, three thousand they say?"

Lucifer looked back passionately. "Yes, maybe a little more. Do you think we can win?"

"Of course we can win. How long till the men from Sandown can march for Villach?" asked Artaxes with curiosity.

"They marched with me. They are setting up camp just outside the walls as we speak," informed the First General surprisingly.

Artaxes looked delighted. "Impressive, truly impressive, now did Milano come with them?"

Milano was the Watcher of Sandown. He was a Captain and a loyal one at that. He put upon the men of Sandown the strict training programme that Artaxes created, the exact one that every son of Meridium spent their life carrying out, that was what made them warriors, incredible warriors.

"He did, my King, Cassius has received him. He is showing him to his quarters by my command," said Lucifer whilst taking a deep bite out of a chicken leg.

"Nonsense, bring them here. I have an announcement. Havada, go and find them. Tell them I want them both here," commanded Artaxes.

Havada pushed out his chair and bowed, making for the door to leave.

"Two to one," stated Dariuss.

Artaxes looked at him as if waiting for more words.

"They out number us two to one, now them odds can be ignored when both sides have small numbers to start with, like when we took Villach, both our forces were small to start with, were they not?" continued Dariuss confusingly.

Artaxes looked at him, resting his chin on his fist whilst leaning over the table. "What is your point?" he asked.

Dariuss clasped his fingers together and rested his merged fist onto the table. "What I'm trying to say is, we may not be able to overcome the odds when we face a larger force. There are three times more men to kill than last time. Yes, we may have more men, but it won't matter. A force of three thousand can swarm us, our men will tire and we could very well lose."

"You think we can't win?" barked Artaxes.

"That isn't what I'm saying," insisted Dariuss.

"You have another plan?" asked Lucifer from across the room.

"I do, a way to make the Oakland Musters panic, a plan that will cause them to flee or surrender," he said hopefully. He had caught the attention of Artaxes truly now.

"And what do you suggest?" questioned the King.

"How many ships do we have?"

"Three," said Lucifer.

"That's enough," Dariuss said. "We will only need two. Right, we should attack them head on, as planned. March into the port and set up the square battle formation at three points. The tactic worked well against the Musters when we used it here. They have proven that they do not know how to penetrate it. Now, whilst they are occupied with us, send two ships along The Sink, filled with archers."

Artaxes, Lucifer and some of the Lieutenants had become very intrigued at this point.

"Go on," said Artaxes.

"Equip the archers with fire arrows, and have them obliterate the enemy ships from behind. Even if the Musters were winning the fight, they would lose heart at the sight of their ships. Their getaway burning behind them would cause panic among their forces."

Some of the Lieutenants and officers shouted out with excitement. They liked this plan.

"We will strand them there, destroy them and take back our lands!" declared Dariuss with passion.

Artaxes smiled widely. He liked the plan also and admired the dedication of his King's Guards to the cause. He stared at Dariuss who sat back down, his excitement having triggered his hangover to kick back in, and his face going white again.

"An excellent plan, Dariuss. Well thought," complimented Artaxes as the doors swung open again causing everyone's heads to turn.

Havada walked in first, marching quickly along the table and taking back his seat beside Dariuss. Cassius and Milano walked in next. Cassius had a certain unstable look about him. He was very nervous to be around the King after the events of the other night.

Milano quickly stepped in front of Cassius and bowed to the King. He was of average height and in his thirties, with a whiskery beard that curved around his tanned face. His head however was without hair, an ugly feature for a man of Meridium to be bald. But his jewel blue eyes made up for it, standing out like a crystal sitting in an abandoned field.

"I assume First General Lucifer filled you in?" asked Milano as he straightened.

"He did. I'm glad to have you on board, my old friend. Now sit, please," replied the King whilst holding his hand out to his left.

Milano walked around the table and sat down to the left of Artaxes. Artaxes then looked at Cassius who seemed too scared to even look at the King.

"Cassius," addressed Artaxes pleasantly as he held his hand out to the left again, pointing to the chair beside Milano.

Cassius scurried around the table and sat down beside Milano.

Artaxes waited until everyone sat silently before he stood up and faced everyone happily.

"First General, have the two ships prepped and ready to sail before the week's end. After that I want you to rejoin me. I need you in this fight, my brother. Can you still swing that sword as quick as you used to?" asked Artaxes with a slight chuckle.

Lucifer stood up passionately. "I can, I will."

Artaxes then looked down to his right. "Havada, go with Lucifer. You will lead the attack along The Sink. Handpick two hundred men and be ready to sail by the end of the week. On the seventh day, Dariuss and Milano, you will march alongside Lucifer and myself."

"It would be an honour to ride beside you again, my King," said Milano as he stood up and latched onto the King's hand.

"Now leave us. Everyone tend to your tasks and be ready to leave the city at the end of the week," stated Artaxes. "Wait there, Cassius. I need to speak to you."

Cassius who was halfway up from his chair, slid back into it, fear beginning to take over. He didn't know what the King would do to him this time.

Artaxes waited till the room was empty before sitting back down.

"Captain, you will not accompany me and the men. You will not fight in this battle."

Cassius nervously lifted his head. "If that is your wish, my King, then I will obey it," he said carefully.

Artaxes frowned as he realised how frightened his Captain had become. "Listen, what I did to you the other night was not acceptable. You have been a loyal lad all your life. I just, sometimes I see her, you know. Sometimes I see my wife, and it changes me," Artaxes said sadly.

Cassius looked a little less frightened now, more surprised than scared. He was surprised that the King confided in him enough to speak to him about his wife.

"What do you speak of, my King?" Cassius asked with caution.

"Never mind all that, we have a battle to prepare for." Artaxes stood up.

"You will stay here and run things for me. I will call for you when you are to return to Meridium," said the King.

"Of course, my King, I am honoured to do so. Rise and rise again, my King."

King Artaxes shoved his chair out of the way, walked for the doors and pushed on them hard.

CHAPTER 15
AN EASTERN INTRODUCTION

There was a steady audience present in the throne room. Tobias Ringfold was sitting on his creamy brown throne, tending to the requests and needs of the Brigantium people.

Once a week, the people of Brigantium would form a line into the Palace and then into the throne room, where Tobias would listen to them. Sometimes he would reward people with workers, to help repair their lands, sometimes he would give the poor people coin and sometimes he would even loan out soldiers to help people fight off bandits or raiders. King Tobias Ringfold was adored by the people because of charities such as this. He, unlike many other Kings in Requirium, put the people first.

The King was sitting in his casual grey tunic and trousers. He only wore armour if he was marching into battle. He did however have a large wolf skin fur draping over his shoulders.

Tobias was in his late forties. He was married with one child, Hector Ringfold. Tobias was a little over six foot, thin around the waist and broad at the shoulders. He had short brown hair that curled ever so lightly at the front but its short length prevented it from dangling down. He had piercing brown eyes that collided nicely with the olive tan that riddled his skin.

"King Tobias, I beg you for assistance. My farm hangs on the border of Brigantium. A flu has swept through my land, killing most of my horses. I cannot plant the crops on my field without the horses," whimpered the old man who was next in line.

Tobias smiled and held out his hand. He waved one finger at the old man, signalling him to come forward. The man stepped up the dark painted steps that led up to the throne, knelt and awaited the King's decision.

"Tell me, do you have any family members, or even yourself, that have a history of providing a service to the throne?" asked Tobias with a delicate but sweet tone.

"I have two sons serving in your army. One is of rank, my King."

Tobias smiled. "Then that is all I ask. If you provide a service to the throne, then the throne will provide a service for you. I will give you four Huskarian horses and six men to help tend to your crop."

There were three different breeds of horses in Brigantium. There was the Huskarian horse that was bred for work, tough beasts, usually a creamy brown colour. Then there was the Buywise breed of horses, bred to transport goods and resources from town to town, with excellent stamina and trained from birth to learn how to control heavy loads. They were mostly grey. Finally there was the Starchitect breed, jet black, tall and powerful beasts that could run faster than any known creature. These horses were bred for war.

The man smiled with delight. "Thank you, Tobias, thank you dearly."

Tobias nodded happily whilst holding his arm out to the right. A man, dressed in thick black robes stood with a scroll between his grasp, was waiting to receive the farmer.

"Next," said another armoured man holding a scroll and feather, standing at the top of the stairs. His job was to keep control of the line, bringing forward the people one at a time. His name was Fangoy. He was of small position, an advisor and assistant to the king.

Another man walked forward and attempted to press his matter, but he was not given the opportunity. The double oak doors swung open causing an agonising squeak. A man dressed in thin chainmail trotted in with an urgent matter.

"King Tobias, a Meridium soldier has entered the city. He is on his way through the Palace as we speak," informed the soldier who went by the name of Enly. The soldier had lily white hair, and was one of the King's Lieutenants.

"Thank you, Enly," said Tobias. He stood up from his carved chair and spoke to the line of civilians. "I do apologise, folks, but I must end today's meet earlier that I would have liked to. Follow Fangoy here out of the Palace. He will make sure that your requests reach my ears once I have taken care of business."

Fangoy looked over his shoulder to the King, seeming annoyed that he had been given the task, but he did not complain. "Right, come on, you lot, out you go. Come on, follow me," he ordered with frustration. The line of about twenty people disbanded quickly out of the throne room.

Tobias sat back down and stared at the doors. It had been a very long time since he had engaged in conversation with a man of Meridium. He wondered who it could be and more so, what could they want.

Tobias continued to wait with the remainder of his staff on shift, Enly standing patiently at the door whilst a group of soldiers stood guard in various locations around the room. The soldiers of Brigantium were not as elegant to look at as Meridium ones were. These soldiers wore very thin brown armour, made of hard leather, string and the odd coil. They believed that a great soldier did not need fancy armour and heavy defensive plates in order to be a great fighter, and also considered that heavy armour would slow down their war horses. The only thing similar between the two armies' appearances was the cape. The Brigantiums also wore a long cape, but theirs was not blue, it was yellow. It scraped across the floor behind each man.

There were three other men present in the room, each standing at attention behind their King's royal seat. Each one of them well over six foot, and well over sixteen stone, they were massive. These men however did wear armour, painted with thick steel plating from neck to toe, and also wearing the long yellow cape down to their ankles. Their most decorative piece of armour was their helmets, smelted silver all over and then mixed in with perfectly forged golden strands that ran in a zig zag formation over the top of the helmet. They were from a town by the eastern coast called Brushup.

The beastly brothers were known as trouble-causers, always stealing and fighting. Some of the soldiers blamed their wild actions on the fact that both of their parents were killed when the men were but young boys.

They were picked up when they were in their teenage years, by a party of Brigantium soldiers trading coin for fish at their hometown. The same soldiers made many visits to Brushup, each time noticing the boys. They eventually told Tobias who suggested bringing the boys to the city, and so they did.

With the promise of food, the boys came willingly. Upon arrival, Tobias tended to their needs. He treated them like his sons for a short while before putting them in an orphanage where they got a proper education and a better understanding of a civilised life. Shortly after, they were also taught how to fight properly where each one of them excelled massively. Tobias became aware of their progress so he gave them a position, to act as Royal Guards, but after some time Tobias realised that the new Royal Guards were wasting away, they were getting no action by following Tobias to his meetings and escorting him to towns, so he devised a new plan.

The eastern King began renting out the men, at a rate per man. Anyone who needed bandits or clans defeating, or even debts settling could hire the men, either one of them or all of them. The 'Three' now looked at Tobias as a father, their loyalty had no limits, and they, along with everyone else in Brigantium, loved their King.

Enly opened the huge wooden door as he heard the footsteps of the visitor approaching. Tobias sat up eagerly, ready to greet the unknown Meridium man.

"Greetings. Our King awaits you," said Enly as the man walked in.

Tobias stood and walked down the charcoal steps in order to meet his visitor halfway.

"It's been a long time, has it not, Koos, son of Tidus?" stated Tobias happily as he finally set his eyes upon the stranger.

Koos blew his blond fringe out of his face as he reached Tobias, holding out his hand and shaking the King's hand.

"Your presence is of great surprise to me, General. What can I do for you?" asked Tobias as he began walking back to his chair.

Koos walked by Tobias's side and began. "I come to ask for aid. I'm sure you will have heard about our Muster problem in the West? Artaxes has marched on Villach. If successful, he then plans to march on Oggsfleet Port."

"Words reached my ears that Artaxes was successful at Villach. He has retaken the city with ease," informed Tobias.

Koos who was not aware of this quickly pressed his next matter. "Then we don't have much time. He will attack Oggsfleet within the coming days. There are three thousand men at Oggsfleet. I fear he may not be so lucky this time," continued Koos.

Tobias had reached his throne. He sat back down and looked at Koos who stood a few feet away from him, glaring with hope.

"And what is it that you want me to do about it?" asked Tobias.

Koos looked at him angrily. "I want you to ride alongside us, help us take back our lands then together we can forge the alliance that we should have made a long time ago."

"Artaxes would not accept my aid. For unknown reasons, the mad man despises us," said Tobias as he laughed sarcastically.

Koos frowned upon Tobias's remark, even though he knew it was true.

Tobias stood up quickly and rested his hand on Koos's armoured shoulder. "Walk with me?"

The two of them trod down the steps and walked towards the double doors, exiting them quickly with Enly at their backs.

They walked through the Palace and travelled down the side of the eastern hall where all the open windows allowed the beautiful view of the eastern countryside to peek through. A sandstone wall and ledge ran right across the hall, separating the walkway from the destructive drop that lay on the opposite side. Large oval cut outs were spread out across the pale wall so that people could look out and admire the view.

Tobias stopped halfway down the hall and leaned onto one of the sandstone window ledges. He looked out into the lime green fields whilst he thought deeply about Koos's request.

Koos refused to take in the scenery, staring at the back of Tobias whilst waiting for his response.

"Okay," muttered Tobias.

Koos's face brightened. "Okay?" he asked with hope.

Tobias stood up straight, turned around and then leaned his back in a slouching position against the window ledge. "How many men do you need?"

Koos planted his helmet on the window ledge quickly, his arm beginning to ache from holding it for so long. "Four thousand. Now I know that sounds a little excessive but we will be able to end the Oakland Musters for good. That way, we will still have men left to defend our city. As you will know, we don't have many left."

Tobias looked at Enly who had stood patiently listening to Koos's demand. Enly assisted Tobias on a lot of his decisions, a loyal lad that served Tobias well.

Enly simply nodded, insinuating that the men could be easily despatched.

"Okay, we will help you. Enly, feed the men and the Starchitect horses. I want two thousand horses and four thousand men ready to march by..." Tobias paused, and looked to Koos for a departure date.

"Within the next three days would be ideal," suggested Koos hopefully. "Artaxes will leave Villach within a week."

Tobias smiled and looked back to Enly. "Have the men treated to whores and wine tonight, and then tomorrow have them prepare the horses and saddle up. The following morning we leave for Oggsfleet Port."

Koos bowed respectfully and held out his hand for Tobias to meet it. "Thank you, King Tobias," he said. "Let this day be the beginning of a new friendship between the East and the West."

Tobias bowed his head in return and added, "Enly, see Koos to his quarters for the coming days."

"Of course, my King." Enly waved on Koos and led him back off down the hallway.

This time Koos observed the scenery, glaring out as he walked past each oval carved window. The forests and fields were spectacular, so green and fresh. Koos couldn't help but feel a little envious. He had no quarrels with the east but he hated how they lived a life of peace and luxury. A life where they didn't wake on a morning and instantly fill with worry and regret. Something that he had experienced every morning for the past seven years.

CHAPTER 16
THE STONE MONUMENTS

The sizzling sun made a welcoming appearance on this happy day. The company had crossed the eastern border and were approaching the city of Brigantium. The mood was a little better. Josanne had heightened the atmosphere with her excitement. It had been a long time since she had been home.

They were travelling across a very wide stone path so clean you could walk on it with your bare feet. This path would lead them right up to the very gates of Brigantium.

Every half a mile or so along the path was a beautifully sculptured horse, one either side of the concrete walkway, the image of a knight holding on tightly as the stone horse jeered up magnificently.

Everyone took the time to inspect the statues every time they came across one.

"Let me down, Gideon. We are close now. I don't want to be carried back through those gates. I walked out of them and I would very much like to walk back in," insisted Josanne. She had been hanging off Gideon's back since they left the camp on that morning.

Gideon slouched his back slightly, allowing Josanne to slide off. She balanced herself nicely and began walking at a steady pace.

"After you then," Gideon said.

Josanne smiled and led the company the rest of the way.

"Are you worried?" asked Faizer. Nuallan and himself were strolling slowly at the back of the pack.

"No."

"You seem nervous."

"I'm curious," Nuallan said. "I'm not sure what is going to happen."

"Josanne is confident Tobias will take us in," reassured Faizer.

"And what about you? Are you confident, Faizer?"

Faizer shrugged his shoulders. He wasn't entirely sure himself. He was also nervous.

"Holy fuck," cursed Nuallan before Faizer could reply. His attention along with Faizer's had been drawn to a mesmerising sight.

"Behold the Kingdom of Brigantium, my brothers," shouted Josanne just loud enough for everyone to hear.

Josanne, Oslo, Andrus and Gideon had just walked beneath the ginormous sculpture that Faizer and Nuallan were starstruck by. The magnificent sighting was of two Starchitect horses standing off, one each side of the path, each one with a knight upon its back, swords drawn. The swords had been crafted in a way that they were clashing against each other.

The detail was spectacular, each structure as tall as three houses. Nuallan and Faizer nearly strained their necks as they continued to stare up at the sight.

"Once you cross beneath the connected swords, you are officially inside the Capitol of the East," said Josanne.

Faizer and Nuallan picked up the pace, and power-walked until they caught up to the company who had already walked under the landmarks.

The two of them continued to observe the horses as they walked under it.

"That's remarkable. I didn't know men could build such things," commented Faizer who was truly stunned.

"No wonder mother couldn't get enough of this place," joked Nuallan, forcing a half-hearted smile for Gideon.

"If you think that is something, then behold the city, my brothers," said Gideon as he pointed out into the distance.

Nuallan and Faizer both turned and looked ahead, and then they saw it. The city of Brigantium.

It was about three miles further down the stone passage, no more woodland or scenery at the side of the path now, it was just an immaculate green field that travelled for miles in each direction.

Every blade of grass seemed to be cut to the exact length, not a dead strand lay upon its healthy ground.

The city stood so tall, it was twice the size of Meridium, the dominating stone wall clean and strong. There was only one entrance to the city and that was through the heavy black door that sat in the middle of the wall. It was so tall and wide, even the strongest battering ram would struggle to make a dent. Most armies would struggle to even get close to it because of all the strategically positioned artillery.

All along the top of the wall were ballista missile pads, trebuchets, pits and dozens of archer teams. Taking this city would be no easy task.

"Over eighty thousand people live in this city," Josanne said as she continued to lead her comrades towards her home.

"Tobias must have a big army?" asked Faizer with curiosity.

"Forty thousand. Most of them live in the countryside, waiting until they get called upon," she said.

"Forty fucking thousand. I wish but half of them had turned up on the Gantry seven years ago," groaned Nuallan who had seemed to have grown bored of Josanne boasting about her city.

"Riders!" alerted Faizer. "Riders, what do we do?" He panicked, gripping the handle of his sword sharply.

"Do not worry," ordered Gideon. "Remain calm."

The daunting black gate had been drawn and a team of five jet black horses had begun racing across the terrain, towards the company.

"This is routine," reassured Josanne. "They are just taking precautions."

The company all came to a standstill as some of them struggled to have faith in Josanne's words. They stood tightly together and awaited the riders.

Each horse was carrying a leather-armoured man. One of the horses stood before the company whilst the other four spread out around them, two at either side.

"What is the purpose of your visit?" asked the soldier upon the horse facing them head on.

"My name is Josanne, my father is Boltrey, and these are my comrades. They seek an audience with King Tobias," answered Josanne.

"Welcome back, Josanne. What are the names of your friends?"

Gideon stepped forward. "I am Gideon Destain of Meridium. These are my brothers, nephew and close friend." Gideon pointed to each member of his company.

The man on the horse looked puzzled. "Hold on, you say you are Gideon Destain?"

"Aye, I am."

"Rumour has it that you lot died long ago." The soldier then looked back to Josanne. He didn't know whether to believe Gideon or not.

"It's true," she said. "I have been with them for a while now."

"Very well then." The soldier nodded at his party members, signalling them to stand down instantly.

"Follow us, we will guide you into the city."

Gideon nodded gratefully and began walking on.

"Open the gate!" yelled one of the riders as they reached the city's entrance.

Slowly but loudly the monstrous gate started to open up. It sounded like a giant wolf growling ferociously in the night. One at a time, the horses edged through the gate, the soldiers instantly demounting. Each one of them handed the reins to a stable apprentice that was stood waiting.

All that could be seen upon arrival was horse establishments. Stables, practise fields, barns and farms, the city's courtyard was surrounded by them. To the right hand side was a series of oak-built stables that was home to hundreds of specially bred horses, to the left was field upon field, with some archery targets, others with practise dummies and some with joisting tracks upon them. The company were fascinated, all except Andrus. He walked in at the back of the pack with his head hanging low, still no words sprouted from his mouth, still no expression printed itself upon his face. Josanne and Gideon however had both seen it all before, but they still thrived off the incredible sight.

Tobias took the raising of his horses very seriously. There were over ten different jobs that people could train to be that involved the care of horses. Young boys and girls would work for free in order to secure themselves a future job.

"Here we are. Now, everyone climb in," said the Brigantium superior.

A wooden carriage came wheeling around the corner, two smoky grey horses skipped at the front of it. They dragged the carriage through the courtyard and over to Gideon and the company.

The carriage came to a standstill, its sharp carved wheels silent and stationary. Nuallan stepped up first. He leapt up through the mahogany door and threw himself inside. Faizer did the same. They slouched lazily inside upon the silky red seats that had been fitted into the beautiful wooden container. Gideon climbed up next. He leaned his body out of the carriage as he realised Josanne was not joining them.

"Are you coming?" he asked.

"Not this time, I must go find my father and my brothers," she said.

Gideon dropped straight out of the carriage and engaged her with a hug. "Thank you," he said.

Josanne chuckled. "For what?"

"I don't know, for this, for opening our eyes, I guess," he said whilst smiling.

Josanne leaned in and kissed Gideon's cheek. "Do you want me to take Oslo? I can watch over him until you and Tobias strike a deal?" she offered kindly.

Gideon thought before answering. He looked at his brother Andrus who stood glaring back at him. Andrus had made no attempt to approach the carriage. He looked confused. Gideon had now put it upon himself to act as Oslo's guardian. Andrus was in no fit state to make any decisions for the boy.

"Yes, take him with you."

"Okay, once you are done with Tobias, ask him were Boltrey lives. If you are to need me for anything, that is where I will be."

Gideon nodded at her. "I will find it, don't worry." He then looked to Oslo who was standing beside Josanne. "I remember when I had to crouch down to speak with you, now you're almost as tall as me."

Oslo smiled, his smile then fading as he noticed his father walking over to one of the sprite green fields. He leaned on the fence and watched the horses galloping around.

"Is he going to be okay?" asked Oslo.

"Like your uncle Nuallan told you, he just needs time. We have seen this before. He will speak again," reassured Gideon.

Oslo looked away from him and at Andrus angrily, before holding out his arm and shaking his uncle's hand.

Gideon boarded the carriage again, this time flinging himself inside, and closing the rich door behind him.

"Is no one else coming?" asked Faizer. He had been too busy stroking the interior to even notice Gideon and Josanne's conversation.

"We will find them once we have spoken with Tobias," said Gideon.

The carriage suddenly swung forward as the horses began their journey to the Palace. Nuallan and Faizer slid back the wooden shutters and glared out of the window, scanning their surroundings with interest.

Brigantium was built on a sharp slope, the roads that ran through the city would angle and curve steeply the further up you travelled. The people were cheerful, the streets exploded with joy and happiness, the citizens of this city had no worries. They had a good King, a rich, sizable city and most of all, no enemies.

Nuallan slammed his delicate shutter shut. He seemed frustrated.

"What?" questioned Gideon simply.

"Tobias has all of this, the luxury, coin and power is limitless here and yet he still never offered Meridium aid."

"Brother, Tobias is a good man, a good King. You have to understand, father does not make it easy for anyone. He is impossible as an ally, you know this," reminded Gideon.

Nuallan knew that the real reason Meridium never received aid from Tobias was down to their father's ways but still, right then, he wanted someone to blame for the misfortune of Meridium. He slouched down into the cosy red cushion and remained silent.

"I have to get myself there. Jesus, look at that place," said Faizer with excitement.

The carriage was passing an incredibly inviting tavern. It was an extremely large settlement with what seemed to be a garden at the front, people sitting outside and drinking ales and rich wine. The people there were not like the ones Faizer was used to. Every tavern he had ever entered was flooded with drunk, toothless peasants. But not this one, the people were sitting chatting happily and slurping sensibly. It was so disciplined.

"Is this what it is like back home? Is this what Meridium is like?" asked Faizer.

"It was once, aye, but not anymore," replied Gideon.

The carriage began to travel a little more smoothly, the tough rubble floor having disappeared from beneath them. They had crossed through the Palace gates and into the Palace grounds. The floor was as clear as crystal and as clean as marble. With every step, the horses hooves echoed like a harmonic audience clapping pleasingly.

"We're here," Gideon said as the carriage came to a standstill. He reached for the door but before he could extend his arm out, it swung outwards away from him. The coachman had leapt down and opened it for them.

"Out you come," he said. "Lord Badstuber awaits you."

Gideon dropped out first, Nuallan and Faizer sliding out

after him. They thanked the driver and began walking across the incredible surface towards an oval cut set of steps. The Palace grounds were ginormous, a circular road engulfing a rather large pond that flowed exquisitely in the centre of the pavement, host to many exotic fish and flowers.

The carriage began its journey back to the stables, gliding past the company and then around the pond. It left the gate leaving the atmosphere silent.

"I have never seen so much green in my life, and I have spent half of that time in a forest," stated Faizer as he observed the wildlife around him. Bushes, trees and other spectacular plants grew neatly by the side of the smooth road, taller than towers and wider than men.

"I feel slightly under-dressed," he mocked.

Gideon and Nuallan chuckled at the comment, but stopped sharply as Faizer pointed over to the entrance of the Palace, where multiple characters were awaiting them on the stair.

Gideon and his two comrades walked the rest of the way and then took their first step onto the stairs, stopping as they reached the top. They were instantly greeted by a man in dark green silk robes.

"Greetings, my name is Stelio. I am speaker and advisor to Dreyo Badstuber," he said nicely.

Gideon shook his hand. Stelio turned to his side and held his hand out, insinuating that he should walk forward to greet Stelios's master. Gideon nodded at him and walked forward where he found himself standing in front of a crowd of five eager people.

"I just had to see this for myself. I didn't believe it at first but here you are," stated Dreyo Badstuber. He was over six foot three, long of hair and bushy of beard. Many unwelcoming grey silky strands slithered through his brown fading hair.

Gideon had met Dreyo before, but he wasn't overly fond of him and his family. He favoured Tobias a lot more and since the Badstuber family rivalled the Ringfolds, it meant Gideon had to chose a side, everyone did.

"This is my wife Joy and my son Riycard," introduced Dreyo.

Joy was a tall woman with nicely plaited brown hair. Age had caught up with her since the last time Gideon had seen her. She courtesied politely and Riycard bowed respectfully. Riycard was tall and strong, but arrogance got the better of him.

"And this must be Nuallan and... Andrus?" said Dreyo. He paused slightly when he looked to Faizer. He had mistaken him for Andrus.

"Nuallan, aye, but that is not Andrus. His name is Faizer, my advisor and friend," said Gideon, clearing the confusion immediately.

Faizer bowed.

"Oh dear, your brother hasn't fallen, has he?" asked Dreyo without hesitation.

"He is here. He will be with us presently," replied Gideon.

A younger man came marching forward to interrupt. "Enough of the formalities, you must be tired, and eager. It will have been a long time since you last met with Tobias, has it not, Gideon, son of Artaxes?"

Gideon had only met this man once before. He was head of the Chalk family, the second rivalling family to the Ringfolds. His name was Farren Chalk.

Farren Chalk was medium height and at least ten years younger then Dreyo. He had very light brown hair that was nice at the back but messy at the front. His emerald green eyes dazzled with the summer sky.

"This is my son, Romford. He has been eager to meet you. Romford is a Lieutenant in Tobias's army," boasted Farren. He stood sideways on when he said it, making eye contact with Dreyo.

The Chalk family and the Badstuber family rivalled each other just as much as they did the Ringfolds, Brigantium was a very competitive place.

Romford was still rather young, only nineteen. If Hector Ringfold failed Selection, he would still be of age to challenge Selection himself, meaning his family could inherit the throne. Dreyo's son however was over the age of twenty, ruling out any chance of him inheriting the throne, but luckily Dreyo had another son, but he was only thirteen.

Romford stepped forward and shook Gideon's hand. He then leaned around him and took Nuallan's hand and then Faizer's. Romford was very similar looking to his father, with the same shade of hair and the same piercing eyes. Romford had his armour on as if ready to do battle. His rank and the fact he was meant to be on duty meant he had to be equipped with the heavy costume. A chore for any man of Brigantium, as it was always so warm in this part of the country.

"Shall we go, then? Tobias will be waiting," said Dreyo who had grown bored of listening to Farren and Romford blab on.

"We shall," said Farren as he turned off to lead the way. He guided them up the second set of steps and in through the solid black door of the Palace. Two carefully sculptured Starchitect horses had been decorated on the face of the doors. Faizer admired them like he had everything else before entering.

The Palace was very different from the Meridium one. There were no marble walls, no ginormous banners and no memorabilia or weaponry upon the walls but it was still an incredible sight. The huge open room circled around creating a bulky bowl-like area. Every fifty feet or so, a hallway led you away into a different part of the Palace. The walls here were rather dark, made from very rich oak that had been excellently designed, and giving off a lovely homely smell.

Dreyo waved off his wife and son before trekking quickly behind Farren and Romford. Gideon, Faizer and Nuallan followed. Farren walked through all the people that were standing around the timber built hall and took the group down one of the eastern hallways. Many of the people stared rudely at Gideon. They had heard the news, and they were also eager to see the heir to Meridium in the flesh. So many of the people in Requirium had believed Gideon and his brothers to be dead, so it came as a great shock to the people to see them alive.

The design down this passage was identical to the main halls, it was just smaller. One thing that Nuallan noticed was the lack of guards. Back home there was always a soldier on guard at every entrance, every door and on every corner. But here there were very few.

Farren angled around the now narrowing corridor until he reached another set of mahogany doors. On either side of the door was a lightly burning torch that had been positioned over a nicely cut piece of parchment.

"Here sits Tobias Ringfold, King of Brigantium and ruler of the East," muttered Faizer as he investigated the parchment.

"Are you ready?" asked Farren, but before Gideon and the others could reply, Dreyo pushed through.

"Get on with it," he snapped whilst launching open the throne room doors.

CHAPTER 17
PROVEN WHISPERS

Dreyo Badstuber led the group into the exquisite throne room, where everyone observed the surroundings as they travelled through the room towards Tobias. Nuallan was the first to realise the huge difference between the decorations at Meridium to here. Back home everything was so over the top, almost everything was made from smooth white marble but here everything was dark mahogany, or perfect oak. The excessive wooden structures gave the throne room a glum but cosy look.

Tobias leapt up from his throne, clattering down the stairs in an attempt to meet his visitors halfway.

"My God," muttered Tobias to himself. He quickened his walk, which struck Gideon as very unusual.

Gideon and Nuallan were both wondering why Tobias was so eager to meet with them, that he couldn't wait another minute for them to travel through the small crowds and up to his throne. Kings would rarely stand for anyone.

"My god, it's true," said Tobias a little more plainly this time. He engaged Gideon by instantly grabbing his face and inspecting him.

Gideon looked extremely confused, along with everyone else.

"It's you," whispered the King. He gently leaned to Gideon's cheek and kissed it, then leaned to his other side and kissed that cheek. "I don't believe it. Once word reached my ear of your arrival, I laughed. Everyone was sure you were all dead." He looked around Gideon, and inspected Nuallan and then Faizer.

"However you seem to be one short. Where is your brother, Andrus, and better still who is this man?" asked Tobias whilst he looked Faizer up and down.

Farren stepped in and offered an explanation. "The lad wanders around the stables. He seemed intrigued."

Tobias latched his eyes onto his rival as he spoke out. "That will be all from you, and you, Dreyo. Leave us."

Farren bowed first and then Dreyo. They both turned and left the throne room.

"Andrus will meet with you soon," explained Gideon. "We have had a few complications... he lost his wife and boy. He needs time."

"My sincere apologies. He will receive the help he needs here," replied Tobias kindly. He then walked around Gideon and shook Nuallan's hand.

"You must be Nuallan, welcome to Brigantium, and who did you say this was again?" he asked as he arrived before Faizer.

"This is Faizer of Vaughan, my advisor and friend," answered Gideon.

Tobias continued to inspect Faizer rudely. "Very well, welcome Faizer," he said less pleasingly, then latched his arm around Gideon. "Come, walk with me," he added and guided him towards the steps at the far end of the homely room.

Nuallan and Faizer were left standing by the doorway. Nuallan was confused. He was puzzled as to why Tobias was so interested in Gideon but then showed very little concern towards himself and Faizer. He decided not to dwell on the matter for too long, he was after all used to this sort of thing.

Dozens of people were scattered around the throne room, mostly people of importance and position. Priests, Lieutenants, bodyguards, business owners and even some of the most respected horse trainers. Many of them gossiped among their groups at the sight of the lost sons of Meridium. Just like Tobias, most of them thought their survival was a lie.

"Come, I want to know everything," said Tobias as he dropped onto his throne.

Gideon, Nuallan and Faizer now stood before him, but Gideon was the only one looking at the King. Nuallan and Faizer were struck on a more interesting sight, three ginormous men, armoured to the teeth standing behind Tobias's seat. Tobias noticed the two men's interest so he quickly provided them with the information they sought.

"Nuallan, Faizer, meet Pscies, Gondogon and Voltor. Also known as 'The Three', they are my Royal Guard. They are also hireable mercenaries," explained Tobias with a smug look upon his face.

"Greetings, men of Meridium," stated Gondogon who bowed politely. Pscies and Voltor who stood to the left and the right of Gondogon bowed after him.

"Greetings, fellas," said Faizer who bowed that quickly he nearly strained his back.

Nuallan however remained straight-backed and simply tilted his head forward.

"I want you to know that we are grateful for your hospitality," Gideon said. "We have been on the road for a long time. We have lost people but also gained people along the way, like Faizer and a woman named Josanne, you might know of her? She led us here."

"You're welcome, my son. Apart from yesterday, you are the first men of Meridium I had seen in a long time."

Gideon frowned with confusion. "Yesterday?"

Before Tobias could respond, a man in his late fifties wandered up the steps and pressed a matter upon his King.

"Apologies, my King, but I heard my daughter's name, Josanne," he said whilst turning to Gideon. "Did she accompany you, friend?"

Gideon turned and offered out his hand. The man shook it roughly.

"Josanne has been an exceptional friend to me," Gideon said. "She looks for you now. Boltrey, is it? We have heard a lot about you."

"It is. I must go find her. I'm sure we will meet again, lad." Boltrey turned to Tobias. "May I take leave, my King?"

"You may. Go and see your daughter," awarded Tobias.

Boltrey bowed and charged down the steps. The man owned many settlements within Brigantium's walls, mostly taverns. Tobias held him as an advisor of coin, since he knew how to make lots of it.

"So where is it that you have been hiding all this time?" asked Tobias.

"We were sell swords for an Earl a little further west," said Gideon, "a man called Earl Oswald. He ran a town called Vanghale."

"Ahh, he is the reason you fled? The reason your brother's family is dead, I presume?" quizzed Tobias.

Gideon lowered his head. "Aye, it is. We lost others. Faizer's brother, a loyal friend, died to save me."

"Your brother sounded like a brave man," Tobias said towards Faizer.

"He was, he was."

"Forgive me, my King," interrupted Nuallan, "but you spoke of another man, a man who came to you only yesterday. You said he was from Meridium also."

Gideon looked at Tobias with interest.

"Yes, he was only young, the son of an old friend of mine, and that of your father's as well. Tidus," announced the King surprisingly.

Gideon filled with hope, a rare expression conquering his face, an expression of delight and satisfaction. "Koos? Koos was here? Are you sure of it?" he pressed with excitement.

"Yes, you know him?"

"We grew up with him. Our father took him in once Tidus died. He's like a brother to us."

"Well, he is still here. I will have my man take you to him if you wish," offered Tobias.

Gideon filled with even more hope then, the thought of seeing his long lost friend again bringing great happiness to him.

"King Tobias, why was Koos here? Was it our father who sent him?" asked Nuallan, who was also smiling but needing to find out more information.

"You don't know? Are you not aware of the trouble Meridium has suffered since your departure?" asked Tobias.

"All we know is that the Oakland Musters have risen up and taken Villach," said Gideon.

"My son, your father has retaken Villach and with great ease, I hear. He now marches on Oggsfleet Port. He has summoned the fighters from Sandown but he is outnumbered."

"So that is why Koos came, for aid," muttered Nuallan.

"Indeed."

"Then who sent him?" added Nuallan.

"Your father, of course, who else?"

Gideon realised what Nuallan was getting at it. He knew Artaxes would never call for aid from the Eastern Horse Lords.

"Believe me here, Tobias, when I say I mean no offence," stated Nuallan boldly, "but you are mistaken. My father would never call for aid from you."

"That thought has crossed my mind, but if Artaxes didn't send him, who did?" asked the King.

"He has come by his own will, which means Artaxes will call for his head. I must speak with him, Tobias, immediately," Gideon said.

"You may in good time but for now we must speak business. I want to offer you a deal."

Gideon stood up straight, staring at Tobias with disappointment. "You want something from me, and in return you will march on Oggsfleet with my father, am I right?" he asked rather furiously. Gideon had grown angry that Tobias would so easily barter the lives of his kin.

"Calm yourself, lad. I have already agreed to send four thousand men to your father's aid. I will keep my word on that. I seek to create a separate deal with you," reassured Tobias.

"The last time we agreed a deal with a stranger, my brother died along with two other people," snapped Faizer.

"A deal with a weak, crazed Earl," said Tobias as he giggled to himself, then his temperament changed, showing his first sign of impatience. "Let me guess, he had a couple of thousand untrained men at his disposal, probably controlled by some Lieutenant or Commander?"

Gideon moved quickly to prevent an argument. "What kind of deal, Tobias?"

Tobias stood up from his chair. He looked towards his advisor Fangoy who had been standing waiting by the door for a while now. Fangoy nodded happily and opened the door at the King's signal. Almost instantly two characters came in. One of them was Enly and the other was Tobias's son, Hector.

Hector was dressed in glistening silver armour, gold trim tracking down the sides of the plate. The bottom of his yellow cape wriggled and spun as he stormed powerfully towards his father. He had soft brown hair like Tobias, and dark menacing eyes like him also. He was exceptionally handsome. His tanned cheeks were hairless and spotless, not a mark in sight, although the Eastern Prince had a certain cocky look about him as he walked across the nicely varnished floor.

"This is my son, Hector, and my Lieutenant, Enly," introduced Tobias. He waited until his son reached the top of the steps before standing up, walking over and wrapping his arm around him. Enly walked off to the side and stood beside The Three.

"A pleasure to meet you. Many of my bedtime stories featured you, Gideon," said Hector.

Gideon looked at Hector, inspecting him.

"Tall, dark and handsome. I bet the ladies can't get enough of you," Gideon said, forcing a smirk from Tobias.

"No time for ladies just yet. Hector has his Selection in the coming weeks."

Gideon released a soft breeze of air through his nose. He had quickly worked out the deal that was to be offered to him. "You want me to train your boy for Selection, yes?"

"Yes, Hector has become very skilled with a sword. I am confident he will win, but he is my only son. If you train him and escort him to Versidia then I will have no doubt," said Tobias.

"And what do I get in return?" asked Gideon.

"You and your brothers will once again experience the life of a noble. You will live like Princes here in my Kingdom. In secret, of course, we don't want Duran Harall finding out that you still live now, do we? I will offer you all a high position among my ranks. This goes for your friend Faizer and also Josanne if she wants it. Your whole company will live out their days here," offered Tobias generously.

The thought swam pleasantly through the minds of Gideon, Nuallan and Faizer, all of them looking overwhelmed.

"Done," agreed Gideon without much of a pause. He offered out his hand.

Tobias looked down at it and smirked again. He latched onto Gideon's dirty hand and shook it.

"Your son will pass his Selection, I assure you."

"Good. Hector, embrace your new teacher."

Hector stepped forward and shook Gideon's hand. "It will be an honour to train with you, Gideon Destain. I will come for you in the morning." The Prince then bowed to his father and left, trotting down the steps and making for the doors.

"Now that we have settled our business, let me fill you in on your father's little war," said Tobias. "Walk with me."

"I think it would be best if I left you to it," said Faizer. "Just point me in the direction of that tavern that we passed on the way in." He looked hopeful and added, "I mean, after everything, I could really use a drink."

Tobias smiled. "Enly, escort our new friend Faizer here to The Swan, will you?"

"Of course, my King." Enly bowed at Tobias before guiding Faizer down the steps and out of the throne room.

Tobias led Nuallan and Gideon out of the throne room by the side passage that sat at the western side of the rich room. The three of them walked out of the door and merged into the hallway. This hallway had cut out walls also, the same as the eastern halls did where Tobias had previously taken Koos.

Tobias walked slightly ahead of Nuallan and Gideon, strolling perfectly with his hands positioned behind his back. Again colourful scenery was on display. Heavily flowered gardens, nicely farmed fields, and even some barracks could be seen through the open cut windows. Nuallan and Gideon took it in, both gawking out as they passed. Nuallan even slithered his bruised hand along the sandstone ledges. He hadn't felt anything so smooth in a long time.

Tobias still remained silent as he led his two visitors around the various hallways that angled off the side of his Palace. If you were to look over the ledges, you would see the true height of where the Palace sat.

As they continued their stroll around the western hallways, they began to hear a load of noise coming from beneath their very feet. Tobias cut off from the curling passage and walked out onto a chunky balcony in pursuit of the sharp noise.

"Take a look," he said as he peeked off the balcony.

Gideon and his brother edged towards the ledge and looked out.

Down below was the Palace's Barracks. It was a flat piece of land that had been built on the side of the hill that was host to the Palace. The area was extremely large. Long stone staircases could be seen a little further to the north of the barracks, leading right back up into the Palace.

Thousands of men were below preparing, the men that had been selected to ride for Oggsfleet. Whenever Tobias would ride into a battle or into any form of fight, he would select the right men and train them in his best barracks. Many preparations would have to be made, and by bringing the men into the Palace, he could then keep an eye on their progress. The selected men were usually treated with whores and wine before being put straight to work. There were of course hundreds of other barracks inside Brigantium, but this was by the far the most advanced camp.

A lot was going in the camp below at that present moment. There were drills, sparring, sprints and many other activities taking place.

"What is this?" asked Nuallan.

"This is the force that has been selected for Artaxes. The horses are being put through the same drills down at the entrance of the city. Two thousand horses, two thousand riders and two thousand foot soldiers, all ready to leave tomorrow," boasted the King.

"Well that should certainly do it," said Nuallan as he continued to observe the men train.

"Tobias," Gideon said. "I would like to say that my father will be pleased with these men, but honestly I don't think he will be. Koos will pay with his life for even coming here and asking you for aid."

"I will keep an eye on him. Maybe once we claim our victory, Artaxes will see us no longer as an enemy. Koos spoke to me of creating an alliance," stated Tobias, excited.

"Koos does not have that authority," said Nuallan sternly. "Now, the past is past, Tobias, but we needed your alliance back then, back on the Gantry. Father will not accept your new goodwill."

"My brother speaks the truth, but still... we thank you for going anyway. Will you lead the army?" asked Gideon.

Tobias paused before replying. He seemed a little disheartened with his mission. He knew that what Gideon and Nuallan spoke of was the truth. Artaxes had always been a difficult person to get along with, especially if you had once crossed him.

"I receive your advice with a welcoming heart, but I ride anyway. I will make amends for turning my back on your father, and I think Artaxes will embrace us. It's been a long time since you have seen your father, I think he has changed, and for the better, may I add," stated Tobias confidently. "We ride in the morning. If you want to see your friend Koos, you better be quick about it."

"Very well, Tobias, I thank you for watching over my countrymen. Now tell me were can I find Koos?"

"Take the carriage back down to the tavern that your friend spoke of. It's called The Swan. Josanne's father Boltrey owns that establishment. Tell him I said that anything you need is free

of charge. I will see to it that Koos meets with you presently."
Tobias bowed. "A guard will show you to your quarters, and when
I return, we will have much to discuss, I expect. Farewell, Gideon,
farewell, Nuallan." Tobias turned and walked back down the hall,
eventually disappearing out of sight.

"A lot has happened, has it not?" said Nuallan. "Seven years
without us and our whole country has fallen into turmoil."

But his words fell upon deaf ears.

Gideon was not paying attention. He was staring back at a
woman who glared at him with fear, anger and hate. She was
standing at the end of the hallway in a dark green dress that
covered her from her breasts right down to her ankles. She was
riddled with golden jewellery that glistened as the summer's sun
gleamed in down through the open windows. She had long brown
hair and loose wrinkled skin, well into her forties. But still she was
an attractive woman. She was most certainly royalty, no normal
noble would wear jewellery as expensive as hers.

"What is she looking at?" questioned Nuallan who had noticed
the woman. "Why is she staring at you that way, Gideon?"

"I do not know."

The woman continued to burn a horrifying stare in Gideon's
direction, holding her gaze for a few more seconds before snarling
viciously, then turning away.

Nuallan laughed loudly. "Come on, brother. It's usually me
making the enemies. What on earth have you done to her?"

He continued laughing loudly, but Gideon did not laugh or
even smile. He was shaken by the incident. Never in his life had
he had anyone look at him in that way.

CHAPTER 18
REUNITED

"Are you nervous?" splurted Faizer who was sitting beside three empty tankards. He had been drinking alone for the last hour whilst Gideon and Nuallan were in the Palace. Gideon and Nuallan had joined him in the Swan Tavern whilst they awaited Koos. Gideon had sent Josanne to fetch Oslo and Andrus so that they could be here in time to greet their old friend.

"I'm excited," said Gideon. Every time the tavern door swung open or slammed closed, Gideon looked instantly. It had been seven long years since he had spoken to Koos, and he was eager to do so again.

"I never thought we would see him again. Strange, isn't it?" said Nuallan. He was sitting opposite Gideon, biting away at his nails. The three of them sat around a table, but it was no ordinary tavern table. The legs were straight and solid, the seats were comfortable and the edges were rounded and sanded. Any drinking establishment that the company had blessed with their presence in the last seven years was diabolical compared to this one. The people here stood in neat queues at the bar, they spoke politely and sensibly and the choice of beverages was limitless.

The room was larger than any household any member of the company had taken refuge in, over a dozen tables positioned in line with each other within the room. The beverages were brought to your table once ordered and instead of rusty old mugs, you had crystal glasses or deep shining tankards, but the sweetest bit of it all was the loving tune that played perfectly within. A group of four young men played little wooden instruments in the corner of the tavern. Faizer had been swaying his drunken head and humming to himself for the best part of the hour. He had never ever experienced relaxation and comfort like this in his whole life.

"Do you think Tobias forgot to tell him?" asked Faizer.

"I think not, brother. He will be here," said Gideon confidently.

"Well, I am very excited to meet him. Any friend of yours is a friend of mine," said Faizer as he undressed the waitress with his eyes. She had just planted a new tankard of sweet ale in front of him. "Thank you, precious," he said.

The woman laughed at Faizer's drunken words as she walked off, eventually looking back over her shoulder to glance at him again.

"My god, I could get used to this place," he added cheerfully.

Gideon and Nuallan both erupted with laughter at their friend, the pleasant atmosphere a rare one of recent years.

"I don't fucking believe it," said a strange but familiar voice. "I was certain it was some sort of trick, a lie, anything. But here you are."

Gideon and Nuallan leapt up into the air, staring towards the tavern's oaken doorway.

"Koos," whispered Nuallan.

Koos was standing in the doorway with a piercing look of surprise on his face. Gideon inspected his old friend, appreciating the sight of his silver armour coated with his sky blue cloak. Gideon waited no more. He pelted over towards him, Koos doing the same, and the men meeting in the centre of the tavern.

The pair of them smashed into each other so hard that their chests echoed with a bang, alerting half of the tavern's customers, people looking over for a second before quietly going back to their drinks. Nuallan came jostling over next, launching himself into the bundle, grabbing hold of Koos's head with one hand and Gideon's with his other. He ruffled Koos's thin blond hair whilst laughing passionately, the three of them continuing to stand there squeezing each other.

"Bloody hell, I have missed you guys," said Koos as he raised his head.

Gideon quickly wiped away the tear that was streaming down Koos's pale face before wiping his own. This truly was an emotional moment for all.

Koos brushed his blond fringe to the side before letting go of Gideon in order to embrace Nuallan individually. The two of them gripped onto each other's faces. Gideon observed happily. This was the best he had felt in years.

Nuallan grabbed hold of Koos's shoulders and swung him around, looking at the cape and observing Koos's armour.

"I have not forgotten this sight, the white lion of Meridium," he said as he stroked the blue cape.

"A General now also. Our father must have finally seen sense," joked Gideon.

"Indeed, brother, but I'm afraid you are wrong. The word sense does not exist in your father's world anymore." Koos's comment dampened the mood slightly.

"We have a lot of catching up to do, brother," said Gideon. "Come and sit down. There is someone you need to meet."

Koos willingly walked over to the table.

"Indeed we do, but first I want to hear everything from you two," replied Koos as he glanced at Faizer.

Faizer was slowly lifting himself out of his chair, the excessive slurping of ale having gone to his head.

Gideon laughed as Nuallan ran around the table to help him up.

"This, Koos, is Faizer, a loyal friend. He has been with us from the beginning," said Gideon.

Koos smiled as he edged around the table to embrace him. He offered out his hand but was met with a welcoming hug. Faizer grabbed him tightly and began laughing.

"What an honour it is. It's good to see you in the flesh," he said.

Koos resisted ever so slightly as the stench of foul breath and dry ale gushed out into his direction.

Gideon quickly saved the young General from his drunken friend. He prized Faizer's grip open and pulled Koos around to the opposite side of the table. Nuallan sat Faizer back down and then planted himself down beside him. Koos and Gideon did the same but on the opposite side.

"Gideon, where have you been? Are you aware that the High King did not honour his deal? Once you, Andrus and Nuallan left the city, he sent riders to track you. I'm sure they still track you now," warned Koos.

"Aye, they do, but we have kept ourselves well hidden, until now," replied Gideon.

"And why is it that you have chosen to reveal yourself now?" asked Koos.

"We had a run in with an Earl that we fought for," said Nuallan. "We lost people, but not as many as he did. We had no choice but to reveal ourselves."

"Then why here? Why Brigantium?"

"A woman led us here. She is part of our group, well, our company. That is the name we went by to help keep our identity a secret," explained Gideon.

"Here she is now, the feisty fucker," burst Faizer whilst taking a break from his newly-filled tankard.

Everyone looked to the door as Josanne, Andrus and Oslo wandered in.

Josanne smiled ecstatically at the sight of her comrades, and everyone glanced back at her in astonishment. She was without her usual armless chest piece and brown leather skirt, instead smothered in a casual gown that only a noble woman would be allowed to wear. She looked beautiful.

It was rare that Josanne was provided with an opportunity to dress up and although she behaved like a man most of the time with her foul words and dry humour, she was forced by her father to act like a lady, which she hated.

Josanne's chance of meeting Koos was stalled. Oslo

rushed past her and dived into Koos who had just stood up to greet him.

"My, you have grown. You were only about eight the last time I saw you. I bet you can't half fight now, can you not?" joked Koos.

Faizer quickly interrupted, leaning across the table and almost knocking his drink over. "You would be surprised. Don't underestimate the little fucker."

Gideon was growing tired of Faizer's drunken behaviour. He glared at him in such a way that Faizer quickly realised he was annoying Gideon.

"I… I'm sorry, I'm going to go and fuck that barmaid and leave you to it," he blubbered comically.

He stood up and wobbled over to the bar where the woman was cleaning glasses. She hadn't taken her eyes off Faizer all day.

"Ugh, she is such a slut. Can you think of anything worse than Faizer crawling on top of you, stinking of ale and ash," said Josanne as she sat down next to Nuallan.

"You know her?" asked Nuallan.

"She's my cousin. My father gave her a job here because she can't find work anywhere else. She always ends up fucking the wrong person some way or another."

"I don't suppose you have any more cousins, do you?" asked Nuallan nervously.

Josanne and Gideon erupted into laughter, even Koos took a moment from staring at Faizer to laugh a little.

"What peculiar friends you have adopted, Gideon," he said, directing his remark towards Faizer. Koos had still not really noticed Josanne, the only person in the tavern who hadn't.

"He is not normally like this. Ale hasn't crossed his lips in over a year. I'm sure you will meet him tomorrow properly," Gideon said cheerfully.

Everyone was in such a good mood, it was remarkable, usually the atmosphere was filled with such sadness and despair. But not today, not until Andrus slowly crept over to the table.

"Andrus, my god, my brother." Koos, who had only just sat

down, jumped back up, holding his arms out as Andrus walked towards him with the most stunned look upon his face.

Gideon watched with interest, even ignoring Nuallan's obvious facial signs from across the table.

Before Gideon informed Koos of Andrus's condition, he wanted to see if any words would spring from his brother's mouth. Gideon hoped that the embracement of Koos would bring the person he was back, but he was wrong.

"So good to see you," said Koos as he kissed both of Andrus's cheeks. It wasn't long before Koos noticed that something was wrong. Andrus's hands remained by his side and his face remained clueless, as if he didn't know his old friend anymore.

Koos stared at his eyes, worried, then turned and looked at Gideon who had already risen to his feet and begun walking over.

"There was an incident, Koos," Gideon said.

Andrus quickly brushed past Koos and wandered past his table of friends and over to the bar. He sat gently on a stool with his back to the company.

Gideon guided Koos back to the table, Oslo moving over so Gideon and Koos could sit down together.

"Ornella is dead, Armel too," said Gideon.

Koos looked back at Gideon with horror.

"How?" he asked, shocked.

"The Earl I told you about, he killed them, he tried to kill us all. We survived but they died. Doxass too, he was Faizer's brother," reported Gideon sadly.

The atmosphere returned to its usual state then. No one smiled and no one laughed.

Koos leaned past Gideon and rested his hand on Oslo's arm. The boy was beginning to deal with the situation a little easier now. He looked up and smiled at Koos.

"And Andrus has been like this since?" asked Koos.

"Yes, he doesn't speak to anyone. He hasn't muttered a word since that day," said Nuallan.

"Like your father," said Koos.

"Exactly like father. We all know Andrus was cut out of father's back, their personalities identical. Andrus has just always been a little more stable and reasonable," said Gideon.

"I can't imagine what you have all been through. At least you're safe now. Have you made a deal with Tobias?"

"We have. I will prepare Hector for Selection and in return we can live out our days here. We have been offered position and will be of rank if we wish," said Nuallan.

Koos laughed to himself. "Selection, what a joke. It is the most ridiculous system I have ever heard of."

Josanne was upset by the remark. "It is tradition, the tradition of these people. Do not mock our ways," she barked.

"My apologies, my lady. I did not mean to offend." Koos had not been introduced to Josanne yet, he hadn't even noticed her sitting there. But now that he had, he couldn't take his eyes off her.

Josanne, who had slightly lost her patience, stared back at Koos, her wicked glance soon turning into a flirtatious one. She had noticed Koos. She had been looking at him from the moment he sat down and she hated herself for it. She never usually paid much attention to men, but there was something about Koos that triggered a warm cosy feeling inside of her.

The whole table noticed the strange chemistry between Koos and Josanne as the pair stared at each other for a few moments before Koos spoke.

"I'm sorry, my name is Koos, General of the Meridium army, and loyal friend to the Destain family," he said.

Josanne blushed a little. "I am Josanne, daughter of Boltrey, advisor and business partner to King Tobias Ringfold."

She stated it competitively, causing Koos to smile. He was blinded by beauty. He had never came across a feisty woman like Josanne before, and was mesmerised by her.

Gideon, Oslo and Nuallan sat awkwardly whilst Koos and Josanne flirted blatantly in front of them. Koos held his open palm out over the table, waiting for Josanne to meet it, which she immediately did. She put her hand inside his grasp allowing Koos to lean over and kiss it but she only allowed his lips a second of contact before she tore it away and stood up.

"I have to help my father with some business," she said. "I will help you with Hector in the morning, Gideon. Goodnight all."

She left the company's presence and made for the door.

"She never usually walks like that," remarked Nuallan as he watched Josanne shake her backside with every step.

He wasn't the only one watching either. Every pair of male eyes on the table watched Josanne wiggle her way slowly towards the door.

"I think she likes me," Koos said. "What do you think?"

"Do not even attempt it. She is the reason we are here, Koos. Save your charm for one of your usual whores back in the west," warned Nuallan.

"Oh I'm sorry. Is she with you?" asked Koos apologetically.

"No, but she had a thing with Faizer's brother for a while, before he died," Gideon said.

"My honest apologies, I didn't know," Koos said. "I will leave the girl alone."

"Word of advice, don't let her hear you calling her a girl either," joked Nuallan.

Everyone laughed but Koos had to fake his. His mind could only concentrate on one thing right now, and that was Josanne. Even though he had agreed to leave her alone, he couldn't get her out of his mind. He dwelled on the image of her long red hair swaying down her tanned back.

"Now tell us about father. I don't believe for a second that he ordered you to come here?" pressed Gideon.

Koos quickly dropped any thought of Josanne and informed Gideon of the occurrences back home. He leaned over the table so that Nuallan could hear his words. "Your father has gone mad. He no longer sees anything as a threat and even worse, he has visions. People have heard him, I have heard him. He calls out your mother's name."

Nuallan and Gideon didn't look as stunned as Koos expected them to.

"He called for my head if I rode for Brigantium," added the Meridium General.

"Then you must remain here. Let Tobias ride to his aid alone," said Nuallan.

"Do not underestimate him, Koos," said Gideon.

Koos looked at the two of them. He felt that they were over-reacting. He knew the wrath of Artaxes better than most, but the King was like a father to him. He was sure King Artaxes would praise him once the battle was won.

"No, I ride home tomorrow alongside our new ally," said Koos decisively. He stood up and stepped away from the table. "I will come and say goodbye in the morning, and will visit you here as often as I can." He turned and walked for the door, resting his hand upon the handle and taking a quick look back. "Today was one of the best days of my life, my old friends."

CHAPTER 19
AN UNEXPECTED VISITOR

"Is that the last one?" asked Boltrey.

"It is, father," replied Josanne. She had just shut the tavern door and latched the lock, the last customer having just left. Josanne had travelled across to the other side of the city and had been helping her father lock up his most recently-opened tavern. It was called the Telstar. It was a little smaller inside compared to some of his other settlements, but it was just as nice. The tables were all nicely positioned and the walls gave off a log burning scent that warmed the air cosily.

"Hurry up with that and come and sit down," demanded Boltrey. He sat down on a small table by the bar. Josanne wandered over with a bored look upon her face. She loved her father but she knew she was about to receive a speech, one that she had heard a hundred times before. She swiped her long green dress to the side and slouched down in the chair opposite her father, the two of them looking at each other for almost a minute before anyone spoke.

"The marriage offer still stands, you know?" Boltrey said surprisingly, causing Josanne to groan heavily.

"I will not marry him, father. Tell Dreyo Badstuber to take his offer and stick it up his arse. I won't marry his cunt of a son Riycard."

"I already did. I didn't want to but I did," he said sadly as he leaned onto the edge of the table with his elbows. "Why are you the way you are? Three years you have been gone, three years, Josanne."

Josanne gave a little look of guilt. "I am sorry I left, father, but I don't belong here. I am an adventurer and a fighter, the same as Lebon and Kalane."

Boltrey expected an answer like that. He looked down sadly.

"And speaking of them two oafs, why haven't they came to see me? Where are my brothers?"

Boltrey looked back up. "Gone," he said painfully.

Josanne yanked her body up with horror. "Gone? Dead?"

"No, no, you fool. Nothing can defeat them, they are like you in that way."

"Then where?"

"They left to join the Lure Alliance. Many lads have, even some young woman. They left about a year after you did."

Josanne really did feel guilty then. Her father was getting older and loneliness crept up on the old ruthlessly.

She sought to reassure her father. "Guess what? I won't be going anywhere for a while. The group I am with have made a deal with Tobias."

"They are to remain here?" asked Boltrey.

"Live out the rest of their days if they wish."

"And what does that mean for you, my girl?"

"That is where I do belong, father. With them. If they stay, so do I." She reached over and pushed her hands into her father's.

Boltrey smiled with relief. "Tell me one last thing, my sweet daughter, how is it that you came to be in the presence of the Princes from the West?"

"They found me on the road. I was out of food and water and they helped me. After that I just stuck with them. Together we survived and travelled."

"The leader, Gideon. He is very fond of you."

"You have met with him?"

"I have. He spoke very highly of you. Is there something there between the two of you?" asked Boltrey boldly.

Josanne giggled cutely. "Gosh, no. He thinks of me only as a sister, that I can assure you, father."

Boltrey held his hands out in front him in a gesture of peace. "If you say so. All I am saying is that he is the perfect match for you. You're going to have to get married someday." He quickly ended the debate. "But anyway, I've set the beds up upstairs. We will stay here tonight. With the place just opening up and all, I want us to stay here for a few nights to make sure no one tries to break in."

Josanne watched him walk over to the bar to get himself drink when she noticed something in the window towards the door. The shape of a man, sneakily spying through. Suddenly it vanished.

"Will you carry out the checks on the windows before bed, my dear? I'm extremely tired," asked Boltrey.

"Of course," she said whilst she still looked to the window. She quickly looked back to her father who had now walked through the bar and into the back of the tavern.

Josanne dived up with haste and charged for the door. She rested her ear against it and listened, but she heard nothing. She decided to open the door as quickly as she could to catch the burglar in the act. She counted to three in her head and then executed her plan, ripping open the door and diving into an attacking stance.

But standing there before her was no burglar, it was Koos.

"What on earth are you doing here? I thought someone was breaking in," she said in a panic.

Koos was standing there with his fist clenched as if he was ready to knock on the tavern door.

"Did you follow me here?" she asked with a flirtatious smirk upon her face.

Koos lowered his arm and dropped the act. "Oh what the hell, fine. Yes, I followed you here. I'm sorry but since I saw you in the tavern earlier this afternoon, you're all I can think about."

Josanne giggled to herself. She had begun twirling her red plaited ponytail with her fingers without even realising.

"Please say something, I feel completely stupid here," Koos said as humorously as he could manage.

Josanne squinted her eyes and stared at him. "Fancy a light drink to end the night?" she whispered gently.

Koos raised both his eyebrows and accepted. "Sure."

Josanne opened the tavern door fully and allowed him to walk past her, observing his body shape but it was hard to make out any real detail with all that armour on.

"Where you come from, does everyone walk around wearing that ridiculous armour all day?" she asked.

"Yes, most of them," he replied.

Josanne continued to stare with her squinted eyes. It had been a while since she had felt the warmth of a man, and she craved it.

"Take it off," she said.

Koos looked at her with confusion.

"Take the armour off," she repeated.

Finally he realised what Josanne was insinuating, and quickly became very excited. In a hurry he planted his helmet down on the table next to him, undid his sword belt and slammed it down. Josanne was watching his every move, her legs beginning to tremble and her thighs beginning to shake as she watched.

Koos unstrapped his chest plate and loosened his grieves, putting it all down on the table. Finally he pulled off his leg plates and quickly reassembled his straight posture, standing up straight, waiting for Josanne to make a move but she still watched him, inspecting him thoroughly. Koos was left waiting in his thin thermal pants and jerkin, the atmosphere fierce with passion and anticipation.

Josanne bit her bottom lip and reached her tender arms round to the bottom of her smooth back. She roughly ripped the string loose, allowing her green dress to slide off her shaking body.

Koos stood amazed. He watched Josanne with pure desire whilst she stood naked in front of him so he could observe her. Her long toned legs stood out beautifully, so long and clean. Koos began filling up with hunger at the very sight, as he inspected every little part of her elegant body.

The young General couldn't wait anymore. He raced over to her and latched onto her lips with his own, his tongue tentatively stroking hers. With his right hand, he caressed her rounded breasts, and with his left he began to explore around to her meaty behind. His fingers and hands were warm at the very touch of his lover's luscious body.

Koos's lips engaged into a ferocious battle with Josanne's. They kissed each other aggressively as if fighting over control of the moment. She groaned loudly as she thrived off Koos's very touch, each kiss, each grope making her weaker at the knees.

Josanne took control of the situation quickly, she had grown eager and impatient. She pulled Koos's thermal jerkin off and reached down into his brown pants. Her fearless hands adventured around his waistline until she discovered her prize, grabbing him hard.

Koos leaned his face into Josanne's trembling neck and breathed out as she grasped him below. In a sudden outburst, Koos bit down on Josanne's neck causing her to react in a way that he didn't expect. It had fired her up and aroused her beyond measure.

She ripped down his pants the rest of the way and launched Koos against the table. Koos retaliated by bending his knees and latching onto Josanne's legs with a meaningful grab. In one solid thrust, he lifted her up and slammed her down onto the warm table.

Josanne moaned out loud as the aggression was turning her on even more. She spread her legs wide and with her arms grabbed hold of Koos's waist. The young General directed himself before lunging in towards her. This time Josanne yelped out. The feeling was extraordinary. She tightened her grip on Koos's hips and began pushing him in and out of her, her legs folded around Koos like the shape of a diamond, and the Meridium General the grain of crystal imbedded between her.

Koos threw his upper body down and again began chewing on the side of Josanne's soaking wet neck. Again she reacted the same way. She moaned, but this time she arched her back and tightened her legs, now tangled around Koos like a snake suffocating its prey.

Koos continued his thrusting. He looked down and observed Josanne's groaning body. She had whipped her arms up to Koos's broad shoulders and began dragging her fingernails in a downward spiral. It caused Koos to tense his arms, making them feel even tighter, his sweat defining the muscles on his pale solid arms.

Koos could almost see his reflection on his lover's skin now. The flames of the surrounding candles reflected off Josanne's sweat-dripping body. He could not keep his eyes still. He watched every part of her body, each wriggle, each tense. Every stride that he made caused her to twitch somewhere or another. He was blinded by beauty.

Koos leaned his right elbow down so that he could rearrange his knees in order to go faster and with his left, he grabbed hold of the side of Josanne's pear-shaped backside. He held her tightly and thrust even faster, causing the table's legs to shake tremendously.

Josanne laid on her back with her eyes closed, allowing Koos to do whatever he wanted to her. Her passionate groaning and exotic moaning had now turned into an uncontrollable scream. She quickly became aware of the noise the two of them were creating, so in one swift, sharp movement she latched onto her lover and turned him. She could now control the pace.

She had completely taken Koos by surprise. The power that she possessed had shocked him. She barely even struggled to turn him from being on top to then being flat on his back upon the table. He had become the victim of Josanne's sexual game.

The now dominating redhead curled her gorgeous naked legs over Koos and sat on him slowly. She let out a long passionate breath as she slowly lowered herself onto her victim. Koos quickly mimicked Josanne's previous action by latching on to her hips and pulling her body inwards, generating a sensational feeling. He slowly pushed his pelvis up and flexed his hips into her as she rode him, but Josanne was in control. She grabbed hold of Koos's hands and pulled them from her curved hips. She pushed his hands above his head and began to stride at her own delicate pace.

Koos was shocked, out of all the women that he had seduced in the past, none would dare take control like Josanne just did.

The Meridium General was playing slave to Josanne, and he liked it. Any time he attempted to travel with his palm-sweating hands, Josanne slammed them back above his head. Koos craved another touch of the exceptional redhead's body, but she called the shots.

Josanne then used her widely-separated legs to joist her body forward, her soaking wet pelvis clashing against Koos's like two shields smashing against each other. The quickening of the pace had taken its toll on her, the constant pulsation causing her to breath out uncontrollably. The smitten redhead tightened up her thighs and raised her arms up above her head. She crumpled up her long red hair and gripped it tightly whilst her hips did the rest.

Sweat was dripping off every inch of both their bodies, the heavy out of rhythm breathing causing the candle flames to flicker all around the room. Koos was now close. He watched Josanne play with her beautiful long hair. The way the waves and curls bounced all around her upper body made him crave her more and more.

Josanne continued to rip at her hair before slashing her hands down, nails first. She slapped down on Koos's chest, mouth wide and eyes shut, breathing out so hard that she caused Koos to flinch. With her hands, she dug her nails deep into Koos's toned chest and began dragging them down towards his abdomen, causing him to squirm with pain, but he dared not resist her and he was seconds away from finishing.

The exotic redhead began to struggle with her rhythm as Koos's position prevented her from doing so. He had arched his back, stiffened his legs and curled his toes.

Josanne moaned gently as Koos latched onto her hips with a vicelike grip. He squeezed so hard that red marks had become visible around the top of her exhausted legs.

"Don't you dare," he murmured as he noticed Josanne's intrigued smile. "Don't you dare laugh."

But it was too late, Josanne had already begun to laugh hysterically. "Did you really just arch your back? I thought I was fucking a woman for a moment there." She slid her wet body off him, trekked over to her dress and began fitting it back onto her desirable body whilst Koos watched her.

"You are the most beautiful woman I have ever seen, Josanne," he said.

Josanne tied her dress and looked back to him. She smiled and walked back over to him. Koos still remained flat on the table, naked, as Josanne leaned over and kissed him passionately.

Koos seemed to be deep in thought. He was dwelling and had decided to think about it before revealing it, but his addictive and obsessive mind caused him to fire it out without much thought at all.

"Come away with me," he said.

Koos had truly caught Josanne's attention.

She took a step back and laughed out like a man. "You can't be serious," she said with an interesting look upon her face.

Koos slid his worn body off the table and marched over to her. "Oh, I am deadly serious. I have never met anyone like you in my life, my lady."

Josanne continued to laugh at Koos's every comment. She did like the sound of what Koos was offering, but she was realistic, she knew that she could never be with anyone properly which was a shame. She had taken an exquisite shine to the young General.

"You ride off to war tomorrow. You could be face down in a ditch by the end of the week," she said jokingly.

Koos grabbed hold of her arms and kissed her powerfully. "If that is what God demands of me then so be it, but hear me now, my lady. If I survive, I will ride back east and I will come for you."

He said it perfectly and that time Josanne didn't laugh. She realised the seriousness of his words. She thought only for a moment of what it could be like and it was very appealing to her, but her loyalties lay elsewhere. She turned from Koos and walked over to the small table where his armour lay. She picked up his helmet and held it out for him to collect.

"Koos, I would love nothing more than to be the woman you want me to be, but my loyalties lie with Gideon and the others. I can never turn my back on them. I won't stray from the company."

Koos looked at her with confusion.

Josanne took a deep breath. "There was another before you. Doxass. He died." The look of sarcasm had faded from her face now. "We were nothing that serious, but his death affected me. I don't think I can go through that again."

"Gideon and the others told me of him, and I understand. But I promise you one thing, I'm not going to die," Koos said. He walked over to the table and began suiting back up.

The two of them remained silent whilst Koos finished up fitting his armour. Once fully dressed, he walked for the door. He grabbed the handle and pulled the door open.

"I will come back for you," he said simply and he left, slamming the door behind himself.

Josanne sat down into the chair. The talk of Doxass had upset her and swept her off into a state of anger and depression. Only one thought helped to keep a tiny glimmer of hope in her heart. And that was the thought of Koos, honouring his word and returning to her.

CHAPTER 20
THE PRINCE'S TEACHER

The day's practice was about to begin, the morning had barely even broke before Hector and Gideon had met up. Gideon had taken Hector from the city and out into the small forest a little way from the city. Faizer and Oslo had tagged along in order to assist Gideon with the training plan he had created over night. Lieutenant Enly had also come along to watch.

Tobias had plenty of training facilities in the Palace but Gideon wanted Hector put out of his comfort zone.

"You know why I have selected this location for you?" asked Gideon.

"I do not," replied Hector simply.

"Because here, you are not aware of your surroundings, the same as you won't be when you go to Versidia. This location will prepare you mentally and physically for your Selection. If we just trained up in the Palace on one of your father's training grounds, it would not benefit you. You need to get used to fighting in a place that you are not comfortable in."

"Of course, completely understandable."

Gideon had selected a medium-sized opening within the trees. He prepared the area by removing all the stray logs, rocks and branches.

Enly stood with his back to a tree and his arms folded. He was dressed in his silver plated suit as always. Faizer and Oslo however were messing around with their swords. They both wore the company's traditional black overthrow. Josanne had had one made for Oslo within the city.

"Okay, in a moment we will begin. Arm yourself," said Gideon as he turned his back and walked away from Hector.

The Prince had been made to wear his full armour, covered from his neck to his toe with his yellow cape hanging nicely. Hector reached for his sword and grasped the handle, but he was engaged.

Gideon had surprise attacked him, swung round and lunged his sword towards Hector, catching him off guard. Gideon lightly tapped Hector on the chest plate with the tip of his sword. He then yielded his sword and began to explain Hector's mistake.

"At your Selection, the people you are fighting will not stand upon ceremony. They will not fight with respect nor honour. You must be ready at all times." Gideon again turned his back to Hector and walked away.

Hector took in his teacher's advice. He quickly drew his sword, just in time. Gideon again had attempted a cheap shot, spinning around and slashing towards Hector. He parried the attack and quickly countered. Hector's footwork was on point and his patient and composed fighting style proved the rumours correct. Gideon blocked all of Hector's slashes and stabs until he spotted a countering opportunity.

Gideon smashed his sword against his student's incoming swipe, knocking him slightly off balance. Gideon was impressed with Hector's countering ability and his attacking ability, and wanted to test out his defensive ability. Gideon spun around and hacked down at Hector, who luckily just managed to block the attack, but yet again he comfortably controlled his footwork and blocked every single attack that Gideon threw.

"Impressive," Gideon said. "You have proven yourself extremely skilled in the arts of a sword fight. Over the course of our training, I will continue to attack you from behind, and when you least expect it. We need you to improve your reaction time."

Hector, who had picked up a little sweat, scraped his brown

hair away from his forehead, revealing all of his face. Gideon looked into Hector's eyes for a little longer than he had intended, and couldn't help but notice how thin and slanted they were, a little like his own.

Faizer and Oslo edged a little bit towards the training area. Enly who was watching the training proudly, noticed their movement. Confusion struck him immediately.

Gideon stepped away from Hector, this time facing him dead on. He secretly nodded to Faizer who stood about fifteen feet behind Hector.

"Let's go again," said Gideon. He raised his sword and stepped towards his student, attacking first.

Hector quickly raised his sword, stopping Gideon's attack, but he had not been successful. He felt a light tapping on his metal back. Hector turned to find Faizer standing there holding his sword directly at his back. Gideon again yielded. He lowered his sword.

"At your Selection," he said, "it is likely that you will be attacked by more than one person. If you become too distracted with one foe, another will most certainly snatch the opportunity and kill you."

Gideon walked slowly around the muddy area with his sword still lowered before looking up and nodding at Faizer again. Faizer backed off and retook his position about fifteen feet away from Hector.

Gideon stopped still as he planned to attack quickly. In an instant, he lifted up his sword and charged at his victim, swinging ambitiously across the front of Hector's chest. Hector prevented the attack with his sword, then quickly spun around and smashed down hard at Faizer who had engaged him also.

The Eastern Prince successfully fended off Faizer before quickly spinning back around to engage Gideon. He battled momentarily with Gideon before again turning to deal with Faizer. Hector had his work cut out, but he eventually managed to create a bit of distance between the two surrounding trainers.

"Good, very good," said Gideon as he brought the practice to an end.

Gideon then planned to execute the final stage of his training. He nodded at Faizer who again retook his position behind Hector. Gideon then nodded to Oslo who quickly grasped his sword and ran into the bushy surroundings. Even though most of the trees were without leaves, Oslo still managed to vanish from sight, mounds of mud and prickly close together trees providing cover for the young lad.

Hector watched him with interest for moment until he eventually lost sight of the boy.

"Hardly fair this, three against one," blurted out Enly.

"Twelve people go into that arena. It could end up being eleven against one if he's not careful," said Gideon.

"Exactly, Enly. Now let Gideon do his job," insisted Tobias who came lurking out through the bushes.

Tobias had come bearing news, but he was eager to watch his son in action. Tobias was accompanied by Gondogon and Fangoy.

"Proceed," he said whilst looking at Gideon.

Gideon nodded. He looked back at Hector and clenched his sword. Hector readied himself also. He lifted up his sword and prepared himself to defend Gideon's attack, but it didn't come.

Hector waited patiently until he heard a soft crunch behind him. In a split second, he dropped down so low that Faizer's unexpected swing went whizzing over the top of him. Hector came back up and hacked down at Faizer, allowing himself about two or three more slashes before he turned to face Gideon who was probably only an arm's reach away. He quickly realised that he didn't have time to parry the attack as Gideon's sword was screaming towards him. He again ducked and bounced back up. Hector swivelled his sword left to right inflicting two damaging bashes against Gideon's sword, then switched his sword hand in order to deflect Faizer's counter attack, which he managed successfully.

Hector then played it smart. He sidestepped from in-between

his two attackers, luckily managing to get Faizer and Gideon on the same side, preventing any attack coming from behind, or so he thought.

Hector heard it again, the light crunch of shattering twigs from behind.

It was Oslo.

Oslo pounced out from the bushes, leaping up into the air and slamming his sword down hard. Hector blocked it immediately. He attempted a counter attack but he had no time as Oslo had taken control. The boy fired attack after attack towards Hector who was suddenly on the back foot. He was running out of options, struggling to control his stance as Oslo moved in closer with every attack, and Hector knew he didn't have much time as his two trainers now approached him like a pack of hungry lions.

Hector thought quickly. He spotted his opportunity as Oslo raised his sword high. He waited for him to strike. As the sword came inches away from him, he dropped to his knees and dived behind his teenage challenger. As he passed the boy, he latched onto his overthrow, yanking it powerfully backwards. Oslo tumbled and splashed against the spikey wood riddled floor.

One down, two to go.

The Eastern Prince managed to prepare himself for Faizer and Gideon who ran across each other switching sides tactically. Gideon attacked first. He lashed at Hector's side whilst Faizer sliced at his leg. In one excellently skilled block, Hector managed to block the attacks with one diagonal swing, but the attack continued. Faizer this time lunged deeply towards him causing him to jump backwards, meaning Gideon could now slash his sword lengthily towards the Princes stomach, but yet again he swiped up sharply in a diagonal motion, knocking both his attackers' swords away.

Hector desperately wanted to impress whilst his father was watching. He knew he could not defeat Gideon, but Faizer on the other hand could be an easier target. So he planned his move.

The royal student slashed sharply in Faizer's direction. He knew that if he attacked Faizer first, Gideon would soon follow with his own attack, and he was right. Gideon came gliding in sword first. Hector, who pretended that he hadn't noticed Gideon, bent down, coming back up elbow first. He connected nicely with Gideon's jaw, knocking his trainer down to the ground.

Hector then had a few moments to attack Faizer alone. He began by kicking out at Faizer's mid region, cutting down and hitting Faizer's defensive sword powerfully. Hector had Faizer on the back foot now. He sliced at him with extreme stamina before eventually hitting his sword so hard that the man dropped it.

Hector claimed his win and held his sword an inch away from his victim's throat.

"Surrender?" said Faizer jokingly.

Hector lowered his sword and smiled. He sheathed his weapon and looked to his father who rewarded his son with a smile.

"Come on, old man," said Faizer as he helped Gideon up.

"Who you calling old man, you old man," replied Gideon.

"Impressive, isn't he?" boasted Tobias as he walked out onto the training area with Fangoy beside him.

"Indeed, there is little skill with a sword that he will learn from me, but I will focus on his fitness for the time being and his anticipation and awareness skills," said Gideon.

Tobias smiled as if satisfied with his son's training schedule. "I'm afraid the meaning of my visit was not to witness the training session." Tobias received a few confused looks as he said it. "I come to say farewell. We ride west within the hour."

Hector was the first to say his farewells as he leaned in and hugged his father. Oslo, Faizer and Gideon stood in a line before the King, waiting until Hector finished before one at a time shaking Tobias's hand.

Gideon went last.

"Again, I thank you for aiding my countrymen. I will watch over yours until you return and I will watch over your son. He will be ready for Selection upon your return," said Gideon honourably but Tobias showed a little look of regret as he prepared to speak.

"I'm afraid I must ask something else of you, my son," said the King.

Everyone looked around at each other with confusion, all except Gondogon, who obviously knew what the King was going to say.

"I won't be back in time for your Selection. You must take him, Gideon." Tobias could see immediately that Gideon did not look happy with this task.

"Impossible," Gideon said. "Darchem soldiers patrol Versidia as if it was their home. I will be recognised, my brothers too."

Hector quickly interrupted, voice thick with disappointment. "You will not attend? The ceremony cannot be completed without your presence."

"I will send word to King Emric and the Elders of Versidia that I will not be attending. The ceremony will take place, I promise you, and I have no doubt that you will pass, bringing even more glory and honour to our family name."

The King said it passionately but Hector looked down, depressed, only to be comforted by his father almost immediately.

"Son, I ride off to war. I am creating an alliance with the West. I am expanding our Kingdom, your future Kingdom."

"Very well. I understand, father," he said sadly. He bowed forcefully and stormed out of the practice area.

"Tobias, do you not hear me? It is an impossible task you set me," repeated Gideon.

"Do not worry yourself. Take Gondogon here, free of charge for protection. He is well known in Versidia. His judgement will not be questioned. Enly will go along also." Tobias pivoted to glare at Enly.

Enly looked back and smirked, bowing lightly and accepting the quest.

"As for your brothers and company," Tobias said, "they will all remain here. I only want you and Faizer to attend. Faizer will act as the lead escort, disguised as a Brigantium General. You are simply there to prepare Hector. You can pose as a coachman whilst travelling through Hornton's Watch and then upon arrival you can act as a servant. There is no risk."

"What you ask of me is extremely dangerous," Gideon warned.

"I could say the same to you, my son, but men must act like men by just simply, doing it," hissed Tobias viciously.

Gideon was slightly taken back by Tobias's first true sign of aggression towards him. He just stared back into the King's eyes before accepting.

"Very well. We will take him."

"Good. Enly tell Dreyo Badstuber that he has command of Brigantium in our absence." The King then looked back at the not so confident Gideon.

"You must leave within the week. It is ten days ride to Versidia. Now good luck to all," Tobias said and left.

Gondogon, Fangoy and Enly stormed after him leaving Oslo, Faizer and Gideon standing alone and frustrated.

CHAPTER 21
THE MANNEQUIN MAN

Geralix, a young servant of the High King had awoken as normal in his lightly decorated room. Today was the day that High King Duran planned to host a meeting with all of his advisors and officers. Geralix had been given the honour of preparing the hall in time for the meeting. The nineteen-year-old lad edged himself onto the end of his small bed and yawned. He was tall and pale with thin eyes and a rough face. He was without hair anywhere, his head and face were both as smooth as a marble floor, but not by any choice of his own… all Mannequin Men were forced to shave their heads and beards daily.

It was extremely unusual for someone like Geralix to have much authority in High Darchem because of his status, the status of a Mannequin Man, not a true born. A Mannequin Man, also known as an Artificial was someone who was taken from his home at a young age to be raised to fight for the High King. Many cities like Brigantium and Meridium had been victim to this evil system since the reign of Duran Harall's grandfather, Deeshan Harall.

Thousands of young lads from both cities had been taken to High Darchem and Geralix was one of them. Geralix, however, had excelled so much in his training and had become so obedient to the High King, that he had earned himself something of a position. He acted as a bodyguard, servant and escort to Duran.

t from their shaved heads and hairless faces, there was
er way that they could be told apart from a normal man of
rchem: a black print of the Darchem tree, burnt onto the back
of the necks of all who were taken from their homes. A painful
process.

The lads were not looked at any differently from any ordinary
soldier, they were all treated with respect. Once they'd passed
the test, that is. Upon arrival each boy was put through a series
of challenging physical tests and mental examinations, the boys
were basically brainwashed and then moulded into the perfect
soldier. When each batch of new boys arrived at High Darchem,
they were quickly put through the tests. Usually a couple tried to
escape in the early days in an attempt to flee back to their homes.
But they were hanged, in order to set an example. It truly was a
brutal way of life, and also part of the reason for the uprising of
the Meridiums seven years previous.

Geralix sat staring at his uniform that hung neatly over a
wooden chair, the chair one of the only pieces of furniture within
his small room. He stroked the Darchem print on his neck then
stood up, naked, before reaching for his thin black under layer,
and beginning to dress. Next, he fitted his red-legged armour
and started fitting his red-layered chest piece. Geralix fastened
all of his straps and looked down to his helmet. He picked it up
and tucked it neatly under his arm before opening his door and
walking out.

The young Artificial walked through an extremely thin hallway,
taking an interesting glance into every small room that he passed.
In every room was a Mannequin Man, also fitting his armour and
preparing himself for the day. The hallway was lined with rooms,
a door to a new room every six or so feet away from each other.
These were the quarters of the Mannequin Men.

Geralix walked through a grey scaled archway at the end of the
hallway and wandered out into a medium sized hall. All the walls
were stone and cold, for they were inside a castle-like fortress,
not a palace. The High King did not have an eye for design or
comfort, only an eye for soldiers and war. The bare concrete walls

gave off no feeling, and if it were not for the scattered fire pots, the soldiers would most likely freeze.

Large groups of Darchem soldiers, all dressed in their legendary red armour marched up and down the hallway. There were no priests or stable merchants, tavern owners or advisors, just soldiers. Some of them nodded at Geralix as he continued his journey to the meeting hall. He followed the dark smoky hallway to the left before tackling a small set of steps that led him down another passage. Geralix instantly felt the warmth as he entered the passage, the flaming torches along the wall giving off a welcoming heat.

The young Mannequin Man arrived at the meeting hall. The doors were already open so he just wandered in and began organising the set up. Geralix instantly dumped his helmet down on a rounded table that glimmered like the moon. The table was so large it took up most of the room's space. There was a perfect gap between each black chair positioned around the table.

"Hurry with that, the King will be on his way," he said as two young girls started unravelling a large fabric sigil of Darchem. They spread it out over the table, covering every inch of black with the monstrous black and red sigil.

"You three, bring the wine and water," he commanded.

Three girl servants who were previously filling the water pots, left their current assignment and tended to Geralix's orders. The girls scurried off into the corner of the room and picked up the jugs. They stood idle before the table until the other two servants finished off dressing the table. Once complete, they planted down the jugs of wine in the middle and placed a jug of water at every seat. The servants continued to rush back and forth carrying the jugs whilst Geralix stood with his arms folded, monitoring their work.

Geralix was very satisfied with the presentation of the meeting hall, and picking up his helmet, he walked around the table, before tucking the helmet under his arm and standing motionless by the side of a chair. This chair was the High King's.

"Stand at your posts and await your King," he said.

The servant girls all scattered off to the edges of the cold, grey room and stood with their backs to the hard wall. The servants all wore long, white gowns that trailed across the floor as they walked. They were children of the poorer families of High Darchem and had been sent to the King's castle to work in order to feed their families.

The Kingdom of High Darchem may have possessed more men, gold and power than any other Kingdom of Requirium but it was not invested in the people, or the city, for that matter. The High King put all his time and effort into the planning of his crusade across the 7th.

Geralix tightened his posture as a group of men approached the open doorway. They walked in and sat down silently around the table. Moments later another two men came in and sat a little further along. Over the space of a couple of minutes most of the empty seats were filled up. All but one.

Most of the men present were dressed in armour identical to Geralix's. Some, though, had thin rectangular streaks of gold sown onto their armour straps. This was their rank. There were, however, three men sitting to the right of the table who wore the Darchem colours but their armour design was a little different to the others.

The whole room remained silent. No one had yet even poured a drink. No one would dare begin until the High King graced them with his presence.

Which he now did.

A shuffling noise ran through the meeting hall as everyone turned to face the doorway... the High King had arrived.

Duran Harall stepped into the hall and smiled forcefully at his officers, who all stood up to honour his arrival. Duran was dressed all in black leathers, and wrapped comfortably on top of the leathers was a long black cushion of fur balanced across his shoulders. Duran's once black hair was now the home of much grey.

"Welcome and thank you all for coming," he said. "Sit."

Everyone sat.

Duran walked around the table and sat down sharply on the chair that Geralix had just pulled out for him.

"Right, first things first, give me the report on the progress we have made further south with the Lure Alliance. Is there any sign of Victor or the Alliance's main camp?" said Duran, looking to his left at a man.

The man looked back worried. His name was Pontus.

Pontus had long grey hair that fizzed between the bald patches. His beard was long but had managed to hold some of its old colour, black riddled the centre of it. Pontus was in his sixties and had been in charge of dealing with the Lure Alliance problem for the last two years or so.

"Erm," said Pontus, "it appears that the Alliance is growing in number, my King. Wherever I send riders and soldiers, they get returned to me almost immediately, dead."

Duran clenched a fist in anger.

"Send soldiers to Woodpine and Willowdale," he said. "Burn both of the towns to the ground, cut off the Alliance's source of income."

Willowdale and Woodpine were two towns that were positioned just east of the Square Wood Forest where the Lure Alliance were based. Victor had had his men strike deals with the people of the towns many years ago.

Pontus looked even more nervous. "We already tried, my King," he said, "our men were attacked before they even got close to the towns. The Alliance protects all of its assets. Word has also reached my ears that Victor's army is expanding further east. They now control some of the other forests across the Midlands."

Duran tightened his other fist, struggling to contain his fury. He stood up slowly and took a breath.

"Pontus, send word to Havideous Destain, the drunken cunt, I want him in Darchem within the fortnight. Tell him to bring five thousand men. He is to be briefed here by me before marching south to Woodpine and Willowdale."

Pontus nodded. "Of course, my King."

Duran turned his focus to the opposite side of the table. "Now, tell me some good news, Seluse."

Seluse was a tall bushy man of forty, his skin darkened by the constant shadow of his lengthy beard and loose black hair.

"Well, the fleet is nearly ready... two months at the most," said Seluse, watching as Duran Harall sat back down. Seluse was the Fleet Commander. His lava red armour had three rectangular gold bars on it. He was one of Duran's highest ranking officers and had been given the job to organise two hundred ships for the King's crusade across the 7th.

"Good, that is good," said the King. "And how many men to a ship?"

"Fifty fighters, easy. We will be able to escort around ten thousand men across the 7th."

Duran thought on the matter, trying to work out whether ten thousand men would be enough to take the lands that his father and grandfather failed to conquer twenty four years ago.

The Schezaar Republic were Duran's main enemy. For decades the Harall family had left their Guardian Kings of Requirium to run their country for them whilst they sought to take over the foreign lands. But the furthest anyone ever got was to the two islands in the 7th sea, one named Marooka and the other Bastiam.

The two islands sat only twenty or so miles off the coast of the foreign land. Duran Harall's grandfather attempted to take the lands twenty four years ago, but they failed. An ambush from the Schezaar Republic forced the Harall family and their army of red cloaks to flee the island. Duran's grandfather and father had died there.

"Very well," said the King. "Keep me up to date on the progress on the ships. Leave now, Seluse. You too, Pontus. Make sure Havideous rides for High Darchem the day he receives the message, and tell him to bring Aphrayer... I miss my daughter."

Pontus stood and nodded, as did Seluse. They left with haste, taking with them a handful of other members of the meeting, their followers.

High King Duran looked around the table at his remaining

officers. "Now, to the more important side of business. Who wants to fill me in on the disturbing movement in the west? What is our troublesome friend, Artaxes, up to now?"

An officer called Crespo spoke up. "Artaxes has retaken Villach and called upon his fighters from Sandown."

Crespo was an officer in the Darchem army. He had no wife or children, nor any desire to succeed in anything but the arts of strategy and tactics. He was in his forties but still kept his youthful colour.

Crespo was graced with a light shade of skin and silky black hair. He was the most handsome man in the room and Duran's most loyal soldier. He was the one who had suggested reaching out to Havideous seven years ago, which of course led to Duran winning the battle against the Meridiums upon the Gantry. Crespo was a highly intelligent man, as well as a master of warfare.

Duran looked at Crespo with confusion.

"His fighters from Sandown? You mean my fighters from Sandown?"

"Of course, my King."

"Continue," said Duran.

"Artaxes is preparing to retake Oggsfleet also," said Crespo, "but movement in the east troubles me. I think Tobias is riding to his aid."

"Nonsense," said the King, "Artaxes can't bear Tobias. I think he hates him more than he hates me." He signalled one of the servants over.

One of the young girls scurried to the table. Reaching for one of the jugs of wine, she quickly poured Duran a goblet and fluttered away.

Duran picked up his drink and slurped away whilst his officers discussed the problem at hand.

An elderly man of about sixty stood up in protest. He was called Hornton. He ran a watch that protected the city of Versidia, monitoring everyone who entered and left the holy city. The old officer had long grey hair and a bushy untended beard and was suited up in his Darchem armour, like most of his companions around him.

"If Tobias is intending to aid the Westerners" said Hornton, "then he must be stopped. If they create an alliance, we will again be at threat."

Hornton was no stranger to the Westerners, he was in charge of taking all the boys from their city after the war, making them into Mannequin Men.

"Calm yourself, Hornton," Said Duran. "Artaxes has an army of barely a thousand. This is not an important issue."

"But, my King," said Hornton, "Tobias possesses over forty thousand, and we all know Artaxes's army of one thousand is as good as an army of triple that amount."

"Right you may be," replied the King, "but for now I want you to return to your watch outside of Versidia. The young Prince of Brigantium has his Selection coming up, I want you to closely monitor who enters the city. I can't help but think there is more to this… someone close to Artaxes must be pulling Tobias's strings."

"Very well, my King, I will take my leave at once." said Hornton. He stood and left the room with his followers at his back.

Very few men remained present. Duran looked around his table and addressed a man who had been sitting quietly throughout the whole meeting. His name was Lumon. He had two companions, one either side of him. Lumon had medium length black hair that dangled messily at his shoulders, extremely tanned skin and dark, demonic eyes. He was also in his flashy Darchem armour, but his was slightly different for melted artistically in the centre of his red chest piece was a golden eagle. It had been forged into the centre of a glimmering shield. Lumon was of course a part of the Eagle Pact, but not just a member. He was in fact the leader of the party. The men to his left and right wore the same strange design of Darchem armour, except their eagles were forged from silver instead of gold.

The Eagle Pact was an elite group of Darchem soldiers hand picked by the King himself. Each member had to be over thirty, as fifteen years of service was required to even qualify. There were twelve members of the Pact, each fantastically skilled in survival, tracking and fighting. The High King would involve the Pact whenever he needed a quest completing quickly. Lumon was the leader of the organisation.

But that hadn't always been the case.

Lumon was once the right-hand man to the leader of the Eagle Pact, a man that was once favoured by so many people within Darchem, including the High King. This man's name was Victor Stran. The same Victor Stran who was now leader of the Lure Alliance, and archenemy to the High King.

When Victor had left the city and created the Lure Alliance, Lumon stepped up and replaced him. Lumon and his Pact had been sent out on a handful of quests in the early days of the Alliance's set up, to spy or sabotage Victor's uprising, but Lumon struggled to even find Victor. Victor was too skilled. After all, he had spent many years leading the Eagle Pact, he knew all their ways and could anticipate all their moves. The High King now left the dealings of the Alliance to Pontus, instead having the Eagle Pact monitor Versidia, especially with the Selection coming up.

"Anything to report from Versidia?" said High King.

"Nothing, my King," said Lumon. "The preparations for Selection are being made, and all visitors and guests are being monitored closely."

"Good, I want you to continue with your work in Versidia. Take the Pact back there at once. I need you to attend Selection in my place. I will send word to the elders and King Emric. Report back to me as soon as Selection finishes. Go, now."

Lumon and his two comrades stood up, nodding one at a time at their King.

"Is there anything in particular I should keep an eye out for?" said Lumon.

"I can't help but think something else is at work here," said Duran, "something stirring in the east and the west, but, for now, I need you in Versidia... although I may have a new mission for you upon your return."

Duran stood up and walked away from the table, to the back

end of the hall, then he looked out of a window, out into his kingdom. The large window offered a view over the misty stone buildings below the King's castle.

Lumon and the members of his Pact bowed even though the High King wasn't facing them, then left. But for Geralix and the High King, the room was now empty.

High King Duran continued to look out of the window, staring down and observing his rocky kingdom. He thought heavily as he tried to solve the riddle that played at the back of his mind. He was confused and troubled deeply about the movement of Tobias's army. He could not think why Tobias would ride west to aid Artaxes. If the reasoning behind it was that an alliance was secretly being forged, then they would have to be stopped. He could not allow an alliance like that to be created.

CHAPTER 22
THE FLEET COMMANDER

Geralix squinted his eyes as the salt from the sea merged with the gusty wind, blowing into the faces and eyes of all upon the dock. He had been asked to accompany the High King while he went down to the Darchem docks to check on Seluse and the fleet. Seluse had made little progress since the meeting three days earlier. He had over half of the ships built and the course and route were being planned.

The Darchem docks were located an hour's ride from the city, along the eastern border of High Darchem. They ran for miles across the coast.

The Darchem Harbour was made from solid wood, its thick legs running deep into the water and securely into the earth beneath. The legs been designed so that they could withstand the ferocious waves that smashed against them every morning. The weather in the Harbour was not as sunny as it was down in Brigantium… at the Harbour, clouds conquered the sky, bringing nothing but wind and rain.

The Darchem docks' extremely large platform eventually split into various different wooden walkways, all supported by legs, each walkway leading you away towards a different part of the marina.

Any ship or boat that entered the harbour would be directed through the zigzagging wharf so that it could anchor at the correct station. Certain tie-up stations all along the coast were home to specific types of ship.

Trading ships and market stall ships were further along the dock and people from the city would come here to attempt to strike deals with the foreign traders. The arms dealer ships were anchored a little closer but further out into the sea. Many other types of boats floated out in the water, each one carrying some form of beneficial material or item for High King Duran.

The dock was Darchem's central source of income. All their food, weapons, silks and even Mannequin Men were transported in through them.

"Do you see him?" said Duran, scanning the crowd.

The dock was overwhelmed with people, all from the city to buy from the latest batch of wine and food. Duran smiled back at the odd passerby, but it was obvious he had grown impatient. He was struggling to spot Seluse and the path towards his Fleet Commander's ship was blocked.

"This way, my King," said Geralix, slithering off into the crowd.

Duran followed.

Geralix led Duran through the commotion and away from the merchant rallies and bartering arguments. He walked up a wooden ramp that supported a long wooden beam leading out over the ocean. It was one of the many thinner walkways that sprouted out off the main platform that was host to hundreds of merchants and tradesmen.

Duran tightened his black cloak around him as the waves splashed up salty jewel blue water up onto the pier-like walkway.

"The bastard better be on his ship," said Duran, angrily.

Geralix didn't reply, but felt the same eagerness to find Seluse.

"Come on, let's get on board," said Duran, passing his guide and tackling the ramp leading up to the Fleet Commander's ship.

The two of them reached the end of the walkway and found themselves at the base of Seluse's remarkable vessel.

The very sails upon the rich ship blotted out the small shy sun, hanging like humongous bed sheets that could only comfort a giant. Many sailors were hanging from the tall tower-like mast, reeling in the sails by tightening them with fine rope. But tying up the sails was proving a difficult task for the sailors... the giant quilts lashed and stabbed wickedly as the wind did its damage upon the pale, milky sails.

The design of the ship's body was of a basic nature. Its only difference from the other naval ships was its size: it was at least three times the size of any ballista or transport ship.

The High King slipped between two Darchem soldiers that stood at the base of the long, swaying ramp that led from the dock walkway to the deck of the battleship. Geralix followed.

Two more soldiers stood on guard at the end of the ramp.

"Your Commander, where is he?" said Duran as he reached the top.

"In his cabin, my King," said one of the men.

Geralix again followed his King across the decking, in and out of all the sailors that scurried around the deck, either cleaning or working to tie up all the loose ropes that dangled like a horde of snakes.

The High King reached the cabin's doorway. He pushed open the doors to find his Fleet Commander standing over a small table, going over a map with two of his Captains. The Commander and the two Captains turned instantly and greeted Duran.

"Leave us," said Seluse to his two companions.

They immediately left the cabin.

"King Duran," added Seluse. "I didn't expect you."

"I want to check on the progress," said the High King, "and I am satisfied."

"I'm glad to hear it. We have built a lot of ships. The crews are all eager and ready. I have them carrying out simple drills and practices on deck. Prepare them for when we set sail."

Duran showed little interest in his Commander's plans. He cared only for information on his crusade. He walked over to Seluse and stood over the little table that tilted lightly, left and then right. The waves below them caused the ship's hull to slowly sway, like a dancer timing out her steps.

"Have you planned our course?"

"I have. Here, I will show you," said Seluse. He placed his hands on the small parchment map that lay on the table. "Right, we are here." He pointed a finger onto the symbol of a fish upon the map. "At the docks, yes."

He then trailed the finger across the blue that was the sea until it hovered over a small, green island that sat in the ocean.

"Marooka?" said the High King.

"Yes. Marooka will save us much time on the journey."

"The enemy will anticipate this move," said the High King. "They will deploy most of their defending force on the beaches of Marooka. Have you thought this through?"

"We are relying on the Schezaar to do so. It means that, yes, we will suffer more casualties, but they will not have enough men to successfully hold the island. If we keep prisoners, we will be able to use their survivors as auxiliary units, which will then help us take Bastiam shortly after."

Duran was slightly more interested. "If the soldiers could be forced to fight as auxiliary units," he said, "then this plan would be effective, but we don't know if they will."

The High King had used the auxiliary method before and it had proved useful... if the captured enemies obeyed, of course. Which they usually did. Most men would if they expected death and were then offered life.

"They will, I am sure of it," said Seluse.

Duran looked back with uncertainty. He took up a more observant stance over the table and looked at Marooka.

"How many men do you think the Schezaar Republic will have at Marooka?"

"A couple of thousand," said Seluse, "maybe five at most. They don't suspect an attack. It's been over twenty years since our two nations crossed swords."

"Very well. But what if they did know we were coming? What if, for example, we had a snake in our garden and that snake informed our enemy of our intentions. How many men could they possibly have then?"

Seluse seemed confused by the question. "Well, our scouts tell me that the Republic has over eighty thousand troops, but that won't be a problem if we take one island at a time. Once we control their two outer defences, we will then have the advantage and can transport the rest of our army over and call on King Emric, King Tobias and whatever the fool Artaxes has left. Together, as a nation, we will destroy the foreign fucks." Seluse sounded as if he had rehearsed his speech.

But still Duran did not look won over. "Tell me, Seluse," he said, "how loyal do you think your scouts are? They are but foreign merchants that spy on the enemy in return for gold. How do you know that they are not doing the same to us?"

Seluse looked nervously at his King.

He didn't have an answer.

"So, if that was so," said the King, "how do you expect our ten thousand men to take on a savage army of eighty thousand?"

Seluse again looked at Duran without reply. Perhaps, he hadn't thought the plan through properly after all.

"You haven't planned this as well as you thought, Commander," said Duran, "but no worry, that is why I am King and you are not. It is my job to think of things like this. I want all your scouts and spies killed. From now on we send our own men to spy upon the enemy. I want ships sent five miles off our coast to create a defensive blockade to prevent any of the enemy's spies to get insight on what we are building. From now on every merchant ship will be searched before entering the harbour and every tradesman, arms dealer or fisherman will be closely observed. I want the dock guard trebled by tomorrow."

He then turned to Geralix who still stood by the doorway.

"Geralix, handpick six thousand Mannequin Men, the best that there is. I trust your judgement. Seluse, I leave the selection of the remaining four thousand men up to you, see to it."

His orders handed down, Duran stormed for the doors, launching them angrily open.

Without another word, he left.

CHAPTER 23
ORDERS FOR PELIOS

Duran Harall stood alone in his throne room. The day had ended, allowing the night to make an appearance. The black sky could be seen through the oval shaped gaps that were positioned all along each wall. For the reward of a pretty sight through the windows came a chilling sacrifice, warmth. The throne room was horribly cold in the winter, along with most of the rooms, halls and chambers inside the High King's fortress.

Duran had wandered over to the eastern side of his cold throne room. He stood before a pleasantly detailed sight, straight backed with his arms folded. He was investigating the artistic feature that had been painted upon the face of the grey wall. It was a map of Requirium, similar to the one that Artaxes had in his council chambers in Meridium, except this one was a lot more detailed and its size excelled the Western King's. Every single town, village, city, field, forest and lake were on this map, painted elegantly in the correct location.

The High King looked a little worried as he read his map, his gaze fixed on the Square Wood Forest that took up a large portion in the centre of the painting. Victor Stran and his Lure Alliance were swimming inside the King's mind. Duran was beginning to understand and fear the threat of the Alliance now. He remembered how persuasive Victor was. Even when he was the right hand to the High King, he ended up with the same amount of followers if not more. Victor's expansion, and his influence in Requirium, was truly worrying him now as more people joined his cause everyday, more than the amount of Mannequin Men that Duran had been taking anyhow.

Duran tilted his body slightly right so that the drawings of the towns Woodpine and Willowdale entered his line of sight. He thought hard on a solution, a way to take the towns which would then allow him to surround the Square Wood. Duran could burn it to the ground with the whole Alliance inside if he could achieve victory over the towns first. But there were few solutions. Victor had now taken the two towns as his vassals. He protected the towns and the people that lived there well.

The High King diverted his attention away from the map for but a moment to see who had just entered his throne room, a creak echoing throughout the room as a small boy prised opened the thick doors. The small boy with black hair began running towards Duran, crossing the silky red carpet that ran from the door to the charcoal-shaded throne. He then dodged in and out of the concrete pillars and columns and tackled the steps that led up to his worried father.

"What are you doing out of bed, Damassius?" asked Duran as his five year old boy skipped up the steps.

"What are you doing out of bed?" replied the child annoyingly.

Duran looked down at him and smiled. "I'm busy, trying to build you an empire, my boy."

Damassius smiled and skipped off to a flaming brazier pit at the side of the map's edge. The boy grabbed a torch from the pit and leaned in, lighting the end aflame. The young child then walked right up to the map and held the torch up so that he could see the pictures upon the wall more clearly.

"I thought the kingdom was already ours?" asked the young boy as he crossed his torch over Meridium and the Western lands.

"It is, but people are beginning to disobey me." Duran walked towards his boy, taking the torch from his little hands. Duran then raised the torch above the Square Wood.

"Here, an old friend of mine has begun rising up against

us." Duran then raised his torch right up into the corner, past Darchem and onto the 7th sea.

"And here, people who were rebellious and resistant towards your grandfather have began rising up also," explained the High King as simply as he could so that the boy could understand.

Damassius looked at his father through his bushy black fringe with confusion. "Then you should go and fight them all in a huge battle," advised Damassius.

The young child then skipped over to the glowing brazier, grabbing another unlit torch from the side, and lunging forward with it as if it were a sword. Damassius continued to play happily as if he was fighting in a great battle.

Duran smiled down at his son who continued to spin and jump around. It was then that he realised that his boy didn't understand the seriousness of the issue, he was after all so young.

"My King!" said someone who had just burst in through the half opened up doors.

It was Lumon.

Duran began walking down the steps in order to meet him halfway, eager to find out why Lumon had returned to the city so quickly after only recently departing for Versidia.

"Lumon, I sent you to Versidia. Explain your return at once," demanded Duran aggressively.

"My King, I came as soon as I heard. My connection in Brigantium sent word to me, I received the message barely a day ago so I rode here as soon as I could," explained the Eagle Pact Leader.

Duran grew impatient. He grabbed hold of Lumon's armoured shoulders, shaking his Pact Leader furiously.

"Speak, quickly!" urged the High King.

"The lost sons of Meridium are alive. The spawn of Artaxes are in Brigantium," announced Lumon, completely shell-shocking the High King.

Duran released his hold instantly and stepped back. "Impossible, they are dead," muttered Duran to himself.

"My King, they are very much alive. My source would not

send me word of this unless he was absolutely sure. And there is more…"

Duran looked into his eyes with pure ferocity.

"Tobias accepted them like they were his own sons," the Eagle Pact Leader said. "My source says they are living in the Palace under the protection of Tobias and his fellow Horse Lords."

Duran this time looked like he was ready to explode. "Treason! Treason! Tobias will hang for this. Is he really that foolish that he would betray me like this? I reward him with a throne in the East and this is how he repays me?"

"My King, Tobias commands over forty thousand well trained men. We can not fight him and the Schezaar Republic."

Duran was quick to reply. "Send out word in the morning, all the crusade preparations are to be put on standby. Send word to Brigantium also, to Tobias. If he does not hand over the children of Artaxes, I will march on his city with one hundred thousand men," declared Duran menacingly.

"As you wish, my King." Lumon bowed and turned in order to leave.

"Wait, I have an idea," said Duran. "One that will truly make Tobias Ringfold pay for his betrayal. Send word to your source in Brigantium. Tell him I am offering him and his family a chance to inherit the Eastern throne."

"But my King, if Hector passes Selection he will have earned the right to the throne. If we were to kill him, the whole of the East would rise up. They are very passionate about their traditions."

Duran smiled back at him with a glimmer of evil in his eyes. "That is why Hector will not pass Selection. Have our little ally in Brigantium send his son. Have him put a mark on the Prince's armour. That way he can be identified in the arena. I will call for 'him', he will do the job no questions asked." The King sounded strange.

Lumon looked at his king with confusion. "Him?"

"Yes, an old friend of the Ringfold family. Pelios," revealed Duran.

The Eagle Pact Leader raised his eyebrows with interest. "Pelios the survivor?"

"Yes, he will jump at the chance to get his revenge," said the High King happily.

"Very well, my King. I will send word for him and take my leave at first light, back to Versidia," announced Lumon.

The Eagle Pact Leader turned from his furious High King and made for the throne room's dark doors.

CHAPTER 24
OGGSFLEET PORT - PART 1

The ice blue banners of the Meridium army whistled as the wind scratched at their silky surface. The white lion of Meridium roared silently all the way across the frontline of the composed army of Artaxes Destain. It sat proudly upon the various flagpoles that were being flown. The Western army had positioned themselves tactically along a muddy mound that sat one mile east of Oggsfleet port, observing their enemy, waiting for their King to give the command.

The Port's new citizens began to fill with panic at the sight of their uninvited guest. It had seemed as though the over confident Oakland Musters had transported many of their women and children across The Sink.

The remaining Oakland women and children that had no time to sail back to their home had begun rushing off, taking refuge in various different stores, boats and inns. Meanwhile, the Muster men had begun flooding out of Oggsfleet, marching slowly out of the small streets and out into the mound-riddled field that surrounded Oggsfleet. Over three thousand vicious savages armed to the teeth leaked out of their newly stolen harbour and began their short walk into battle.

Oggsfleet Port was one of the biggest ports in Requirium. It was a huge marketplace, dock and fishing port. There was also a long wooden pier that ran out over The Sink. On a rare warm day, the pier would be rammed with fishermen, however the port held even more settlements on the land that encircled the water and docks. Over two thousand Meridium civilians lived there before the rebels invaded the western lands. People actually lived there comfortably, meaning there were many houses and a few streets within Oggsfleet. Taverns and even brothels had been built there also so that the fishermen could enjoy more than just the fish on a cold night.

"Look at them, look!" snarled Artaxes furiously. The Guardian King in the West was sitting upon his famous white horse at the front of his lines of men. The horse's breath was more than visible as the baltic air rushed into its lungs, the only bit of warmth that the masculine stead received from the thin blanketed Meridium sigil that had been smothered over its pale markless back.

Three other horses stood patiently beside Artaxes, all carrying men of position. Milano, First General Lucifer and Dariuss all sat upon their beasts waiting for a command. All of the other officers and Lieutenants were mooching about the frontlines of the Meridium and Sandown soldiers, checking that everything was in order. They patrolled quickly, treading heavily into the soggy mud that supported the thinned line of brave Westerners. The Lieutenants handed out extra blue banners to the men and patted the odd man who looked nervous on the shoulder, but there weren't many soldiers who showed signs of nervousness. The Meridiums were ferocious, eager and extremely brave, even when outnumbered massively.

Artaxes and his honourable comrades observed the shadow of grey emerging from their port. The Musters wriggled out of Oggsfleet in a reckless formation, their frontlines scattered and their flanks exposed. The Meridium King smiled soundly to himself as he watched the uneducated enemy crawl slowly towards him.

"Prepare the block formations," ordered Artaxes finally.

Dariuss was now the only remaining companion beside the King. Lucifer, who had become a stranger to battle, had ridden off to the western flank and Milano had ridden off to the eastern flank. They were to command their own separate block formation. Unlike at Villach where there had been only one, this time there was to be three. Lucifer and Milano could both be heard roaring out their orders at the forces they had been given command over, their powerful voices echoing throughout the silent Meridium post.

The Meridium army of around one thousand three hundred broke the silence and began creating an awfully loud ruckus as they all broke off into their sections. The bang of their shields and the clatter of their swords caused the risen mound that they stood upon to hummer and vibrate. Lengthy gaps had begun appearing between the frontlines as the three line thick block formations had begun forming in the east and the western flanks of the silver force. It was obvious that this formation had been practised and used many times before. The men merged into their designated positions among their selected leaders' formation. There was no fuss nor confusion.

Artaxes remained motionless. He still stared out at the Muster force that had completely left the port and had made their way within half a mile of himself and his army. Three thousand men hadn't sounded like much to Artaxes back in his feasting hall, but now that he could see them in the open field marching whilst they shouted, cursed and screamed at him, a feeling of uncertainty and dread took over a little. But Artaxes Destain was a brave King, an insane one at that but a brave one none the less. His insanity was probably a good thing at this present time. No King who was even remotely sane would have attempted a retaking like this.

The King as usual looked the part in his battle armour, the same suit that he usually wore when riding to war, however the chest piece had been re-forged because of the damage it took retaking Villach. The lightning bolt slash down the centre had been connected and varnished flat. Dariuss too looked rather spectacular, coated in his excellent silver armour which was cloaked with his blue King's Guards cape. He still sat upon his valiant horse awaiting the Oakland threat to reach him.

The central portion of the Meridium force tended to its task.

They had waited until the other two box formations had fully formed before they began. They without order began swarming around Artaxes and Dariuss like a mother wrapping up her new born in a wolf quilted cover. The final preparations were being made, and with Artaxes's block almost fully connected, the men were ready to battle. Each box formation consisted of about four hundred men.

The men's mouths were silent but their glistening bodies created an unpleasant tune as they marched around their King creating a perfect square. Artaxes still didn't move. He didn't even seem to be paying attention to his assembling men.

The corners of his man-made square were tightly fitted with the bodies of Meridium men, the rows securely set strong also by the bodies of Meridium men.

They were ready.

Each Commander and his regiment waited patiently, everyone's eyes fixed on the movement of the closing enemy that had picked up a light jog.

The three superb formations all continued to observe, each with their Commander sitting high upon horseback in the centre of the squared formation, and the Western army yet again took up its silent stance. The professionalism of the formation excelled anyone else's, their rows were so straight, each front man's shield was perfectly level with the man's next to him and every swordsman stood with his hand upon his sword handle. It was a pure spectacle to even see, not a whisker out of place and not a foot out of formation.

Individual men began picking out their own targets as the faces of the Oakland rebels became visible. It was an immaculate sight, every soldier's chest piece still managed to shine from afar, even with the demonic dark weather creeping above them. It was probable that a heavy downpour was going to play audience to the bloodbath that was about unfold.

Each block had three rows of men to the east and the west and, to the front and the back, all rows were connected at the corner. The first row consisted of spearmen, who held their long shields up from the ground and pointed their lancing spears outwards. The second and third rows were the swordsmen infantry, their job to cut down any enemies that managed to break in through the shield wall, or to replace any spearmen that were killed. The key to this formation being successful was that the first row would hold strong and not be breached. If the box formation was breached, the battle was more or less lost.

The view for any bird that hovered above would be breathtaking, three rich silver boxes moving out to claim back their lands.

Artaxes finally moved his body, leaning to his left to address his most favoured King's Guard, Dariuss.

"Rise and rise again, my son," said the King for the first time since the war. Artaxes had no interest for a speech this time, he just wanted the job done. His men already knew what to do, and what was at stake. They would fight just as gallantly without one.

Dariuss however did feel the need.

"Rise and rise again!" he screamed as he pulled out his sword and held it up into the now drizzling sky.

The men took these words as their command to mobilise, and so they did.

The surrounding hills and fields growled angrily as the footsteps of over a thousand outnumbered Meridium soldiers smashed their metal heels deep into its surface. Artaxes's regiment led the attack, the Meridium's planning to meet their foes head on.

Artaxes was making a habit of entering his battles first lately, not a regular tactic for a King. He swayed his hips back and fourth gently to match the pace of his trotting horse. His formation had picked up a light jog also.

Milano's regiment also jogged towards the Musters, slightly to the King's left, about a hundred yards behind. Lucifer was positioned to the King's right hand side, picking up more and more pace with every stride. It had been over ten years since First General Lucifer had swung his sword at a living being. It was time to see if the stories about his fighting style were true.

"Hold the formation upon impact!" screamed out Dariuss as the Oakland Musters now sprinted recklessly out towards the three approaching death boxes. The Musters charged with no strategic plan, their lines were broken and thinned and they were without officers. But still they charged bravely, seconds away from Artaxes's force.

The battlefield cried out in agony as the first smash of the Musters colliding fiercely against the shields of the King's front row shocked it tremendously. The smash of the bodies bouncing against the Meridium shields sounded like an old volcano rupturing its bowls.

The formation came to a standstill as they could not fight properly whilst moving. The best way to completely use this tactic to your benefit was to have every man stand strong and dig his heels into the ground whilst holding his shield up powerfully. By doing this, the second row could hack their swords over the top of the spearmen, slaughtering all who dared break the brick wall formation.

Dariuss quickly kicked his horse into action. He strode forward until his horse was at the back of the third row of the northern face of the regiment. He screamed out inspirational words and also many curses to the frontline of spearmen that were fighting. They would push their shields out, disorientating the enemy before quickly stabbing out with their spears, a tiring but effective technique against even the strongest of foes.

The spearmen held their ground well despite the constant forceful bash and push that their shields received. Hundreds of Musters swarmed Artaxes's regiment, and the regiments to the east and west were also engaged. The wrongful invaders attempted a different technique to breach the shield wall, crouching down low and trying to swipe their rusty weapons at the legs of the spearmen. But the long hefty shields covered the whole of the soldiers' bodies, right up to the wielder's neck. The reckless Muster technique provided an opportunity for the spearmen to tower their lances over their defensive shields, lunging down into the foolish Oakland soldiers.

The air filled with screams and yelps, most coming from the skewered Musters that bashed pointlessly against the Meridium shields. Any Meridium soldier that did fail to hold his shield up was almost instantly cut down, a horde of enemy swords almost instantly seizing their rare opportunity by killing the weakest of men in the shield wall.

Any spearmen that did fall were almost immediately replaced, their shields and spears picked up by one of the swordsmen in the second row.

The bodies of the Oakland Musters began piling up right at the very feet of the Meridium frontlines.

The tactic was working.

Artaxes began patrolling the centre of his man-made square. He moved up and down, checking to see if all of his rows were remaining intact, checking for any weak points that might be used against them. The Oakland numbers were greater than the Meridium's still, despite the hundreds of dead they had suffered already. They had sacrificed so many men just by trying to create an opening in the formation, they knew that if they were able to breach the box formation, the Meridiums would face certain defeat.

The Meridium King suddenly focused his attention on the eastern side of his force. A few familiar cries and screams came from that side of the regiment, and then he saw it. A gap forming. The frontline was losing men rapidly as a pile of Musters had successfully forced four spearmen to the floor, stabbing them as they breached. Before the second row of swordsmen had managed to pick up the spears and shields in order to replace their dying comrades, they were attacked. They now duelled desperately against the small mob that had found their way in.

Artaxes leapt from his horse and pulled out his longsword. He pounded over to his struggling fighters and slithered into the lines of men. He began pushing his way to the front where the troublesome Musters were fighting with his swordsmen.

Some of the surrounding swordsmen had managed to pick up the bloody shields and squeeze into the frontline, but still a small gap remained unfilled, allowing the odd Muster to breach. Artaxes was forced to step over a couple of dead Meridium soldiers on his quest to the frontlines, which only angered him more.

The King reached the gap that had been created by a group of Oakland fighters who seemed to be breaching even further along the shield wall. They were swinging their axes hard against the tough armour of the spearmen's backs. The spearmen had no choice but to retain their strong stature. They could not break from it, not even to defend themselves against any soldiers that managed to break in behind them. They had to lay full trust in the swordsmen behind them to deal with the problem.

Artaxes quickly jumped into action. He stabbed out, piercing the flesh of the first Muster that he targeted. He then pulled his sword from the dying body and slashed left, cutting the side of a man and then right, cutting the throat of another, his sword causing devastation to the enemy.

The King was soon aided by some of the swordsmen from the second row. They cleared out the breaching Musters by stabbing into them as they attempted to pull the defending frontline away from their stern foothold. The agonising screams from the final foes faded as the Meridium swordsmen slayed them skilfully.

Artaxes had the honour of killing the last one. With two hands, he raised his sword, hacking down, knocking the enemy's axe out from his grasp. The King then spun around beautifully, whipping his sword upwards as he turned, ripping open his victim's chest brutally.

The Meridium soldiers seized their opportunity by quickly replenishing their frontline. Artaxes offered more aid, picking up a shield from one of his dead comrades and squeezing himself between two spearmen that lunged out, stabbing their victims ruthlessly. Artaxes slammed his shield into the ground and closed up the gap on the front row with his presence. The King was now fighting on the frontlines.

"My King, the north and south side are secure," urged Dariuss who had ridden his horse over to the eastern side as he noticed his King fighting. "Pull back to the centre."

But he was not rewarded with a reply. Artaxes continued to fight. He was enjoying himself.

The Meridium King was without a spear so he could not mimic the attacks that his surrounding companions carried out, so with his sword he would step out into the open and slash out to the left then out to the right, usually taking down two enemies each time he did this. Each swing was so swift and sharp, the handle of the sword rotated and spun brilliantly as he twisted his wrist around.

The battle was most definitely dealing in favour of the Meridium army. The King's armoured block was coping well now that the small weak point had been dealt with, and from Artaxes's position, he could see that Lucifer and Milano too were both dealing with the assault well enough.

Hundreds of dead Musters littered the battlefield, but their overpowering numbers slowly began taking their toll on the frontlines. Although the Meridium men were fighting well, they were beginning to tire and their strong stance was beginning to weaken, just as Dariuss had predicted.

Artaxes slashed out at an ugly enemy who came leaping towards his shield. The dirty wild of beard Muster ducked beneath the King's slash and cut out at the man beside him, killing him instantly. Artaxes slashed again, but yet again the Muster avoided the sharp swipe and engaged in a duel with a Meridium soldier to the King's right, also killing him dead rather quickly. Artaxes lowered his shield so that he could extend his arm out a little further. He stabbed his destructive foe right in the top of the chest with frustration, the crack of his enemy's collar bones loud enough for everyone nearby to hear.

King Artaxes's frustration was not because of how slimy and difficult the Muster were to kill but because of how easily his men were now being killed. Meridium soldiers were known to be very difficult to take down. But they were tiring, they were not fighting as they had been at the beginning of this battle, and with not enough men to take shifts between the lines, that meant the same men had to continue fighting right to the end. Many of the second line of swordsmen had been forced to pick up the scattered Meridium spears and take up a new position in the first row.

The northern front face was no longer secure. The Oakland fighters pushed up harder and harder and began overwhelming the spearmen that had so far held the shield wall up well.

"King Artaxes, we have been breached," Dariuss shouted, having again ridden his horse to the eastern flank of the regiment.

This time Artaxes turned to listen to him, but what he saw as he turned worried him deeply. His eyes locked onto the attack at the front of his regiment.

It was a final but desperate push from the Oakland rebels. They completely surrounded their box formation, the northern and western faces were completely outnumbered. He had to act fast.

Before the King could devise a new plan with Dariuss, the King's Guard dropped from his horse down to the ground, landing hard on his back, Dariuss's horse yelping agonisingly as a spear hung loosely from its belly.

The Musters had breached.

Artaxes looked to his northern point, forced to take his focus away from fighting the men in front of him so he could lean on his toes to see over his third row of swordsmen. Dozens of grey-clothed enemies had forced their way in, raiding the centre square with only the third row of swordsmen to challenge them. Most of the spearmen were dead and the second row of swordsmen had replaced them on the front row. The King needed to end this problem quickly before it was too late.

"Soldier, defend this point as best as you can," commanded Artaxes as he grabbed hold of one of the swordsmen who stood slightly behind him.

"Yes, my King," he confirmed. The soldier and Artaxes shuffled up against each other as they swapped positions. The King then wriggled through the second row and then the third row, falling into the open square of the formation. He ignored Dariuss who was fighting on foot, hacking away against the shield of a cowering enemy that was unlucky enough to have found himself battling against him. Artaxes quickly calculated the men he would need to take out the conquering Musters. Luckily it wasn't many as the number of intruders slowly stopped increasing as the northern face swordsmen had managed to stop the intrusion. They yet again held a strong shield wall against the enemy, trapping the Oakland infiltrators inside.

Artaxes wasted no more time observing. He gripped his sword handle tightly and sprinted to the southern face of the formation. They had not seen much action yet. Artaxes addressed the back row of swordsmen, as these men were to accompany him on his rescue mission.

"Swordsmen, with me. Come quickly with me," he ordered as he began tapping countless men on the back. Artaxes then had a small company of about thirty five men at his back. The selected soldiers stood facing the Musters that hassled the northern face. They frowned, growled and spat in an attempt to rile themselves up for a proper fight.

Artaxes stood in front of them passionately.

"There are men at the northern face that need our help! Charge, men, charge!" he screamed.

Without hesitation, the men leapt across the battered turf with their swords held high.

Artaxes led his blood-starving pack the short distance to the breaching soldiers, hitting hard against the dozens of Oakland filth that were hacking at the back row of the northern faced warriors. A wild bloodbath erupted the second the glimmering western warriors smashed sword tip first into the uninvited rebels.

The Meridium rescuers fought excellently against the straggling enemies, slicing and cutting quickly as their fresh and untested arms swung brilliantly. Unlike the rest of the King's regiment, these men hadn't had much action so they were still fresh, eager and just as vicious as their heroic King.

Dariuss was fighting his way out of a tight threat. He managed to quickly cut across an enemy that was about to lunge in towards him, and then ducked down away from another attacker whose axe was aimed for the head of the King's Guard's but it closely missed. Dariuss swung his hips around, bringing his arm and menacing sword along with it. The blade ripped open the man's side, causing the blood to gush from the wound. His blue cape swayed from side to side. Each time Dariuss swung at an enemy, his King's Guard cape flung itself around like a bannerman signalling a retreat.

The King's Guard pulled off his helmet and allowed his soaking wet black hair to dangle free. He was breathing so hard that his helmet had become a heated furnace.

"My King, look!" alerted the King's Guard who, in the process of scraping his lengthy dark hair out from his face, had found his gaze locked upon The Sink.

"Ships! Havada is here!" he shouted.

Artaxes who was currently kneeling down, forcing his blade into the heart of a young soldier, lifted his head. His face brightened at the sight, two wooden vessels gliding in across the River to aid their allies.

"See that men? Victory is close! Fight on, fight on for Meridium!" yelled the King.

Some of the surrounding soldiers finished off their duels with a deadly stab or slash and began thrusting their swords in the air passionately.

Victory was close for the Guardian King in the West.

The first attack from Havada was dispatched, a hundred flaming arrows from each ship flocking through the air like a thousand baby dragons breathing their first breath. The arrows quickly locked onto their grey targets and lunged deeply into their worn bodies. Many Oakland Musters at the back of their ranks fell unlucky victim to Havada's surprise attack. The arrows continued to hurtle through the dark spitting sky and into the unlucky foes, killing them barbarically, but the range of the ships' archers was already beginning to decrease as the Musters pushed up closer to the Meridium box formations.

CHAPTER 25
THE PRINCE'S DEPARTURE

Enly barged in through the sturdy doors and into the Prince's oval-shaped chambers. The room was tidy and wealthy, designed the same as the rest of the Palace. All the furniture was rich bark, and the walls were sanded beautifully. They were littered with golden picture frames that held painted pictures of royal legends or noble family members. It was overall a cosy lived in room, and Hector had had the honour of spending every night there since he was but a small boy.

"My Prince, the escort is ready and the nobles are awaiting your presence in the main hall," said Enly who was wearing his full suit of armour.

Hector was standing still, looking over his bed and up onto the walls, inspecting a painting of his father. He was still disappointed that his father was not going to attend the ceremony in Versidia, even though he knew it could not be helped.

Hector was dressed in a creamy pale tunic that had neat golden tassels dangling down from his shoulders. He had dressed himself in the most comfortable clothes he owned. He was after all about to embark on a ten day long carriage ride to the holy city of Versidia. Enly on the other hand, and the rest of the escorts, would have to play on tradition and travel in their full armoured suits.

Hector had been waiting for his servants to finish off carrying out the boxes that he was to take with him to Versidia, monitoring what they were taking and telling them what he wanted to be left. He took a break from ordering his servants when he heard Enly speak.

The young Prince began marching across the room towards him. As he walked, his attention was diverted to Riycard Badstuber who had just walked in the room and over to Hector's boxes. He was also in his full armour which aroused suspicion.

"Is he coming with us?" muttered Hector as he embraced his friend and escort with a strong handshake. Enly received his Prince's hand and shrugged, turning to Riycard and pressing the matter.

"Are you coming along as part of the escort?" he asked loud enough so that Riycard could hear him.

Riycard picked up the biggest box in the pile, the one that had the Prince's battle armour inside. He walked off towards the door and stopped. "I am, my father deemed it wise to increase the security and escort."

"Does Dreyo have that authority?" asked Enly.

Riycard smiled sarcastically. "He does in the absence of the King."

Hector quickly interrupted the petty discussion. "No need for that box. I am not to wear my own armour. The Versidians provide me with armour on my arrival," he said.

Riycard looked back at the Prince with confusion.

"It's so I cannot be identified in the arena," he added. "All twelve of us are to wear identical helmets and armour so that alliances may not be forged within."

Riycard held onto the box for a few more moments, then slowly crouched down, dropping the box back down on the dustless floor.

"Oh I see," he said strangely, the fact that Hector was not bringing his armour along seeming to have struck Riycard strangely. He behaved very peculiarly as he latched onto a different box. "This one?" he asked.

"Yes, thank you," replied Hector.

Riycard forced a smile before leaving the Prince's chambers.

"Well, that's that then," said Hector who didn't seem too fussed about dwelling on Riycard's strange behaviour.

Enly shrugged with disinterest. "Been in the whorehouse all night, I reckon," he mocked.

Hector laughed as he put his hand on Enly's shoulder, guiding him over to the door.

Hector led the way as they left the chambers and headed down along the royal halls. Enly kept his distance as the two of them travelled down the small steps that led from the royal halls, down into the eastern halls. Hector remained silent for the whole journey. As much as he tried not to think about his Selection, he did. It was in fact all he could think about, and now he had to face everyone he had ever known one last time before departing.

Enly came to a standstill as the two of them approached the end of the eastern hall. Hector was to walk out alone into the fishbowl-like foyer where everyone awaited their future King.

The small chatter instantly stopped as the Brigantium heir wandered slowly through the archway, stopping before them. Two perfectly shaped lines of people had formed from the archway leading right up to the double doors that would take him outside. The floor of the main hall wasn't visible, so many people had crowded behind the noble line of men and women. Everyone in the city had shown up to pay homage to Hector, and those who could not fit in the Palace swarmed the Palace gate.

Dreyo Badstuber awaited the Prince by the door. He stood proudly looking down the long lines of silent people, finally locking his eyes onto Hector. The two lines of people consisted of every person that held position within the city of Brigantium, every General, Knight, advisor and military expert stood awaiting Hector to walk between them. This was another tradition of the Eastern Horse Lords. As far back as the existence of the Ringfold family this tradition had existed. It was in a way one last farewell in case the Prince did not return.

Hector took a deep breath as he stared out into the royal lobby, staring dauntingly at the hundreds of faces that all burned their eyes into him. Brushing the nerves aside, Hector took his first step with Enly a few feet behind him. The Prince remained straight-faced, ignoring all the compliments, farewells and congratulations that he received from the supporters. He felt like a lost child wandering nervously through a haunted forest.

As Hector continued to walk through the middle of the hordes of people, he suddenly felt the reality of what was happening. A sickly feeling sprang through his belly allowing fear to take over. He desperately tried to keep a solid stern face, even though he would have liked nothing more than to go back to his chambers and curl up.

Hector eventually showed some acknowledgement of his supporters as he passed Voltor and Pscies, two of the Royal Guards. They both bowed lightly to him and were rewarded with a gentle wink. The sight of two of his Guardians and friends managed to steady the Prince's swaying mind for a moment, at least until he reached Dreyo Badstuber.

"Prince Hector, you leave this Palace today as a Prince and a boy," said Dreyo Badstuber as Hector finished his walk of Selection. Dreyo was filling in for Tobias, as part of the leaving ceremony should have involved the Prince's father speaking the words to the Selection challenger.

Hector turned to the people, preparing himself to speak the words.

"I, Hector Ringfold, son of Tobias Ringfold, today set out on my journey to the holy city of Versidia. I leave this Palace a boy and a Prince but I will return as a King and a man." The Prince spoke brilliantly. Despite his nerves, he managed to speak the honourable words without a stutter. Hector then bowed deeply to the lines of noble people.

Dreyo began the applause, slapping his hands together and signalling everyone else to join in, which they did. Hector re-straightened his back and turned for the door.

The sound of applause still ruptured from the Royal Palace as Hector trod out onto the Palace grounds, where his escort waited.

The day was as pleasant as any other day. The sun blazed in the sky, shining down brightly on the gardens of the Palace, whilst Hector took in what could be a final look at the extraordinary surroundings of his father's home.

Gondogon was standing by the first carriage that had just pulled up, alongside Riycard Badstuber, both fully armoured in silver plates, each with their yellow cape covering their backs. Hector was to ride in the beautiful golden carriage with them, but first he was to embrace his teachers.

Gideon and the whole company were present, all except Andrus. Word had reached Gideon's ear that his brother had taken refuge down by the city's entrance, living in a stable. He had begun tending to the horses in what Gideon hoped to be his way of grieving. Gideon was still hopeful that Andrus would soon return to his natural state.

"Hector, are you ready?" asked Gideon who stood beside Nuallan, Oslo and Josanne. Josanne was first to embrace her Prince. She stepped out and shook his hand roughly before he could provide Gideon with a false reply.

"May God watch over you, my Prince," Josanne said sweetly before stepping back into the line.

Oslo stepped out next. "You're a great fighter, Prince Hector. I wish you all the best."

"I admire your courage, lad. Good luck," said Nuallan who embraced Hector also with a strong handshake. Nuallan although speaking respectfully, was in a furious mood. He was not happy that he was being left behind. It was very rare that Gideon and Nuallan had been separated for more than a day since their banishment, and he did not like it.

Nuallan stepped back allowing Gideon to say a few words.

"I will be in the carriage behind you," Gideon said. "Every night we will go over the steps I have taught you. You have nothing to worry about. I can assure you your sword fighting skill will exceed the ability of anyone who will go up against you. Now, are you ready?" Gideon was as usual dressed in his rugged black overthrow, except this time he had a metal chest piece hidden under the black newly sown cover up.

Hector nodded before thanking the company for their kind words. "Thank you all for your support. When I return and eventually come into the throne, all of you will be held close, that is a promise," he announced kindly. He then turned from them and trotted down the steps towards the second carriage.

Faizer was standing there dressed in solid sliver armour with the Brigantium cape flowing behind him.

"You truly do look like a man of Brigantium now, General," said Hector as he held out his hand.

Faizer laughed loudly as he met the Prince's soft grasp.

"Nothing he hasn't earned," said Gideon as he attempted to climb into the second carriage.

"My Prince, wait. Wait, Hector," shouted Farren Chalk who came bounding out of the Palace doors.

Everyone halted what they were doing in order to see what the noble man wanted.

"My son Romford is to accompany you, my Prince," insisted Farren as he strutted down the steps with his son at his back. Romford was dressed in his armour, the same as everyone else who was participating in this voyage.

"No need for that," said Riycard Badstuber who came wandering over from the first carriage. "I am to help escort the Prince to Versidia, along with Gondogon, Gideon and Enly. There is no need for Romford." He was desperate to prevent the company of Romford.

Farren verbally attacked Riycard harshly. "That is not for you to decide, boy. My son will ride alongside you, by request of the King," snapped Farren.

Riycard cowered back and kept his mouth closed. He turned and walked back to his carriage, boarding it anxiously.

Gideon and Faizer seemed slightly taken back by the brief argument that had just erupted between the noble families of Brigantium, but Hector seemed less bothered. He was used to it.

"By word of my father, you say?" asked Hector.

"Indeed, my Prince. Now, we have no time to waste. You must be on your way," replied Farren sternly.

Gideon observed Farren closely. Although Hector and the others didn't think much of Farren's desperate attempt to get his son on board, he did. He found it very peculiar indeed. One of Gideon's many talents was spotting when something was out of place, a talent that he had inherited from his father Artaxes.

"Very well," announced the Prince. "Romford switch with Enly, you will ride up top with me. Enly, you will ride with Gideon and Faizer."

"Very well," agreed Enly. He stepped up and climbed into the second carriage, his loosely fitted armour clattering nosily as he stretched his leg up the wooden steps, throwing himself inside. Faizer waited till the steps became available before climbing inside also.

Romford left the presence of the Prince and his teacher and walked to the first carriage, trailing his hand across the back of one of the creamy Huskarian horses that led Gideon's transport. He seemed rather pleased about the fact he was coming along. Romford glided around the backend of the first golden carriage before boarding it after Gondogon who had just climbed inside.

"Don't look so worried," Hector assured Gideon. "It's just a power battle between the Badstuber family and the Chalk family. Neither of them can stand being left out of any of my father's plans."

Gideon stared at the back of Farren Chalk. Farren, satisfied with his work, left the Prince without a proper farewell, walking back up the steps only to be met by Dreyo Badstuber.

"I see you swindled your son a place, then," snapped Dreyo who really didn't look too happy about Farren's late arrival and need to add to the escort.

"Well, someone has to keep an eye on your corrupt son now, don't they?" countered Farren brutally.

Before Dreyo could reply, Farren barged past him, walking back into the Palace.

Dreyo's frustration was growing, but he contained it. He was in fact acting in King Tobias's stead, and he had to tend to the final part of his job. He stood with his feet close together, looking down at the carriages.

The coachman upon the carriage waited for the doors to slam shut as Gideon and Hector climbed the steps. Hector climbed into the carriage first, and then Gideon, but Gideon stalled. He caught sight of a woman dressed in a black dress standing by the Palace doors. It was the woman who had haunted Gideon's thoughts with her strange behaviour. Yet again, she was staring at Gideon, burning her hatred into him with her very stare. Gideon looked back with confusion. A few moments passed as the two of them stared each other out, until eventually Gideon broke from her line of sight, ducking down and entering the carriage.

Once the slam of the doors shook the carriages, the coachmen whipped gently on the Huskarian horses' backs.

Faizer and Enly sat beside each other in the gorgeous carriage. Even though they were both armoured, they could still enjoy the silky soft of the velvet layered interior. They both stared with envy at Gideon who was dressed only in his overthrow. He lounged across the cosy seats happily.

"So Gideon, Hector and myself discussed a plan for when we reach Hornton's Watch," revealed Enly.

"And that is?" asked Gideon.

"Since you're still lurking about in your scruffy overthrow," joked Enly, "you can act as the coachman. A few miles prior to our arrival at Hornton's watch, we still stop, allowing you to get out and take control of the reins."

Gideon, who still didn't seem confident about the plan, shrugged, uninterested. "If they notice me, we will all be killed," he stated boldly.

Faizer gulped hard. The disguised General had grown tired of fighting. In fact even the thought of clashing swords worried him. He worried that it was only a matter of time before he met the same fate as his brother Doxass. Faizer craved peace, and Brigantium was willing to provide. One last mission, one last quest and Faizer could live out his days in peace.

"Hornton wouldn't dare attempt an attack on the Prince's escort. He would hang for it," said Enly, who as usual overestimated the authority that his people had in Requirium.

"And you think The High King would so easily allow one of his most favoured puppets of war to be hung?" quizzed Gideon whose mood was truly one of a miserable nature.

"The High King's strings do not reach as far as Brigantium. He does not hold as much authority in the East as he thinks," argued Enly.

"Well, one day we might find out for sure," added Gideon patronisingly.

Enly looked back with a touch of anger at his new comrade's words, but he said nothing. He slid open his shutter and took one last look at his home before he left.

It seemed as though the full city's population was out to wave farewell to Hector by the time his carriage reached the main gate. Women and children threw cut flowers at the two bowl-shaped carriages, screaming the Prince's name proudly as they threw.

Faizer as usual was mesmerised by the sight. He admired the loyalty of the eastern people greatly. He would have never experienced anything like this where he was from, the town of Vaughan. Faizer's home was a small town, even smaller than Rhoden. They had no Kings or great halls, massive feasts or royal tournaments. Faizer along with the rest of the population of Vaughan spent their days scavenging, farming and fending off raider gangs. This was a whole new world to him, and he liked it.

"We're at the gate," stated Enly as the carriage came to a standstill behind the Prince's.

Gideon sat up and opened his shutter, looking out as the screaming, cheering and chanting got louder. Thousands of people had swarmed the city's entrance, all ecstatic in celebration for their Prince's Selection. Gideon smiled as he scanned the crowd. He too admired the loyalty and love of these people.

"Andrus!" alerted Faizer who was looking out of his own shutter.

Gideon dived across the carriage and looked out of Faizer's window.

Andrus was standing leaning against a wooden fence of a practice field, pale faced, glaring over at Gideon's carriage.

"Hopefully on our return he will be the man that he once was," said Faizer sadly as he struggle to see out of the window. He slid back into his chair, rearranging his plated shoulder piece as he slouched. Faizer fell into a similar mood to Gideon. Every time he saw Andrus, it reminded him of that dark day inside of Vanghale, a tragedy that no living member of the company would ever forget.

Gideon remained on Faizer and Enly's side of the carriage, his head as far out of the horse lead escort as he could manage. He looked sadly back at his young brother who was staring into Gideon's eyes from afar, still no emotion or reaction taking hold of his widowed brother's once characterful face. Gideon squeezed his head out even further as he slowly began losing sight of Andrus as the horses kick-started the journey again, the gate having been opened and the carriages trundling out of city and off across the Eastern lands.

Their journey had begun.

CHAPTER 26
OGGSFLEET PORT – PART 2

"Loose!" commanded Havada's Lieutenant with a deep and clear tone. The archers upon the newly-arrived ship continued to set their arrows ablaze, launching them across the river and port, down onto the Oakland Musters. The archers were positioned all along the deck of the ship, their bows not of a delicate fashion, the wood rather chipped and the string not as tight. The Meridiums were not known for their skill in archery, and nor did they want to be. It was rare that King Artaxes would ever take a legion of archers into battle in fact.

Havada stood by the edge of his Meridium-flagged ship, staring out at the battle. He watched angrily as his countrymen remained surrounded. Despite some of the northern streets of Oggsfleet being in the way, Havada could still clearly see the battle unfolding. Artaxes and his Commanders had fought very well so far, but with their numbers shrinking and the Musters not shrinking fast enough, they truly faced a daunting challenge, especially if Havada's attack was not successful.

"More arrows. Fire at will," declared Havada as he grew hungry for blood. The out of favour King's Guard was dressed up in his scaly silver armour, his blue cloak whipping at his ankles as the wind and rain really began beating on The Sink. The sword clashing sounds in the background could easily be mistaken for thrashes of lightning as the clouded sky darkened.

Although the two swaying ships rained down storms of arrows, the Musters continued to fight. They did not flee as quickly as Dariuss had previously predicted. The back of their ranks were being slaughtered but the front of the force still battled viciously against the strong Meridium shield walls. Havada could see from his position upon his vessel that one of the box formations was struggling, Milano's. Artaxes seemed to have his under control and Lucifer also, but Milano was not handling the attack anymore. He had lost too many men.

There was only one way for the other Commanders to save Milano. If his box formation became completely overrun, the other two formations would be forced to disband, breaking the formation and falling into an open fight. It would leave the flanks of the two remaining box formations open and exposed. The men would be completely overwhelmed. This was not what Artaxes wanted to do, but if he wanted to save his Commander and men, he would have no choice.

Havada squinted his eyes as he noticed the little blobs of grey flooding in through the various gaps that Milano's shield wall had revealed. Milano himself could just about be made out as he fought upon horseback in the middle of his broken square. Without help, Milano would soon fall.

"Signal the other ship to target the boats in the dock. Terrify the filthy fucks," Havada ordered his Lieutenant. He remembered back in the feasting hall when Dariuss suggested trapping the Musters by burning their ships that currently all floated in a messy bundle around the harbour. Havada hoped this tactic would cause the Musters upon the battlefield to panic, relieving some of the pressure on Milano's broken force.

The Lieutenant accepted his orders and trotted across the packed deck with two white flags in his hand. The flags were used to send orders from one ship to another. The Lieutenant would hold them and wave them in a certain motion to deliver a specific order or command.

Havada's second in command crossed the decking, slipping between the concentrating bowmen as he ducked, dived and dashed in and out. The armoured Lieutenant then climbed up the ladder to the Quarter Deck, moving to the end of the ship and waving both flags in an angled motion.

This signal to anyone who was not part of the Meridium naval fleet would have meant nothing, but the sailor on the opposite boat whose job it was to await commands from Havada understood the message almost immediately. The white clothed sailor pelted across the opposite ship to inform his Lieutenant what Havada had ordered so silently. Within the minute, the scorching blaze of arrows flooding from the second ship changed its direction. The burning death sticks now swooped down in the direction of the docks. One by one, the unmanned Oakland boats set alight, crackling as they singed.

"The command is given, the enemy ships have already begun sinking to the riverbed," informed the Lieutenant as he marched back across the deck.

"Good, now focus our attention on the western blockade, towards Milano. His wall is failing, but we must get closer so that our arrows are more effective. We can risk sending the ship a little closer to shore. Do it now," commanded Havada who set out to save Milano.

The blue and silver of the Meridium army upon the battlefield was beginning to fade as even Lucifer and the King's shield walls were shrinking drastically in number. Artaxes, due to his own private struggle, had failed to see the pressure that was being applied to his western force. If Milano fell then so too would Artaxes. The battered Musters still drove hard against the Meridium ranks, bearing a little less than half of their original three thousand man force that they started off with.

Havada's ship continued to shoot gangs of arrows up into the dark sky as the vessel glided ever closer to shore. The ship bore left as it flanked the dock and found itself close to a green field that surrounded the tiny sandy shore just to the west of Oggsfleet's central market and dock.

The archers were scattered all across the ship, many of them sailors that would have to tend to the ship until they reached their destination. They were not that well educated on how to use a sword. Their skill set was archery and sailing, although they could still swing one if needed. They were dressed in very light chainmail that covered only portions of their chests, thighs and back, the rest of their body in cheap black fabric. Considering most of these men were sailors, they possessed an excellent shot. Some of them had already confirmed a dozen kills which was pretty impressive considering the distance between them and the rebellious Oakland Musters.

"My Lord Havada, look!! Look!" bellowed one of the officers who darted across the ship's deck.

Havada prised his view away from the scrappy fight on the west side to see what was the matter.

"Look!" the man repeated whilst pointing his shaking finger out into the centre of Oggsfleet Port.

Havada removed his helmet, allowing his stringy blond hair to fall free. He squinted lightly so he could pinpoint what the Musters were doing.

"Turn us around! We're too close. Turn us around!" he announced, horrified.

The Oakland Musters, well aware of the ships causing the destruction, had sent a squadron of men back into the heart of Oggsfleet and they had begun dragging something out onto the dock. A catapult.

A single catapult would not normally frighten an invading fleet, but with just two ships present, a weapon like that could cause a devastating blow to the King's plan. A single shot if launched accurately could tear a ship like Havada's in two.

"Archers target that catapult. Take it down, take it down," ordered the King's Guard as his ship slowly began drifting back off away from the western shore. One at a time the frightened bowmen began redirecting their aim towards the squadron of over a dozen enemies assembling the catapult.

"Quickly, destroy them!" he commanded ferociously as the unsettled look on his face increased.

The archers took aim and released their arrows high in the

sky towards the counter-attacking siege men. The odd arrow managed to drift into the bodies of the attacking Musters, but most just dug into the wooden frame of the loading catapult.

They had run out of time.

The first they heard was a terrible wicked whip as the mountainous flaming bolder came sizzling through the stormy winds towards Havada's ship.

"Brace yourselves!" ordered Havada desperately as he jumped back from the edge of the ship, diving onto his belly just below the mast.

Everyone on the battlefield stopped for a moment as the rupturing smash of the boulder ripped through the ship's mast, the impact creating an earthquake-like rumble. Havada removed his protective hands from his face as the demonic creaking above frightened him, but what he saw terrified him. Havada's eyes widened. He tried to pull himself to his feet as the destroyed mast collapsed, dropping down heavily onto the deck.

The Meridium surprise attack was failing, something that the people of Meridium were all but too familiar with. Havada again pulled his bruised body up and desperately attempted to rally his men.

"Focus fire on the catapult!" he screamed as loud as he could, but he was not rewarded with positive results. The catapult's shot had devoured the ship's sails and mast, causing the archers and sailors to panic horrifically, some men even diving overboard as parts of the ship set aflame.

Havada knew he must react quickly. With his archers abandoning their posts, he attempted to signal the other ship. He looked around in search of his Lieutenant. He needed the command flags which he suddenly saw, lying on the floor in the grasp of his crushed Lieutenant.

The collapsed mast had fallen down onto him. He was dead. Havada ruthlessly snatched them from his dead officer and charged beneath what remained of the burning mast in an attempt to reach the Quarter Deck.

"Incoming!" warned a terrified sailor who dived from the

centre of the burning ship's deck. Havada curled around to see where the missile was coming from, but it was too late to take cover. As he turned, the ginormous boulder smashed down through the top deck, ripping all the way through the ship and out of the bottom. The ship was doomed.

Havada who again found himself on the floor, now found it a little more difficult to stand up as the ship crumbled in on itself, creating an increasing slope leading down into the water. The ship was sinking and it was taking everyone down with it.

A devastating moan vibrated the gentle waves in The Sink. Every crack that the wooden decking made disturbed the water even more, causing it to slam harder against the riverbed-destined ship. With all his might, Havada grabbed hold of the base of the wooden mast as the ship broke in two. With his foot, he lunged out, digging his heel behind a wooden ledge. The King's Guard needed to keep on the ship until he could remove his armour. If he failed to do so, he would drown. But he was short on time, the water lurking up through the middle of the ship as it devoured the wooden vessel with ease.

In a state of panic and quick thinking, Havada quickly released the straps on his armour. The water was rising even faster through the middle of the boat like an abyssal nightmare crawling up to snatch its victim. Havada shuffled his body desperately as he still tried to loosen the armour's hold on his body. He was destined for the water and he knew it. He also knew that if he didn't remove his armour before he slid in, he would die an unpleasant death so he continued to gnaw at his straps with his one free hand whilst his comrades slid past him at speed, disappearing into the man-devouring water.

With one last shrug, Havada managed to wriggle out of his armour. He then rolled onto his back as he held onto anything that could keep him on the snapped ship. But it was to no avail, he lost his grip as the invading water splashed at his hands, forcing his grip to fail. The King's Guard began sliding with pace down the risen deck and down into the hellish river.

The freezing temperature of The Sink took its toll on Havada as he fell into the water. Because of the speed that he slid, he found himself rather deep beneath the surface. His vision was blurred as the water pressed against his eyes, but the one thing he could make out was the scattered soldiers and sailors around him. They too struggled to remove their armour, but some of them were not as lucky as Havada had been, their straps were too tight.

The minority of the sailors and archers that managed to free themselves from their armour, swam for the shore, keeping hold of only one thing, their swords. As for the ones who didn't manage to remove their armour, the river soon became their grave.

Havada made for the surface, his cheeks swelling as he began running short of air. His arms created a motion like a baby bird trying to fly for the first time, but he was tiring. The harder he thrust, the heavier his arms and body became. But he had no choice but to thrust more, his life depended on it.

As Havada almost reached the surface, he heard an unusual tune coming from above. It sounded a lot like a chorus of beaked birds singing happily. But the tune was a little too deep for it to be birds. Although the war cry-like tune intrigued him, he had more important things to worry about.

The drowning King's Guard swam the small distance, eventually lurching out of the water like a trout escaping a net. He gasped so hard that the skin on his face sucked right into his cheekbones.

The screaming and crying of the burning Meridium sailors shocked the river, but that sound slowly got drowned out as the strange horn-like sound erupted again. Havada pivoted his body around in the freezing water and looked to the hill beyond Oggsfleet. That was where the noise was coming from.

"My God," he muttered to himself as the sound of war horns attracted his attention to the yellow caped reinforcements. Tobias Ringfold and his army of horses and infantry had arrived.

Tobias was sitting upon his gallant horse facing out over the scrappy battle. General Koos sat astride his horse beside the Eastern Horse Lord King, dressed in his Meridium armour. What a rare sight it was to see a yellow-cloaked warrior and a blue-cloaked warrior preparing to ride into war together, as allies.

"Look men, reinforcements are here. Now swim, swim to shore and take up arms. I want that catapult taken out," urged Havada, grabbing the attention of any man close to him. Many of his crew were scattered about in the water, but with the inspirational words from their Commander and the sight of the Eastern Horse Lords marching over the mound, they found the strength and power they needed in order to drag themselves from the water to fight on. Their ship may have been sunk, their bodies armourless, but they were men of Meridium, and they would fight to the very last man.

Every survivor splashed though the water in an attempt to reach the shore. They didn't have long to take out the catapult before it destroyed the other ship. Fortunately the remaining ship sat a little further out across The Sink. The catapult would struggle to hit its mark at such a distance, but nevertheless it tried. The bombing sound of the catapult still shook the river as it tried to crush the final threat, but each shot smashed into the murderous water.

The ship still rained down its hellish arrows upon the Oakland's fading transport ships. Very few remained. They managed to burn the boats with ease whilst keeping clear of the rounded missiles that splashed inaccurately around them.

"With me, men, take out that catapult!" ordered Havada as he pulled his drenched body up and out of the rough water. He signalled every man around him that had managed to make it out alive. Almost thirty men all picked themselves up and clutched their swords.

The catapult sat in the centre of the port just before the docks, not even half a mile away from where Havada and his remaining force had just emerged. Wasting no more time, Havada led his team across the small sandy shore and then the misty grass towards the surrounding huts that encircled Oggsfleet's southern point.

Havada moved in silence, his men too. The catapult team had no idea that Havada was approaching from the west. The team crossed through the thin streets of Oggsfleet, diving, slithering and darting through the alleys until they burst out onto the docks, taking the Musters by surprise. The catapult had fired its last shot, and a vicious one at that, the burning boulder skimming the ship's mast.

The Oakland catapult team whipped out their swords as the drenched Meridium team sprinted towards them. Havada made sure he led the pack and hit first. His victim hadn't even drawn his sword in time before Havada slashed devastatingly across his face, dropping him to the floor. The rest of the men smashed hard against the helpless Oakland fighters that attempted to flee without resistance, but the Musters had just destroyed the men's ship along with many of their friends. Havada's men wanted revenge.

Out on The Sink, the Lieutenant on the second ship had noticed Havada and his rallying force so he decided that he would dock the ship so that he could link up with Havada's men.

Having successfully destroyed the Musters' transport ships and boats, he sailed towards the harbour, avoiding the burning blaze. Although the battle for Oggsfleet was being fought out brutally a mile away from the port by the King and his best fighters, a small squad of naval units could soon take it back before that battle was actually won.

At the docks, Havada's troops quickly tracked the catapult team, catching them almost immediately. These Musters were probably the most unfortunate ones of all as they got cut down. They endured a barbaric execution as the Meridium men stabbed constantly into their breaking bodies. The crunch of the dying men's bones echoed through ghostly streets that were all that stood between Havada and the Meridium King.

"Turn that catapult around quickly, turn it!" he ordered his men.

Havada did not participate in the task he set out for his men, his mind was dwelling on the sight his eyes had laid upon only minutes ago. He was not sure but he assumed that the yellow riders upon the hill were the Brigantiums. In a desperate need to find out, he ran out of the square and up a street, moving with speed and precision as he pelted up the steep empty street, armourless and alone.

"Koos, you did it. I don't believe it," he whispered to himself as he saw the battlefield. He'd travelled through the streets that surrounded the port and docks and set his eyes upon the gruesome field that was the home to over a thousand dead men. The massacre was only about a mile or so away from where he stood.

Havada observed the Brigantium reinforcements upon the hill in shock. He still couldn't believe that Koos had managed to get the support of the Eastern King. Havada stood with his sword by his side, staring off over to the towering hills. He noticed a rider galloping across the frontline with his sword in the air, and Havada could only assume that it was Tobias.

The King's Guard looked at the thick wide line of black horses, standing looking down about two miles away from Artaxes, Milano and Lucifer. All of a sudden confusion struck Havada. Milano's force who he had recently witnessed being breached had been completely scattered. The shield walls were no longer existent and the men fought in a scattered ball to the left of Artaxes's still coping block.

The failure of Milano's block formation meant that Artaxes and First General Lucifer had to break their formations, creating a long line. Artaxes would no doubt be furious that he had to break the formations, but if he wanted to claim the glory of this battle, it would have to be done.

The men from Artaxes's force broke the shield wall and linked up with Milano's regiment whilst the right side of his force linked up with Lucifer, his shield wall now disbanded. The Meridiums were making a last stand, and unless Tobias rode soon, the westerners could well be defeated.

Havada continued to watch with frustration as he saw his countrymen hang on for dear life. Suddenly a screech whistled over his head. In a state of panic, he cowered as the missile rushed above him. The burning boulder fired from his enemy's catapult by his allies smashed devastatingly into the back of the Musters that still out numbered Artaxes two to one. The Oakland Musters had a little over a thousand men whilst Artaxes had around six hundred. As much as the Meridium King would deny it, he needed Tobias and he needed him now. His men were exhausted, they had fought non-stop for over an hour.

"Havada, me and my men are with you. What is your move?" asked the Lieutenant from the second ship. He had docked his boat and brought his one hundred men to the exhausted King's Guard's position. The survivors from Havada's ship had come also.

Havada turned as the sound of mobilising men startled him. He looked at them and felt a great sense of pride. He was going to charge the back of the Musters with only a little over a hundred men.

The King's Guard tried to speak but his voice was drowned out as a demonic war horn shattered the battlefield. Yet again Tobias Ringfold signalled his presence, except this time his army began to mobilise. The ground shook like a volcano as two thousand Starchitect horses began picking up the pace, the horses magnificently forming a perfect spearhead formation as they slowly trotted down from the hill. The great black and yellow force strolled across the field. The obliteration of the Oakland Musters was about to begin.

Havada turned and spoke to the men. "I say we go out there and give these Oakland fucks one last hammering. What do you say, men?" he asked passionately.

"Yeahhh!" screamed the force.

Havada smiled at the courage of his men.

"To victory, sons of Artaxes! Charge!" he yelled. The men erupted as the thought of victory excited them. They drew their swords and immediately gave chase after Havada.

"No, noooo!" squawked Artaxes furiously as the Brigantium war horns signalled again. The Western King now saw Tobias and his horses hurling down the hills towards him.

The aid from his new ally was not as welcome as King Tobias would have expected.

Artaxes was fighting in a thin line against what remained of the Oakland Musters. The three box formations held off for a long time before they were forced to disconnect, due to Milano.

The Meridium King lunged at a soldier, stabbing his sword straight into his belly. He pulled it out and instantly looked to the west as the galloping two thousand horses shook the ground agonisingly.

"My King, it's General Koos and King Tobias. Do we pull back?" asked Dariuss who was fighting beside the King.

"We do not pull back. This is our victory. The Eastern Horse Lord thinks he can steal this day from me. Well, he is very mistaken," declared Artaxes, entering his demonic state.

"Fight on, men!" he screamed as he began rushing west through his exhausted men. The Meridium soldiers were so fatigued that their swings and lunges were dispatched with only half the energy that they usually had.

Artaxes wriggled through the less populated part of the crowd in search of First General Lucifer, but there was no sign of him. Artaxes was forced to head into the more action-packed duel that was occurring further to the east.

The King made his way through the fight until he found his First General. But his search was cut short as a group of Musters cut down at the surrounding soldiers, killing them brutally, and charging to the King who had his back to them.

The Meridium King swung around as the approaching sound alerted him. He lifted his sword, but it was not needed. Lucifer lashed at the attacker nearly cutting him in two, and almost immediately after dealing the blow, he swivelled his sword round, wiping out the other Oakland fighters. First General Lucifer had saved the King just in time.

Lucifer tore his sword around and cut down again at another attacker. He then leapt beside the King and began slashing incredibly at the tired enemy. Every swing he dealt inflicted a devastating blow. Even the Musters that managed to get their swords defensively in the way still fell. Lucifer's power and precision was far too superior for any Oakland Muster on the field.

"The dogs think they can steal this day from me, Lucifer. Order the men to kill any man that gets in their way, Muster or Easterner. I want the men to push forward," ordered Artaxes as he turned to his First General.

General Lucifer sliced at what was to be his final attacker of the day. He then looked at his King with confusion.

"My King? The men are tired. Let them Brigantiums finish it. Why put the men through more suffering?" asked Lucifer.

"Do as I say! Get the men to push forward!" yelled Artaxes angrily, but there was no time for the order to be given. Tobias had arrived.

Tobias Ringfold was at the very head of his army. He rode terrifyingly at the front of a massive triangular spearhead horde of horses, the formation gliding excellently across the grassy plain, not a black hair out of place.

Tobias was in his gold-trimmed metal armour, with red royal shoulder plates that had rich colourful tassels hanging down. He rode without a helmet but with a silver curled crown upon his head, the Brigantium crown. Tobias's arm was raised with his longsword pointing out, ready to claim the lives of the now panicking Musters.

Artaxes, Dariuss and Lucifer observed the destruction unfold right before them. The Oakland Musters no longer engaged the battered line of Meridiums. They either turned to their side to try and face the four-legged swarm or fled back to Oggsfleet. But whatever they decided to do would still result in their death. Tobias had not even signalled his two thousand infantry to march into the battle. They were not needed. They all stood upon the hill, watching, the same as the Meridiums were.

The bravest of the Oakland fighters stood and awaited their doom as a yellow cloud of power smashed barbarically into the brave enemies that had picked up the Meridium spears in an attempt to skewer the Starchitect horses. But with the pace in which they moved, and with the brown leather armoured warriors upon their back, they stood no chance.

The night black horses burst through the Musters, killing almost half of their force upon impact. King Tobias, who still rode at the front, swung down from his horse, severing the head of his first victim, his horse having already trampled a dozen enemies. The Brigantium fleet of beasts had crushed the Oakland Musters only seconds after engaging, the horses continuing to ride through to the west without a casualty. Tobias and his cavalry were now riding away from the battle towards the most far away hills.

"Who is that?" asked Lucifer as he pointed towards the open exit to Oggsfleet, ignoring the bypassing crusade of black beasts. A man and around one hundred and fifty men had engaged the fleeing five hundred Musters, catching the attention of The First General in the process.

"That's Havada. It's Havada," shouted Dariuss who swung his head towards Artaxes. "What do we do, my King? Are we to aid him?"

Artaxes turned his head to the west. He watched Tobias and his force as they began curling around by the base of the hills, preparing another spearhead charge.

"Yes we do, yes we do," replied the King softly whilst he stared at the reforming Brigantium army with pure hatred.

The Meridium King stepped out in front of his force, a little more than four hundred remaining. He raised his sword and turned to them.

"The Brigantiums will not take this day from us! Pursue the enemy! Charge!" said Artaxes ferociously. He then turned and began laying chase. The Meridium men growled and barked like wild dogs as they sprinted across the graveyard field behind their King. They had only a few yards to travel.

Artaxes raised his sword and rotated his wrist. He slashed out at the back of an already wounded Oakland fighter that was trying to escape. His body slammed down against the rest of his defeated brothers that Havada and his men had taken out, but that was to be Artaxes's final kill of the day. Just as his men were about to engage the fleeing enemy, the roaring stampede again engaged.

Tobias again crushed into the side of the Musters, this time absolutely obliterating the remainder of the men. The horses slowed down after the impact as the warriors began lunging down, stabbing the enemy.

"Get into it, lads," ordered Dariuss who felt like he had to give the command, his King paralysed, motionless as he watched Tobias smash into the Musters again.

As his force sprinted off into the mayhem, he quickly lost sight of them, the black of the horses swallowing up the battle as if a night sky had taken over, blotting out the sun. Artaxes lowered his sword and walked into the abyss with a need to track his old friend.

He roamed through the battle in search of Tobias, in search of anyone in fact. His face remained still as the screams and roars of the Musters and the Brigantiums chorused through the blood-drenched area. He couldn't see anything except the mountainous horses and their yellow-cloaked companions. Artaxes noticed a bleeding out Oakland fighter on the floor, so he approached him despite the dashing horses all around. He dug his heel into the man's spine and raised his sword. Slowly he took out all of his anger and glided the stained sword inch by inch into the enemy's back.

Artaxes continued to stroll through the pile of wounded Musters, stabbing each one harshly in the spine. No challenges remained, so he had no choice but to feed his addiction with weak Oakland souls.

"King Artaxes, the Musters are defeated, we have reclaimed our land!" informed Dariuss who came pushing between the now stationary horses.

"See to the men, Dariuss, and then find Tobias. I would very much like to speak to him," ordered Artaxes as he slowly began walking off towards the port.

"What of the survivors?" asked Dariuss quickly before he lost sight of his King.

Artaxes halted his escape as he conjured up a plan in his mind. He smiled psychotically before continuing his walk.

"Kill them all, but keep one alive. Bring him to me in my tent after nightfall," commanded the King as he disappeared into the mob of horses.

The men of Meridium were ecstatic on the battlefield. This battle meant a lot to them, and the victory meant even more. The surviving soldiers of Artaxes Destain shoved their blood-coated swords up into the air. They stood on a well-deserved field of victory.

CHAPTER 27
MURDER

The weather calmed drastically as the Meridium army stood inside their reclaimed port. It was as if God himself had cleared the skies to celebrate King Artaxes's victory. Although Artaxes did not feel like he had won a victory today. Tobias had stolen it from him, or so he felt.

Tobias, a couple of his Lieutenants and Koos were present among the victorious crowd of Meridium survivors whilst the rest of his army had begun setting up a massive mob of tents out on the battlefield.

The men inside the port stood looking up towards a small wooden platform. It was in the centre of the port's belly where the Oakland Musters had set up their catapult barely an hour ago. The men were awaiting their King who now made an appearance. He wandered out of one of the surrounding buildings with Dariuss and Havada at his back. They had been debriefed whilst the rest of the men awaited their King's speech.

Artaxes strolled slowly through the crowd, towards the risen podium. He walked with his sword still drawn and with his other hand, trailing it out to his side, he touched the awaiting hands of his brave men. It was a rare show of emotion from the Western King.

Tobias glanced over his shoulder as he looked for the approaching King. He was standing with his hands clenched together in front of him and was still equipped with his golden-trimmed armour. He smiled lightly at Artaxes as he passed by, but he was not rewarded with a smile back. He was not even acknowledged, nor was Koos who stood with the same posture beside the Eastern Horse Lord King.

The small chatter from the men who greeted and praised their King died down. The whole port was silent. All that could be heard was the gentle crashing of the blood-painted river slamming up against the docks. Artaxes began tackling the wooden steps up to the platform. He banged the tip of his sword off every step that he climbed. Once he reached the top, he stopped and took a deep breath. He seemed to be in a bit of a distant state, again.

The King gathered his thoughts and continued his walk. He picked up his feet and wandered to the centre of the podium. He then burned his glance into the eyes of all his men that stood beneath him looking up passionately.

"Men of Meridium, today we stand on a field of victory, the second victory that we have claimed within the fortnight. Once again the people of Requirium are beginning to understand that we will not be so easily conquered. We have retaken our lands with barely fifteen hundred men!" Artaxes erupted as he fired his murderous sword up into the now clearing sky.

The surviving Meridium men of around four hundred screamed ecstatically, drowning out the bash and slash of the wicked waves off The Sink.

"Now drink, eat, and have your way with some of the beautiful woman of Oggsfleet Port if that is what you desire, you have earned it. You men are the greatest fighters that this world has ever seen. No one could accomplish what we have." He arched his back and bowed honourable to his men.

The silence below was broken again as the creaking of four hundred chest plates rang as the Meridium soldiers bowed back to their King.

"Now go, go," he added with a straight face.

Artaxes left the podium faster than he arrived. He stormed

248

down the steps and approached Tobias who remained still beside Koos.

"Follow me to my quarters, if you will, King Tobias," Artaxes said as he walked past, refusing to wait for a reply.

Tobias looked to Koos who held a worried look upon his face. Koos knew Artaxes better than most, and he knew Artaxes was not happy.

The two of them stared at each other silently until Tobias addressed his Lieutenants.

"See to the horses and prepare my tent," he commanded. "I will be back shortly."

The officers nodded and left.

Koos led Tobias off down the streets of Oggsfleet Port towards one of the inns that Artaxes had taken as his temporary keep.

'Let me do the talking, Tobias. He is not in the best of moods.'

'Not in the best of moods, General? We just rode to aid his people, risking our lives in the process," argued Tobias as the two of them climbed the three solid steps that led up to the inn.

'You don't know the man as well as I do. Just let me talk, okay?" insisted Koos.

Tobias didn't reply. He just smiled forcefully and held out his hand towards the door. Koos slid between the two guards and entered first.

"King Artaxes," greeted General Koos as he entered the inn. The room was of a plain nature, the Meridium men having just touched up the room for the King by planting a few fire pots and a table inside the inn's main room.

Artaxes sat in a hefty wooden chair at the head of the long rectangular table. Havada, Dariuss and First General Lucifer were present, all sitting along the left side of the table. Artaxes stared at Tobias who stood slightly behind Koos.

"King Tobias, join me round here," ordered Artaxes who like the rest of his comrades remained fully suited up in armour.

Koos had not been rewarded with a greeting or an offer to sit at the table, so he remained standing. He looked to Dariuss and

Havada who both looked down at the table, confusion striking him. Their actions had struck him as very strange indeed. These two men were two of his closest friends yet they refused to even look at him, never mind embrace him.

"I guess thanks are in order. Do you care to sit in with my council?" asked Artaxes seriously.

"No thanks are needed," said Tobias. "I seek to forge an alliance with the Westerners. That is the reason for my aid. Your General here spoke on your behalf. He is confident we can create something promising."

Artaxes glanced over at Koos, this time struggling to control his fake emotions. His eyes executed Koos where he stood.

"Seven years ago maybe," hissed Artaxes whilst staring at Koos still.

"Excuse me?" replied Tobias.

Artaxes then whipped his head around and growled back at the Eastern King.

"Seven years ago upon the Gantry, Tobias, that was our chance to create something promising. If you had honoured your word, we would both be ruling Requirium now."

Tobias looked back at Artaxes with shock. He had no words.

Artaxes then changed the subject to address his King's Guards. "Military report, Dariuss?"

"Four hundred and thirty two Meridium men survived, my King."

"And Milano, how severe are his wounds?" asked the King.

"He's dead. His wounds were too severe, my King. He died for the cause," announced General Lucifer from the opposite end of the table.

"Milano of Sandown?" asked Koos who still stood. He seemed to be affected by the news.

Artaxes, ignoring Koos again, spoke to Havada. "Havada, you are beginning to prove yourself massively since your betrayal with the traitor Koos. Your work upon the River despite losing one of our ships, was commendable, and I thank you for your efforts." He said it as if Koos wasn't even there.

"Betrayal? Traitor?" asked Koos with frustration. "You foolish old man…"

"Silence," screamed the King, viciously cutting Koos off immediately. "Leave us," he ordered his King's Guards and First General.

The three of them stood up and headed for the door, not one of them making eye contact with their friend and General on their departure.

"Artaxes, I hoped that we could put the past behind us, and create a new beginning," said Tobias calmly.

"It's too late for that, you fool. We don't need your help and we didn't need your help today. You think you can just ride in here with your fancy horses and steal my victory?" said Artaxes angrily.

"We rode to your aid to help you secure your lands, not to steal your victory, and from what it looked like, you needed our help. Your men fought well, yes, but you were still outnumbered," argued Tobias.

"Do not mock me, you peasant. Your presence insults my men's victory," shouted Artaxes as he pushed his chair out, launching himself to his tired feet.

Tobias was not one to cower down, and he too dived into the air and faced his threatening foe. He stared with fury at Artaxes who stood barely two feet away from him, smiling psychotically, but their stare off was quickly interrupted as the furious Meridium General bombed over to the head of the table.

"Traitor? Have you lost sense? I rode to Brigantium to assure our victory. I am more loyal to Meridium than you are," he exploded.

Artaxes slowly turned to face the young General.

"Do you remember what I said would happen to you if you rode east, General? Do you remember?" asked Artaxes with a deranged look.

Koos looked back at him as he thought back to the conversation the two of them had had in the marble throne room of Meridium. He remembered the King's statement telling him that if anyone rode for Brigantium, he would call for their head. In an attempt to avoid saying the exact words, he instead spoke calmly to Artaxes. "Is that really the kind of King you have become?"

"Yes, a good King must honour his word. Arrest him," bellowed Artaxes without mercy or gratitude.

Two guards came marching in through the door and approached Koos, who most certainly resisted. But they overpowered him quickly, hitting him in the back of the head with the handles of their swords and dragging him out of the room whilst he screamed and cursed at his deranged King.

"Artaxes, this is unnecessary. Release him, you bastard!" shouted Tobias as he leaned across the table and latched onto Artaxes's arm, but he was countered immediately. The Meridium King pushed his attacker's hand away and grabbed hold of him aggressively.

"You should not have come here, Tobias Ringfold. You should have stayed in the East where you belong," he whispered as he pulled Tobias's head in close.

Tobias tried to resist but Artaxes's grip was too solid. Tobias then attempted to speak but he held his tongue as his attention was diverted off towards the doorway as the inn's door was flung open.

It was Dariuss, and he had brought with him an Oakland Muster prisoner. The man's hands were bound and his body was battered.

Tobias looked at the prisoner with confusion, until he realised what was about to happen. He then looked back to Artaxes who towered over him with a knife in his hand.

"You fool, my people will go to war over this. Your city will burn," threatened Tobias desperately.

Artaxes ignored Tobias's weak threat and spoke to him again. "You should not have come," whispered Artaxes again as he tightened the grip on his dagger. With one lunge, he stabbed Tobias Ringfold, the Eastern King.

Tobias let out a devastated yelp as the dagger slipped through a gap in his armour, tearing into his body, but the attack didn't stop there. Artaxes pulled out the knife and retightened his grip, and again he thrust it deep, twisting the knife as it entered. As Tobias screamed out again, blood spurted from his mouth, spraying onto Artaxes's face, but the Western King didn't flinch. He continued to stare into Tobias's eyes, watching as the light began to leave the Eastern King.

With one last blow, Artaxes yanked Tobias's body in close so that he could rest his lips on his ear.

"Now die, like the dog you are." He dug the dagger one last time into the ribs of the dying King. Artaxes then ripped the blade out and allowed the body to drop to the floor.

"Bring him," commanded Artaxes to Dariuss.

The King's Guard dragged the Muster over and threw him to the floor beneath the murderous King.

"We thank you for your noble sacrifice," said Artaxes as he loosened the straps on his armour, dropped the plate from his body and held the knife up to his own arm. Artaxes slid it painfully across his arm, dealing a bloody blow to himself, whilst Dariuss watched without surprise. The young King's Guard was aware of the plan, in fact he began assisting his King to complete the set up. He tipped up the table and the various chairs around the room, and once satisfied with that, he began screaming ferociously for the guards.

Artaxes quickly cut the ropes around the Muster's hands and then threw the dagger at him, launching himself to the floor beside Tobias, who was now dead.

Dariuss prepared himself to execute the final part of the traitorous plan. He raced over the room towards the Muster.

"Guards, guards! Prisoner escape," screamed Dariuss as he drew his sword. The ruffling outside the door insinuated that the guards were approaching.

Dariuss kicked out hard, knocking the Muster back down to the floor as he tried to drag himself up, then with his sword, he aimed it down and stabbed right through the falsely accused Oakland fighter, kicking away the dagger as the guards walked in.

"Quick, get the medicos, quickly!" alerted Dariuss.

The two guards looked with horror as the two Kings lay

bleeding on the floor. They scurried out of the door and began screaming, alerting everyone of the events of the evening.

Dariuss stood breathing heavily. He looked down to his faking King and then to Tobias, feeling a little tinge of guilt for the Eastern King who lay dead on the rug. Dariuss had committed a traitorous act, and it wasn't something that he had wanted to do, but he was a man of Meridium, and a King's Guard to the Meridium King. He hadn't been given a choice.

CHAPTER 28
THE WATCH

"Okay, are you ready?" asked Hector.

"Yes," replied Gideon as he climbed up to the carriage's coachman seat. He slid up beside the coachman and took hold of the reins after putting up his hood.

"Right, off we go then," said Hector as he climbed back up onto the wooden steps of the leading carriage.

The escort were only two miles away from Hornton's Watch. With Gideon upon the carriage disguised as a coachman, they could approach the watch and hopefully enter the realm of Versidia without any problems. Hector and his companions lunged forward in their comfortable royal seats as the carriage kick-started again. It carried them the remainder of the way through the country roads that the people of Versidia had built over one hundred years ago. Many quiet paths had been built through these lands that all led to the same bit of open land, a rocky terrain that was split in two by a long wall, Hornton's Watch.

"Upon arrival, you will all proceed to the Palace and await me there. Faizer will accompany me to the Citadel whilst you all begin the preparations, understand?" stated Hector.

"Understood," confirmed Gondogon.

Hector then looked to Romford and Riycard who both stared at the Prince.

"Are you sure? A one man escort is not very effective were something to go wrong," argued Romford.

"Silence, Chalk," Riycard said. "The Prince has spoken. We will tend to his needs in the Palace. Or so you can, I am under orders from my father who is under orders from your father, Hector. I am to go to the Arena and inspect your quarters in which you will be getting ready, and other things too, like your armour."

Romford looked at Riycard angrily. He seemed to be disturbed by the fact that Riycard would be inspecting the Arena without him.

"Perhaps I should accompany you to the Arena?" he asked.

"No, I need someone at the Palace with Gondogon," Hector said. "You will go with him, and Riycard, you will obey your father's command, go to the Arena." Hector slouched back into his cosy seat. "It seems like both of your fathers have received a lot of orders from my father, yet the words have failed to fall upon my ears." He opened the shutter on his carriage.

"The Watch is dead ahead," alerted Gondogon as he pulled his head away from the open shutter to refit his helmet.

"Okay then, everyone remain in the carriage, but be ready," said Hector.

No one replied. They all seemed to be a little nervous as the carriage was getting closer and closer to Hornton's Watch.

The watch was a fifty foot tall concrete wall that ran right along the realm of Versidia. No one could enter unless it was through the main gate that was manned by fifty red-cloaked Darchem troops. Two thick red flags bearing the black tree of Darchem swayed in the calm breeze, attached to either side of the gate entrance.

"Take another look, Gondogon. Do you see Hornton? Is he here?" asked the Prince.

"I see someone. It could be him," reported Gondogon.

Hector grew a little uneasy at the news. If Hornton was there and he took one glance at Gideon's bare face, he would discover him at once, and the escort would be vanquished for harbouring the fugitive.

The two golden carriages came to a standstill just outside of the main gate, and a squadron of Darchem guards approached. Hector quickly opened his small door and dropped outside to greet them. As he stepped down, he noticed Faizer stepping out of the other carriage. Faizer, disguised as a General, walked over to Hector.

"Is that him?" whispered Faizer.

Hector gulped worryingly. Hornton was here.

"Yes."

"Prince Hector, we have been expecting you, although if I may say so, your escort is rather small considering the threat of the Lure Alliance," said Hornton.

Hector knew the Lure Alliance were no threat to anyone who didn't wear a red cloak, but to keep Hornton happy and the conversation blunt, he agreed.

"Yes, word has reached my ears and those of my father that the Alliance has expanded. We hear also of their soldiers and how they terrorise these beautiful lands," he replied. "But I assure you that my escort is strong enough to withstand a raid from the rebels."

"Nonsense, you have no horses to cover your flanks. No matter. The Eagle Pact will escort your convoy the rest of the way. The people of Versidia await you."

"The Eagle Pact?" asked Faizer.

"Is that a problem?" interrupted a voice. It was Lumon, walking towards the carriages with six other members of his highly trained organisation.

"No problem, just curious as to why you feel the need to do so. The Alliance does not venture this far north," argued Faizer.

"Have you not heard? The Lost Sons Of Meridium have returned, emerged from the shadows they have," said Lumon. Lumon knew that the Brigantiums knew of their return. He knew that Tobias had allowed them into his home, but Lumon felt that it was necessary to keep it a secret and play on the fact that he didn't know of the Brigantiums' betrayal.

"The Lost Sons are dead, that's what we heard," said Hector, just as Lumon had predicted he would.

The Eagle Pact Leader smiled, satisfied that Hector lied to his face, and that gave him the clarification that he needed.

"I'm afraid you are mistaken. Now back in your carriage. We will escort you in." Lumon turned and walked back to the gate.

Hector and Faizer nodded at each other nervously before going their separate ways. Faizer took a little glance up at his carriage as he approached it. Gideon remained still, silent and hooded. He hadn't flinched or even twitched when Lumon and Hornton were present.

"Hector, why are horses surrounding our carriage?" asked Romford as the two royal carts wheeled through the Watch's gate and off across the tree scattered terrain.

"The Eagle Pact insisted on guiding us in," he answered.

"Oh well, that's just what we need, not like we're harbouring the most wanted man in Requirium," moaned Romford as he made eye contact with one of the armoured Pact riders. He slammed the shutter shut and slouched back in his seat.

"Keep your voice down. We will be alright," said Hector.

"Do you hear that?" said Riycard, rudely interrupting the debate.

Everyone listened keenly. The sound of ecstatic cheer and bellowing drums could be heard faintly in the background. They were closing in on the city.

The city of Versidia was home to over two hundred thousand people, each one of them holy to the bone. The people here worshipped God more than any other in Requirium. The religion ran deep here, every child brainwashed from birth to believe in God. Soldiers would pray before and after battle, and the Kings would sacrifice their healthiest livestock just as an offering.

The city was surrounded by a lake of blue, the only way into the white city over the long wooden bridge that extended out to the island. Versidia's position and strategic defensive system made it nearly impossible to conquer. The lake was attached to no ocean so fleets could not reach it, and no more than a thousand men could fit on the bridge at a time, even then they would be so ram packed together, the city's defensive trebuchets and catapults would obliterate them.

The city was flat. Only certain points rose up into the air, and those were the white watch towers that controlled the city's wall, and the Citadel that could be seen from afar, in the centre of the city and home to the Elders and the Moth Priests.

The cheer was now high in volume as the carriages crossed over the bridge and headed towards the opening doors of Versidia. A soldier still galloped at every point of the carriage, with Lumon leading the escort.

The carriage almost instantly became covered with flowers as it entered the city, thousands of people gathering in the courtyard to greet the Brigantium Prince. Selection here was more important than it was back in Brigantium. The Versidians had always hosted it, so it had became a tradition for them too.

"Look at them all, so many," said Hector as he peeked out of his shutters.

"They're here for you, my Prince," said Romford.

"I've never seen so many people gathered in one place," added Hector as he stared out at the masses of people all crowded around. The surrounding buildings could barely be seen as people hung from balconies, stall roofs and any window within five miles.

The Eagle Pact broke off as the carriages travelled down the steep roads, down towards the centre of the city, taking up a formation with three horses at the back, three at the front and one at the front of the leading three. Lumon was the one leading the convoy. He guided them through the crowd of people as he led the convoy towards the Citadel.

"Okay, upon arrival," the Prince said, "I will get out with Faizer. The rest of you go to the Palace, except you, Riycard, you tend to whatever business it is you seek to do at the Arena. Have this carriage guide you there once the others have been escorted to the Palace."

259

Everyone stayed silent as they accepted their orders.

"Okay good," added Hector.

Gondogon looked at him. He could tell the Prince was nervous. "Prince Hector, be courageous and brave and do not show weakness," advised the brutish Royal Guard. "The people of Darchem and Versidia will be watching."

Hector looked at him and smiled.

"We must be here," said Faizer as the second carriage stopped. "Have a look will you."

Enly, who seemed to be getting tired of taking orders from Faizer, groaned as he slid open his shutter. But his mood soon changed as he laid his eyes upon the famous Citadel.

"What, what is it?" asked Faizer. "Go on, speak."

Enly still didn't reply, forcing Faizer to look for himself, but because of the carriage's angle he couldn't see out of his shutter, so he opened the door and stepped outside.

Faizer was fascinated at the sight. He stared up, along with everyone from the first carriage who had already exited their ride. The Citadel was a sight, a sight like no other. It was as white as a new born baby and as large as the 7th Sea. It was built up of hundreds of columns and pillars that ran around in a cylinder shape. The Citadel's body sat heavily between the maze-like columns.

"King Emric of Versidia and the Elders of the Citadel await you, Prince Hector," said Lumon who was the only man there to stand unimpressed by the sight.

Hector and his followers released the strain in their necks as they looked to Lumon.

"Of course. Faizer come with me, I will see the rest of you tonight," said Hector.

"Yes, my Prince," said Faizer as he slid between Riycard and Romford. Lumon led Faizer and Hector along the white bricked surface towards the mountain of steps that lay beneath the fortress. Faizer glanced over his shoulder as he watched the carriages trot away. The plan had worked. Gideon had gone unnoticed.

The three of them stepped onto the glowing staircase and began hiking up to the top. One hundred silver steps lay before them. This was the first challenge, to gain entry to the Citadel, the second challenge awaited them at the top.

"King Emric Kane, it is my greatest pleasure to introduce you to Prince Hector Ringfold of Brigantium," stated Lumon.

Hector, with Faizer at his back, climbed the last step and walked towards King Emric and the Elders.

King Emric was by far the most reasonable, calm King in the whole of Requirium. His sole purpose was to run his Kingdom peacefully, whilst obeying the High King's commands, and more importantly, obeying God. But he was not the sole leader of this city. Any decision he had to make went through the Elders first, of which there were seven.

"A grand pleasure to meet you, Hector, son of Tobias," greeted the green-cloaked King. He went towards Hector and held out his hand.

Hector bowed his head as well as taking the King's hand, to gently kiss it.

Emric was of medium height, with long brown hair and a clean shaven face. He was well over the age of forty, but he still kept a youthful glow about himself.

Emric took back his hand and held it out to his left where three extremely old men in white gowns stood looking at Hector.

"Prince Hector, I introduce to you, Shevion, Dothron and Belyon. The three speakers and Elders of Versidia," said King Emric.

One of the men walked forward at a decent pace considering his extreme old age.

"I am Dothron, and I wish you good fortune in the Selection to come," he said as he offered out his hand.

Hector without pause grabbed his hand and kissed the wrinkled knuckle of the Elder speaker.

Dothron was the main speaker of the company of Elders. He had been one of the Elders for over fifty years, and had the final say in everything that the Versidians did, and also a lot of what anyone did outside of the city also.

"Tell me, my son, how is your father? I had a terrible dream about him last night," announced Dothron.

"He is well, or at least he was the last time I saw him," replied Hector who seemed slightly taken back by the Elder's mention of a dream.

"I will pray for him," declared Dothron as he walked away, entering the blockade-like doors to the Citadel.

Next Belyon stepped up and offered out his hand which Hector kissed quickly.

"An honour it is to meet you, so young but yet so strong, or at least I hope. Are you ready for your Selection?" asked the croaky old man.

"I am."

"Good, I wish you good fortune in the Selection to come," said Belyon as he too walked off into the Citadel.

Finally Shevion stepped up. He didn't move with as much pace as the other two did. Shevion was a man of few words. He was one of the three elected speakers, but he always enjoyed observing and listening more than speaking. He simply offered his hand out and pulled it back once kissed.

"I wish you good fortune in the Selection to come," he said simply as he turned and walked for the Citadel.

"Good, good, now that they have had their meeting with you, we can speak a little more plainly," said Emric with a pleasant smile on his face. He walked towards Hector and put his hand upon his shoulder. "It is an honour to meet you, my son. I have been a good friend to your father since he won his Selection, and what a day that was, earning the right to the throne at the age of sixteen. Remarkable, was it not?"

"Indeed it was. King Emric, I would like you to meet my General and close friend," said Hector as he stood back.

Faizer then stepped forward and walked towards the King. Lumon watched Faizer closely. He knew many of the Brigantium ranking officers, and he didn't like that he didn't recognise Faizer.

"Pleasure to meet you, King Emric," said Faizer as he held out his hand.

"A General, yes, still so young. You must be very good at fighting, my son?" said Emric as he shook Faizer's hand.

"He is," interjected Hector.

Lumon stared at Hector. His quick and reckless interruption had aroused suspicion. Lumon flicked his eyes back at Faizer and thought carefully on the matter, but without any evidence or reason, he decided to forget about the issue and took his leave.

"I have preparations to make in the Arena," he said. "I will be attending in Duran Harall's stead. He can not make Selection, and sends his apologies." He continued his journey back down the steps.

"No Tobias, no Duran, no Artaxes," said Emric. "I hope this doesn't have an effect on Selection. It would be a tragedy if it was to be, shall we say, dull without their presence." Emric turned and walked towards the giant Citadel doors. Realising that he was taking the trip alone, he turned back. "Well, come on, you two. It's time for the tour of the Citadel. It is tradition, after all."

CHAPTER 29
THE HIGH KING'S RECALL

High King Duran stood shivering with his hand on Dammasius's cloaked shoulder in the courtyard of stone at the main gate of High Darchem. Geralix and a number of other officers were present, awaiting the arrival of Havideous Destain and the High King's daughter, Aphrayer.

The Darchem courtyard was a flat with a tall proud stone carving of the tree of Darchem sitting solidly in the centre. It was, or so Duran believed, the symbol of all life in Requirium. The main entrance was surrounded by many concrete buildings and archways that led off to some of the city's archery ranges, fighting pits and barracks. Only one thick walkway led back up through to the heavily populated city.

The heavy gate began rattling as the soldiers began drawing up the gate, Havideous and his escort waiting on the other side. He had brought the five thousand soldiers that Duran had called for. They were setting up camp on the abandoned wasteland outside of High Darchem.

"There is your sister, Damassius. Run to her, she will like that," said Duran as the large unbreakable gate was drawn all the way up.

Damassius smiled and, whipping back his black cloak, he ran across the puddle-riddled courtyard, leaping at Aphrayer's legs as she entered her home.

"Sister, sister," cheered the small boy with excitement.

"Greeting, Damassius. I have missed you," expressed the beautiful young woman as she embraced her over-excited brother.

Aphrayer was very tall and very beautiful. She was Duran Harall's oldest child, married off to Havideous as reward for the information he provided against his own countrymen seven years ago. Her brown wavy hair fell out of her hood and whipped wildly in the cold wind, covering her high cheek-boned face.

Havideous stumbled past Damassius and Aphrayer and belted over to the High King and his small crowd.

It had been two years since Duran had last called upon the Meridium traitor and his daughter, so the King was extremely eager to see Aphrayer, but first he had to associate himself with the drunken barbarian that staggered towards him.

"High King Duran, I am at your service," pledged Havideous as he dropped to his knees before him.

Duran looked down at him with disgust, immediately noticing the stench of ale spewing from the brutish man's breath. Instead of acknowledging Havideous, the King opened his arms to embrace his daughter who approached her father sheepishly. She buried her head deep into Duran's black covered chest.

"I have missed you, father," she muttered.

Duran held her head tightly before taking a peek at her face. He brushed the hair out of the way and gazed upon her, but what he saw surprised him.

"How did you come by this?" he asked as he rubbed his gloved finger over Aphrayer's bruised eye.

"A fight broke out in the kitchens at Thort between two servants. I was unlucky enough to get tangled amongst it," she said persuasively.

Duran switched his eyes back to the floor, staring at the still-kneeling Havideous whilst gripping his daughter's face tightly.

"A fight, you say?"

"Yes, Havideous had the servants whipped and flung out into the street. Nothing to worry about."

Duran released her and stepped in front of Havideous. He had the urge to cut off the drunken oaf's head where he knelt. He knew him responsible for this act but with no proof he decided to leave the issue at hand, for now.

"Rise, Havideous," ordered the High King.

Havideous pulled his fat body to his soaking feet and looked cross-eyed into Duran's wide black eyes.

"Drunk?" asked Duran even though he already knew the answer."

"Sorry, my King. It was a dull journey."

"Dull? How can that be when you have the beauty of my daughter to gaze upon?" snapped Duran.

"Apologies, my King. I meant no offence. I bless God everyday for allowing me to lay beside your daughter," slurred Havideous.

"God? It is I who allows you lay beside her, not God," growled Duran.

"Of course, my King. I brought the men you requested," said Havideous in a desperate attempt to calm the High King.

"Five thousand?"

"Yes, my King."

"Good, you are now relieved of command. The soldiers are under my order now. Get yourself up to the castle and sober yourself up. I expect to see you at breakfast in the morning," ordered Duran with disappointment. "Geralix, take Havideous up to the castle and report to me after. I want to go through the new military report on the soldiers from Thort."

He waited until Geralix and Havideous had gone, then reached for his daughter's delicate hand. "I promised Damassius a look round one of the archery ranges. Do you care to join us? I would very much like to know how that drunken traitor has been running my city."

Damassius tugged on Aphrayer's green gown annoyingly. "Yes, come with us, dear sister."

"Of course," she replied happily as she tucked her hand between her father's chest and arm, linking him gently.

Duran allowed his guards to lead the way off down one of the western archways, Damassius pacing after them. The young boy was eager to practise on the archery range. He had a passion for a bow, even at such a young age.

The evening wind still managed to slash at the cold backs of Duran and his family as they all travelled through the cold torch-lit walkways of the military section of Darchem. Although not all of Darchem was as dull as this, the deeper into the city you got, the more rich it became. Still it would never compete with the luxury that the cities of Versidia and Brigantium held, but that was because the High King chose not to.

Unless a settlement could provide training, weaponry or space for soldiers to live, it was not required. It was a difficult task for even the most adventurous of men to find a tavern or brothel within the city's walls. High Darchem was just one big circular military camp.

The gentle moaning and bash of swords swam annoyingly over the conversation that Duran had with his daughter. It was indeed evening but the soldiers still trained until dark.

"So tell me about your marriage, my love. Does the Westerner treat you with respect?" asked Duran.

"Of course. I mean, he's not much to look at but I am doing my part for the cause. I keep him happy so that you may continue your rule over the Kingdom," she said as if rehearsed.

"If you're not happy, you can tell me. Other arrangements can be made. The reason I married you to Havideous was because we needed him, but we don't need him anymore. He can be replaced," stated Duran boldly.

Aphrayer remained straight-faced. "I love him, father. I have grown to love him. I hated you for it at first but now I understand," she said as the escort arrived at the archery range.

Duran looked at his daughter with a little bit of regret, thinking of how he so easily signed her life away in order to win the war against Artaxes Destain, but her maturity and honour filled his heart with warmth.

"What a woman you have grown up to be. Your mother would be so proud of you," praised Duran.

"I know she would, father."

The warm conversation between Duran and his daughter was interrupted as Damassius yelped with excitement. He sprinted through the fenced range and charged for the bow rack. He snatched a short bow and a quiver of twenty five sharp bronze arrows.

Now that Damassius was occupied and the rest of the guards were observing the little lad, Duran could now speak to Aphrayer alone. He hung back and latched onto her arm, then pulled her towards him and gripped her tightly.

"If I find out that drunken bastard inflicted that bruise upon your eye, I will cut his head off and hang his disgusting body from the city gate," snarled the High King.

Aphrayer denied the accusation less persuasively than the last time, and she looked nervous as she peered teary-eyed into her father's eyes.

"He did not do this to me. I promise you, father."

Duran released his hold and looked down. His daughter had never lied to him before but he still felt like she was keeping something from him. Luckily for her, Damassius again interrupted the conversation.

"Aphrayer, come look. I hit the bull's eye first time," he shouted with excitement.

The young lad was pretty skilled with a bow considering his age. Ever since he could walk, he would wander about with a toy bow until he got to the age of five and began practising with a real one.

"I see you have been practising whilst I've been away," she shouted as she paced around the fence and headed towards him.

Duran watched his daughter walk away, his mind deeply troubled. Although his daughter had promised him that her bruise was not inflicted by her husband, he still felt angry. He felt like there was more to it, and he intended to find out.

"I am going back to the castle. See to it that these two get back in time for dinner," he ordered his guards who stood observing the young boy.

"Yes, High King. As soon as the moon rises, we will head back," confirmed one of the guards.

Duran smiled and walked over to the archery range where Aphrayer was volleying arrows down towards the targets also. He put a stop to the archery session to say his farewells. He rubbed Dammasius's head.

"Keep practising, my boy. But soon, you will take up the sword."

"I will, father."

"Aphrayer, it's good to see you again," Duran said as he leaned and kissed her softly on the cheek. He then turned and marched off out of the archery yard.

Aphrayer watched her fuming father escape their presence with pace, and she filled with fear as she knew her father had read her lie.

CHAPTER 30
A GIFT FOR AN OLD FRIEND

Duran Harall ripped through his morning bacon aggressively as he sat at a long table in one of his feasting halls. Damassius too indulged himself in breakfast, but no one else had attended. Duran dug deeper into his food whilst keeping a watchful eye on the hall's grey doorway. He was waiting for Aphrayer and Havideous who had still not presented themselves.

"Tell me, Damassius, how was the rest of your archery practice last night?" he asked.

"Yes, it was good. I'm getting better."

"That's good, son, but the time will come when you must practise with a sword. The finest Generals in the army do not shoot bows, they swing swords," informed Duran, dampening his son's mood slightly.

"But I like the bow," he argued.

"Yes, and so did I when I was a boy but your grandfather made me see sense…" said Duran. He zoned out, and looked down. "He made me see sense," he muttered to himself before quickly regaining his senses. "It is a weapon for the less skilled fighters. Now I will hear no more about it. Starting next week when Lumon returns from Versidia, you will begin your training. You are nearly six years old now. It is time."

Damassius looked down at his food sadly.

"Yes, father," he replied as Aphrayer finally made an appearance.

The double doors slid open slowly as she walked in with her sober but hungover husband. She lingered by the doorway for a moment or so, holding open the door for her husband to enter. He bulged through and stormed straight across the hall, smashing himself down in a chair close to Damassius.

Havideous slammed his arms down and began digging away at the plate of food in front of him. He still hadn't made eye contact with the High King. He seemed in a hurry to finish his food, as if he wanted to cut breakfast as short as he possibly could.

Duran watched him from across the room with disgust. Duran truly hated Havideous. The only reason he lived was because of the deed he did for Duran at the Gantry. The High King continued to stare angrily at the already chewing beast, before Aphrayer caught his eye.

She wandered slowly to the table and guided herself to the opposite side of Damassius. Duran was forced to lean slightly to one side to get a glimpse of his strangely shy daughter. The manner of her arrival struck Duran as a peculiar one. She too kept her head down as she tucked her dress under the chair, sitting down neatly. He again leaned to his left as he tried to get a glance of his daughter's face. He smiled as he did so, but that smile soon vanished.

Duran had noticed something, something upon his daughter's face. It was a purple bruise twice the size of the one that was visible only yesterday. He squinted a little harder as he tried to extend his line of sight through the forest of hair that hung over Aphrayer's face. Suddenly Duran leapt into the air. He had seen properly the destructive marks upon her face.

Everyone flinched as the High King fired himself up from his chair, the very table shaking. Damassius stared at his father as he began his journey along the side of the table towards them. Aphrayer and Havideous continued looking down as the High King's footsteps struck fear into them both, their attempt at concealing whatever it was that Aphrayer was hiding having failed.

Duran slowed his walk as he reached Aphrayer. He positioned himself behind his daughter who could be heard sobbing lightly.

The High King slowly slithered his hand across his daughter's neck and tightly gripped her hair. With one whipping slash, he threw it from her face and pivoted his body around until his face almost touched hers.

Duran's eyes narrowed at the horrific sight upon his daughter's face, a large purple bruise circling her eye.

"You lied," he whispered as he closed his eyes and breathed out angrily. He stood up straight and slowly released his hold on Aphrayer's brown knotted hair.

"Father, please don't."

"You lied!" he screamed as he locked his gaze onto the motionless Havideous.

Havideous Destain still looked down to his plate, too much of a coward to even face his wife or her father. Duran growled quietly as he processed what he had seen. Suddenly he slid his cloak back, revealing a concealed dagger that was tucked into his belt. Havideous had not yet noticed, but Aphrayer had.

"Father, no! It was an accident. Don't!" she begged.

The tone of Aphrayer's begging now aroused the suspicion of Havideous. He lifted his head with worry as he expected an attack from the High King who towered over him with the dagger in his grasp, and he was right.

The High King's victim had no time to react as Duran lashed down with the knife like a snake snapping out at an innocent mouse. The feasting hall vibrated loudly as Havideous's agonising screams echoed within.

Duran Harall had speared his knife down tip first through the hand of his daughter's husband.

"You bastard! How dare you lay a hand upon my only daughter?" screamed the High King as he wiggled the knife around Havideous's hand with cruelty.

The knife had gone through the oaf's hand and then deep into the hard wood, the tip of the knife making an appearance on the under side of the table. Damassius watched with horror as his father dealt the almighty blow. Frightened, he leapt from his chair and sprinted for the door.

"Stop him, bring him back!" ordered the High King. "It's time you grew up. You will watch and you will learn," he demanded brutally.

One of the guards at the door restrained the kicking and screaming boy and carted him back over to his chair.

Duran tightly gripped the knife again. He ripped it from the bloody hand giving the terrified woman-beater a moment's rest, but only a moment. Before Havideous could throw his heavy body to the floor, Duran slammed the knife down again, creating a separate bloody hole in his prey's hand. Havideous again screamed agonisingly as his butchered hand squirted out a new batch of blood.

"Father, stop!" screamed Aphrayer who now attacked her father. She tried to prize his grip from the dagger but she was nowhere near strong enough.

Duran released the handle of his knife and grabbed hold of her, leaving the knife securely in Havideous's hand.

"You fool, you would protect the man that beats you!" he screamed with hatred.

Aphrayer didn't answer, she just gripped her father's arms and sobbed.

"I was wrong yesterday what I said about your mother," hissed Duran. "She would not be proud of you, you have grown weak."

He turned and shouted, "Take her, and send in the guards."

One of the guards walked over and grabbed hold of the High King's daughter, dragging her screaming body from the feasting hall, leaving Havideous to the wrath of the High King and the newly arriving guards.

"Father, please let me go," begged Damassius, who was crying hysterically at the sight of Havideous's hand.

"Silence! You are to be The High King of Darchem one day. You need to learn. Now watch." Duran grabbed hold of Damassius and pulled him away from the bleeding mess. Duran then looked to his door and nodded at the three armoured guards who awaited their turn. In an instant, the mob bounded over. The first guard ripped the knife from the blood-drenched hand of Havideous whilst the other two pulled him to the floor.

The three guards encircled Havideous who whimpered on the floor, and one at a time they began kicking out at Havideous who curled up into a fat protective ball. But that didn't last. One of his attackers prized his arms out wide so the other two could deal blows to his face. Havideous groaned and began shouting for help as the three guards beat him bloody.

"Father, stop them!" begged Damassius who had never seen such things, but he got no reply.

The High King just smiled crazily as he watched the soldiers stamp deeply onto Havideous's broken face.

"Father!" screamed the young boy again.

Havideous lost consciousness, lying in a pile on the floor as the guards smashed their fists bluntly against his skull.

"Stop!" ordered Duran suddenly.

The three guards refrained from beating the half dead man and stepped away. Duran released his grasp on his son and wandered over slowly to the table. He reached over and dragged a silver goblet towards himself, and then pulled a jug of wine over. The High King then filled the goblet and walked over to Havideous. He knelt down and stared into the black eyes of his victim.

"Thirsty?" he asked as he poured the goblet of wine onto the motionless body. "You still alive in there?" Duran had an evil smile on his delighted face as he shook the body. All of a sudden the delighted look turned into a worried one, worried that Havideous was actually dead. Duran didn't worry because he was concerned about the man's well being, he was worried because he had other plans for Havideous. He wanted to ensure that the woman-beating beast endured a slow and painful death, and he knew just the man who would take pleasure in committing this act.

Duran shook him again, and again until Havideous eventually coughed and half opened one of his swollen eyes.

"Ah, there we are. Glad to have you back, Havideous."

"Please," muttered the beaten man desperately. "Please," he repeated from his blood-flooded mouth.

"Please what?" replied the High King.

"Please don't kill me," begged Havideous whose words could barely be made out.

"Kill you? I'm not going to kill you, Havideous," reassured Duran.

Havideous forced his eye open a tiny bit more with surprise.

"You... you're not going to kill me?" he croaked.

Duran smiled at him and stood up.

"No, I will leave that to your brother, Artaxes," he announced shockingly.

Havideous Destain rolled onto his back, groaning and moaning as his broken ribs stabbed his insides as he turned. He wasn't sure if he had heard the High King properly.

"What?" he mumbled.

Duran ignored him and stepped over him. He approached his guards quickly. "Prepare an escort, take Havideous to Meridium and give him back to Artaxes. Tell him an old friend sends a gift."

The guards bowed and tended to the condemned man upon the floor, leaving Duran standing feeling very pleased with his plan to put Havideous to a long and unpleasant end.

CHAPTER 31
THE PRINCE'S CHAMBERS

The afternoon sun blazed down on the streets of Versidia. It irritated the plated bodies of Enly and Faizer who walked with speed through the busy streets towards the Arena. They passed many wattle houses and even more stone churches on their travels, multiple priests roaming around outside of the holy settlements, some praying and some greeting the civilians that passed by.

Faizer was leading the small group to sign the papers confirming Hector's Selection challenge. Gideon Destain travelled with the two men, still disguised in his black overthrow. He, however, was not going along to assist in signing the papers, he had a matter of his own, something he wanted to tend to himself.

Many of the Versidian people halted their daily tasks to witness the three men making their way to the Arena. They recognised the yellow capes that dangled from the sweating backs of Faizer and Enly. The civilians smiled and shouted out happy remarks with excitement as the men walked past. It was the eve of Selection, and the people were ecstatic in celebration. Over fifty thousand of them would be able to attend the event in the morning.

"My god, that's a sight," said Faizer as the three of them crossed over the people-cramped road and headed down a slope of slanty steps. The Arena was situated in the centre of an open square that the steps led down to. Many buildings encircled the

Arena with large streets leading away to the east, west, north and south. Although the Arena sat in a circular space, the way that the buildings and streets formed around it created a square-like display.

Each open street was carved off with the set of sloping stairs that Gideon, Faizer and Enly travelled down at the north side of the Arena section. The Arena section was dug down deeper than the city's over populated surface, the steps running down twenty five feet to the sand-spread ground.

"It's so much bigger than Tobias had made out," said Enly who was mesmerised by the Arena.

"This is the first time you have seen it?" asked Faizer.

"Aye it is," he replied.

"What about you, Gideon? Have you seen it before?" asked Faizer.

"I have seen it, once," he responded from beneath his hood. He walked lightly behind Faizer and Enly.

As the group reached the bottom of the steps, two guarding soldiers locked their spears together and addressed Faizer. The soldiers were Versidian Guards. They wore lightning white body armour that curled beautifully at the shoulder plates, the armour also smothered by a smoky grey cape that ran down the men's backs. The helmets however were oddly-shaped, covering the full head of the soldier, but not the face.

"What is your business?" demanded one of the soldiers sternly. It was their job to monitor who entered the Arena section. Two stood guard at each of the four passages into the section.

"We represent Hector Ringfold. We are here to sign the papers," announced the disguised General Faizer.

"State your names," requested the grey-cloaked soldier.

"General Faizer, Lieutenant Enly and our servant."

The soldier peeked his head around the two Brigantium officers and looked at Gideon. He frowned before locking his eyes back at Faizer.

"Very well, they are expecting you," he announced, finally letting them through.

Faizer nodded and passed between the two soldiers, walking out onto the sandy flat towards the Arena.

"Tell me again, why is it you insisted on coming with us? You risk compromising us," said Enly as he looked to Gideon.

"I need to check out where Hector is to get ready. I want to inspect his armour and discover how I am to watch Selection without being discovered," Gideon said.

"And do you think that is wise? You risking being caught just to watch the games? You have already done your part. I don't even know why Tobias asked you to attend in the first place," snarled Enly.

"I could ask you the same thing," replied Gideon from under his hood.

"Quiet, you fools. More soldiers," snapped Faizer.

The three of them approached the Arena where dozens of soldiers stood straight-backed on separate podiums that provided support to the terrifying structure.

"Are you here to sign the papers for Hector Ringfold?" enquired a robed man who came wandering out of the main archway entrance. He smiled delightfully as he awaited a reply.

"Indeed we are, and a good day to you," replied Faizer.

"I thought so, I recognised the capes. Follow me," he said.

The three men obeyed and trod through the brown archway, entering the lobby of the Arena.

"Where does your servant go?" asked the white robed escort.

Enly and Faizer stopped and turned. Gideon had turned left upon arrival and had begun making his way down the long walkway to the left.

"He is to check on the Prince's quarters for tomorrow. No need to worry. Proceed," answered Enly.

"Again? I will say to you the same as I said to the man who came before you, I assure you our facilities are well above standard," chuckled the man as he turned away from Enly shaking his head.

"Wait, what do you mean again? What other man?" pressed Enly with concern.

"Another man came the other day and then again barely an

278

hour ago, demanding to see the quarters also. He entered the city with you," he said, groaning with impatience.

Enly looked to Faizer who looked back with confusion. Enly was clueless as to who it could have been that the old man spoke about, but the man brushed off the matter.

"Come, we have work to do," he declared. "Follow me."

Gideon travelled with pace along the decorated hall way towards the Challengers' quarters. Although he didn't have an exact idea of where he was going, he used his logic to follow the corridors until the walls and floors became a little more rich. Hector's quarters would without doubt be in the nicest part of the Arena's halls. Gideon was truly taking a risk wandering alone around the halls. All it would take was for one Darchem soldier or officer to wander past and notice him, and all hell would break out.

Gideon slowed his walk all of a sudden as he came to a passage to the right of the corridor that he travelled down. The new passage led upwards towards a large oval cage door that allowed a gentle ray of sunlight to burst through. Gideon stopped completely. This could be the location where he could watch Selection. He took one look over his shoulder to make sure no soldiers were present, and once satisfied he stormed up the stained ramp towards the cage, quickening his movement by turning his walk into a jog. If any soldier saw a servant sneaking about alone, it would most certainly be questioned, so Gideon had to be quick.

With a rattling slam Gideon reached the top of the ramp and gripped hold of the cage. He'd found his place of viewing. This was where he would watch Selection take place. He looked out through the square cage door onto the ginormous Arena, the stands thrusting up into the sky and the sandy ground sizzling in the sunlight. It was breathtaking.

Without lingering too long, he scurried back down the ramp and turned back onto the corridor.

"You lost, slave?" barked an unfamiliar voice.

Gideon turned sheepishly to find two soldiers staring at him.

"Speak!" barked the soldier again.

"I am heading to Hector's chambers. I am his royal servant," muttered Gideon whilst keeping his head down.

The soldier huffed and looked to his accomplice who locked his eyes onto Gideon's hidden face. He slowly stepped forward and reached for Gideon's hood, spreading his fingers and opening his palm as he made contact with Gideon's cover.

"What do you think you are doing? You understand that you are harassing a servant under the protection of Tobias Ringfold?" interrupted a familiar voice, just in time.

The soldier halted his grasp and stepped back.

"And you are?" mocked the Versidian soldier whilst hovering his hand over his sword handle.

But that didn't frighten Gideon's saviour one bit. Instead of cowering, he stepped forward and pushed up against the white armoured man.

"I am Riycard Badstuber, son of Dreyo Badstuber, the noble and lord of Brigantium. Now turn around and piss off or my father will have both of your heads," threatened Riycard viciously.

The two soldiers looked back at Riycard.

"Apologies, my Lord," one of them said before turning and leaving along with his comrade.

"What are you doing here, Riycard?" asked Gideon.

"What am I doing here? I could ask you the same thing. If you get discovered, we will all be killed. Have you not seen all of the Darchem red cloaks that roam the city?"

"I have reason. I need to check the Prince's armour, his quarters too."

Riycard looked at Gideon nervously.

"No need," Riycard said without making eye contact. "Everything is order. I would not deem it wise with all the soldiers about either. We should go."

Gideon looked into Riycard's eyes wisely. Gideon as usual could tell when something was wrong, and he could sense Riycard's unnecessary panic, the panic that his eyes revealed the moment Gideon announced that he was to inspect the Prince's quarters.

"Riycard, I am going and I'm going alone," he said with slight aggression.

"Yeah, sure… I'll… I'll see you back at the Palace," he replied with a broken stutter. He then quickly took his leave, storming off down the corridor.

Gideon watched Riycard leave before tending to the matter. He now had a greater urge to inspect the chambers. Riycard's unusual behaviour left him intrigued. He waited until Riycard was out of sight completely before walking off, following the walkway round until it came to a dead end. Only one door sat in that corridor, the Prince's chambers.

Gideon turned the doorknob and entered the room. As he entered, he took a moment to take in the room's historic offerings. The walls were painted with pictures of previous Brigantium heroes that had completed Selection. Dozens of Ringfolds were imprinted on the wall, but one in particular took Gideon by surprise. A huge painting that took up the full back wall was an image of Tobias Ringfold, slashing down at his older brother Helix. Gideon took down his hood and observed the exquisite image upon the wall closely. He thought it was bizarre that the Versidian people honoured Tobias's Selection so much. It was considered a disaster back at Brigantium. The Brigantium heir was dead due to his sixteen year old brother, the King was devastated and the people in uproar. The Easterners had never suffered a tragedy like it before. It took Tobias years to win over the people when he came into his throne at the age of twenty one. It really did take the people a long time to get over what Tobias did to the Kingdom's favourite, Helix.

Gideon broke his trance-like gaze from the painting and approached the Prince's armour. It was hung over a wooden cross that stood in the centre of the room. Gideon slammed his hand on the silver steel chest plate, and then inspected the helmet that hung over the top of the cross. It was a silver oval shaped helmet that covered every inch of the face of whoever wore it. Gideon, pleased with the armour's condition, turned to the sword provided.

As every fighter that entered the Arena wore the same identical armour, they all used identical swords. Gideon stroked his fingers down the spine of the sword. It would do.

"Tomorrow then," Gideon whispered to himself as he planted the sword back on its holder. He then turned for the door and left.

CHAPTER 32
SELECTION

It was the day of Selection and the fast-beating heart of Hector Ringfold thudded ecstatically. He was extremely nervous, but no one apart from himself knew that.

Tobias stood in line beside his challengers inside of the glistening Citadel. He kept his chin high and his back straight in an attempt to look as calm and brave as possible. Hector and the other Selection challengers were attending the first part of Selection, which was a speech from the Elders and King Emric Kane.

Hector had lived his whole life without seeing the Citadel, now he had seen it twice in two days. It seemed even bigger and more beautiful now than it was the first time he seen it. All the walls were crystal white, along with the floor and the flower carved ceiling. Hundreds of columns ran perfectly up to the distant ceiling, a similar style to Artaxes Destain's throne room, but almost twenty times as large. There were also dozens of doorways, archways and passages all leading off to different locations within the building. The Citadel was home to more than just priests and holy crosses, it also held libraries, alchemy studies and many galleries.

Although many soldiers patrolled the city, Arena and Citadel grounds, none were actually present within the Citadel itself. This holy house was home to the Elders, and they did not want the likes of common soldiers patrolling God's house. As such, they had created their own form of protection, the Moth Priests.

The Moth Priests were a group of men that dedicated their lives to serve the Elders and God. They would begin their training and religious education from the age of fifteen, and would spend their lives practising the ways and beliefs of God. Over one hundred of the priests protected the Citadel. They were led by Chaudrey, a man of very few words. His sole purpose was to train the boys and turn them into loyal and religious Moth Priests, although there was a lot more to being a Moth priest than just praying, guarding and training. The Moth Priests were actually the most exceptional fighters in the whole city, some would even say in the whole of Requirium, although many felt their ability to be exaggerated.

Every Priest was without hair and without beard and they wore creamy white robes that covered them from neck to ankle. The robes were extremely baggy. They had to be to hide the silver plate body and the curved, silver scimitar sword that were hidden beneath them.

The twelve Selection challengers stood in a line, looking up at a thick sandstone podium where the seven Elders were awaiting King Emric to present himself. The King walked to the edge of the podium with his hands raised by his sides. He was wearing a golden crown and a long silky blue cloak that looked so heavy it seemed to be weighing him down.

"Challengers, challengers," he said, "I welcome you to Versidia and wish you all good fortune in the Selection to come. At stake today we have the claim to the Eastern throne of Brigantium, and also the Victor's purse of ten thousand gold pieces should anyone defeat the Prince."

Everyone applauded the King's words as he smiled down at the twelve challengers.

"As you all know," he continued, "we have royalty with us today… Hector Ringfold, who today tries to extend his father's legacy. But he is not the only man of popularity here today who fights in front of this crowd of fifty thousand."

Many of the attending officers and a lot of the Moth Priests that stood guard at scattered locations around the hall looked up to the podium, interested to see who it was the King spoke of.

Surprisingly, Hector was the only man in the packed hall to remain straight-faced. He was surprised but remained calm in an attempt to not show any weakness in front of the other challengers. He continued to stare up, awaiting the King's next words.

"Ladies and Gentlemen," announced King Emric, "I give to you... Pelios the survivor, a true enemy of the Ringfold family."

Chatter echoed around the hall, as the name worried many of the challengers. Everyone had heard of Pelios and his story.

The Eagle Pact Leader, Lumon, leaned on his elbow against a glimmering podium, smiling psychotically as the name was announced. He was the only man present, apart from his Eagle Pact members, that knew the real reason why Pelios was present.

The startled crowd stuttered into applause again. It had been a long time since the name Pelios had lingered on the tongues of the people of Versidia. For a time it was all the people spoke about... how he interfered with the shocking fight between the two Ringfold brothers twenty years ago had set all the Versidian tongues wagging.

Hector still remained straight-faced, even though the name frightened him. His father, Tobias, had told him of the story of Pelios long ago. But, although most people in the room knew the story of Pelios and his attempt at Selection, Hector was actually the only man who knew the real story. No one knew that Tobias tried to contact Pelios once he'd found out about the man's survival. He'd wanted to help him, but Pelios couldn't be found anywhere within Versidia.

Hector repeated the story over and over in his head, he felt the urge to approach Pelios and try to explain that his father tried to find him. But Hector stopped himself, fearing it would show weakness.

King Emric stepped down, to be replaced quickly by Dothron, the main Elder speaker.

"I wish you all good fortune in the Selection to come," declared Dothron, before bowing his head and stepping down himself.

All twelve men bowed back.

It was King Emric's turn to speak again. "Challengers, your carriages await you outside. May God watch over you all and reward the greatest warrior with an epic victory."

As he finished, the double doors to the Citadel swung open... it was time for Hector and the mercenary volunteers to leave.

Hector led the line of challengers out of the Holy House and onto the lengthy stair to find that hundreds of people had gathered outside to pay their respects. They too were ecstatic, and clapped so loud it sounded like a horde of Starchitect horses trampling across the concrete.

The people threw flowers and ribbons up into the air as the twelve brave men marched down the steps towards their round, white carriages. All the men remained straight-faced as they reached the bottom of the high-built stairs. They then, one by one, walked off to their designated carriages. Only they, and they alone, could board the carriage, any support or family they had would already be seated inside the Arena.

Hector walked through the chanting crowd, towards the leading carriage. He was to arrive at the Arena first. The shaking Prince now took his first steps towards glory as he lifted himself up into the carriage. Once inside, the door was quickly slammed shut behind him.

Hector breathed out as he finally had a moment alone.

"Remember your training," he muttered to himself.

The young Prince was terrified. For the whole morning, he had remained calm as the traditional speeches had taken place, but now that he was alone, he was overwhelmed by fear. The nineteen-year-old wanted nothing more than to do his father proud, but his life was at risk... eleven tough foes that had spent their whole lives fighting now stood between him and his rightful claim to the Eastern throne.

It was Pelios that troubled the Prince's mind more than anything. Although the Selection survivor had made no indication that he was out to get Hector for the actions of his father, Hector knew that he was. Why else would Pelios volunteer for Selection? The only glimmer of hope was that Pelios would have no way of targeting Hector in the Arena as everyone would soon be wrapped up in the same steel armour.

Hector was jolted forward as the horses started their journey to the Arena. It was only a short ride from the Citadel, so Hector didn't have long to gather his thoughts and compose himself. In an attempt to take his mind off the bloodbath that would soon unfold, he opened his shutter and stared out at the swarming crowd. It seemed to thicken the closer the carriages got to the Arena.

The Brigantium Prince smiled gently to himself at the heart-warming sight. The support from the Versidian people was incredible, but it was only an incredible sight to him, the other eleven challengers would find the sight daunting. After all, the people chanted Hector's name, not theirs.

The Prince slid his shutter closed slowly, deciding that he wanted to experience the final moments of the journey alone. He slouched slightly and closed his eyes. He pictured his father's face, his mother's face, Enly's face... all the people closest to him. These were the people that he wouldn't see again if he was not victorious. There was, in fact, only one more friendly face that he would see before the games, and that was Gideon who awaited him in his quarters within the Arena.

The journey was coming to an end and Hector found himself thinking about his father. For a moment, he had forgotten that the King Tobias was not attending. In fact, for the first time in history only one of the four Kings in Requirium were attending, the event was to be absent Artaxes, Tobias and Duran.

Hector dwelt sadly on the thought of his father fighting in the West. He had still not received word from anyone. He was sure that Artaxes and Tobias would have been victorious but a little reassurance wouldn't go amiss.

The carriages came to a halt. They'd arrived at the northern entrance to the Arena. Suddenly, Hector's carriage door swung open. The Brigantium Prince took one last nervous breath before assuming a forced posture of bravery, and then stood up and climbed down the carriage's wooden steps. Almost instantly, he was pelted with roses and ribbons as the ecstatic crowd declared their excitement.

Every challenger stepped out of their carriages and faced the overwhelming crowd, but they were only allowed a moment to soak up the atmosphere, before they were each led off by four Versidian soldiers, creating a protective square around each man.

A horn erupted from the front carriage, signalling the soldiers to guide the challengers to the Arena, and, for most of them, their end. In one synchronised movement, the soldiers and the challengers stepped forward and made their way to the Arena.

The chanting from the Arena shook the very ground as the challengers stampeded down the steps and crossed the sandy brown terrain toward their doom. The structural beams and columns vibrated incredibly as the crowd of fifty thousand continued to chant and stamp their feet. They knew that Selection was now approaching. They knew that the challengers had arrived.

Hector continued to lead the brave line of volunteers up the bronze steps and into the Arena lobby where twelve old men with identical bowl haircuts awaited the challengers. One by one, the heavily robed men approached Hector and the other warriors. These men had been assigned one Selection challenger each, their job to escort the men to their quarters where they would have ten final minutes to ready themselves.

"Hector Ringfold… this way," said one of the men, going over to the Brigantium Prince. Hector nodded and followed the man off to the left and into a dark corridor.

The Prince walked nervously behind his elected guide as the roof above him shivered to the stomp of the crowd. His mind was only taken off the thought of the bloodthirsty crowd by the sound of slapping footsteps from behind. He looked around and saw two escorts leading fighters that would soon face him in the Arena. One of those challengers was Pelios.

He stared with hatred at Hector, who continued to look over

his shoulder as he walked. Pelios made it pretty clear that he was blaming Hector for what Tobias had done to him over twenty years ago. His eyes screamed vengeance.

Pelios had long, greasy, black hair and a face of true menace. He was over six feet tall and a little wide, the years had added beef to him. The Selection survivor had managed to remain calm right up until this point but he now broke and showed his hatred towards the Brigantium Prince.

Pelios had good reason to hate the Ringfold family. He'd been a volunteer to Selection back when Tobias was declared victor. He'd volunteered to win the purse to feed his two sisters and mother. They lived on the streets of Versidia, begging daily. Pelios taught himself how to fight so that he could one day enter Selection and change the lives for himself and his family forever.

Tobias and his brother Helix had defeated all their opponents in the arena except for Pelios, who was proving to be very difficult to defeat. The two brothers had to work together in order to defeat him, which eventually they did, but when Selection had finished, Pelios was found still alive. He had received a deep cut to the leg and a wide slash across the chest from Helix, but Tobias attacked the eldest Prince from behind before he could finish the job on Pelios.

Peilos had survived but his family had died of starvation. He had sworn revenge and now he was going to take it.

Hector, not wanting to give the beast a reason to lash out, turned back around and focused on the task ahead. He wanted desperately to reach his quarters so that he could discuss the Pelios situation with Gideon. He hoped that his friend would have some advice on how to kill the beast if he was to come across him in the Arena.

"Here you are, Prince Hector," said the guide, bowing. "I wish you good fortune in the Selection to come."

Hector bowed back and waited for the man to leave, then quickly opened his door and darted in.

Gideon was sat, looking down at the floor, but leapt to his feet at the arrival of the Prince. "Greetings, Hector."

"Greetings, Gideon," said Hector. "There is something I must ask you."

Gideon wandered over to the cross that held up the Prince's Selection armour. "What is it?"

"Have you heard of a man called Pelios? He survived my father's Selection?"

Gideon groaned depressingly. "Yes, why do you ask?"

"He is here. He has volunteered for Selection."

Gideon groaned again and sat down, his head in his hands.

His reaction instantly struck fear into Hector. "Is he really as good a warrior as they say?"

"That is not what we should be worrying about right now."

"Then why do you look so worried?"

"I believe there is more to this," said Gideon. "I do not think he would just volunteer for Selection. I think someone has urged him to do so, maybe even paid him to do it. And only one man would arrange something like that."

"Who?"

"High King Duran."

"We have no quarrels with High Darchem," said Hector. "The High King supports my father's claim and his traditions."

Gideon was just as clueless as Hector as to why the High King would organise something as vicious as this, but, all of a sudden, something occurred to him.

"Unless," said Gideon.

"Unless what?"

"Unless he knows of mine and my brothers' return," said Gideon. "If he's found out that your father took us in, he would declare war on Brigantium and his first move would be to ensure that you do not pass Selection, leaving Brigantium without an heir."

"That is a bold assumption, Gideon. How would Duran Harall even know of your return? There are no red cloaks within the eastern realm."

"Just tell me, Hector, do you trust everyone? Can you vouch for everyone under your command?"

"If you speak of Enly or any of the officers, you are mistaken."

"No, not Enly. Not Gondogon or Fangoy. I'm talking about the Badstubers, Dreyo and his son Riycard. Are they foolish enough to plot against you?"

Hector looked to the floor as he thought on the matter. "I don't know," he said. "I need to speak to my father. I need to send message to him at once."

Hector was in a state of panic.

Gideon leapt towards the Prince and grabbed him. "Focus, Hector! Focus! I could be wrong but there is no time to do anything now. You have to go out there and you have to win. The second it is over, we will leave for Brigantium and get to the bottom of this." He released Hector and stepped back.

"What about Pelios?" said Hector, trying to compose himself.

"You may not even have to fight him, but if you do, you will have to kill him. Do what your father and uncle failed to, my Prince. You can do it."

"But how will I even know it's him?"

"If you come face-to-face with him, I'm sure he will let you know who you're fighting."

Hector looked at his teacher with confidence. "You have become a good friend, Gideon. And a great teacher. I meant what I said back in Brigantium, you and your company will be held close for the rest of your lives should I pass Selection."

Gideon smiled and approached the young Prince, embracing him like a brother. "You will pass Selection," he said. "You will."

Hector walked over to the cross and pulled off the leg plates, fitting them nicely. Next he fitted his armoured grieves and then his chest plate. Once suited up, he opened up his arms and stepped back.

"How do I look?" he said, slowly sliding on his helmet and hiding his face from the world.

"Like a King of Brigantium," said Gideon, going over with the sword laid over his wide spread arms.

Hector smiled and received the sword. He drew it quickly and held it up in front of his face.

"I'll be watching from the dungeon, Hector," said Gideon. "I will see everything. Remember to anticipate your opponent's attacks. And watch your back."

Hector nodded, then walked to the door and knocked. It swung immediately open.

"Greetings, challenger," said the Versidian soldier outside. "Follow me."

As Hector walked, he focused on his breathing. They reached the left turn that led up to the cage door that Gideon had chosen as his viewing point only the day before. Hector's escort stood at the base of the stone ramp, holding out his hand towards the inclined passage.

Hector was to take the final steps alone.

He took a gentle breath inside of his tomb-like helmet then climbed the ramp.

Gideon, who had followed Hector out at a distance, now stood behind the Versidian soldier and watched the Brigantium Prince walk toward glory. Gideon raised his covered head slightly, allowing a little more of his face to show than he would have liked, in order to witness Hector's final steps. But then horror struck the Western Prince, and it struck him hard.

Gideon noticed a mark upon Hector's armour, a mark that most certainly should not be there. In a drastic decision, Gideon lunged forward and attempted to pursue the Brigantium Prince.

"What the fuck do you think you're doing?" snarled the Versidian soldier, grabbing hold of Gideon and pushing him up against the wall.

The soldier reached for his sword. "Your ten minutes are up, slave. Now back to the challengers' quarters, pig."

Gideon desperately had to speak with Hector before he went into the Arena, and into a possible trap. But it was impossible. Hector was slipping from his reach, and unless Gideon left now, the Versidian soldier would most definitely cut him down.

"Apologies, apologies," said Gideon, "I'll be on my way." And with that, he slipped off back down the hallway, leaving Hector to his doom.

The nineteen-year-old challenger wished that the trek up the ramp would last forever, but it ended much sooner than expected. He now found himself facing out through the cage dungeon door, and out onto the sandy Arena surface. Eleven other cage doors ran around the base of the Arena in a circular shape. Each one had an armoured fighter on the opposite side, each fighter in identical armour to the Prince of Brigantium. The roar from the crowd was explosive, fifty thousand Versidian civilians bounced from their seats with passionate excitement as the cage doors began rising.

The time had come.

Hector was the first of all the fighters to step out onto the battlefield. He walked out ignoring the ear-blistering crowd. He walked only so far before coming to a standstill, and took one glance up to the left where the King's box was positioned. Every man or woman of position attending the event were either stood or sat in the rich, quilted box. Hector spotted Faizer and Enly toward the front of the box. They leaned, elbows first, against the sandstone ledge that protected the people within.

Hector then looked to the higher tier of seats in the box, where he spotted Gondogon, Riycard and Romford. They sat behind twelve red cloaks, twelve members of the Eagle Pact. It seemed as though every ranking man in Requirium was present except for the three absent Kings.

The Brigantium Prince looked away from the happy sight of friends and shifted his gaze to the newly-formed circle of mercenary warriors upon the sand. There was a gap of about twenty feet between each Selection fighter. Each man stood with their swords gripped tightly, staring each other out. The atmosphere was tense. Before the moon would rise this very night, eleven of these men would be dead.

The noise of the crowd slowly died down, into a nervy silence as King Emric Kane stood up. He held his hands out wide and prepared to speak. Every single man, woman and child in the crowd sat back down in their seats and listened.

"People of Versidia, officers of Darchem and Brigantium,

Selection challengers! I welcome you all here today to either take part in or witness a one thousand year old tradition. Selection! I speak on behalf of every person in the city when I say to you challengers. I wish you all good fortune in the Selection to come... begin!"

The crowd erupted menacingly and Hector quickly tightened his grip on his sword then charged into the circle, along with every other man. The first slash of swords came from the left of Hector as two vicious men engaged each other barbarically.

Hector quickly picked a target. He selected an opponent who ran at him with his sword in the air. The Prince lunged at him but his sword was deflected. Instead of repeating the attack, he thought back to Gideon's teaching and quickly ducked then sliced. Hector cut his opponent's leg, dropping his foe to the floor.

Hector then dived back up and parried an attack. Then another. But it was not a repeated attack from the same enemy, two men had now ganged up on the Prince, which confused him beyond measure. He was puzzled as to why two men were targeting him from behind. The skilful Prince managed to deflect the swings that came from the left and the right, but he struggled to find space as the two men continued to go at him. Hector was being targeted, and he knew it. But how the men knew it was him he did not know, although someone did, and that someone watched from the dungeon entrance.

Gideon, still disguised as a servant, gripped the dungeon door with frustration. He beat himself up, hating himself for not managing to warn the Prince in time. He felt even worse that he could do nothing now but stand and watch, powerless.

Gideon scowled as two decently skilled fighters targeted Hector. It was obvious they knew who they were fighting. Gideon had quickly sussed out how the men knew who Hector was.

The mark upon the Prince's armour.

Gideon looked up to the royal box. He noticed Lumon, the Eagle Pact Leader, smirking happily. Gideon's eyes widened as he put together all the pieces. He now had the clarification he needed to pin this act on the High King.

Duran Harall must have had Lumon hire someone to put the mark on the armour, but who? A spy? A servant? Or maybe even someone of position within Brigantium who could get close to the Prince's amour?

Gideon looked to the floor as he thought, his very brain pounding with the desperate struggle to solve the traitorous riddle.

"Oh my god. Riycard. Riycard Badstuber."

Countless times had Riycard panicked when questioned about certain things, many times had he been caught acting suspiciously.

Gideon filled with anger, debating leaving right then to find the traitor. But the sight of Hector cutting into one of his attackers calmed him slightly.

Hector was doing well. He'd killed one of the two hired fighters and now smashed against the second opponent with aggression. Gideon observed the rest of the fighters... only two others had fallen to other swords around the Arena's reddening ground.

He locked his eyes onto a meaty warrior who had just ripped his sword out of the injured fighter that Hector had cut at the beginning. The fighter now focused on Hector. He was watching Hector smash away at the mercenary.

Gideon was sure that the observing man was Pelios.

Hector controlled his breathing and stayed on top of his footwork as he continued to duel with his opponent. He noticed the fatigue in his enemy's arm, so he planned his finishing move.

He allowed his enemy to attack so he could counter quickly, which he did brilliantly. The Prince's challenger lunged recklessly in, falling into Hector's trap. Hector spun his body round, smacking his sword off his challenger's blade, knocking it to the side, then switched back inside with his sword tip aimed at the man's chest. He thrust his hips forward, forcing the sword through the man's armour and into his chest.

The Prince dragged his sword from his second kill with a

venomous tug, then stumbled back and looked around. He counted the dead bodies on the ground. Two from his sword and three from the other warriors. Seven remained, including the Prince himself.

Hector was then engaged by one of the largest warriors upon the deathly sand, tackled from the side and taken to the ground hard. He felt like he had been run over by a chariot as he tussled on the ground with the man who now forced his body on top of Hector. The challenger lifted his sword up high with the tip aiming downward. It was only a foot away from the Prince's chest.

The young Eastern heir had to act fast before his attacker eliminated him from the battle. Hector smashed the man in the head but the blow barely moved him. He again bashed the man in the head, this time knocking him off balance slightly before his opponent could force his blade down. Hector realised no amount of bashing to the helmet was going budge the beast, so he changed his approach.

He thrust up with his hips and rolled his enemy onto his back. Once on top, he instantly targeted the man's hand, slamming it off the floor repeatedly until the beast's grasp loosened and he let go of his sword. The Prince then dived to his feet and slashed at the man, who just managed to roll out of the way.

Hector whipped down repeatedly, trying to catch the legs of the foe that now managed to grab his sword and regain his posture. The man quickly attacked Hector again. He slashed down hard before pulling back the sword and slashing upwards, but Hector was too skilled to be defeated by a simple attack like that. He anticipated his opponent's next move, waiting for the lunge which he slid backwards from, before lunging forward himself to grab onto the beast's shoulders. He held on tight as he pulled his head back and with one shocking thrust, Hector smashed the front of his helmet off his weakening foe's metal face.

Once again the man barely even budged.

"You will die now, Hector," said the man. "Like your father should have long ago."

Hector now knew… he was fighting Pelios.

He was horrified and confused as he took in the poisonous words. He knew now that it was Pelios but he did not know how Pelios knew that it was him, but before he could think about it anymore, Pelios released his grasp on his sword and wrapped both of his arms around the startled Prince. He then squatted, springing back up sharply and launching Hector up into the air and across the bloodstained sand.

The Brigantium Prince smashed against the ground hard, quickly cushioning the impact and rolling onto his back. He tried to reach for his sword, but he couldn't.

He now expected death. Any second, Pelios's sword would find his way into his broken body. But the blow did not come and Hector shifted his body onto its side, looking up in an effort to spot out his enemy.

Luckily for Hector, Pelios had been engaged and he duelled messily against an unlucky challenger that had got in between the lion-like warrior and his prey.

Hector had a chance to take a breather. He pulled himself up onto his knees and reached for his sword. Once grasped, he stood back up and observed the fight in front of him. Another warrior had now fallen, leaving Pelios fighting against one man and two other challengers duelling against each other. That left one other fighter who was knelt down on his knee, wounded. The fighter noticed Hector and suddenly he sprang to his feet and sprinted as best as he could toward the Brigantium Prince.

Hector planned to meet his foe head on in the centre of the Arena between the two separate duels that still went on. He charged towards his next victim, waiting until he was only a few feet away from his opponent before swinging his sword in a windmill motion, slamming his enemy's sword straight out of his hand. He then spun around and hacked at the man's throat, nearly taking his head off.

The man dropped to the floor, gasping for air, as his red blood spurted from his deep wound. Hector put the man out of his misery, standing over him and aiming his sword down. He then dropped to his knees, bringing the sword down and stabbing his beaten foe in the chest, screaming menacingly.

The Prince neared victory now as he stood back up and attempted to pick out his next opponent. As much as he wanted to end the threat that Pelios posed, he would have to wait. Pelios had his work cut out with a strong foe of his own. He had only just defeated his last competitor before involving himself in the separate duel that went on between the other two warriors. Pelios had slammed his sword through one of the men's backs and then turned to the dead man's opponent.

Hector approached the duel with caution. No one else was left to fight so he stepped over the fallen challengers and approached the two left. Both had taken injuries to the arm.

Hector had a problem. As he got closer to the fight, he could not identify which one was Pelios. Both men were large and of similar shape.

The Prince was now only about twenty feet away. He really didn't want to stab one of the men in the back, but he was going to have to. He couldn't just observe the fight and wait so he approached with his sword held out in front of him.

All of a sudden a haunting scream ripped through the Arena. One of the men had stuck the other with his blade. Hector halted and watched the runner-up slide from the sword and onto the floor. His death was applauded by the crowd, who expressed their delight as the final two men prepared to fight to the death.

The large man turned to Hector who stood over a dead warrior that still bled heavily onto the ground. Hector stared at the only surviving man with interest, wondering if the final opponent was Pelios.

He figured he had a way to find out.

Since there was only one opponent left, he decided to reward the crowd with his presence. The Prince stuck his blood-drenched sword deep into the ground and reached up to his helmet, gripping it tightly before sliding it off.

The crowd gasped with shock as the Prince took off his helmet, revealing his identity and also his survival. The gasp soon dissolved as an ear blistering cheer erupted, the people overwhelmed to see that Hector was still alive. Their screams and cheers gave him the courage he needed to finish the task.

Hector blotted out the crowd's roar, looking to his left to the dungeon door that he had only recently emerged from. He looked at Gideon who stared back with his fingers wrapped tightly around the cage bars. Hector looked only for a moment then turned from his teacher and began to compose himself, breathing out hard and focusing on the final part of his task.

He glared at his opponent with interest. He hoped that removing his helmet would encourage his enemy to do the same. But the large man simply stared back at Hector, motionless.

Finally, he reached up and pulled off his helmet.

Pelios.

"Now, you die, Hector Ringfold," said Pelios. "Your father's line ends today. Just like mine did long ago."

Hector's stomach sickened at the sight of Pelios. He had hoped that he wouldn't have to face him.

"My father tried to find you, Pelios," he said, "when he learned of your reason for volunteering for Selection all those years ago. He wanted to help you."

The crowd bristled with anticipation.

"Your father rides to war, I hear," said Pelios. "I hope he lies face down in a ditch, dead." He gripped his sword and began stalking towards Hector.

Prince Hector stared at the approaching beast with anger. He too gripped his sword handle and walked forward in order to meet his enemy head on. He now had no choice but to finish his father's job by slaying the beast once and for all.

The first slam splintered the ears of the crowd as Pelios struck first. Hector slashed straight back, trading blows with his opponent.

Every time Pelios swiped, Hector swiped. Whenever Hector slashed, Pelios slashed. But neither men allowed an attack to reach their body.

The Prince decided to change his style, he side-stepped and cut diagonally, aiming for Pelios's leg but the attack was blocked and he was then forced onto the defensive. Pelios slashed in an angled motion, one attack after the other, even diving up into the air and slamming heavily down at Hector, who looked to be panicking all of a sudden.

Pelios was seemingly not tiring. Usually when someone lashed so many blows in quick succession, their arm would begin to tire, but not Pelios's. He was as fit as a Buywise bred horse.

Hector tried to devise a plan to get out of the situation that he found himself in. He was struggling to find a way to attack. He had no time to even angle his sword as he only just managed to block the flurry of slashes in time. Every swing of his sword had to be a defensive one.

Pelios swivelled his hips and brought his sword hand around every time. Hector had to act. It was only a matter of time before one of these deathly swipes got through so he decided to target Pelios's already cut left arm.

Hector deflected his enemy's sword again, this time using his signature counter attacking move by ducking down and attempting to spin and slash, but he was booted hard as he ducks. Hector fell to the floor, his usual technique of ducking, then countering disposed of with ease.

Nothing that Hector attempted could beat Pelios, but he didn't give up. He rolled back as Pelios smashed down, narrowly missing him. The Prince rolled and rolled as Pelios followed him, smacking down constantly with his sword.

The bulldozing footsteps that Pelios made with every attack helped Hector pinpoint exactly where his bombarding foe was as he continued to roll away from his finally tiring pursuer, like a wounded snake sliding away from its predator.

Hector decided it was time to strike.

He rolled one last time then pivoted his body around, digging his heels into the sand. Then, like a startled fox, he leapt into the air, ripping his sword upwards.

He had Pelios off-guard, sword cutting up through his enemy's wrist, taking the hand off in one clean cut.

Pelios screamed into the sky, dropping to the floor, holding his bloody stump.

But he was soon silenced.

Hector swivelled his sword, aiming its tip at Pelios's pain-filled face.

"It is in fact you, Pelios, who lies face down in a ditch, dead."

Hector leaned all his weight onto his right leg, thrusting forward to push his sword into his foe's mouth.

The crowd screamed with surprise as the sword ripped through Pelios's face and out of the back of his head, leaping from their seats and bouncing up and down in the stands as Hector claimed his victory.

They chanted his name ferociously.

Prince Hector Ringfold had passed his Selection at the age of nineteen. He had earned the right to one day be called King.

CHAPTER 33
BROKEN SILENCE

Nuallan walked through the sunny streets of Brigantium, heading to the Swan Tavern. He craved a pint of the rich tasty ale that Josanne's father served every morning, evening and night. With intent to quench his thirst, he had travelled down into the city from the Palace where he had been since Hector and Gideon left for Versidia. He had been soaking up the rich comforts he had been deprived of for so long.

Nuallan chose to retain his black overthrow. He rejected the colourful royal clothing that the servants in the Palace had offered him. The poor-looking rug trailed behind him as he clattered up the steps to the sweet-smelling tavern. Nuallan opened the door and entered, immediately spotting Josanne and his nephew, and, to his surprise, his brother Andrus, who sat beside his son, slurping gently on an ale.

Nuallan, although relieved to see Andrus, decided not to declare his excitement. Instead he walked calmly over, zigzagging between the maze of benches, eventually sitting down in the empty seat beside Josanne.

"Have you only just woken up?" said Josanne. "It's the middle of the afternoon."

"Just because heartache keeps you up all night, doesn't mean the rest of us should sleep any less."

"Heartache?" asked Josanne.

"Don't play innocent with me," said Nuallan. "Something happened between you and Koos. You've not been the same since he left and we've all noticed your change in mood." He waved over the barmaid.

"You are mistaken, friend," said Josanne. "I simply worry about Hector and your brother. Still no word has travelled to my ears. His Selection was yesterday."

"I'm positive Hector will pass," said Oslo, pulling apart a tough chunk of bread. "I trained with him and Uncle Gideon. Faizer too. Hector is one of the best fighters I have ever seen."

"Exactly," nodded Nuallan, looking over at Andrus.

"You're still mad that you were not asked to go along, aren't you?" said Josanne.

"Well, of course I am," said Nuallan. "Gideon may seem strong but he needs me. We never do things separately."

"You can't protect him forever," spoke a rare voice.

Nuallan looked across the table in disbelief. The voice he had just heard was not Josanne or Oslo, but Andrus.

Nuallan couldn't find words to say back to Andrus. It had been almost a month since his brother had uttered a word.

Andrus released his grasp on his ale and stood up.

"No one can," said Andrus. "My wife, my son and Doxass all tried to protect Gideon. And now they are all dead. Just like you will soon be dead unless you let him go." Then, refusing to give anyone a chance to reply, he turned and left the tavern.

"Why was I not informed that he was speaking again?" hissed Nuallan, turning on the shell-shocked Josanne.

"Hold your fucking tongue," she spat. "That is the first time I've heard him speak since Vanghale."

Nuallan turned to Oslo, but before he could ask him anything Oslo spoke out.

"He spoke," said the lad. "You said he would. He spoke." He then jumped up and attempted to chase after his father. But he was quickly stopped.

"No, Oslo," said Nuallan. "We don't want to harass him.

He might still need more time. He knows where we are if he needs us."

Oslo looked down sadly before sitting back down in his chair.

"Sometimes I think he forgets that he still has a son," the boy said angrily. "He forgets that I too lost a brother and a mother. It wasn't just him who felt the loss." He reached for Andrus's half-full tankard.

"Your grandfather went on like this," said Nuallan. "Your father looked up to him like no one else, he watched Artaxes do the exact same thing. He's acting the only way he knows how to, Oslo. But he will come back to us properly. Look at today, he spoke."

"It's not good enough," snapped Oslo. "It's selfish. He's lucky he has a son. You would make a great father, Uncle, but yet you don't sire a son and Uncle Gideon doesn't even know if his son lives."

At that, Oslo launched himself out of his chair and stormed for the door.

Nuallan buried his head in his hands. He feared for Oslo deeply. Although no one else could see it, he could. Oslo was exactly the same as Andrus, just like Andrus was exactly the same as Artaxes. The same aggression, the same hatred and volcanic personality of Artaxes and Andrus lived within Oslo.

"Do you care to explain?" asked Josanne.

"What's to explain?" said Nuallan. "The boy is troubled. His father has abandoned him."

"Not that. He said that Gideon didn't know if his son was alive or not. Nuallan, does Gideon have a son?"

Nuallan looked at her blankly. "It's not my place to share my brother's business."

"Not your place? I'm sorry, but do you mistake me for some stranger? Do you forget who I am? If Gideon were here, he would tell me. You know he would, so proceed. Now."

Nuallan gave a gentle nod. "Gideon had a son, yes," he said. "Whether he still does or not, we do not know. Even Gideon doesn't know."

"But how can that be?" said Josanne.

"After the battle upon the Gantry, after we were defeated, the High King ordered all of our boys over the age of twelve to be offered up to him. To be trained as Mannequin Men, I think he calls them. We had no choice. Father had already agreed. Agreed to banish his three sons, replace the Darchem losses with our own troops, and offer up every boy over the age of twelve."

"Rather steep demands, I must say," said Josanne.

"Well, yes," said Nuallan. "Andrus took it the hardest as he looked up to our father more than anyone else." He paused to retrieve the ale that he had only just received from Josanne's barmaid cousin, and then continued. "So… straight from the Gantry, we rode home with a Darchem party led by Hornton who runs the watch outside of Versidia."

"Carry on," urged Josanne.

"Upon arrival, we rallied up the boys for Hornton, but there was a massive panic. Mothers, fathers, they all fought back. There were riots in the streets, and our father sat back and ordered the soldiers to not intervene. To let Hornton do as he wished. The men that fought back were killed. Women too, if they resisted. By nightfall the Darchem soldiers had taken almost all the boys, chained them up and prepared them to march to High Darchem, but then a brawl broke out in the square. The square where Gideon was trying to hide his family. You see, Gideon didn't trust Hornton, so he was trying to hide his son in the sewers beneath Meridium when Hornton's men raided the square. Gideon fought back but his wife and son were dragged away. He watched as they beat his wife to death with clubs. His son, too."

Josanne looked at Nuallan sadly. "You poor men. Your whole life truly has been a misery. Did the boy survive?"

"We don't know. Gideon said they carried the boy's body away and took him anyway. His wife, however, was pronounced dead on the spot, her skull bashed in by Hornton himself. Gideon insisted that Hornton followed him and planned the whole thing."

"And what do you think?" said Josanne.

"I think that, for three brothers, we have seen too much pain for one lifetime, and right now I would like to just enjoy what we have because you never know when something like that may happen again." He picked up his drink and slurped at it hard. Once finished he gently put the tankard down on the table and looked back to his redheaded friend.

"In some places of Requirium," he said, "they call us the Lost Sons of Meridium. I think The Cursed Sons of Meridium fits far better. At least that's how it seems to me anyway." He wrapped his hands around his ale again.

Josanne looked at Nuallan who somehow managed to retain a pleasant face after explaining the horrific story. She closed her eyes and leaned in towards Nuallan, kissing him ever so gently on the cheek.

"There are no more dark days for you and your brothers now," she said. "Gideon will soon return, Andrus is talking again and you have the favour of the future King. You can live happily here in Brigantium. No more fighting and no more death."

"For all of our sakes, I hope you're right, Josanne, I really do." He put his hand on top of hers. "You're a good friend. And an even better drinker."

Josanne laughed and stood up. "I'll get us a bottle of port and prove you right then, shall I?"

She turned and went over to her father's bar.

Nuallan took the moment alone to think about Gideon's son.

Although he seemed calm whilst speaking, the story had upset him. He truly had had enough of the pain that he and his brothers had suffered in their lifetimes. He wanted nothing more than for Josanne's words to be right… no more fighting, no more death. But Nuallan was a realistic man. He knew it was just a dream. As long he and his brothers lived, they would always be surrounded by pain and death.

CHAPTER 34
THE PROMISE CROWN

Hector stood patiently behind a thick golden curtain whilst listening to the muffled voice of King Emric Kane. It was the day after Selection and Hector was waiting to take part in the final part of the traditional event... the Crowning.

Everyone of power, reputation or popularity was inside the Citadel's theatre room. They awaited the Versidian King to finish his speech so that the future King of Brigantium could step through the glowing curtain and out onto the stage.

For the first time in a fortnight Hector felt worry free. The only thing on his mind was the thought of returning home to inform his father of his victory. He was to now go down in history as another Selection victor.

Although Hector felt no guilt for killing four men in the arena, he did feel something. He felt curious, curious as to how Pelios and the first two attackers knew who he was. Hector wanted answers, but, for now, he was going to enjoy his victory.

For the occasion, Hector had suited himself back up in the armour he wore for Selection. He left the helmet off and added a new homily touch: a long, sunny yellow cape. The cape would match the golden crown he was to receive. But the crown was not his only reward. He was to also receive the ten thousand gold pieces, the victor's purse. Hector was a prince and soon to be a king, ten thousand gold coins was nothing to him, he did not need the money so he planned to give it away.

He looked up from the stage floor as King Emric spoke his name. Suddenly the golden curtain glided open, revealing the massed crowd, applauding his arrival.

The Prince walked onto the stage where he was to meet and greet all the noble men and women, whilst the Versidian civilians watched from the seated area below. Present on the stage were Dothron and the Elders, Chaudrey and the Moth Priests, as well as King Emric and his whole family.

The seven Elders stood in a neat triangular formation to the left of the stage whilst Chaudrey and a squadron of Moth Priests stood beside them. To the right was King Emric Kane, his wife, six daughters and a son.

Out of all the people in this section of the Citadel, Hector could not find a single friendly face, but that was his own doing. He wanted to set back off to the east as soon as possible so he had all his friends and accomplices off preparing the carriages.

All except Gideon, who waited in one of the backrooms for Hector to finish the ceremony. He had told Hector before he left that he needed to speak with him as soon as it was over.

Hector went out onto the heavy, wooden stage. He was embraced by King Emric. The King then leaned in and kissed Hector on both cheeks, before presenting the victor to the crowd of cheering people.

"Ladies and Gentlemen, I present to you our victor, Hector Ringfold of Brigantium!"

The crowd stood up from their pew-like seats and applauded sensationally.

The Prince bowed to the crowd before facing King Emric, who waited until the crowd had silenced before speaking.

"May all of you witness the crowning of Hector," said King Emric. "In a few moments, I will place the Promise Crown upon the head of the future King of the East." He then turned to the left where one of his royal servants stood with a purple cushion laid across his arms.

On the cushion was a pointed, oval-shaped crown... the Promise Crown.

The Promise Crown was a temporary crown given to the Brigantium heir should he pass Selection, to confirm that their claim was deserved. They would wear this crown right up until the death of the King. They would then return the Promise Crown to Versidia and take up their father's crown to become King.

The servant walked over and stood before Hector who knelt down on one knee. He then bowed his head and stared at the floor.

King Emric stepped slowly over to the servant and picked up the crown. He turned to the crowd and lifted up the Promise Crown with excitement, before lowering it slowly to waist level.

"Hector," he said, "you entered this city as a boy. You bent that knee as a boy, now rise as a man and a King." He delicately placed the crown on Hector's head.

The crowd roared like an army of lions as Hector rose to his feet, applauding so loudly the crystal chandeliers shook.

Eventually, the cheers died down and Hector walked past Emric, to the end of the stage.

"People of Versidia," he said, "people of High Darchem and people of Brigantium, I thank you all for your attendance. And I thank you even more for your support. I came here to honour a tradition and to extend a legacy. Although this is a happy day for most, some would deem it a dark day. Eleven warriors died yesterday. They didn't have to die but they took the risk. They took the risk because they sought the victor's purse of ten thousand. Or at least most of them did. I know for sure that one man volunteered so that he could end my father's bloodline. And for that his family will not receive a taking in my good gesture. But for the other ten men, I reward their family with one thousand gold coins each, from my victor's purse. Let their families go on surviving for as long as they can."

The crowd clapped gratefully and respectfully, although some chatter could be heard, as it seemed that some did not approve of Hector's gesture. The volunteers that fought in Selection were usually homeless men, or servants that were accustomed to the swing of a sword. They usually only volunteered for Selection so that they could win the victor's purse in order to feed their starving families. That was the reason for Hector's kind act, but some people in Versidia saw it as an insult that he would give away his reward to the likes of someone that they classed as a slave or beneath them. But still, the majority of the crowd clapped pleasantly.

The generous Prince turned from the applauding mob now and approached King Emric, who stood beside the Elders. They were deep in whisper.

"I trust that I can leave you in charge of tending to the matter, King Emric," said Hector. "Will you see to it that the families receive the gold?"

"Of course, my Prince," said Emric. "And might I add what a fine gesture that is."

Dothron stepped forward. "Congratulations, Hector. Your father will be very proud."

"I'm sure, he will," replied Hector.

"I had another dream about him last night," said Dothron, "a very strange dream. And it was not only your father I saw, Hector. You keep strange company."

Hector looked to Dothron, waiting for more, but no more words came from the old man's mouth. He simply bowed and walked off with the rest of the Elders.

"Word has reached my ear that you plan to leave today," said Emric. "Most people take the rest of the week to enjoy the celebration, my Prince."

"I leave at once, actually. My escort are preparing the carriages. I need to get back to my father."

Emric nodded. "Very well then. I will have my servant here take you back to your quarters so that you can prepare yourself for your trip back up to the Palace to gather your effects."

"No need, my King," said the Prince. "My men have already retrieved my things. I need only to go get my servant from the back room and I will be on my way."

"Very well then," said Emric. "Congratulations again. You will be looking for a wife soon, no doubt?"

"I haven't really thought about it."

"Well, take a look. I have six daughters. Some more beautiful than others. You can take your pick should the day come soon." Emric pointed over to a swarm of people that chatted upon the stage.

Hector looked heavily uninterested as he gazed over to the flock of young women, but one of them caught his eye immediately, wiping the look of disinterest clean from his face.

A tall woman, who could only be a few years older than himself, looked back with a dazzling smile. She was elegantly postured and long of blonde hair. She was called Kendle Kane, or at least she was before she got married. Hector gazed at her as she looked back, smiling as she did so.

"Any one of my daughters but that one, I'm afraid," said the King. "She is married to Lumon, the Eagle Pact Leader. Duran Harall felt he was securing a strong alliance by marrying his right hand to one of my daughters."

Hector looked away immediately. "I see."

The King smiled sadly.

"King Emric," said Hector. "I thank you for your hospitality. I now take my leave." He bowed and turned from the King.

The Brigantium Prince walked back through the golden curtain and trotted down the steps towards the theatre's back rooms. He hurried through the black sheets that dangled down, then trekked through the corridors to the room that he had got ready in before the crowning ceremony.

Hector pushed on the door and entered.

"Thank God that is over," he said. "Are the carriages ready?"

"They are," said Gideon, looking out of an open but barred window.

The wind outside had become fierce. It was lashing at the people who scurried past the Citadel. A storm was brewing. The wind was so strong that it burst through the window taking Gideon's very breath away. He was forced to turn from it.

"A miserable day to be a coachman," he said.

Hector laughed as he began to pull off his armour. "At least you only have to bear the reins until we pass back through Hornton's Watch."

But he was not rewarded with a reply or even acknowledged for that matter.

Hector looked up at Gideon who stood, arms folded, with one of his fingers between his teeth.

"Gideon? What's wrong?"

Gideon broke from his trance and looked to the Prince. He tried to think of the best way to lay his case against the traitor, Riycard Badstuber, upon Hector.

"It was Riycard," he said. "All of it. Probably his father too."

"What do you speak of?" asked Hector with great confusion.

"Pelios…" said Gideon, "and the two men that attacked you at the beginning of Selection too. They were able to identify you."

"You noticed it too. So I wasn't just imagining it. Wait. What has this got to do with the Badstubers?"

"My Prince, there was a mark upon your shoulder blade. Someone had put it there before Selection. I am confident that it was Riycard."

"And you didn't think to tell me this before I entered the Arena?" growled Hector.

"I tried," said Gideon. "My Prince, don't you think I tried? I was stopped by a guard. You were in the Arena already. There was nothing I could do, believe me."

Hector understood, but he still wanted to know why Gideon assumed that the Badstubers were responsible for trying to sabotage the Selection.

"What makes you think Riycard is involved? Do you think he put the mark on my armour?"

"I think he did more than just put the mark on the armour. I think he and his father are working for Duran Harall," said Gideon.

He had Hector's full attention now.

"What?"

Gideon explained. "If Duran had found out that your father took us in, he would declare war on the East. But with his crusade almost in action, he can't risk the men, so his other option would be to end Tobias's line, allowing the Badstuber family to inherit the throne. Providing the Chalk family did not send Romford off to challenge Selection, of course. That way, with you dead, and Tobias with no other sons, the throne would then pass to the Badstubers. Or the Chalks should they want it."

"So you think the High King wants me dead," said Hector. "You think that he hired Pelios and those other two men to volunteer for Selection so that I could be killed with no questions asked?" He stood up and went over to the barred window.

"Hector, I saw Lumon in the stands. I saw the look on his face when the two warriors allied against you. He knew that it was going to happen even before it did. I am sure of this."

"Very well," said Hector. "I will arrest Riycard now and he will stand trial."

"I would recommend waiting until we arrive back at Brigantium. We do not want to make a mockery of our image within Versidia. Say nothing until we set foot back in Brigantium."

"So be it," declared Hector. "Let us take our leave."

He was massively affected after hearing Gideon's theory. Riycard was his friend and, if this were true, Hector would have to execute him. And that was not something he wanted to do.

Hector and Gideon walked out of the theatre corridors and back out into the open hall of the Citadel. They walked through the magnificent space in silence. Gideon had his hood curled around his face as he followed behind the Prince, still disguised. They headed toward the massive double doors that rattled loudly as the wind outside thrashed against them like an army trying breach a fortress. It was going to be a bumpy week's ride back to Brigantium for sure.

Gideon and Hector slowed their walk ever so slightly as they reached the doors. The guards on duty lifted the latch and began dragging the doors open as they noticed Hector and Gideon approach. But their efforts were assisted as the wind pushed the doors all the way open, allowing an angry blast of wind to breach the Citadel.

The wind ripped through the hall, whipping at everyone's faces.

But, worst of all, it almost tore the hood from Gideon's head.

Gideon composed himself. He pulled the hood close to his face, holding it against the wind. He slipped over onto Hector's left, so that the approaching squad of Darchem red cloaks that were now entering the Citadel guards couldn't lay eyes upon him.

They passed, a couple of them looking with vague curiosity at Hector.

Gideon kept calm, refusing to look back as he felt the burning stare of the Darchem soldiers burning away at his back. Seven years he had managed to keep his identity hidden. This had been too close. He had been too close to being discovered.

"Hector, we must leave," he said. " We must leave right now."

CHAPTER 35
THE STAND OFF

"Okay, so that is the overall cost of Selection. The hire of the armour, the upkeep of the fighters and hire of the chariots are all included, yes?" asked King Emric as he read through a scroll that his financial advisor had just handed him.

"Yes, every penny spent by the crown has been noted down here," replied the advisor.

"Very well then. That will be all," said Emric as he rolled up the scroll and handed it back to the banker. As the banker turned to walk away, Emric all of a sudden remembered something that Hector had asked him to do.

"Oh wait, one more thing before you go. See to it that the volunteers' families are given one thousand gold pieces. It was Prince Hector's command."

"Of course, my King." The advisor bowed and walked off down a curved set of steps.

King Emric walked over to a short comfortable throne and sat down in it, exhausted. The King of Versidia indeed had his own throne room, but unlike the other Kingdoms in Requirium, it was not within the King's Palace. King Emric Kane's throne room was tucked away in the centre of the Citadel, a medium sized room with curved walls. There was only one entrance, a twin double set of doors, nothing like the one at the entrance of the Citadel. The King's throne room was more like a nursery sitting inside of a large school that was the dominating Citadel. The walls within were however decorated the same as the other throne rooms that lay scattered around Requirium. Large silky grey sigils of Versidia hung from large metal beams, and a long white carpet ran from the door to the circular steps before the risen throne platform.

King Emric was indeed shattered, but he still had a matter of business to attend to. He rose again from his throne as Chaudrey and five other Moth Priests entered the throne room quietly. The six of them moved across the white carpet in silence as they approached King Emric.

"Greetings, Chaudrey, what news do you bring?" enquired the Versidian King.

"Dothron sends word, your grace. The church is to aid in the financial payment of Selection, exactly half," informed Chaudrey in a twanging accent.

"Is that so? Tell him I said thank you. That will most certainly aid the crown. Will you tell him I will meet with him tomorrow to discuss the matter further?" asked King Emric.

"I shall inform him at once," obeyed Chaudrey as he bowed along with his five followers. He stood. "That is not all, my King. Dothron… Dothron sent word that you must take care."

"Take care why?" Emric said, puzzled. The elder was often vague and mysterious in his speakings. But why such a warning?

Chaudrey looked uncomfortable.

"Tell me."

"My King, Dothron wonders at the wisdom of sheltering one such as the heir to the Meridium throne in our city."

"Gideon Destain? Here?"

"Disguised as a servant, my King, so that he could be here for Hector's Selection."

"You must be mad. I haven't seen the boy in over ten years," argued Emric persuasively.

"Dothron is certain. And he sends warning."

King Emric clattered down the steps and began his short walk to the throne room exit with the six Moth Priests at his back, but someone else had entered. The double doors slammed open as a mob of angered red cloaks stormed in. Lumon, accompanied by his eleven other Eagle Pact members, burst in through the doors and approached the King. Something had truly angered the Eagle Pact Leader, his furious shivering face and his pacey walk confirming that.

Emric, clueless to Lumon's ferocious march, attempted to greet him.

"Lumon, what can I do for you?" he asked as he opened his arms out wide.

But Lumon wanted nothing from him but answers. Lumon clenched his fist as he reached the King, and with one hefty blow, he smashed King Emric in the nose, dropping him to the floor. What he had just done was punishable by death. Chaudrey's protective instincts kicked in. It was their job to put an end to any threat that arose inside the Citadel. It was their sole purpose.

"Swords!" commanded Chaudrey in defence of the King and the Citadel. In one synchronised movement, Chaudrey and the five other Moth priests reached under their gowns and pulled out a curved Scimitar, the shivering slide of the swords being drawn echoing around the throne room.

Lumon, who looked hungry for a fight, retaliated instantly by hacking out his own sword, the members of the Pact doing the same.

The two small forces stared each other out venomously.

"Shall we find out if the rumours of you and your people are true, Chaudrey? Can you really swing that toy sword as well as they say?" hissed Lumon wickedly.

Chaudrey ignored the threatening talk from his possible opponent and remained calm. So did his men. He awaited the command from King Emric before engaging.

"Wait, wait, Chaudrey, don't!" yelled King Emric as he gripped his nose tightly, blood dripping from it.

Lumon looked down with disappointment at Emric's struggle as he pulled himself to his feet.

"What, what is the meaning of this?" asked the King who seemed completely disorientated from the blow.

Lumon pulled his gaze from Chaudrey and sheathed his sword. He stepped forward, pushing himself up against the King.

"Did you think you would get away it? Did you really think that we wouldn't find out?" he growled.

"Find out what?" quizzed King Emric in a state of worry.

"That you've been sheltering Gideon Destain right here under our noses."

"That's not true."

Lumon stepped back and looked deep into the King's eyes. He tried to interrogate his eyes in an attempt to see if he was lying. He gestured towards Chaudrey. "Your own elder sent warning with this priest. Do not deny it."

"I assure you that I was not aware of it. My loyalties lie with Duran Harall, not Artaxes and his lost son," argued Emric, this time persuading Lumon of his innocence. The King turned back to the Moth Priests and signalled them to stand down. He lowered his hand and smiled at Chaudrey who instantly drove his blade back into its hidden sheath. The five other Moth Priests mimicked the action, yet the Eagle Pact did not. All but Lumon stood side on with their swords drawn.

"Tell me, King Emric, where is Hector and his escort?"

"They left, only recently. Hector was in a massive rush to leave the city. He said he needed to speak with his father," said Emric.

Lumon frowned with frustration. He knew that he needed to catch Hector's escort before they passed through Hornton's Watch. Lumon would need the men that guarded the wall otherwise he would not have the strength to overpower the full escort.

"Quick, ready the horses. We go after them right now," ordered the Eagle Pact Leader as he turned to his Pact.

Without question, they charged out of the throne room.

"Duran Harall already knew that Tobias was harbouring the Lost Sons," declared Lumon, closing in on King Emric again, "and in doing so he has decided the fate of himself and his people. They will now die. The High King will send an army of seventy thousand to march on his city before the week's end." He pushed right up against the King as he threatened him. "If Tobias is expendable then so are you. If I find out that you are lying, Emric, your daughter, your city and your Citadel will burn right before your very eyes, do you understand?"

"Yes, I understand," stuttered Emric helplessly.

"Don't make me come back here, King Emric. If I have to, it will be with an army at my back."

Lumon left the throne room, leaving King Emric, Chaudrey and the other Moth Priests standing there bewildered beyond measure. King Emric had had no idea that Gideon Destain had even stepped foot in his city, and although confident that he had persuaded the High King's right hand man of his innocence, he still dwelled on the horrific threat that he had just received.

Lumon paced noisily through the Citadel, his red armour clattering with every step. He fiercely ignored every single person he passed until he arrived at the Citadel's double doors that still rattled angrily as the storm winds attacked it. He took a gushing slap of wind to the face without showing an expression as the soldiers opened the Citadel doors to let the Pact Leader leave.

"My horse, quickly," he ordered as he bounced down the steps towards his prepping company. "Come on, hurry up, hurry up," he commanded again with impatience as he finally reached the bottom of the stairs. Upon his arrival, one of the members of the Pact dragged over a black horse. Lumon without question dived up onto its back.

"Mount up, men," he commanded his men.

The other eleven members of the Eagle Pact mounted their black horses and began lining up behind their leader.

Lumon, aware of his Pact's presence, swivelled his horse and faced them.

"We have been deceived by the future King of Brigantium. See to it that he does not live out the day. His friends too. Slay them all. Except one. Duran Harall wants Gideon Destain alive. Ride hard and true, my friends, for if we do not reach them before they pass through the Watch, we will have failed. Now ride!" said Lumon, and without wasting another moment, he kicked his horse in the hip. Almost instantly it catapulted off down the concrete path. Lumon had begun his chase with his whole Pact at his back. Hector and the others would soon have to face them in another fight till the death.

CHAPTER 36
THE POWER OF THE PACT

"Hector, is something the matter?" asked Riycard Badstuber. "You have not spoken a word since we left the city."

Hector looked up from the carriage floor and stared viciously into Riycard's eyes. He wanted to leap across and throttle him where he sat, but he remembered Gideon's advice and kept the traitor's act a secret. Instead he looked back to the floor ignorantly.

"I'm fine."

Gondogon looked to the Prince who sat beside him. He too knew that something was wrong but he didn't say anything. He just opened his shutter and looked out at the overgrown forest that they were riding beside. They were about five miles away from Hornton's Watch.

Hector thought about the theory that Gideon had told him back at Versidia. He wanted to discuss it more but the opportunity had not arisen. Gideon was up top driving the carriage behind. Gideon's theory troubled him, although the Badstubers rivalled the Ringfolds, him and Riycard had always gotten along. They would spar together when they were children, and then drink together as they got older. The idea of betrayal devastated him, but he was to one day become a King, and Kings had to make the difficult choices. In this case, his choice was to decide whether to kill Riycard or let him live. Hector so far had dismissed any thought of his friend's innocence even though he wished it possible, but Gideon had sold a pretty believable theory, and he was rarely wrong about anything.

The strong wind that had harassed every tree within fifty miles since the morning was heightening even more, the arriving storm bullying the landscape as it made its presence known. It wobbled the carriage annoyingly as it blew against the wooden wheels that carried the Royal escort back home. Gondogon closed his shutter as the wind whistled off the open gap that the shutter provided.

"I feel sorry for the coachmen," said Gondogon. "The storm is worsening."

"Maybe we should stop for the night once we pass through the Watch?" suggested Romford.

"That makes sense. We can take shelter beneath the mountains that we passed on the way in," recommended Riycard, adding his input to the conversation.

"What do you think, Prince Hector?" added Riycard.

Hector again looked up with venom towards Riycard. "That sounds fine. How far out are we?"

"About three miles," said Gondogon.

Hector nodded slightly before going back to silence.

"So what is your plan now then that Selection is over?" asked Enly who sat opposite Faizer in their carriage.

"Not a damn thing, Enly," he replied with a smile stretched across his face.

Enly smiled back at him and continued to listen as Faizer spoke again.

"I'm tired," he said. "I have fought my whole life. I'm afraid this was my last quest. I am retiring early."

"I don't know, I don't see it," said Enly cheerfully.

"See what?"

"You, sitting calmly in the garden of a tavern, drinking yourself into an early grave. You need the fight in order to survive," said Enly, making Faizer smile widely.

"You don't know me, my new friend. I have more about me than just a strong arm."

"I've known men like you my whole life. You wouldn't know what to do with yourself if you had no sword to swing, no one to protect, nothing to fight for," said Enly passionately, sending Faizer into a daydream.

Faizer zoned out as Enly's words reached him deeply. Faizer half-believed what Enly was saying to be true. Faizer had known nothing else but the fight, but for his own sake he had to try.

"Right you may be, Enly, but I have to try. The thought of drinking myself silly in Josanne's tavern appeals to me greatly.

"If you say so, maybe get yourself a woman too? A woman that will provide you with a family of sons and daughters?" added Enly happily.

But that remark did not please Faizer. He shook his head sternly. "No, none of that for me."

"Why not?"

"I have witnessed the people closest to me fall apart, lose themselves in their own minds, over losing a woman, or a child," said Faizer sadly as he thought about Andrus.

"You speak of Andrus and his family? I heard the story."

Faizer nodded. "Not just him, others too. I don't want to have the worry of keeping them safe, not in this world, not in this life."

Enly, who sympathised with Faizer, sought to provide comfort. "Hector is a man of his word. He will let you all stay in Brigantium and live the high life if you chose to. If you truly want the fight to be over, it can be," he said kindly.

Faizer smiled at Enly without words. The trouble was, Faizer didn't know if he was truly ready to leave the fight behind. Enly's words had made him realise how daunting a life would seem without the company and without the danger and the risk.

Gideon stopped the carriage harshly, and Enly and Faizer stuttered forwards slightly as they arrived at Hornton's Watch,

"Are we here?" asked Enly.

Faizer slid open his shutter and peeked out.

"Yes," he confirmed. "Hector and the others are getting out, come."

Enly and Faizer climbed out of the carriage and walked over towards Hector and the others.

"Prince Hector, word reached the Watch of your victory in the Arena. Congratulations," said Hornton kindly as he approached Hector with a squad of three men.

"Thank you, Hornton," replied Hector.

"I must say I am surprised that you have left the city so quickly. Usually the victor stays for at least a week to soak up the rewards," added Hornton.

"Well, I must return to my father."

"He fights in the west, I hear, with Artaxes?" said Hornton.

"He does," replied Hector bluntly as the news seemed to have slightly angered Hornton.

Hornton, like most men from Darchem, despised Artaxes, so it was pretty obvious that he did not approve of Tobias aiding him. An awkward silence took over as the two looked at each without words until Hornton finally yelled out to his guards that stood by the black caged gate.

"Open the gate!"

The extremely heavy gate croaked intimidatingly as it slowly began sliding up.

"Fair well, Hornton," said Hector as he turned from the red-cloaked watchmen.

"Fair well, Prince Hector. Send my regards to your father, will you?" said Hornton.

Hector nodded and smiled vaguely at Hornton before turning again and signalling his men to get back in their carriages.

Faizer was the only person who remained stationary as something in the distance grabbed his attention.

"What's that?" he asked.

Hornton also noticed and slid between Gondogon and Hector, staring out into the distance at the black smudge that approached at a high speed. Hornton squinted, trying to make it out.

"What's he doing here? He was to ride back to Darchem today," said Hornton as he relaxed his eyes and turned to one of his soldiers.

Hector, who heard Hornton's words, quickly looked up to Gideon who was already staring at him. They both knew that the approaching mob was Lumon and The Eagle Pact.

Gideon had risked raising his head slightly in order to send a silent message to Hector. He stared at the Brigantium Prince. He needed to yell out to tell Hector of the danger that was closing in, but he didn't want to risk discovery. Luckily for him, Hector had read his worry. He knew it was time to leave.

"Hornton, we must go. Fair well," repeated Hector as he tried to hurry Romford and Riycard back into the carriage.

Hector's sudden need to leave caught the attention of Hornton who ended the quiet discussion between himself and his guard to walk over and address Hector.

"If you wait a moment, I'm sure Lumon will willingly escort you across the Versidian border. After all, you still haven't strengthened your escort like I advised you to upon your arrival. You know the Lure Alliance occupy many of the villages and towns south of here," offered Hornton with slight suspicion.

"No need," replied Hector quickly as he approached his carriage. "My father is expecting us before the week is out. We have no time to waste."

Hornton turned back to the approaching cavalry as a distant noise attracted his attention.

"Close the gate!" screamed Lumon from afar, but the wind suffocated his words, making it clouded to Hornton's ears.

Hornton squinted his eyes and stepped forward in an attempt to make out what Lumon was shouting.

"My lord, he is telling us to close the gate. What do we do?" asked one of the soldiers, his hand on his sword hilt.

Hornton looked at him with his eyebrows raised. "What?" he asked.

Old age had taken its toll on Hornton, his eyesight fading and his hearing weak. He relied deeply on his guards and soldiers to aid him with simplest of tasks.

"My Lord, he is telling us to shut the gate," repeated the soldier who looked up to Hector.

Hornton looked with confusion at his soldier for a moment and then looked back out into the distance as Lumon's words become a little more clear. He was in a state of shock as he finally realised the seriousness of The Eagle Pact's return. Each member of the Pact was riding fiercely with their swords drawn.

Without knowing the reason for Lumon's aggressive approach, Hornton made a quick decision.

"Close the gate, close the gate!" he screamed as he spun round. The gate door was more than halfway open now as Hornton shouted his command.

"Hornton, what is the meaning of this?" barked Hector as he jumped down from the carriage steps.

Hornton replied to Hector without the use of words but with the sight of his sword. He drew it, along with the three soldiers that had accompanied Hornton. Hornton was not taking any risks. Until he found out what Lumon wanted with Hector, he was not taking any chances. He signalled the full watch guard to prepare themselves for a fight.

"Arm yourselves!" he screamed in an attempt to alert the guards that swarmed the Watch's wall. Suddenly fifty swords ripped out of their scabbards, the red cloaks abandoning their Watch and making for the various stone stairwells that ran down the inside of the concrete wall.

Hector and his escort were on the verge of a massively outnumbered fight. If they were to stand a chance, they would have to engage the Darchem troops before the Eagle Pact arrived, but they were running out of time.

"Remain calm, Prince Hector. I am just taking precautions. It appears that Lumon has an urgent need to speak with you." Hornton stood back, allowing the three soldiers to step in front of him.

Hector took his worried glance from Hornton and turned to the left as the Eagle Pact rode with menace in their direction. They were only half a mile out now.

Hector then looked to the right where over forty soldiers scattered down the steps with their swords drawn. He didn't know what to do. He flickered his fingers as he thought about drawing his sword, but he resisted. He then swung his head to the right where he watched a squadron of guards attempt to close the gate. He was running out of time.

Romford and Riycard stood either side of Hector. They both stared at him nervously, awaiting a command that he had still failed to give. He was frozen.

Luckily for him, Gideon saved him the decision, by making it for him.

In one decisive lash, Gideon whipped the reins, signalling the two horses leading his carriage to bolt forward, breaking out into an instant sprint. Hornton and Hector along with both of their accomplices looked with horror as Gideon drove his carriage with menace towards the lowering gate. For a moment, Hector thought Gideon was making a run for it, that was until the carriage veered left slightly and headed towards the stone stairwells where a large portion of Darchem men clattered down in an attempt to reach their commanding officer.

Hornton watched with shock as Gideon drove his carriage into the crowd of men, witnessing helplessly as almost all of his force became victim to the quick thinking Meridium Prince. Gideon had made the important decision that Hector had not. He was giving the escort a chance. Gideon knew that the Eagle Pact were not coming to sit down and chat. He knew they were coming to kill the Prince and the escort, so before they arrived he knew he had to take out as many of the Darchem soldiers as possible. That way Gideon and his friends had a chance.

The screams of the crushed men haunted the Watch as they bled out beneath the smashed carriage. Gideon had gone through more than half the men, squashing, crushing and flattening the red cloaks as he collided with the wall. Gideon had given his comrades a fighting chance. No more than fifteen Darchem guards were left able to fight. Even the guards that were closing the gate broke from their posts to engage Gideon who was crawling from the wreckage.

"Kill them, kill them all!" screamed Hornton as he watched

the horrifying sight unfold to his left. The three soldiers beside Hornton charged towards Hector, but they stood no chance. Gondogon was first to act as he ripped out his sword and slashed it around, cutting across the chest of the first man. But he was not to be left alone in this fight. Enly and Faizer had now charged over from their carriage and had hacked away at the other two men.

"Romford, Riycard with me. Let's get to Gideon, quick!" ordered Hector as he clawed out his sword. The three of them sprinted over to the wreckage, to be met by the scattered survivors head on. A dozen red cloaks sprinted towards the Brigantium Prince and his two allies.

Hector slashed out first. He cut across the first man, ducking down as he connected. He then lunged forward at the second soldier stabbing right through him. Luckily for Hector, Romford and Riycard cut in at the two men that tried to swing at the occupied Prince. His sword was so deeply jammed into the soldier's body that he wouldn't have been able to pull the sword out in time to deflect any other attack. But he then had to repay the favour. Romford and Riycard had not killed their foes as quickly as Hector had. He tightly gripped his sword handle and pulled it from his dead victim's body, swinging to the left and right taking down his two allies' foes.

Gideon, although in pain from the crash, pulled himself up. Hector needed aid. Gideon dragged himself from beneath the destroyed carriage and entered the battle with nothing but a knife he had hidden beneath his overthrow. The fierce Westerner instantly got to work by cutting at the leg of a soldier who was running towards Romford. He dealt the first cut before swivelling his knife and hand around, ready to finish his first foe. Gideon stabbed hard as he forced the blade down into the man's chest. As he died, Gideon took his sword. He was ready to embark on a vicious killing spree.

Gideon's murderous adventure was inspired by the presence of Hornton. Gideon had an unhealthy obsession for Hornton that no one knew about, no one but his brothers. Hornton had wronged Gideon once before, taking everything from him that he had ever loved. This was the Meridium heir's chance to get revenge.

Gideon destroyed another victim as he stabbed into him. He fought his way to Hector and his comrades with ease, all of the Darchem soldiers disposed of, all except Hornton. Hornton was still alive, but not because he had kept himself alive with skilful swinging of his own sword. He was in fact rather poorly skilled in combat, he was simply too old. The last time he had swung a weapon was upon the Gantry seven years ago against the Meridiums. Hornton was in fact alive because Gondogon had disarmed him and decided to leave his fate to the Prince.

Hector, Romford, Riycard and Gideon charged over to Faizer, Enly and Gondogon in order to regroup. The Eagle Pact, despite losing the advantage of the Watch's guards, continued to ride towards them, and they were almost upon them.

"What do we do with him?" asked Gondogon who kicked out at the back of Hornton's old leg, knocking him to the floor. He then grabbed Hornton's long grey hair and pulled him to his knees.

"My Prince, what do we do with him?" repeated Gondogon.

But once again, Gideon saved the Prince from making the decision. He slid between Romford and Faizer and grabbed hold of Hornton's hair, snatching him from Gondogon's grasp. He dragged the old body of Hornton towards the horses that were almost upon them, then he stopped still and aimed his sword down at Hornton's throat.

"You, you?!" bellowed Hornton as he looked up into the eyes of Gideon. Hornton in a state of rage spat up grossly at Gideon before wriggling about in an attempt to break free, but he got nowhere.

Gideon wiped the spit from his face and smashed down with the sword handle, splitting open Hornton's old wrinkled head.

"Be still, Hornton, you will soon be dead for what you did to my wife," promised Gideon viciously. "To my son," he whispered as he looked down with a demonic gleam in his eyes.

Hornton looked up a little more frightened as he took in the threat. The only hope that the Watch Commander had of survival was the sight of the twelve members of The Eagle Pact demounting in style.

Lumon dropped down from his horse along with his eleven companions, storming towards Gideon who stood with a blade to Hornton's throat.

Lumon walked a few steps before stopping at a distance he felt was decent enough to trade conversation before engaging. He looked sympathetically at Hornton for a moment before acknowledging Gideon and his companions.

"So you have returned after all these years," stated Lumon.

Gideon did not reply. He glared into the eyes of the Eagle Pact Leader whilst tightening his grip around the Darchem sword handle.

Lumon smirked as he looked down to his hands. He delicately pulled his black gloves off, one finger at a time. Once he finished taking them off, he tucked them into a side pocket beneath his red armour. Lumon then looked back up whilst sliding out his longsword casually. The perfect line of eleven Eagle Pact members mimicked his action, all tearing out their swords together.

"You're very clever, Gideon Destain. You had the instinct to take out the Watch before we got here. You knew that you would have stood no chance. Very clever. I don't think your new Prince would have had the instinct to do that, would he?" mocked Lumon as he smirked at Hector. Lumon then looked to Hornton who stared at him with desperation, his eyes begging for him to save him, although his mouth remained closed. But Lumon held no sympathy for his beaten ally. He was in fact embarrassed at how easily he had been overrun by just seven men.

"Lumon, speak quickly and tell me what is the meaning of this. Why do you come after us?" asked Hector as he stepped forward now.

"Oh dear Hector, you and your traitorous father are harbouring fugitives. You have betrayed your High King and will now pay the ultimate price," stated Lumon as he looked over to Gideon again. "Are you going to kill him or are you going to just keep on standing there with your blade to his throat?"

Gideon looked at Lumon furiously, but in order not to show weakness and to also settle a long owed debt, he dug the blade into Hornton's neck horrifically, keeping eye contact with the smiling Eagle Pact Leader. Gideon felt relief as he ended the life of the man who had destroyed his own. In order to retrieve full satisfaction, he extended the attack. He gripped the buried sword tighter, and with one swift tug, he pulled the blade to the left, completely taking out Hornton's throat. Gideon released his hold on his old enemy, allowing him to fall to the bloody floor.

Lumon laughed lightly as he watched Gideon kill his comrade. He then turned to his men and nodded. "The High King wants the Westerner alive. Kill the rest," he declared ruthlessly as he took the first steps towards Gideon with his men at his back.

Gondogon had had enough of Lumon. He brushed between his Prince and Enly and ran at Lumon. Hector and Gideon now charged in also with the rest of the escort. The first swords that clashed were that of Lumon and Gondogon, the shatter of the weapons ringing around the small battlefield sharply, causing the horses on the only able carriage to jeer up nervously.

Hector and his royal escort were out-numbered almost two to one, but every man present was more than capable of taking on more than one foe at a time, even if the foes they faced were members of The Eagle Pact.

Gondogon immediately got to work on Lumon, using his strength and size to instantly put Lumon on the back foot as he swung his blood-hungry sword around and smashed it in the direction of Lumon with ferocious speed. The Eagle Pact Leader was in fact on the back foot, but he was not worried, he was blocking the attacks with ease, awaiting his moment to strike.

Gideon, who had drifted off to the right side, was happy to engage into a duel with two enemies. He lunged forward at one before leaping back, swinging his fist into the face of the other attacker. The recovering soldier awarded Gideon with an opportunity as the punch knocked him in the other direction, leaving his whole back on show. Gideon was surprised as he slid his blade through the back of his first kill without much effort.

The Eagle Pact were known for their excellent skill in combat. Gideon turned and focused on the second attacker, gripping his sword with two hands and slashing at his victim from every angle.

Hector fought in the centre of the commotion with Faizer. They had their backs to each other whilst they fended off four attackers, and overall were coping. Enly and Riycard had taken up a similar tactic by fighting back to back against a number of Darchem enemies also. The only person who seemed to be struggling was Romford.

Romford controlled his sword well as he blocked the attack from his single challenger comfortably, but for some strange reason he was not attacking back. He couldn't take his gaze off Lumon who controlled the fight between himself and Gondogon. Romford's lack of interest almost cost him his life and he only just avoided death as the Darchem warrior slashed at him, only narrowly missing his throat. He then tackled Romford hard, slamming up against the side of the carriage. Romford who still seemed confused as to why they were being attacked was in need of aid which finally came.

Riycard Badstuber who had wounded his last foe, had left Enly alone to fend off the others so he could save Romford. Riycard peered behind Romford's attacker, and in one slash he cut across the red-cloaked man's back, dropping him to the floor.

"Romford, what are you doing? Fight!" barked Riycard who had noticed Romford's strange behaviour. He had also noticed more than just Romford's behaviour, the Prince had been downed, pulled to the floor by his enemy.

Hector looked into the eyes of his attacker as he lay flat on his back, looking up at his doom. He had tried to pull the soldier in close to prevent him from getting the distance he needed in order to lift up his sword, but Hector had failed. The soldier had wriggled free of Hector's grapple and straightened his back. Before Hector could react, his enemy spun round his sword and aimed it down, ready to deal the finishing blow. A blow that did not come.

The only thing that did come was a spray of blood that squirted from The Eagle Pact member. Hector lowered his arms that he had shot up defensively only to see the murderous sword tip that had burst through the Pact member's chest. Someone had saved Hector, but who he did not know.

The body fell to the left with the sword still inside.

"Up you get, my Prince," said Riycard, who had surprisingly saved the Prince. He offered out his hand and lifted him up.

"Riycard, thank you," said Hector, shocked that Riycard of all people had just saved him.

The sound of horses snorting and kicking sounded close. Romford was struggling to control the reins of the stolen mounts.

"Everyone on, let's get out of here, come on!" screamed Romford. "They're closing the gate!"

Enly and Faizer were the first to jump onto the back of a horse, breaking free from their duels and riding for the gate. Riycard ran for it next dragging Hector along with him, leaving Gondogon and Gideon alone.

Hector stopped and turned, shouting, "Gideon, Gondogon, quickly!"

The gate was dropping.

Gideon quickly dodged an attack and rolled to the side. He then chased after the horses, catching up to Hector and pulling him into a run. The two of them mounted, doubling up, ducking under the gate as they fled. Hector turned around to see where Gondogon was. He couldn't see him on a horse, frantically turning. The gate was still closing.

He lay his eyes upon a disturbing sight. Gondogon had been cut and had dropped to his knees.

"Stop the horses," demanded the Prince desperately. "Go back for him!"

"My King, if we go back, we will all die. We move forward," shouted Romford.

Hector snarled.

Gideon wheeled the horse around and spurred it on, back towards the gate. But it was too late. The gate slammed against the ground before they could get there.

There was no escape for the Prince's guardian and friend.

"Hector, there is nothing we can do. We must go," insisted Gideon who gripped hold of the Prince tightly as the horse danced beneath them.

Hector was forced to watch as the Eagle Pact got stuck into Gondogon. One at a time, the men dived in, sword first, stabbing the Royal beast. Gondogon's screams blistered the ears of all every time a sword entered his body. The stabbing only stopped as Lumon involved himself, the members of his Pact backing off and allowing him to end Gondogon himself.

Lumon pulled the helmet from his victim's head and stared at the men on horses on the other side of the gate. He grabbed hold of Gondogon's head and aimed his blade at his throat, making sure Gideon was watching when he dealt the final blow, and he was. Everyone watched.

The Eagle Pact Leader smirked wickedly into Gideon's distancing eyes as he pushed the sword deep into Gondogon's throat, holding it there for a second before ripping it to the side, mimicking Gideon's killing technique.

"No!" screamed Hector hysterically as he watched Lumon end the life of one of the greatest warriors in the East. Gondogon was dead.

CHAPTER 37
PREPARE THE ARMY

The Eagle Pact galloped exhausted across the dark land back towards High Darchem. They had been riding for four days non-stop with very little rest. Lumon had left three of his Pact members behind with the order to return to Versidia with the two wounded members and the two dead members. The wounded could then be tended to with the hope of survival, and as for the two dead members, they could be buried properly.

The Eagle Pact Leader had made for Darchem with the other four members, riding their horses half to death. Lumon had to get back to the High King to inform him of the events that had unfolded at Selection and Hornton's Watch.

The horse that carried Lumon breathed harshly as he pushed it harder and harder as they crossed over the border. The riders were closing in on the grey city of High Darchem.

The Pact and their horses had only been granted a couple of hours sleep a night with barely any food or water. Their need to get back to Darchem was desperate.

Lumon had a brown sack hanging on the right side of the horse. Inside was a gruesome gift for the High King, a heavy ball-shaped object that rolled about in the rough-looking sack as the horse smashed its hooves across the dark earth beneath.

Lumon went over the speech he was going to present to his King upon arrival, his mind swelling as the matter overloaded his brain. So much had happened in Versidia and Lumon was going to have to explain it all to the High King shortly, who without doubt would be very unimpressed with the news.

A loud blistering ringing erupted from the great walls of the city, ringing noisily to signal the return of the riders. Lumon and the Pact rode dangerously through the red and black camp that Havideous's men had set up. Thousands of tents had been put up in a big square shape just outside of the city walls.

The gang of horses glided through the camp, attracting the attention of the soldiers that patrolled the muddy camp with their spears clenched tightly.

With the annoying ring of the city bell came the creaking of the hellish black gates of Darchem city, the guards inside opening the doors for the return of the Eagle Pact. Lumon tugged on his reins, dragging his horse to the right as he aimed for a clear penetrating push through the city's gates.

"The High King, where is he?" asked Lumon as he breathed rapidly, pulling up his horse in the courtyard of stone to greet Pontus who awaited the Eagle Pact.

Pontus had returned to High Darchem only yesterday to give another report on the Lure Alliance, and as predicted he had made no progress. He had already informed Duran Harall that the Alliance expanded further which had obviously angered him.

"I warn you, though, he is not in the best of moods."

"The Lure Alliance?" asked Lumon.

Pontus nodded as he observed the amount of horses that were gushing in through the gates.

"Where is the rest of the Pact? You're seven men short?" asked Pontus.

"I will explain later but first I need to speak to the High King," insisted Lumon as he urged his horse to trample through the courtyard.

The Eagle Pact tracked their leader as his horse cracked the very concrete beneath it as it sprinted off the courtyard and up into the wide street that led into the heart of the city. The rushing flock of horses stampeded through the street without care as people were forced to dive out of their way. Some people screamed with surprise as the horses spewed through the streets knocking over stands, people and anything else that got in their way.

The inner streets of Darchem widened and filled with population the further the horses rode into it. The buildings became slightly more clean and each house began bearing more windows and doors, creating a half welcoming feeling. Every building was camouflaged with the ground, the same shade of grey and the same rocky material built up the floor and every building within the city.

Lumon slowed the horse down slightly as he approached the wall surrounding the King's castle. A small black gate sat in the middle of the wall, the only way into the castle grounds and the only way to reach the High King's castle.

Lumon and The Eagle Pact did not have to wait too long as the gate was quickly drawn up, and as soon as it rose above head height, Lumon again kicked his horse, forcing it to sprint the final stretch before they could finally rest. The five horses galloped across the castle grounds before each man slid from his horse in a hurry, each one of them dropping their reins, leaving the horses to wander around the castle grounds unattended. Lumon unhooked the brown sack from the horse and swung it over his shoulder.

The Eagle Pact Leader flew up the rubble steps to the brown wooden door entrance to the castle. Lumon almost sprinted up the concrete hill whilst his accomplices stalked him eagerly. Lumon pushed on the cold doors, entering the freezing castle. Lumon had not missed Darchem at all. He had been making preparations in Versidia, soaking up the heat and sun that blazed down on the holy city for more than three quarters of the year.

Lumon blew into his cupped hands as the torches upon the walls failed to warm him up. He walked off through the stone archway and made for the thick hallway that led to the High King's throne room.

"Let me do the talking, comrades," said Lumon to his four

Pact members as he held his hands out in front of himself, ready to push on the doors.

The whipping lash of the doors swinging open startled Duran Harall as The Eagle Pact entered. The High King was standing to the left of his throne room observing the world map. He had once again been feeding his addiction of The Lure Alliance by staring at the Square Wood Forest that was drawn upon his wall. He finally pulled his gaze from the map as he noticed Lumon's arrival. He travelled through the stone columns and down the steps towards Lumon.

"Back again?"

"My King, I bear news, bad news," announced Lumon as he walked forward. For the first time in four days, the Eagle Pact didn't track his movement. They stood at attention by the doors.

"Speak!" demanded Duran who seemed ready to explode.

Lumon breathed nervously as he prepared to fill the High King in.

"My king, the plan failed. Our agent indeed managed to mark the armour and Pelios did target Hector, but he fought very well. He still won Selection."

"How?" asked Duran calmly.

"How what?"

"How did he win Selection? He is not capable of taking on Pelios and the two hired men that we paid for?"

"He must have had training. He knew exactly what to do and when to do it. Our agent's reports were false," said Lumon.

"Then I trust the Prince and the agent are both dead?" asked Duran, looking at the round shaped bag that hung over Lumon's red armoured shoulder.

"They would have been, if…"

"If what?" snapped Duran as he grew impatient.

"If Gideon Destain had not been there." Lumon lowered his head.

The High King shivered with anger as he walked towards his right hand man.

"Gideon Destain?"

"Yes, my King. He was disguised as a servant, in Versidia for Selection. As soon I found out, I chased the escort and caught them just before the Watch, but Gideon is clever. He took out the whole Watch before we could arrive. Hornton too," reported Lumon bravely.

Duran looked past Lumon and stared at the Pact with interest. So far he hadn't reacted as aggressively as Lumon expected.

"And more than half of your Pact as well?" asked Duran as he looked at the four straight-backed Pact members before looking down to the brown bag again.

"Two dead and two wounded, my King. I had three members take the bodies and the wounded to Versidia to seek medical attention and a proper burial."

"What is in the bag, Lumon?" asked Duran, ignoring the Eagle Pact Leader's words.

Lumon dropped the bag and pushed out the bloody battered head of Gondogon onto the floor with his foot.

"Who is this?"

"I am not sure of his name, but judging by the screams of Hector when I killed him, he must have been of some importance."

Duran turned his back, disappointed, and walked away from Lumon and the gruesome sight on the floor. He walked back up the steps and walked over to the map.

"Lumon come here."

Lumon hurried up the steps and stood behind the High King who looked to the East on his map.

"Send a squad of two hundred men to the Watch. Tell Pontus he is to take command of the Watch for the time being, then send word to Seluse. Put a stop to all preparations fully on our crusade, I want his men to link up with the force from Thort."

"Yes, my King."

"And as for you, I want you to prepare the army."

"Prepare the army, my King?"

"Yes, seventy thousand soldiers ready to march on Brigantium within the fortnight. We are going to war, Lumon," declared the High King ruthlessly.

Lumon looked shocked at his King before bowing to Duran deeply.

"I will see to it at once, my King," he announced as he turned back to his Eagle Pact.

CHAPTER 38
A MEETING OF SUSPICION

"Havada, bring them in," ordered King Artaxes. The Western King was sitting at the head of his table inside the inn where he had murdered Tobias only days ago. He was wearing a black tunic, the sleeve slightly lumped due to the bandaging beneath. He had made sure that the self-inflicted injury to his arm would stand out to the audience that he was about to receive. The news of Tobias Ringfold's death had spread through the camp, causing panic, heartbreak and question. The Brigantium Lieutenants were not happy as the news came so unexpectedly.

Artaxes had agreed to meet with them to explain how it was that the Oakland Muster prisoner was able to sneak past the Meridium guards. The King had his story straight and his responses prepared as he was going to have to deceive the soldiers that would no doubt attempt to interrogate him.

Havada, obeying his King's command, stood from his seated position beside Dariuss and First General Lucifer. He then walked through the heated room and over to the door. The King's Guard opened the door and greeted the Eastern Lieutenants, but he was quickly ignored as three yellow-caped officers stormed into the room. The men stood straight-faced at the opposite end of the table to the King, the look of fury and need for revenge striking a tingle of fear into Artaxes.

The three men consisted of two Lieutenants and a General,

the General was now in charge of the Brigantium army until they returned home. His name was Matias. Although his helmet hid his hair well, some blond strands hung out of the bottom.

"General, please sit," offered Artaxes who made sure the General was aware of his wound by squinting as he raised his slashed arm towards the empty seats opposite his King's Guard. Without a word, the three tall men walked around the table, sitting down to the King's left.

"My sincere condolences. The death of your King is indeed a tragedy. Hopefully Hector Ringfold passed his Selection, so the Ringfold legacy can continue," said Artaxes even though he had no real interest for the Brigantium Prince's progress in Versidia.

"Hector won Selection, but he is a boy. There was much he needed to learn from his father before coming into the throne," announced one of the Lieutenants.

Artaxes managed to control his facial expression by hiding his look of disappointment. He had secretly hoped that Hector would have fallen in the Arena.

"That's good. The people of Brigantium will need some good news after hearing about the death of their King."

"We have not yet sent word. We don't want to tell our people until we find out what actually happened," stated the other Lieutenant whose attitude was a little more fierce that the last man's.

"You know what happened. We had a prisoner escape who wanted revenge," argued Artaxes.

"And tell me, King Artaxes, how was it that a simple Muster Prisoner who was unarmed managed to slither past your guard, injuring one King and killing another?" barked the General now with aggression.

"Watch your mouth," hissed First General Lucifer who sat directly opposite the Brigantium General.

Matias looked to Lucifer degradingly before locking his gaze back to the Meridium King.

"I find your story a little off. It just doesn't add up," stated General Matias.

"Are you suggesting that my blade ended the life of your King?" asked Artaxes with a sarcastic smile on his face.

Matias smiled back whilst locking eye contact with Artaxes. "Maybe. Everyone knows of your hatred towards Tobias. It makes sense really."

Lucifer leapt up from his wooden chair. "How dare you insult our King. If I was you, I would take your leave at once or you will join your King in the afterlife," threatened the First General.

Matias groaned as he rotated in his chair so that he could address Lucifer. He rose slowly to his feet. "Careful, old man, it would be very unwise for you to earn yourself another enemy, an enemy that could rain down forty thousand troops on you and your precious city," threatened the Brigantium General harshly.

"Is that a threat?" growled Artaxes from the head of the table.

"I don't make threats, I make promises and I am very close to making one," snapped Matias.

King Artaxes gripped his wounded arm tightly as he lifted himself up from his chair. Dariuss and Havada noticed the look in their King's eye, and stood up quickly as he did, readying themselves for a fight.

"Take your leave, General. I want your men off my land before tomorrow morning, and do not ever march them west again unless you want a war," said Artaxes slowly.

Matias grinned to himself. "A war? Against whom? You and your four hundred strong?" he mocked, his grin turning into a chuckle. "We will leave, but I want answers, Artaxes. This is not over." Matias stood, curling his cape around his waist, and spinning off out of the room, his two Lieutenants quickly following.

"We should kill that sharp tongued bastard before he has a chance to leave," growled Lucifer.

"You're right, but the Easterners have suffered enough loss. Any more of it and it would certainly arouse suspicion," said Artaxes.

Havada risked a dangerous question as he grew bored of listening to the King and The First General whine on about the Easterners.

"My King, what is to happen to General Koos?" he asked sheepishly.

Artaxes looked with shock at Havada. He had almost forgotten about Koos, so instead of snapping, he answered the question calmly.

"I have not yet decided, but he is to return to Meridium with me and Dariuss in a couple of days."

"You and Dariuss? What of myself and Havada?" asked Lucifer with confusion.

"I have another quest for you, the final push to ensure our safety and to put an end to the Oakland Musters forever."

Lucifer and Havada both looked at the King with intrigue as they awaited to receive their new orders.

"In two days, I want you both to take one hundred of our best men and sail across The Sink in our last ship. I want you to burn the forest to the ground. Leave none alive, women, children and especially the men. All dead," declared Artaxes barbarically.

Lucifer who still stood, accepted his orders. "Very well, I will begin selecting the men now. Come, Havada."

"What a mess this is," muttered Dariuss who had been quiet for the whole dispute between the Brigantium General and Artaxes.

The King walked over to a table to the left of the room where a jug of wine and a dozen silver goblets awaited him.

"What troubles you, Dariuss?" asked Artaxes as he poured himself a drink.

"Nothing, my King. The recent days have been long. I'm just very tired."

Artaxes slurped his drink whilst staring at Dariuss who remained seated with his back to his King. He was growing suspicious of Dariuss's behaviour that had changed since they plotted against Tobias.

"You know Tobias deserved to die? How many people did you know that were killed upon the Gantry because of the Brigantiums' betrayal. How many children related to you were stolen and taken by the High King as a result of losing the battle? Which we lost because of the betrayal of the Eastern Horse

344

Lords," explained Artaxes, pausing to take another sip before continuing. "He deserved to die."

Dariuss took a deep breath and stood. He turned to Artaxes. "I hate the Easterners, just like my King. I do not regret aiding you in killing Tobias, if that is what you're hinting about?"

"I am not hinting, I am simply reminding you.

"Reminding me of what?"

"Of who the enemy is."

Dariuss looked plain faced at his King. "I know more than most who the enemy is. I have stood with you for a little over ten years."

"Indeed you have, now go. Get some rest. You look hideous," ordered Artaxes as he finished the rest of the cup.

Dariuss bowed and left without words.

Artaxes watched Dariuss leave. He knew the King's Guard had been awake at night. He knew that the murderous plot that he had aided in had affected him. Dariuss was a loyal soldier and Artaxes had great plans for him, but he was not a murderer. He was not like Artaxes.

The Meridium King poured another half cup, and drank it quickly in one heavy gulp. Artaxes then placed the goblet gently on the table and marched for the doors. He pushed them open and walked down the warm corridor that led him to the inn's main double doors. He stopped before them. He didn't open them nor did he have the intent to do so. He looked to his left at a wooden panel spread in a square shape on the floor. It seemed to be some form of cellar or dungeon. Artaxes blotted out the cheer that could be heard coming from the streets outside as the victory celebrations continued. He ventured down the rest of the corridor, snatching one of the lit torches from the smooth wooden wall as he passed.

Artaxes waved the torch over the oaken entrance before kneeling down, gripping the black cobweb tangled handle. The Meridium King ripped open the door noisily as the cracked cellar door screamed as it was forced open and the King entered.

Artaxes cautiously dangled his leg down until it made contact with a wooden step, then put his other leg in and began climbing down the set of old steps that led down into the darkness of the basement. He held the fire lit torch in front of himself as he began his journey down the stairs, all the time waving and brushing the cob webs from his black attire.

Artaxes landed at the bottom and began walking through the wide black room, dodging in and out of the piles of boxes that were rammed to the lid with empty bottles of port, whiskey and rum. Although the darkness of the room made it very difficult to see, the King still seemed to know exactly where to go. He had been here before.

The deeper into the basement he travelled, the worse the smell got, the stale stench of mouldy bread and human faeces attacking the nostrils of the King. Artaxes covered his nose and mouth with his free hand whilst guiding himself through the basement with his torch.

Artaxes picked up the pace a little now as his visibility increased. He was approaching a small lit area as he ventured to the far back end of the long spider-infested space. The area was lit by two burning torches that were fitted upon the back wall that seemed to be the uncomfortable home of a blond-haired man.

The small flickering flames revealed a beaten man sitting cross-legged on the floor, the only thing holding him being two tight rusty shackles. It was Koos. The young Meridium General was chained up to the wall. He had been forced to urinate in his own torn cotton chaps. He was a mess and he smelt even worse.

"Who goes there?" muttered the exhausted General.

Artaxes didn't provide him with an answer as he stood looking down at his weak body. Koos had been beaten before being chained up here since the night of the murder. The King had a guard bring him small portions of bread and half a cup full of water a day, and the only reason he had received that small gesture was because of who he was to Artaxes.

"You?" groaned Koos as he forced his head up from its hanging position. He set his swollen eyes onto his King before spitting gruesomely at him. The white slippery spit gushed through the

346

air, landing on Artaxes's black leather boot. The King looked down calmly at his stained boot before walking over to Koos, and wiping his boot off the bent knee of the General, dirtying his vile stained trousers even more.

"Have you come to kill me?" asked Koos bravely. He then looked down and sniggered to himself. "Go on then, kill me. What do I have to live for if I am without my position and my home. Go on!" he howled whilst he glanced up tear-eyed.

"There is no need for me to kill you. Your debt has been settled," said Artaxes confusingly.

"My debt?"

"Your punishment for betraying Meridium. Instead of killing you, I killed Tobias." Artaxes said it as if it was a completely normal thing to have done.

This news completely shocked Koos.

"You did what?" growled Koos viciously.

"The Eastern throne will be inherited by Hector. He apparently passed Selection. I can only hope that he is a better leader than his father was."

"You fool, you utter fool," chuckled Koos as he began laughing psychotically. "Meridium is doomed, you useless fool. The Brigantiums will march on our city and destroy us!" He burst into a series of vile coughing.

Artaxes waited till Koos settled down before replying. "No one knows that I killed him, only you and Dariuss. And neither of you will speak of it to anyone. Not if you don't want what you predicted to happen. If you care for Meridium and its survival then you will keep it a secret."

Koos, realising that what Artaxes said was true, shuffled his body up to a kneeling position.

"And how is it that I am to go on keeping my mouth shut? Am I to live?" asked Koos who hoped for a chance of survival himself.

Artaxes stepped forward and leaned down to Koos's left hanging arm. He pulled out a key and undid the lock on the shackle, moving across and undoing the other one.

Koos dropped forward instantly, rolling into a ball, caressing his wrists painfully.

"You are to live, Koos. I made your father a promise long ago, now re-join your brothers. We ride for Meridium in three days," announced Artaxes.

"You expect me to just go back to how things were before you tied me down here, leaving me to piss and shit myself?" challenged Koos.

"Take this as a warning. If that still hasn't sunk in then I can refit the shackles?" said Artaxes as he held out the key.

Koos lowered his head again, the thought of fresh water and food overpowering his need to argue with the King, so he said nothing.

"I thought not," mocked Artaxes, then he turned away and walked back off into the darkness.

"They live, Artaxes. They live," informed Koos quickly before his King fully evaporated into the shadow.

Artaxes halted as Koos's words confused him, but only for a moment. It didn't take him long to become aware of who Koos spoke of. He quickly spun around and marched back towards the shimmering light. He stared at Koos as the General rose slowly to his feet.

"I saw them with my own eyes, Gideon, Nuallan and Andrus, your sons."

"My sons?" asked Artaxes with a glistening tear in his eye.

"Yes, in Brigantium. Tobias let them in. They were on the run from some town chief a little to the East. Andrus's family died there. His youngest son and his wife, it changed him. He does not speak anymore," reported Koos sadly.

The tear in Artaxes's eye dried up. It vanished the second Koos mentioned Brigantium.

"Brigantium? My sons?" he asked again. "If they have become citizens of Brigantium, then they are no longer my sons. I have no sons," whispered Artaxes shockingly before dropping the torch and turning away from his General.

CHAPTER 39
A LONELY CELEBRATION

The mood was dark as Hector and his party rode back. Over the last couple of days, they had been taking brief rests before forcing the horses to ride on. They were almost home.

Hector broke the silence. It had been quiet since the escort began their final day's ride that present morning.

"How am I going to tell my father about Gondogon. How will I tell his brothers Pscies and Voltor?" muttered Hector.

Gideon and Romford both lifted their heads up as the words surprised them.

"He loved him as much as he loved me. My father brought Gondogon and his two brothers up into the Palace from a young age. They are like stepsons to him," mumbled Hector.

"Not to sound blunt or rude, Hector, but that is the least of your worries right now," said Gideon whose worried mind lay fixed on the events at Hornton's watch. The only good thing that came out of that day was the death of Hornton. Gideon had finally settled a long owed debt to his most hated enemy.

Hector wiped the thought of Gondogon from his mind as Gideon's wise words brought him back to reality, back to the thought of the Eagle Pact. The Brigantium Prince feared that something had been sparked between Darchem and Brigantium. The last thing the future Eastern King wanted was a war.

"Do you really think Duran will go to war with us over this?"

asked Romford Chalk who seemed to be deep in thought also. He was overly frightened also at the thought of the Darchem army, and even more frightened of Duran Harall.

"Duran Harall finally has his excuse, the excuse he needed to end the threat of Tobias and the Easterners," informed Gideon without explaining properly.

Romford looked at Gideon with confusion.

"Him, Gideon and his brothers," stated Hector, finishing Gideon's sentence for him. "It makes sense now. With Duran Harall invading the foreign lands so forcefully, he would need more soldiers. I mean, my father would offer him tribute warriors, yes, but not the number that he would ask for. So if Duran had me fail Selection he could then march on my father, killing him and taking control of our forty thousand strong. If father fell, Duran would seat his agent, the traitor, on the throne who would then become the High King's puppet." Hector seemed to be figuring it out himself with each word. He looked puzzled at his own comments, the theory confusing himself as well as Romford who looked extremely nervous at the comments his Prince had just made.

"I believe this to be true," muttered Gideon, "but the plan failed. Duran Harall failed to eliminate you, meaning Tobias still has an heir, but there is still one worry."

"Which is?" replied Hector.

"Duran Harall could still march on Brigantium. He took a risk plotting against you. He will now have no choice but to declare war." Gideon began biting his mud-stained nails.

"Wait? Agent? You mean there is a traitor among our people?" asked Romford who for some reason looked terrified.

"I do not care to discuss the matter just yet, Romford," said Hector, remembering Gideon's advice about keeping it a secret until they returned.

"Yes, of course, I... I understand," said Romford who still looked bewildered and frightened by the remark.

Hector then looked to Gideon. "If Duran Harall does march on the city then we will meet him head on. He would be a fool to engage our horses in open battle. Let him come," boasted Hector comfortably before sitting back.

No one spoke any more words and the riders fell back into its silent state as they approached the city.

Gideon tried to relax his tired muscles. He knew the wrath of the High King, but he admired and respected the Prince's bravery. Maybe such a battle could be won.

They pushed the horses to the limit as they passed over the fresh grassy terrain towards Brigantium. They were very close. The air had now cleared and the scenery had brightened. For weeks the escort had been away, suffering the murky miserable surroundings in the less populated areas of Requirium. Finally they could breathe in the sweet healthy breeze of the beautiful Eastern lands.

One thing had struck them as very strange indeed as they closed in on the Eastern city. There was no celebration, no cheer, no clapping or screaming. Nothing at all could be heard coming from the city's courtyard, in fact the only noise came from the solid city doors creaking open, allowing the carriage into the city.

The muddy horses entered through the doors and wheeled out onto the courtyard of Brigantium. They were greeted but not by Brigantium people excited to celebrate the Prince's passing of Selection. Instead twenty armoured soldiers sitting upon horses waited for the escort. The lonely courtyard whistled as the breeze wriggled through the unexpectedly empty courtyard.

An officer broke from his line of armoured knights and quickly trotted over to position his horse beside Riycard and Faizer.

"Lord Badstuber, your father awaits you at the Palace. We are to escort you there at once. There has been a tragedy," informed the Brigantium officer who spoke very shyly.

Faizer and Riycard looked at each other, worried as they both wondered what the tragedy could have been, and glancing back at Hector, but before they could ask, the officer rode off and began waving his hand at certain riders. The yellow-caped soldiers began directing their horses in a square shape around the riders.

"Where is everyone?" Hector said, looking around. "Where on earth is my father?"

"This is a mystery to me," muttered Gideon gently as he looked at all the closed shutters on the settlements and buildings that they passed, even Boltrey's tavern, The Swan, was closed. The beautiful garden that surrounded the tavern was as dead and quiet as a graveyard.

"To hell with this," said Hector as he jumped off the horse and pushed through to the officer.

"My Prince, please," ordered the officer who had recently spoken with Faizer and Riycard. "I ask that you come with us. We will escort you in."

"No," said Hector. "Give me your horse."

The soldier without question slid off and handed his reins to Hector who climbed up and without a word dashed off alone.

Hector blotted out any thought that wasn't one of his father as he raced up the sloping grey streets towards his Palace. The reason for the city's silence was unknown to him. There should have been an army of civilians, officers and family members awaiting him at the city's gates to celebrate his victory in Versidia, but still not a soul made an appearance.

Hector's fresh horse smashed its hooves hard across the stone floor as it approached the Palace gates. The Starchitect horse was almost as eager as Hector as it ran powerfully without fatiguing. Hector noticed two Palace guards standing by the thin steel pole gate. He stared at them as he gained ground on them. The two men finally heard the smashing steps of the Prince's horse and began unlatching the locks. Once done, they swung open the gate, allowing Hector to flood through and out onto the Palace grounds.

Hector rode over the smooth markless ground and curled his horse around the spring water fountain that trickled fresh water into its pond. He spared no time to appreciate the lovely garden of his home, instead he bounded over to the steep steps and attacked them. Still mounted upon his black beast, he raced up the steps and made his way to the Palace entrance where

Dreyo Badstuber, Farren Chalk, and Gondogon's two brothers, Pscies and Voltor were standing. There was also a woman who stood in a thin black dress with a black veil hanging down over her face.

The Brigantium Prince held on tight to the reins as his backside began sliding off the back of the Starchitect horse. The horse lunged and arched its back as it reached the top, delivering the Prince to the very feet of the Brigantium nobles.

Dreyo bent the knee first, followed by Farren Chalk, Pscies and Voltor almost immediately. The only person who remained straight-backed was the woman who wore the black dress and cloak, standing at a small distance from the pledging squad.

Prince Hector reached the kneeling men and attempted to discover why his father was still not present, but he was greeted first.

"Welcome back, my King," said Dreyo, striking confusion into Hector with the words.

"King? I am a Prince not a King, not yet," corrected Hector with a sideways smile.

Dreyo remained looking down. All that the Prince could see was the black and grey forest of hair that sat nervously on the top of Dreyo's bowing head.

It only took Hector a moment of thought before his eyes teared up shallowly. He then choked lightly as he prepared to speak. He had an idea of why he was being called King. Hector turned from the kneeling squadron of nobles and knights and approached the black-hooded woman who had still not looked in Hector's direction.

Hector paced over to her, ripping up the black veil upon arrival. Her brown hair escaped the dark hood as the veil removed its defensive cover from her face. Her thick brown hair gushed out.

"Mother, where is father? Where is he?" he screamed impatiently.

Luna strangely spoke out without struggle. She seemed to have already dealt with the horrifying news.

"He's dead, Hector. He is dead, my son."

Hector stumbled back, the news hitting him like a battering ram.

"No, how? How!" he bellowed as he fell to his knees at his quiet mother's feet. His scream drowned out the noise of the other horses riding in through the Palace gates, finally catching up to Hector.

Dreyo Badstuber and Farren Chalk clattered over to Hector, leaving Pscies and Voltor looking puzzlingly down to the horses where everyone was dismounting. They were confused as to why their brother Gondogon was nowhere to be seen. The remaining two of 'The Three' looked with hope to the riders.

The screaming continued, drawing the attention of Enly and Gideon who sprinted up the steps and began scurrying over to the manic Prince. Gideon was distracted as he slowed his run down to a walk, his gaze now diverted to Luna, Hector's mother. The dry-eyed woman turned for the first time as Gideon's presence attracted her attention. She glared menacingly, twisting her lip and squinting her eyes. Luna again had declared her hatred for the clueless Westerner. Unable to bear the sight of him anymore, she turned from him, leaving her hysterical son behind. She stormed between two leather-armoured soldiers and entered the Palace.

Gideon watched her storm off, abandoning her son in his most desperate time. He half wanted to chase after her and demand answers, her unknown hatred continuing to strike confusion into the Meridium heir. Brushing off the matter for the time being, he knelt down and grabbed hold of Hector's tear-drenched face. Gideon stroked Hector's short curly hair out of his face and gazed into the boy's slanted eyes.

"Hector, what has happened?" he asked, receiving no answer.

Gideon released Hector and looked to Dreyo.

"Dreyo?" he asked.

The Brigantium noble looked to Gideon and told him.

"Tobias died in Oggsfleet. We received word this morning. The battle was won but they had a prisoner escape. An Oakland Muster prisoner escaped and attacked your father and Tobias.

Artaxes suffered a wound but survived, but not Tobias. The King is dead," informed Dreyo who truly looked shocked and a little frightened.

Gideon stood up with horror. He took a step back, allowing Enly to spew down to the floor to comfort his new King.

Gideon became curious and fell into a spell of wonder. 'A prisoner escape?' he repeated to himself in his head. He knew there was more to this. Gideon feared the worst. He had a feeling that his father was responsible for this, in fact he was almost certain of it.

Gideon intended to one day find out the truth about this, but for now he needed to help Hector sort himself out. He leaned down and grabbed hold of Hector's shaking hand, pulling him to his feet.

"The Prince will be crowned within the next two days. He passed Selection and has earned the right to the throne," announced Gideon, drawing the attention of all present. Even Voltor and Pscies, who had just been informed about their brother's death by Faizer, cleared their minds and turned to Gideon.

"With the passing of Tobias Ringfold," announced Gideon loud enough so that everyone can hear, "his son and heir will be crowded King Hector Ringfold of Brigantium, Horse Lord and Guardian King in the East."

Everyone who wasn't already kneeling, did so then. Riycard and Romford who stood at the bottom of the steps still bowed, then Faizer who was speaking to Pscies and Voltor knelt down also, all facing their new King.

The only man left standing was Gideon who received a devastating stare from the hysterical Prince. Gideon dropped down to his knee finally, allowing Hector to take in the atmosphere, but he seemed disinterested. Instead he looked over to the two Brigantium soldiers who stood at the Palace doorway. Hector was not accustomed to this sort of power, but in a state of rage and vicious nature, he made his first commands as King.

"Guards, arrest that man," he announced.

Everyone's heads sprang up as the words took them by

surprise. They all looked to Hector who pointed down towards Riycard and Romford.

Everyone now swung their heads down in their direction as the two soldiers from the door clattered down and approached the two of them.

"Riycard Badstuber assisted in aiding the Eagle Pact, a vile Darchem organisation that sabotaged my Selection in an attempt to kill me within the Arena," Hector declared as he watched with venom as the two soldiers grabbed hold of Riycard.

They grabbed his shoulders and dealt a heavy punch to his stomach before dragging him up the steps.

"My Prince, you are mistaken," insisted Riycard who failed to grab the Prince with his plead. "You are mistaken, Hector!" bellowed Riycard again desperately.

Everyone watched with confusion and frustration, all except Gideon who knew the reason. Even though he felt the manner of the arrest to be very public and very dishonourable, he knew it was necessary. But like everyone else, he kept his mouth closed, all except Dreyo who attempted to beg for his son.

"Prince Hector, what is the meaning of this? Whatever my son is accused of, you are mistaken. He attended Selection to protect you, not to plot against you," argued Dreyo who had no idea he was to be next.

"Silence, you fool!" screamed Hector. "It makes sense to me now. Riycard would interfere with my Selection, taking me out of the question whilst you, Dreyo, you would plot against my father in the West. You are both working with Duran Harall to unseat the Ringfolds. Well, you failed, Dreyo, you failed."

Although everyone was not understanding or following Hector's theory, Gideon was. Gideon felt that it all made sense.

"Pscies, Voltor, you were loyal to my father all your lives, now I ask that you will be loyal to me. I am sorry for the loss of your brother, he was my friend. But now I need you prove your loyalty and arrest that man." Hector stepped back, pointing at Dreyo who pounced up to his feet.

As expected Voltor and Pscies stood without question and

charged towards Dreyo. They latched onto him with a vice-like grip and dragged him off.

"You fool, you are wrong. You are wrong!" pleaded Dreyo Badstuber as his echoing voice faded as he was carted off into the Palace by the monstrous brothers.

CHAPTER 40
THE RETURN OF A TRAITOR

King Artaxes moved his hips in sync with his horse's movement as it led the returning Meridium army back to their home in the West. Artaxes smiled as the sound of his city's bells blistered the surrounding fields and overgrown forests of Meridium. The men that stood with either a spear or the Meridium flag upon the Meridium wall or in the white watch towers shouted down to the gate masters. They then began ringing the city's bells to welcome back the King and the remainder of the regiments dispatched over a month ago.

Dariuss and Koos rode, one at the left of Artaxes and one at the right. Their strong horses walked at a steady pace, following their over-pleased King back to Meridium.

Marching happily, behind the General and the King's Guard, were three hundred or more soldiers, all smiling cheerfully and engaging in gentle conversation with each other. The threat of the Oakland Musters was over. They had fought, they had bled and they had won. They could now go back to farming their fields, running their taverns or drinking themselves to death in the many settlements within the city of Meridium.

The threat of the Oakland Musters was in fact over. King Artaxes had led his men to victory in two different parts of the Western Realm, and now Lucifer and Havada sailed across The Sink to end the threat for good.

Artaxes turned to his left slightly and looked at the bruised face of Koos. The young Meridium General had luckily escaped death after his so-called betrayal, but now he had been given a second chance.

"Take it in, General Koos, the city that you love so much. Let it be a reminder of what you have to lose should you betray me again," said the King.

Koos ignored the words as he stared off into the far distance. He felt guilty and responsible for the death of Tobias. He felt that if he had just listened to Artaxes's order back in the marble throne room all those months ago, they may still have won the battle and Tobias would be alive.

Koos had hoped to create an alliance between the East and the West, but the young General now understood the true hatred that his King had for the Easterners. Artaxes, Koos and the whole of Meridium would fight alone and live alone for the rest of their existence.

Artaxes directed his loyal white horse that had guided him into battle so many times through the arched entrance to Meridium. The Western King's regiment was forced to thin out their ranks forming a four man thick rectangular shape, before they could enter their home, stamping and crunching as they passed through the gate, back into the white city.

Many officers and Lieutenants stood within Meridium's statue-filled courtyard.

"Greetings, King Artaxes," said one of them who awaited the return of the King.

He walked over to the snow-like horse that carried the King and took the reins.

"Greetings, Lieutenant, I trust everything is as I left it?" said Artaxes with a smile, but he was not given one in return. "Speak," he urged sternly as the nervous look on his Lieutenant's face vexed him.

The armoured Lieutenant removed his helmet and looked into the King's vengeful eyes. "All is exactly as you left it, King Artaxes, but there is something else, a gift."

"A gift?"

"From Duran Harall. He sent you a gift, and with the gift was a message. He said, 'A gift from an old friend'."

Artaxes looked to the floor as he thought on the matter but he stopped himself quickly. He had something else he had to tend to first. He wanted the men debriefed and rewarded for their service. Once that was tended to he could continue to speak with his officer more about this gift.

Artaxes waved over Dariuss and Koos who slid down from their horses at once. The King walked back into the courtyard where the soldiers stood in groups discussing what they were going to do that very night.

"Men of Meridium!" shouted the Meridium King.

The soldiers instantly stopped their talking and stood looking towards him.

"I thank you for your loyalty and your will to fight for your lands. Tonight we will honour the dead. We will drink to them and their sacrifice. As for you, all of you will be rewarded with a seven day ticket that Dariuss here will provide for you." The King held his hand out towards Dariuss. The King's Guard bowed and walked off towards section two of the city. Dariuss was heading to the taverns and brothels to give them the royal order to allow the soldiers the seven day ticket.

"This ticket will allow you free entry to any brothel or tavern within these walls, take as many ales and women as you wish over the next week, but do so with respect, of course," continued Artaxes with extreme generosity.

The Meridium soldiers cheered happily and began racing down into section two after Dariuss. Artaxes smiled to himself as he watched his men's faces fill with happiness for the first time in a while. He then addressed Koos who had not yet smiled.

"I have a job for you, General. I need you to send word to Villach, to Captain Cassius. Let him know that we were victorious in Oggsfleet and that I request his presence back home in Meridium."

Koos frowned at the order but he did not resist. Koos hated

Cassius that much that he couldn't even stand to hear his name spoken out loud, but instead of refusing or arguing, he simply bowed and walked off towards the Palace.

Barely anyone remained in the courtyard now, just the King and the Lieutenant that had provided Artaxes with the city's report. All of the other officers had followed the soldiers through the courtyard and off into section two.

"Tell me more about this gift?" the King asked as he leaned right into the armoured man's ear.

"I would hardly call it a gift, my King. It's more like…"

"More like what?" interrupted Artaxes who wanted details immediately.

"A man, more like a man," stuttered the soldier.

The King flinched and leaned back as he heard the shocking words.

"Who?"

"My King, it is Havideous, your brother. He wronged the High King so he sent him back here. He has given you permission to do with him as you please."

King Artaxes was in pure shock. Not a day had passed where Artaxes hadn't thought about destroying the traitor that was his brother. Everything that had happened to the Westerners in the last seven years was because of Havideous, all the pain, all the suffering and the loss of the three Western Princes. It was all because of Havideous Destain.

"Lieutenant, where is he?"

"He is in the cells in section one, barely a few minutes from here. I can take you if that is your wish," offered the soldier.

"I need only one thing from you," said Artaxes as he reached down to the man's waist. Artaxes grasped the soldier's sword handle and tore it from its scabbard. He then brushed past his informant and left the courtyard.

Artaxes was going to section one. He was going to reunite himself with his brother. He was going to kill him.

CHAPTER 41
THE DARKEST OF DAYS
ARE YET TO COME

The throne room was silent as Farren Chalk walked slowly up the small steps towards Hector Ringfold who was seated on his father's throne. Hector had managed to gather himself for the occasion even though the news of his father still brought him much pain. Even now he sat thinking about Tobias.

Farren Chalk was taking over the job of Dreyo Badstuber since he had been arrested. He was to crown the new King. Laid glistening across his wide spread arms was a purple cushion that held the crown of Brigantium. The Chalk family leader wore a dark green jerkin and a pair of leather chaps. He looked extremely royal. He had to stand out as he carried out the important task.

The floor was invisible as hundreds of people covered it with their rich capes and flowery gowns. Everyone had come to witness Hector's crowning. Before noon this very day Hector Ringfold would be crowned The King of Brigantium. Anyone close to Hector had the honour of standing up on the platform beside his seat.

Pscies, Enly, Voltor and Faizer stood straight-backed with their hands clasped in front of them, standing behind the throne looking straight ahead at Farren as he slowly climbed the royal steps. To Hector's left stood Gideon, Nuallan and Oslo. Then to his right stood Josanne, Boltrey and Fangoy. Everyone on either side stood sideways on looking at the straight-faced Prince, soon to be King.

To the very edge of the platform stood Romford Chalk. He balanced motionless beside Dreyo's wife, youngest son and their family speaker Stelio. They had been made to attend even though Dreyo and Riycard were being held prisoner. Their faces were miserable, and it was obvious that their attendance was forced.

Farren Chalk had now reached the top base of the platform and had begun walking slowly towards Hector. Hector was dressed in a dark red outfit, sewn and crafted from soft cotton that provided much comfort. Hanging over his shoulders was a night black gown with quilted fur that looked to weigh as much as a wild dog. It ran from his shoulders to the floor where it lay messily by his feet like a pile of thick pythons.

"Hector Ringfold, I bear the honour today of replacing the Promise Crown that sits upon your head, with the crown of Brigantium that once sat upon your father's head," said Farren loud and clearly.

The Brigantium crown was made from solid gold, although it was very thin unlike most. It was a circular golden bar that had two tiny golden horses sprouting from the rich metal. The horses signified the love that the Easterners had for horses.

"Today we remember Tobias who was a great King and like Hector a victor of Selection. But tonight we honour a new King, Hector Ringfold," said Farren clearly as if he had rehearsed this speech a dozen times. Farren Chalk held out the crown and looked to Fangoy. The Advisor to the King stepped out of the line and walked over to Hector. He leaned down and removed the Promise Crown from his head, allowing Farren the space to position the new crown on his nicely curled head.

"Hector Ringfold, I declare you King of the Horse Lords and watcher of the East," announced Farren Chalk as he planted the crown on Hector.

The crowd cheered and clapped as Hector received the crown. He then stood up, forcing Farren and Fangoy to move out of the way. The new King walked to the edge of the risen base and prepared to speak out to the people that applauded him. The sparkling chandeliers that dangled from the ceiling wobbled as the earthquake-like applause ricocheted around the throne room.

"I vow to continue my father's legacy, and I will treat the people and our realm with respect and love, just like he did. I will bear his routine. Once a week, the people may come to the Palace with their needs and wants and I will try my best to help you," said the new Brigantium King happily. He then nodded neatly and walked back to his seat.

The crowd cheered again and began throwing roses and flowers up towards Hector. Some of the soldiers were forced to intervene as the crowd erupted with that much excitement they felt like they needed to calm down the situation.

Hector forced a smile out as he took in the love and respect that his people offered him. He then looked up to Gideon who stood in a navy blue tunic looking back, Nuallan standing behind Gideon, ruffling and tugging at his tunic irritatingly as he wore an identical outfit. He had managed for so long to reject the royal clothing, but that day he had no choice. All of the company had been forced to remove their overthrows and replace them with suitable clothing, even Josanne had no skin on show for a change. She wore a lemon yellow dress that tightly sucked at her waist.

Hector allowed a small smile to invade his face as he looked down at the ecstatic crowd. The people were obviously confident that he was to be a good King, and this pleased him. In fact there was only one thing that troubled him, the absence of his mother. The strange few-worded woman had not made an appearance. No one actually knew if she was pleased or devastated about the death of her husband. She had not shed a tear and she had barely even spoken.

"Do you hear that?" muttered Enly from behind Hector.

The King looked up and replied to his friend. "I cannot hear anything over the sound of clapping, my friend."

"No, listen," insisted Enly who walked around the throne, drawing the attention of Gideon and Nuallan in the process.

They both listened carefully.

"My King, Hector, listen... bells, I hear bells," said Enly worryingly.

Hector rose from his throne, releasing the quilted fur from his back. He too could hear the bells vaguely in the background of the cheering.

"What is it? Is everything alright?" asked Gideon who could not hear the noise but could see the worry that was taking over Enly and Hector's faces.

"It's the city bell. Everyone with me! Now!" ordered Hector quickly.

Gideon, the whole company and Enly chased after Hector who raced down the steps and tried to squeeze through the crowd. The people that still clapped suddenly stopped as the rushing and panicking behaviour of the King intrigued them.

The soldiers present began pushing the civilians and nobles aside forming a straight path to the throne room doors, until suddenly the double doors swung open causing a devastating bang. The noise shocked the whole room, forcing the heads of everyone inside the dimmed throne room to swing their heads in the direction of the doors.

A Brigantium soldier entered, his yellow cape flapping as he walked in. He was panting desperately for breath and he was not alone. He was assisting a wounded farmer who groaned and moaned with every step.

"My king, an army is at our gates!" bellowed the soldier. He then dropped the man and approached Hector who was at a standstill with all of his accomplices at his back.

Gideon did what he did best and took over the situation. He stepped in front of Hector and spoke to the approaching soldier. "Who has come? Of whom do you speak? The High King?"

"Yes, Darchem soldiers, legions of them stand at our gates, ready for war. Who leads them I do not know, but they are too many," informed the soldier, striking fear into everyone present.

"Who is that man?" asked Hector as he involved himself, pointing down to the wounded man who sat on his knees by the door.

"He has a farm just outside of the city," explained the soldier who looked like he was ready to soil himself. "The Darchem soldiers beat him and gave him a message. He flooded through the gate begging an audience with you. He told me that the soldiers offer you a way out, my King."

"A message?" asked Hector as he brushed past the soldier and ran to the wounded farmer.

"Speak, sir. Tell me what message they gave you," pressed Hector as he helped the man up to his feet.

The farmer coughed hard before speaking. "He said he will burn your city to the ground if you do not comply," the man said with a struggle. He grabbed his ribs hard as he coughed again painfully.

"Comply?"

"He wants Gideon, the Western Prince. He wants the heir of Meridium," said the battered man again, squinting with pain as he spoke.

The man's words only reached as far as Gideon's and Hector's ears. The others could not hear over the panic and mutter of the crowd. Many of the people had overheard the conversation and were now screaming as the sound of The High King terrified the people.

"Enly, Pscies, Voltor, I want them out, all of them. Get the civilians out," ordered King Hector as he began carrying the man over to the throne. The struggle became real now as people attempted to flood out of the throne room as if a dam had broken.

Pscies, Voltor and Enly instantly got to work, ordering the people out, making them leave in their dozens. The ones who failed to leave quickly enough got pushed by the surrounding soldiers.

Before long, almost all the people were being escorted out of the Palace. Dreyo Badstuber's family had also been forced to leave, leaving only the trusted people to Hector present. Everyone who was not back up on the throne platform now made their way there.

"What did he say? What did the man say?" asked Nuallan as he charged towards Hector who had just reached the throne.

He sat the man down in his newly inherited seat.

"He wants me. Of course he does," muttered Gideon who stood beside Faizer on the edge of the platform. His words shocked everyone.

Faizer turned to him with a horrified look upon his face. "You can't," said Faizer.

"No, he can't," said Hector firmly. "We will meet The High King in open battle if we have to." He then signalled Enly, Pscies and Voltor who were on their way back across the room. "Prepare the army at once. Get the archers on the wall and saddle up. Now!"

The three of them nodded and quickly turned. They raced back for the door and left the throne room.

"Will you all ride out with me? Together, we will save the city," asked the King as he looked to Gideon and the company.

Josanne and Faizer smiled and nodded passionately, but before they could speak Gideon interrupted.

"That will not be necessary," he said in a quiet voice.

Everyone looked to Gideon.

"You cannot win this war. Not even with forty thousand strong, Hector. I will offer myself up to him in order to save the city and all of you."

"No, you fool. No, Gideon!" burst Nuallan who raced across the mahogany floor.

Josanne and Hector were the first to back Nuallan by disagreeing with Gideon's words.

"Gideon, don't do this," said Josanne, holding his arm with a shaking hand.

"She's right, Gideon. Don't you dare. We have come so far," added Faizer, tearing up, but he knew already that Gideon had made up his mind. He lowered his head after speaking.

"Gideon, we will fight for you," insisted Hector, charged with emotion, "as you have fought for everyone here. I beg you to reconsider."

But Gideon wasn't given a chance to argue as the soldier that had brought the wounded man interrupted the conversation. He knelt down and bowed to the king before speaking.

"My King, Duran Harall's men said we have but only a few minutes to offer up the Meridium heir or he will unleash his wrath."

"Tell him I accept. Go now. Send an envoy," said Gideon before Hector could reply.

"What is your plan here, brother? After everything, you're going to make it this easy for him?" asked Nuallan who stepped back and sat down on the steps next to Oslo, a gentle tear running down Oslo's young face.

"You can all live happily now," muttered Gideon as he turned from his company, family and friends. "It was always going to end like this."

"It doesn't have to end like this!" said Nuallan as he watched his brother walk away. He burst into tears, anger erupting. "Don't you walk away from me!" he shouted. It was only when he managed to say, a little quieter, "What about Andrus? This will break him again," that his words managed to bring Gideon to a standstill.

The soon to be Darchem prisoner turned and looked to all the faces that he loved so much. "He is in your care now, Nuallan. You can lead these people far better than I can. You will make me proud."

"Don't you turn your back on us, brother. Do not do this," begged Nuallan in one last attempt to sway his brother.

"This is goodbye, for now," said Gideon as a tear trickled down his soft black beard. He slowly raised his hand to the mob of sobbing people before turning and leaving for good.

Gideon Destain walked off down the hallway, trailing his hand across the smooth wall, taking in one last home comfort before he was to no doubt endure the rough touch of a cage for the rest of his days.

Gideon's sole tear had dried up as he walked to his doom. He did not regret his decision but he did regret not saying goodbye to his little brother Andrus.

But his thoughts were cut short as a mysterious woman stood at the end of the hallway, staring at the approaching Meridium heir. It was Luna.

Gideon noticed her and picked up his walk. He half expected her to run or at least turn away but that time she did not. It was as if she was waiting for him. Hector's mother was wearing the same black robe that she had worn when Hector and the escort returned from Versidia, only this time she was without the veil. Her brown hair hung down over her shoulders and over her breasts.

Gideon slowed his walk and took the time to have one last conversation, and this was one that he had wanted to have for a while now.

"You stuck around this time?" he asked.

Luna, without words, just glared back at him.

"You are Hector's mother," he said. "I am Gideon Destain, but I think you already know that, don't you."

"Yes, I know who you are, but it seems like you don't," she hissed.

"I don't what?" he asked with confusion.

"You do not seem to know who you are. You just said you are Gideon Destain," she added strangely.

"Well, yes. That is my name," he argued simply.

"Gideon maybe, a Destain, no," she said, striking more questions into Gideon's mind.

"What do you speak of? Your words arouse much confusion," snapped Gideon.

But again she did not reply and this time attempted her escape.

Gideon refused to let her leave this time, he wanted answers. Too many times had she stared at him from afar, too many times had her unexplained hatred battered his mind. It was time for her to talk.

"Tell me, why do you hate me so? Why do you look at me

with evil? I want answers!" he demanded as he grabbed hold of her arm, spinning her back towards him.

"I did not always hate you," she barked as she spun back around. "It was your mother, you little worm, I hated your mother. But then you were born and as you grew, you reminded me so much of her, and... and you remind me of him."

"Who? Who is him? Of whom do you speak?!" exploded Gideon as Luna's words only brought more questions.

Luna twisted her lip and frowned as Gideon's raised voice angered her. She again tried to leave.

"I do not know what you speak of," he said, "but I want answers. Who am I? You say I am not a Destain then who am I?" He again reached for Luna's arm, grabbing it tightly and again spinning her around and making sure he kept tight hold of her.

"If you should make it back alive from the dungeons of Darchem, come and find me. And I will tell you everything," she teased.

"To hell with that. I want to know right now."

"If I told you now, you would not leave. Seventy thousand Darchem soldiers stand ready to reign fire upon my home, my son's home. You must leave," said Luna, weakening Gideon's grip with her words.

The words struck so much fear and confusion into the Meridium heir that he had no choice but to watch the woman who knew so much about his life walk away, vanishing down into the darkened halls, dragging with her hidden answers and Gideon's soul.